HAPAX

K.T. Bryski

HAPAX

K.T. Bryski

DRAGON
MOON
PRESS

DEDICATION

To my grandparents... all five of them.

ACKNOWLEDGEMENTS

I wrote this book in an empty room with the door closed, but I did not write it alone. Thank you to Susan Hall, Victoria Dawe, Michael Butler, and Michael Johnstone for starting me on the path; to Erin Scothorn, my friend and beta reader; to my editor Gabrielle Harbowy and publisher Gwen Gades, for championing this story and for making it the best it could be; to all the writers who helped along the way; and to my family, for everything. And, of course, thank you to my podcast-cast: Gavin Douglas, Sydney Gautreau, Simon Bild-Enkin, and Blythe Haynes. This journey was far different than we expected. Thank you for staying with me.

I

The time, at last, had come.

A new star ignited over the City. Like a drop of blood glinting in the darkness, it blazed in the Serpent, brighter than any other star in the constellation. Under the starlight, the City crouched in the night, perched atop its plateau. Sheer cliffs fell away on every side; if not for lack of water, it could have been an island.

No breeze stirred the warm air. In narrow alleys, shadows stretched as quiet and endless as the gorges beyond the City.

Time passed. The stars danced on.

Then, the low sound of a bell echoed through the night. In the central square, the towers of a pale cathedral loomed over neighbouring buildings. The bell tolled again, summoning the City's people. One by one, doors opened, and their occupants flowed through the streets. The wind picked up, carrying hushed voices on its back.

The cathedral doors creaked open and embraced the flood, though more than a few passed into the Ecclesiat's narthex with a shudder and fearful glances towards the east. Gloved monks ushered them in, but an anxious edge sharpened their reassurances.

Many paused at the public chapel, where crowds surged at the stone feet of an angel's statue. Candles illuminated stained glass windows portraying the same angel and a snarling beast. Children clapped to see the flickering lights. The old and the pious knew better—it was premature to rejoice before the end of Candlemass.

The bell tolled a final time. Monks escorted the last of the congregation into the pews and secured the cathedral doors. Most of the City now waited within the Ecclesiat's walls, straining forward, eyes fixed on the People's Altar.

And so, no one saw the new star fall to earth.

In the cloisters adjoining the cathedral, Brother Gaelin tried to organize the monks and choristers. With his silvery hair and dignified bearing, the sub-prior usually found a single order sufficient. That night, however, anticipation ran high and attention wandered. Candlemass came so rarely, bore so much weight. Tension knotted in Gaelin's chest. The night could not end soon enough for him.

He had allowed enough time for talk. Gaelin cleared his throat and raised a hand. "We will process into the cathedral shortly," he said. "Please get in line."

The monks assembled themselves quickly enough; with three services per day, finding their place was second nature. The choirs were another story. White-robed choirboys scrambled into line, half with surplices crooked and the other half missing their prayer books. Their high voices bounced off the old stone walls; some weren't even facing forward, but twisted around to chatter to their friends or gaze out wide windows to the gardens beyond. Gaelin caught a passing boy and straightened his robes. "Mind yourself, Praeton. Time to go."

"Yes, Brother." Praeton looked at the floor. Though he had grown up in the Ecclesiat, the orphan still had trouble meeting the clergy's eyes. His book trembled in his hands. "Brother Gaelin, the sun...it's coming back, right?"

He patted the boy's shoulder. "Well, we have Candlemass to find out. But I should think so, it's never failed yet."

"So, it's just like a normal service? Only late at night?"

"For you? More or less—you just get a few more anthems while Sister Alesta and I light the fire. Speaking of which, where is she?"

"There."

The sub-prioress strode down the cloisters, corralling choristers as she did so. "Aren't they organized yet?" she demanded.

"We have time, Alesta." He hid a smile. The boys had fallen silent at her appearance, as they so often did. Gaelin wondered whether it was her waves of honey-coloured hair, or the bite in her voice. Probably both.

She ignored him and clapped once. The sound ricocheted in the narrow cloisters. "Attention! Line up—boys first, then the adult choirs, then the Order. At the signal, we will enter the Ecclesiat through the cloister door."

A monk in the back raised his hand. "Please, sub-prior, won't Father Osvald be leading?"

Gaelin took a breath and looked to Alesta. Her sharp face betrayed no hint of worry as she spoke. "No, the Throne will not be attending Candlemass." Immediate mutterings broke out. Alesta raised her voice. "He remains ill. I advise you to pray to Ael and the Angel for his recovery."

High in the belfry, the Ecclesiat's bell rang again. One hour to midnight. One hour left. Gaelin's fingers tightened around his standard, his palms sweating in his silk gloves. Despite his words to Praeton, a lump had settled in the pit of his stomach. As Candlemass came once every twenty-seven years, this was only his second Candlemass vigil. He shook himself. Alesta had been a mere child her first Candlemass, and she seemed as self-assured as ever.

"May we be pure," she said.

After adjusting her robes a final time, Alesta nodded to Gaelin. Together, they opened the door separating the cathedral from the rest of the Ecclesiat. The cloisters' low ceiling seemed to fall away as Gaelin crossed the threshold, the cathedral's vaulted roof soaring upwards. A ghostly blue tint brushed the walls and columns, punctuated with the brassy gleam of firelight on metal candleholders and statuary. Incense stung Gaelin's nostrils; he muffled a sneeze as he marched down the aisle with Alesta. The congregation turned in their pews to glimpse them through towering pillars.

The sub-priors raised their emblems. The oaken staff felt heavier every year, but Gaelin ignored his aching arms and focused on the gold symbol atop his standard. A gilded triangle, point down, crowned the staff, with another, point up, inscribed within it. Three within three: Ael in All.

Directly behind the People's Altar loomed another statue of the Angel. Larger than the one in the chapel, and fashioned of the purest white marble and gold, it was the Ecclesiat's pride. Gaelin had walked this route enough times that he could mount the chancel steps without ever looking away from the Angel's blind, milky eyes.

In the candlelight, Gaelin could have sworn the Angel's vague smile broadened. The sub-prior continued around the Altar and placed his standard at the rear of the chancel. Until the choirs and monks had settled in their stalls, he could rest and pray. *O Ael, protect us this night.* Attempting to shift to a more comfortable position, he eyed the small door at the back of the chancel. His heart beat faster. *O Ael, do not abandon us this Candlemass.*

Alesta sat beside him, her fingers clenched on the wooden armrest. When the last monk seated himself, she rose with a curt nod, and perhaps a hint of satisfaction. With Father Osvald ill, she had been chosen to lead the service. *To be so young, but so favoured by Ael,* Gaelin mused. For she was not only the youngest sub-prior, but also the youngest to complete an anchorage: one year of prayer and study in a small cell. In the old days, anchors had been cemented in their cells for life; even with the change in practice, few succeeded on the first try. Alesta had done so at twenty-three.

Frankly, Gaelin might have preferred the ancient form of anchorage to leading the Candlemass service. Uneasy anticipation lit every face that craned towards the chancel. His own fear felt heavy enough; he doubted he could shoulder theirs, as well.

Alesta stood in front of the altar, hands outstretched. "On this night, we keep vigil as the old age of Ael ends, and we await the coming of the new. We pray for the sun's return, that life may continue"

Mumblings and pleas to Ael and the Angel filled the great building. From his chair, Gaelin watched Praeton. Despite his earlier nerves, the boy was singing well. That, or he was doing a fine job of mouthing the descants. Ael only knew how his voice would ripen; eleven was still too early for the richness before the breaking.

As the last notes of a descant faded, Alesta stepped forth again. An acolyte fumbled with Father Osvald's stole; she dismissed him and placed it about her own shoulders. The blue and gold of the stole took on further richness in contrast to her white sub-prior's robes. Composed, swathed in rich embroidery, she looked like the Throne already.

She must have felt it, for her back straightened and her voice carried to the farthest recesses of the Ecclesiat. "Ael, hear us reaffirm our knowledge of you."

The Ecclesiat's small sounds, the scrapes of shoes and cracklings of flame, drowned under the unison intonation: "Ael is That Which is All. Because the nature of Ael surpasses our understanding, Ael became the Angel, who is male. And Ael became the Seraph, who is female. And Ael remained Ael."

Incense wafted through the chancel and mingled with the dying echoes. After a short pause, Alesta resumed, "The Angel, the Preserver, was purified into goodness, and became Angelus Rex, the Angel King. The other, destructive part of Ael degenerated to evil. She became the Beast, and was cast out from the Angel and Ael, and now tempts souls to Her ways. May the Angel protect us this night, and restore the sun to us."

A breathless moment as all retook their seats. Alesta alone

stood, hands still outstretched. eyes closed, mirroring the Angel. The choir began another hymn as Gaelin joined Alesta before the Altar. Acolytes silently handed them each an ornate silver candlestick.

Two monks approached bearing lit candles. Twinges shot down Gaelin's arms as he hefted his candlestick. The monks touched their candles to the sub-priors'. The nearness of the flame sent a flush of heat across Gaelin's face and made him forget about his various aches. Beautiful, the sight was so beautiful. Aside from the whisper of fluttering flames, the Ecclesiat was absolutely silent; both chancel and nave looked like scenes carved from stone. Gaelin bowed his head as the fire took hold on his candle and smoke curled to the ceiling. The passing of fire had always touched his spirit. He almost tasted holiness on the air.

"May the sun come again," Gaelin murmured. Sweat prickled between his shoulder blades. His cassock stuck to his skin.

Alesta hoisted her candle. Carvings of saints and the Angel covered the rear wall, but every eye was drawn to a small door set squarely behind the People's Altar. Swirls of gold trimmed its edges, but it lacked the main doors' intricate decorations. Though it had been years since he first passed through it, Gaelin's awe never abated. This was the dwelling of Ael.

A monk eased the door open. Gaelin heard only his footsteps, saw only Alesta's golden hair through the dancing flame he carried. The dark corridor opened into a small, seven-sided chamber. A divine presence washed over him, as though a hand rested upon his shoulder, and Gaelin sighed.

Another altar waited in the chamber's centre. Unlike its public counterpart, the High Altar was devoid of colourful coverings. It was carved of the same white marble as the rest of the inner sanctum, gleaming ghostly pale in the gloom. Careful not to trip on the trapdoor over the crypts, Gaelin took his place at the Altar of the Angel King.

Only the wait remained. Words seemed blasphemous in the expectant silence, so Gaelin held his tongue and concentrated on the altar. Wood lay heaped in the centre. His heart thudded in his throat as the last minutes of the old age ebbed away.

The bell tolled midnight.

"Time has run out." The words made Gaelin's breath catch. "Grant us another generation, Angelus Rex, and let not the end of the world fall on us." They touched the candles to the altar. "May the sun rise again."

The wood shifted slightly. Alesta leaned forward, face alight, while exhilaration swelled in Gaelin's chest. He waited, the candles shaking in his hands.

The fire failed to light.

A cold wave of dread rolled down Gaelin's throat and into his stomach. The room lurched; Gaelin forced himself to take deep, even breaths. He poked his candle further forward, jabbed the flame against a thin piece of wood. With all his heart, he willed it to catch.

Not even smoke.

Across the altar, Alesta's candle shook as she too thrust it deeper into the pile. Murmurings penetrated from the outer sanctuary and nave. The congregation would be getting restless, wondering where they were, hardly daring to imagine that the impossible had happened.

"Ael help us all," Gaelin whispered through numb lips. It hurt to look at the sterile altar, and he turned away, trying in vain to swallow. "Come, we must tell them, we must be there to offer counsel..."

Alesta's head snapped up. "We must continue the service."

"The fire has failed, the sun—"

"If the sun is dead, they will need the Angel's word more than ever."

Gaelin shook his head. "Time has run out. Our ritual has not been accepted. Don't you see? Alesta, we have not bought ourselves another cycle. The end has come."

The fever returned to her eyes. "Well, the Angel tests our faith in these final hours, does He not? Let me see to the people."

"Let us see to them." Gaelin tried to keep his voice mild. "During this time of trial, we all have something to offer."

Neither spoke as they left the altar. As Alesta emerged into the chancel, she reminded Gaelin of a predator: hungry, but patient. She saw him looking at her, and smiled. Her teeth flashed in the candlelight.

Yet she spoke to the people softly, serenely. Her words did not ring out into the vast Ecclesiat so much as seep into every crevice. Her words soothed the agitated masses like a hand stroking a frightened child. Yes, the fire had not lit. No, the ritual had not been completed. Cries rang out, and Alesta shushed them, pacified them. The people listened to her description of the mysterious ways of Ael and the Angel, of the oath the Angel had taken to save His people from impurity.

Now, with the apocalypse itself upon them, they must trust in Him more than ever. To do otherwise was to give victory to the Beast. In this time of uncertainty and fear, would they turn from the saving Angel? No, they must be calm, but watchful, until He chose to reveal more.

Many of the monks nodded along from the stalls. Gaelin bit his lip. It was true: the Beast had meddled with Ael's plans before. Consider the way She had unleashed magic—She had deprived the world of innocence. Was this another temptation? Only the sunrise, or lack thereof, would offer insight.

As Alesta finished, Gaelin stepped forward. "The clergy will, of course, remain in the Ecclesiat to keep the morning watch," he said. "We will wait for dawn, and offer guidance and solace to any who seek it. Do not fear, my friends. Ael protects us."

"And the Angel purifies us," Alesta said.

Though officially dismissed, few of the congregation returned home. Many threw themselves before the chancel railing, wailing their prayers before the Altar. Others crammed the chapels. Gaelin helped where he could, though he too cast frequent glances to the Angel.

Halfway down the nave's centre aisle, the stone calendar attracted much attention. Markings for each day of the year, and each year in an age of Ael, ran along its outside. Both sets of markings had a groove engraved beneath them. The grooves held stones which moved to show the day and year. Currently, the stones remained stuck on the last day of the twenty-seventh year. Gaelin's heart sank at the sight of it. None dared touch it, but they stared at the stones as though they could will them to move.

Praeton lurked at the edges of crowds, his prayer book dangling from his hand. Gaelin patted his shoulder. "It's very late," he said. "You must be tired."

"I know. It's just...Brother Gaelin, why?"

The sub-prior folded his hands within his sleeves. "I will be honest, Praeton. I don't know."

"And in the morning...What then?"

"I don't know that, either."

For a moment they looked at the stone calendar in silence as people continued to crowd around. Then Praeton said, "I knew this would happen."

"Oh?" Gaelin steered him to a quieter corner of the Ecclesiat. "How?"

The boy refused to meet Gaelin's face, staring at his shoes instead. "A dream."

"A dream?"

"Yes." How could a boy with such a pure singing voice speak so indistinctly? "I dreamed it would end up like this."

"We know little of Ael's ways," Gaelin said. "Were you anxious about this? Daytime fears often follow us into sleep."

"Maybe." Praeton shrugged. "Anyway, I'm used to them."

He looked so pathetic standing there with his quivering chin and oversized robes that Gaelin wanted to sweep him into the arms of a loving parent. But the best he could do was say, "You know where my quarters are, if you need me."

"Yes, Brother." The boy yawned and passed a hand through his hair, making it stick up in every direction. "Will things be all right?"

"I trust in Ael and the Angel. Now go to bed, you'll be woken early."

Once Praeton had left, Gaelin's smile slipped. What he would give to be a child again, to have his own doubts so easily assuaged. He returned to the chancel and knelt before the Angel's statue. For a moment, he didn't try to fit words into prayer. Instead, he concentrated on the cool stone beneath his knees, the lingering scent of incense. "Angelus Rex," he whispered. "Ael. Please, help me in this time. Fill me with strength to comfort those who sorrow, and to give courage to those who fear."

He heard a cough behind him. Alesta acknowledged the Angel, and then turned to Gaelin. "I trust I'm not interrupting?"

"Not at all."

"Good." She glanced around the chancel before leaning close to him. "Father Osvald hasn't been told."

"By Ael!" Gaelin could only stare at her. "Why not?"

She shrugged, and her hair rippled like waves of gold. "He coughed blood last night, and the shock would do him no good."

"He has to know. Before dawn."

"Of course."

From the back of the cathedral, a man charged to Alesta's side and flung himself to the floor, clutching the hem of her robes. Without hesitation, she blessed him and then extricated herself from his grasp. He remained in his face-down sprawl, murmuring a stream of pleas to Ael as Alesta motioned for Gaelin to follow her further along the chancel. When they were a safe distance away, Alesta stopped, tapping the chancel railing. "I'll tell Osvald myself; it may be easier with fewer people."

Gaelin nodded. "Then I'll remain here. What's the time?"

"Three past. Another two or three hours, and we'll see if there's a reprieve before the end." Her face clouded. "The Angel must be displeased. I wonder, do you suppose it could be those tainted magi?"

"Strong words," Gaelin said.

Her smile was closer to a grimace. "Could it be those... morally ambiguous magi? They use gifts given by the Beast, their experiments are heretical and probably illegal. Would it be surprising if they corrupted us all in the Angel's eyes?"

"I've known some honourable magi," Gaelin said. "Decent, fair, and loyal. Besides, magic has been with us so long, why should it cause Candlemass to fail now?"

Silence lapsed between them. Gaelin fingered his sleeves. The cuffs were fraying—a few hours more would tell whether he should bother having them repaired. Suddenly, Alesta spoke.

"Magic is old, but they're using it in new ways. They're assuming the role of Ael over there, Gaelin. It's the same story: the arrogance of man in accepting the Beast's magic, the arrogance of man as he uses it." Her lip curled. "*And the sinners amongst them sought the bosom of the Beast.*" Before Gaelin could speak, she continued. "I shall inform Father Osvald of tonight's occurrences. May the Angel find you worthy."

She left Gaelin alone before the great statue. The scrape of acolytes shifting pews back into place and faint prayers from the public chapel echoed in the warm, still air. Shadows from the nave's columns crept over the chancel and crossed the Angel's face. The play of light and darkness almost gave His features the appearance of movement; firelight painted the Angel's marble wings with the warmth of flesh and blood. Gaelin felt that if he glanced away, even for a moment, the statue might well breathe.

In the half-light, His smile was pure contentment.

"Did you hear about last night?" Tamus dumped a stack of books on the table.

Davi shrugged, reached across the table to grab a roll and a pat of almond butter. "No," he said. "What happened?"

Tamus had to shout to be heard. Between the clink of utensils and chattering of students, the dining hall was always loudest at breakfast. "The Candlemass fire didn't light. I could have told them it wouldn't. However, since the world still seems to be here, I'm declaring it a miracle."

Davi peered out the hall's long windows. From where he sat, he could just see the crowns of swaying trees. Rain fell in sheets made practically horizontal by gales. He hadn't actually been outside yet, but he knew he'd have to face it soon. In less than an hour, to be precise.

"Pretty cliché if the world ended today anyway," he said. "Still, campus is always nicest when it rains."

"I'll say. Bet this is causing a few crises of faith." Laughing, Tamus rummaged in his bag. With a grunt, he heaved another thick book on the table. His plate jumped when it dropped. "Here's my reading. Pity me."

"*Aither and Anatomy: Medicinal Magic.* I don't know, Tam, looks pretty standard."

"Well, what about you?"

He could allow himself some smugness. With exaggerated care, Davi dribbled some honey to his tea. Stirring it, he said, "Oh, nothing much. Just a chat with Professor Volpes."

Though he loved his tea, rendering Tamus wordless was almost as good a way to start the morning. Having both was even better. Davi sipped, enjoying his drink and his friend's sputtering.

"You got a one-on-one with the Fox? How'd you manage that?"

Davi shrugged. "Easy, really. I'm a student in his Faculty, so he knows me, and when I explained what I'm studying..."

"Right, right. Any closer to finding out where aither comes from?"

Davi groaned and grabbed his tray. "Right now, I want to say the Beast. But the Ecclesiat's probably wrong about that, too. Good luck, Tam."

Cool air washed over Davi's face as he left the dining hall. He shivered a little, and wished he hadn't left his jacket in his dormitory. Still, who wore jackets at the beginning of summer? He hurried to the Regis Building, home of the Faculty of Experimental Magic. Worried that the wet lawns would muddy his shoes, he abandoned his usual shortcut and stuck to the paved paths, going the long way around the campus pond.

He paused outside the Regis Building to catch his breath. From its front steps, he couldn't even see the buildings across the pond. Some fog. It crawled over campus, engulfing the familiar trees and buildings, and turning them to alien shadows in the mist. When he deemed himself sufficiently composed, Davi strode inside and across the mosaic on the foyer floor. He winced as his wet footprints splattered the Magistatiem falcon, and looked for a mat to wipe his feet. No such luck.

Frowning now, he withdrew a scrap of paper from his pocket. *Volpes: 442.* Of course it would be on the fourth floor. Davi took the stairs two at a time, grateful for the carpeting. At least his shoes would be dry.

Although many of Davi's classes had been held in the Regis Building, he never felt entirely comfortable on its upper floors. Maybe it was the silence—you could almost hear pens scratching behind heavy office doors. Maybe it was the portraits—dead professors judged his haircut and scrawny build, and wondered why students never wore academic gowns anymore. Or maybe it was the knowledge of what lived here. As he rushed through the dark halls, he felt his heart thud in his throat. But that was silly; he knew they weren't here. Not now.

Still, he lingered by their door, pretending to tie his shoe. Then he straightened up, and brushed a finger over the brass nameplate. *MCBs.* A smaller, painted sign was affixed beneath: *Unauthorized Access Strictly Prohibited.* A heavy lock, the only one on the floor, reinforced the sign's message.

Directly next door, the name plate read *Doctor Conael Volpes.*

Davi straightened his tie, checked for his notebook, and knocked. He hoped his hands would stop shaking before Volpes answered.

The door opened too quickly to give them a chance. Cold fish eyes dissected him. "Yes?"

"Please, I have an appointment with Dr. Volpes."

The secretary blinked. "And you are...?"

"Sanders. Davi Sanders. I'm a student in Aither Studies."

Across the waiting room, Volpes's door flew open, and the professor himself beckoned Davi. "Sanders!" he said. "Quick now, I've double-booked myself. Should have time to squeeze you in, though."

"Of course, sir."

Volpes cocked his head. Lean and shrewd, his nickname— the Fox—suited him.

"You're the origin of aither, right?" Volpes said.

"Well yes, where it comes from...but also why some people can use it and others can't."

"Ah, yes. Come, make yourself comfortable. She'll be here shortly."

Davi sauntered past the secretary with a smirk and followed Volpes into his office. Rain lashed the windows, but a crackling fire warmed the room. Volpes took his place of honour at his desk, while Davi sank into a luxurious green chair. If only the dormitories had furniture like this. While Volpes busied himself with papers, Davi amused himself by reading the titles on the bookshelf opposite. Leather-bound texts stood to attention in neat, alphabetized rows. He got up to examine them more closely. Quite a few spellbooks, their spines thick and glossy, dotted the shelves.

"Sir? Are these the spells for creating an MCB?"

"What? No, those are kept safe in the vaults." A wave dismissed any further questions. "Let's talk about you. I assume you've traced magic ability through family trees?"

"Uh, yes, of course." With great effort, he pulled his thoughts back. "Genealogical study has helped; magic seems to run in families. It's strange..." He trailed off. "I wonder if certain traits are shared by parents and offspring. Like eye colour—my parents both have brown eyes, and so do I. Maybe magic is similar."

Volpes frowned. "That depends on where the aither's coming from. It's easy enough to say *I just reach for the blue fire.* The question is, where exactly are you reaching? Is the aither within us, somehow? Or is this 'passable trait' of yours the ability to access aither, rather than the aither itself?"

"Well, there was a paper recently, by Sorel, I think it was...it seemed to prove that aither isn't inherent in us."

Davi's pencil flew across the page. The problem of aither was one he'd been working on for a while. Besides which, the innocent question "What is the difference between magi and non-magi?" had led him down some treacherous paths of research. In some cases, the data simply didn't exist, leaving Davi to formulate his own theories, such as that of "passable traits," to help create his central thesis.

In the middle of a long, elliptical explanation of a recently-published paper, a knock sounded at Volpes's door. The professor cursed. "That will be my next appointment. An MCB evaluation. You know how important those are."

Davi swallowed. "Yes, sir."

The stare with which Volpes fixed him turned incisive. "Do you have much experience with MCBs?"

"No, sir."

A moment passed in which Davi heard his own heart. Volpes motioned him to stay seated. "Would you like to sit in on this eval? Might give you a new perspective on your research."

"Really? I can do that?" Davi clutched the armrest. "All right. Which one is coming?"

Volpes peered at Davi over his spectacles. "River of Knowledge."

"River?"

The professor raised an eyebrow. "You know her?"

21

Davi gulped and nodded. All three of the Magistatiem's MCBs worked in the library, which by this point was practically his second home. River was his favourite: her dark eyes had captured him the moment they first met his. And for some reason, it was most often River who offered him assistance. More than once he had daydreamt that she'd drop a book while shelving and their fingers would graze as he handed it to her... Stupid, pointless nonsense, but he couldn't help himself.

The knock repeated. "Come in," Volpes called, as Davi smoothed his hair.

The door opened to reveal a young woman. Short and slight, with dark hair that just brushed her chin, she stepped into the office, but froze on seeing Davi. "My apologies, Dr. Volpes. I was unaware you had a guest."

"No, no, River, he's observing your evaluation. Take the other chair, there."

Her movements were quick, sharp. Davi marvelled at the time and skill that had gone into her. Even close up, she looked human. What's more, she looked beautiful. Taken separately, her features were common enough: dark hair and eyes, hint of bronze to her skin, delicate face. Mixed together, they created a most uncommon result.

Suddenly conscious he was staring, Davi focused on the window behind Volpes. Tracks of rainwater coursed like spider webs. He willed his breathing to slow.

Volpes flicked open a notebook. He hunched forward, vulture-like. "Magically Created Being L/A 10-284," he said. "Otherwise designated River of Knowledge, otherwise called River. You are here for a standard examination and evaluation."

II

Balancing some paper and a pencil on his knee, Davi did his best to look serious and scholarly. If only he had a beard to stroke.

Behind his massive desk, Volpes shuffled papers, eyes narrowed. "Well then, River, how are you?"

"I am experiencing nominal function, thank you."

"Good." The professor scratched a note. "And Glory and Keeper? How are they?"

"Relationships between the Magically Created Beings continue to foster a maximally efficient working environment."

Her face was so still, not quite what Davi was used to. While he scrutinized her, pretending not to do so, Volpes continued his questioning. "Are you happy in your work?"

A slight pause this time. "I fulfil my duties within the library and archives as I was designed to do. If I did not, I would have no purpose. As I successfully complete all aspects of my work, I can therefore be said to have purpose."

Volpes wrote for several minutes. Where humans might have fidgeted, River sat straight and motionless. No crossing of legs, no tucking hair behind an ear. Contrary to stereotype, she did blink, but Davi noticed it was at regular intervals.

The evaluation resumed, but Davi's attention wandered. If he shifted just slightly, their knees would brush. *Stop that!* He berated himself. *Yes, she's so uncomfortably close, but she's an MCB. Not alive. Not a real woman.*

Oh, but she could fool me.

From time to time, Davi jotted something down. In truth, he couldn't grasp the significance behind some of Volpes's questions, nor River's answers. But Volpes was searching for something, he was sure of it. Davi stole another peek at River. Was it his imagination, or were those fine worry lines creasing her forehead? Surely her voice was just a little less flat?

Eventually Volpes paused and polished his spectacles. "River," he said, "I'm giving you some statements to consider. I want you to tell me whether they are informative, illogical, or…" A fox's grin split his face. "Humorous."

Davi jerked upright. MCBs and humour?

"First statement: The boy ate milk."

"Illogical."

"Second: The vineyard is in the valley."

"Informative."

They continued in this vein for some time. Davi's eyes darted from River to Volpes. So far, all the statements had been deemed illogical or informative. He waited, poised on the edge of his chair.

"Ninth." Volpes flicked a page over. "The astronomer married a star."

"Humorous," River said promptly.

"Explain." Volpes's words were honeyed poison. "Explain your reasoning."

For an instant, River's eyes widened. Before Davi could decide whether or not he'd seen it, she composed herself, her face impassive. "The word *star* has two meanings," River said. "It may refer to a celestial body, or to a talented and celebrated individual. In this context, the word refers to the latter meaning. However, astronomers are generally associated with the former. The simultaneous attribution of both definitions is a rhetorical device intended to evoke amusement."

She was no longer blinking. Instead, she maintained unbroken eye contact with Volpes. Tension tightened the room, as though half the air had been sucked out. Davi realized he was holding his breath.

Volpes considered River, playing with his ink bottle. "Thank you," he said at last. "Dismissed."

River wasted no time in leaving. The sounds of her rapid footsteps disappeared down the hall. Volpes continued to roll the ink bottle around his fingers, his mouth set in a thin, straight line. Davi bit his lip, afraid to break the silence. Then Volpes shook his head and sighed.

"Pity. She was our best one."

A cold weight settled in Davi's stomach. "Did she...pass?"

"She'll be kept under observation." The professor rubbed his temples. "Looks like she's becoming emotion-capable."

Emotion-capable. The words hung in the air, their implications as chilling as the rain outside. "How do you know? She seemed normal."

Volpes laughed. "You really don't have much experience with MCBs. The astronomer statement tipped me off. Most MCBs misidentify it as illogical. Once we had one that froze up, and then rambled on about how it could be informative, illogical, *or* humorous. But seeing the humour so quickly is a warning sign."

Davi felt like his mouth belonged to someone else. "What will happen to her?"

"We'll watch her. She's running out of chances, though. We've had reports of peculiar behaviour from her already. If she is emotion-capable... well, we don't want another Emerald on our hands."

"I guess not." He'd been an infant during the days of Emerald, but the stories haunted him. Driven to lethal rage after becoming infatuated with a mage in her department, Emerald had set experimental magic back years and alienated magi from the Ecclesiat even further. Since Emerald, any MCB which developed the ability to feel was killed.

Not killed, Davi reminded himself. *Destroyed.*

He barely heard Volpes's goodbye as he trudged back into the rain, head spinning with half-remembered hypotheses and crystal-sharp details of the evaluation process. Work. He had to work, to fill in those gaps in logic Volpes had shown him. A long session in the library was clearly in order.

The library. Davi stopped dead on the path, one foot drenched in a puddle. Fog obscured the clock tower, but presumably River was on duty by now. He increased his stride, dodging clumps of wet and miserable students.

In the distance, thunder rumbled.

The scent of Father Osvald's sick room made Gaelin gag. The room itself was spotless: a cold cup of tea was the worst offence to cleanliness. But sickness pervaded the freshly-washed linens and vases choked with flowers. It skulked in each breath Osvald took, cloaked his bed with the taste of death.

Osvald's eyes were closed, limp curls of hair plastered to his forehead. No matter how often Gaelin wiped his skin, it quickly grew hot and clammy. A dull flush bloomed on the Throne's cheeks, yet he shivered under heaps of blankets.

Gaelin checked the windows again, anxious to keep the rain out. Hand on the latch, he looked into the gardens. The pond's surface roiled. Even from inside the Throne's cottage, he heard wind shriek through the cloisters.

The sound briefly grew louder, and then died away as the Throne's front door opened and closed. Brother Baeor entered, the ends of his robes dripping water on the floor. "Any change?" he asked, seizing a towel to wipe his face.

"No." Gaelin took the towel and hung it near the fire. "Not in the time I've been here."

The Ecclesiat's healer placed the back of his hand on Osvald's forehead, only to snatch it away. "By the Angel! Have you gotten him to drink anything?"

"Alesta did. Some water." Gaelin hesitated. "But I don't think he knew what it was."

"As long as it went in him, that's fine." Baeor fussed over the Throne, feeling his pulse and lifting his eyelids one at a time. For such a large man, Baeor's movements were surprisingly graceful. "He was conscious last night?"

"According to Alesta. She was able to tell him about the ritual."

"Looks like Ael's spared us, eh? But it's odd things happening lately." Deftly, Baeor plucked a lemon from a small table by the window. He sliced it as he spoke, squeezing the juice into a cup of water. "The ritual. Father Osvald. Not to mention, we're seeing the last of the spring colds. How those boys spread them, I have no idea..."

Osvald interrupted with a hacking fit. His upper body rose off the bed, though his eyes remained closed. Gaelin rushed to him and held his shoulders. "Come, Father, it's all right."

Baeor grimaced as though the lemon were meant for him. "That's happening far too often."

"I know." Gaelin's own breathing calmed as the Throne's coughing subsided.

"What exactly did Alesta say to him?" Baeor asked.

"I don't know the exact details, only that she told him the ritual had failed. She returned to the morning watch so quickly, I doubt she told him much beyond that." Rain hammered the roof, filling the silence as the two men dribbled lemon water between Osvald's lips. "I've been speaking to him," Gaelin added, "just in case he can hear. I let him know that the sun did rise."

"Not that you can tell it from this weather."

Despite himself, a small smile escaped the sub-prior. "Perhaps. But I have faith it's there, behind the clouds."

"Well, we're still here, and that's enough for me." Baeor dipped his hands in the wash-basin. "You don't need to stay, Brother Gaelin. I can look after him."

"I don't mind."

Droplets of water splattered him as Baeor flicked his hands. "It's my duty. Anyway, there's quite a crowd in the cathedral. Seems they want explanations as to why the world didn't end last night."

"It should have."

Baeor shook his head. "Just no pleasing some people, I suppose."

"I do want to know *why*. Something in the natural order of things has broken. Frankly, that worries me almost as much as the failure of Candlemass itself." He tucked the blankets more securely around Osvald's chin. "I want to delve into the matter more, see if the ancients said anything on the subject."

"St. Memoyah?"

"Her prophecies do seem the best place to start. But if there is need for me in the cathedral..." Gaelin paused, his cowl half over his head. "Don't hesitate to send for me if things get worse."

"I will. Go serve the people."

The cathedral seethed with bodies. Wet, panicked, crowded bodies. Young children cried as their mothers pushed them before statues of the Angel. Young lovers cried, wondering if they'd been impure. The elderly remained quiet, beseeching the Angel with knotted hands and eyes filled with dim fear. He intended to find the answers they sought, but for now, Gaelin walked through this fear, and tried to dispel it with his words, to disarm the terror by listening to it.

"The sun didn't go out!" one woman shouted. "Is it the Beast? Is She preparing us for something worse?"

"No!" Her friend made the sign of the Three. "No, it is the Angel. In His mercy, He has prevented the apocalypse."

Silent as a spectre, Alesta glided beside Gaelin, making him jump at her touch. "Brother Gaelin, how is our dear Father Osvald?"

"Sleeping. Baeor is with him."

"Good." She peered into the crowded chapel. "Oh my." Without another word, she strode into the chapel and assumed a place at the front. A hush fell.

"My people," Alesta began. She sounded even more confident than the night before, her voice as strong and vibrant as Osvald was weak and sick. "My people, these are strange times in which we live, are they not?"

Nervous laughter broke out. But the sense of camaraderie shattered when a man yelled, "So why didn't we die last night? Is this all a fraud, then?"

Alesta smiled at him. Collected, controlled, she radiated calmness. She spoke louder. "The ritual fails, yet the sun rises again! Now, my people, who has seen the stone calendar?"

From the back of the crowd, a red-haired woman said, "I have."

"And? What did you see?"

The woman blinked. "The day stone has been moved," she said. "But not the year. According to the calendar, it's a new day without being a new age."

"Precisely!" Alesta smacked the back of one hand against her palm. "The old age has ended, but the new has not begun. We currently live in limbo, time outside of time. And why?" No answer came. "Because time has run out, yet the Angel has deemed us unfit for His new world. Thus He has given us time to purify ourselves, to make ourselves worthy of His mercy before He brings the Final Day."

Relieved smiles replaced frowns; hope flowed to people's faces and drove out the fear. "How do we purify ourselves?" another man shouted. "How long do we have?"

His question seemed to burst a dam. Similar shouts flooded forth, threatening to drown Alesta. For a moment, she wavered. Gaelin was about to step in when her hand brushed the Angel. Apparently, she drew strength from Him, for she straightened and said, "We shall be purified according to His words. Pray to Him, fast for Him, keep His spirit within you. But be warned." Her face darkened. "The end approaches, and in these last days, the Beast is here also. Be vigilant, lest you be led from the Angel's path."

"What about the Throne? Can Father Osvald guide us?"

"Ah, Brother Gaelin would know better than I."

At her gesture towards him, the masses swivelled as one. Countless pairs of eyes fixed on his own. The chapel suddenly felt much hotter, and Gaelin swallowed. "Father Osvald remains ill," he said. "We are, however, doing all we can to restore his health. Time shall provide answers, but I ask for your thoughts and prayers."

The impromptu sermon gradually disintegrated. People went to Alesta, to touch her and speak to her personally. Gaelin lingered for a time before returning to the nave. There, he reassured a family around the stone calendar, before kneeling at the People's Altar himself. He prayed, putting all his strength of mind into reaching that quiet place of divinity. But for once, his heart remained agitated. The Angel's blank eyes held no warmth for him. *Am I worthy, Angelus Rex? I cannot heal the Throne. I cannot bring solace to the people. How can I perform your will, Angel King? Please, Ael Who is All, show me the path.*

Someone cleared their throat. Gaelin turned to find the red-haired woman from the chapel, her mouth in a faint twist of amusement. "So," she said. "This world is in limbo, is it?"

"It is possible." He remained on his knees. "As Sister Alesta said, the new age is not begun, yet the world continues as if it had. Troubling days, indeed."

The woman sat beside him on the step below the chancel railing. She was young. Maybe in her twenties, a few years Alesta's junior.

"My apologies," Gaelin said. "I forget myself. I am Brother Gaelin."

Blood-red lips parted in a smile. "Serafine. Likewise." She offered a hand. Gaelin took it, but he cringed on touching her. The coldness of her skin made him want to wipe his hand on his robes. Serafine smiled again. "Sorry about that. I've been outside all day."

"Have you nowhere to go?"

She shook her head. Deep red hair tumbled down her back, catching the light. Celibacy had not completely deadened Gaelin's instincts. The thoughts didn't stay long, though. He had only so much energy; he had decided long ago to channel it into his ministry, rather than to individual members.

"First time in the City. I knew a family, once, that lived nearby. But they've long since left."

A traveller, then. Probably an Islander, judging by the looks of her. Though most remained fairly isolated, especially as so much of their mythology emphasized the Beast, a few wandered through the City every so often. It would explain much: not only the curious glances she shot at the Angel's statue, but also her name and colouring, so different from the mostly dark-haired, dark-eyed people of the City.

From what he'd heard, while the islands had little use for the Angel, they did value their kin groups. Travelling alone would be difficult for her, and he winced in sympathy. "My dear..."

Serafine shrugged. "Don't worry, I can find an inn. Are there any nearby?"

"Never mind an inn." He rose and gestured for her to follow. "The Ecclesiat does not turn away those in need."

She raised an eyebrow. "Are you suggesting I stay here?"

"I am." Gaelin surprised himself with the forcefulness of his voice. If he could speak like this in front of a crowd, he'd sing the Angel's praises from the bell tower. "Not here in the cathedral, but in the priory connected to it. There are always extra beds."

"They won't mind?"

"We ask our guests to help where they can; we'll be pleased to have an extra pair of hands."

After showing Serafine to the dorters, Gaelin went to the library. Questions dogged him, demanding answers. Were they in limbo, as Alesta said? He had to discover what was happening, how to prepare for it. Gaelin poked into books chained to their shelves, hoisting them onto lecterns for a closer look and running his hand along ancient, leather-bound spines. He was sure he remembered rightly, but there was a gap where his books should have been. The clink of rustling chains grew louder as he pulled volumes out faster and faster.

"Need help?" Sister Liana, the library's guardian, tapped his shoulder. She had to stand on tiptoe to do it; the top of her head barely reached Gaelin's chest.

"Yes, actually. You seem to have a book missing."

Liana glared at him. Giant spectacles magnified her expression into something far more menacing than a person of her stature could normally achieve. "Missing?" she hissed. "None of my books are *missing*."

He held his hands up. "Of course not! What I meant to say is, I can't find it."

She relaxed. "That's a different matter. Which one?"

"*The Prophecies of St. Memoyah*."

"What?" Liana withdrew as though from a serpent. Behind her spectacles, her eyes narrowed. "Memoyah was an insane old hag, and probably worked for the Beast to boot. What do you want her work for?"

"She wrote about the End Days. Liana, I need to know for certain whether or not the final times are upon us."

"I see." Liana's nose wrinkled. "Sister Alesta says the end's been postponed. We have to get cleaned up first."

Gaelin pulled a chair from a nearby carrel and sank onto it. The rain wasn't helping the twinge in his hip. "I know. But I think that, given the circumstances, we should consider all possibilities. Blessed is he that hears the wise man's whisper over the shouting of fools, no?"

The librarian cackled. "I think you just called Alesta a fool. I won't tell," she added, catching Gaelin's stricken expression. "Now, let me see..." Without warning, Liana darted down the aisles. Gaelin eased himself up and trailed her to the front of the library. She hopped onto a small box set before a wooden lectern, upon which lay a book so large, Gaelin doubted Liana would be able to carry it. A chain, thick as two of Gaelin's fingers, snaked from a loop at the back of the book's cover to another on the lectern. It jangled against the wood as Liana flipped pages.

"*St. Memoyah, St. Memoyah.* Ah, here we are. *The Prophecies of St. Memoyah.* Author: St. Memoyah of Oris. A collection of visions on the last days of this world and the return of Ael." She looked up. "Funny, *the return of Ael.* She implies Ael is gone. Interesting, how even centuries ago, we see Ael's influence wane. Did you know some sects don't even worship Ael anymore? Either Ael is dead, or Ael is become the Angel. Personally, I..."

"Sister," Gaelin said gently. "The book?"

"Right." She squinted at the page. Sighed. Polished her spectacles. Squinted again. "According to this, it's not here anymore."

"I beg your pardon?"

"No, it's gone." Liana stabbed the page. "About thirty years ago. Needed rebinding. Of course, that fool Cardo ran the library then. He couldn't rebind books to save his soul."

Gaelin slumped. "So it's been destroyed."

"Not exactly." A soft curse burst from Liana. She absent-mindedly made the sign of the Three, and then cursed again. "Cardo couldn't rebind it, so he sent it to someone who could. Idiotic move, of course, because he never dared to go get it back." She heaved the massive volume shut. "Brother Gaelin, your book's at the Magistatiem."

"Very well," Gaelin said. "I shall pay them a visit."

Liana laughed. "Go on, tell me another!"

Her mirth passed over him. "For all she has been discredited, St. Memoyah remains the authority on the End Days. If there is any value at all to her prophecies, we owe it to our people to read them."

"Fine!" Liana shook her head. "I still think she's a rambling old bat, but you're right. What am I saying? Of course you're right—you're Gaelin."

He smiled on his way out.

"Let us pray the Magistatiem thinks likewise."

—⌣—

Blackness cloaked the cathedral. All was silent. Hardly surprising considering the hour; even the most devoted monks were in the dorters, deep in sleep.

Save one.

The door between cathedral and cloisters creaked. Alesta froze, listened for approaching footsteps. No one came. The nave was empty. Clutching her lamp, she crept up the centre aisle, past the Altar, and to the back of the chancel. There, she pulled on her gloves and eased the door open. No tell-tale creaking this time. These hinges were always well-oiled. Another glance backward at the cathedral's shadowy vastness, and she disappeared down the corridor.

Upon reaching the inner sanctum, she ignored the High Altar. She set her lamp down and tugged at the trapdoor. It swung upwards, revealing a shadowy square in the marble floor. Uneven steps descended out of sight. Without hesitating, Alesta retrieved her lamp and went down. The walls narrowed, pressing in on either side until it seemed inevitable she would be crushed between them. She paused a moment to measure the distance between the rough-hewn walls and wait for the dizziness to pass. There was enough space. There was enough air, even if it smelled of long-forgotten dust. The Angel outweighed her petty fears.

At the bottom of the stairs, passages went off in three directions. She chose the centre one. A musty scent thickened the air, and for a moment, she could not breathe. It was a tomb. Her tomb. The urge to flee to the great open space of the cathedral above curdled into despair of ever escaping the pressing darkness. Her thoughts gathered their legs and broke from tortured crawl to frantic gallop. The passage was closing on her, consuming her. Whisperings from the rock. A pit of spirits, all of them circling her like vultures.

She thrust her hand to the wall. Felt the rough, solid stone. It wasn't moving. No whispers. The tightness in her chest eased, but she closed her eyes against the panic. Her fingertips could guide her. In any case, there was little to see, no carvings or paintings. The dead had little use for such things.

Bumps in the stone under her feet pointed the way as effectively as signs. The passage had stopped sloping. The pads of her fingers slipped into gashes in the rock as she continued on her way; she could trace the runes as easily as if all the Ecclesiat's candles were trained on them. Now she forced her eyes open. It would not do to run her hands over an ossuary.

She reached another door, massive and unmarked. Ebony wood contrasted with the grey stone of the catacombs. Few ever saw it. Fewer still passed through it. Alesta did so with a prayer to the Angel.

After all, it was His sepulchre.

Light from her lamp skittered off the gold of the interior. Despite its weak flame, the reflection dazzled her. Gold tiled the floor, walls, and ceiling. The eye, overwhelmed, clung to the sole object within the Angel's sepulchre: another statue of Him. It was carved not from gold, but some white stone that was not marble, or crystal, or any mineral ever found in the ground. He loomed over Alesta, shadows streamed behind Him to cover the rear wall.

All was perfectly silent. All was perfectly still.

Alesta collapsed before the Angel, her forehead pressed against the precious floor. She cleared her mind, and her thoughts faded to an expectant void. This was where the Angel truly lived. When He was ready, He would come.

In the depths of her mind, she felt something stir.

Angelus Rex! Alesta cried mutely. *O, my Angel King!*

An alien mind grazed her: curiosity without joy, a clinical questioning that challenged her presence here.

Tears pricked the corners of her eyes. *I am frightened, Angel King. The fire did not light, but the world did not end. Why, my King? I feel the people's faith dissolving. I try to guide them back to You, but—*

The otherness turned sibilant, beguiling. Alesta's eyelids drooped. Events were following some plan of His, she sensed that much, but... "I don't understand."

The Angel's cold anger filled the chamber.

Alesta's spirit quailed, and she writhed on the ground. It was true. She had known it all along. They were impure, perpetually doomed to failure. Even her own monks; she had heard them discussing Gaelin's red-haired stray, without care for their vows of celibacy. Even she—but she would atone for all her transgressions, both great and small. Yet atonement was impossible. They were imperfect sinners, every one of them fallen from the grace of Ael.

Hints of triumph. Quiet scorn as she thought the name *Ael.* "Angel?"

He waited. Let her reason her way to the truth. "Ael is all," she said hesitantly, "pure and impure. If you are the stainless part of Ael... As Ael became you, you purified even Ael..."

The flame strengthened in her lamp, threw more light upon His face.

"Then you...you are greater than Ael."

Satisfaction replaced the anger.

"But if the people worship Ael, they also worship that part of Ael which is the Beast."

Assent.

Horror suffused Alesta's veins. Every time she had prayed to Ael, she had also offered prayer to the Beast? Her wicked, foolish flesh and soul were more contaminated than she had believed.

The Angel reached for her, and she felt her spirit burn under the scorching heat of His hand. What was left of her floated, savouring the perfectness of the Angel. She had no idea how long she lay there, on the floor of the Angel's sepulchre. But at last, she lifted her head to His statue.

I am your servant, Angelus Rex.

III

He hadn't found her. Directly after his meeting with Volpes, Davi went to the library and searched for River. He conceded defeat only after combing through the stacks for so long that the other two MCBs had given up asking if he needed help.

Not that this stopped him from returning the next day. He loitered by the library until the clock on the Chancellor's Tower showed one past dawn. The storm had intensified overnight and stiff wind flung rain against him like tiny pebbles. Soon, his jacket dripped water, and his shoes and socks squished as he shifted from foot to foot. When Keeper of Truth came to unlock the doors, he nearly knocked her down in his rush to get inside.

Soft lamplight made the library into a cocoon of warmth and cosiness. Any other time, he would have succumbed to the urge to lose himself in the stacks. Not today. He sprinted to the information desk. Behind it, Glory sorted a pile of newly-returned books. She stamped the date on each one, so engrossed that she didn't notice Davi until he coughed.

"Good morning. May I be of assistance?"

"I'm looking for River," Davi said. "Where is she?"

No emotion flickered over Glory's face. "She is shelving this morning. I would suggest you try the upper floors."

Not a soul stirred on the third floor. Davi supposed it was awfully early for anyone to be working. His stomach rumbled, and he groaned as he climbed the central staircase, shoes squeaking on the marble. It was a cruel world in which the library opened before the dining hall. The fourth floor was equally empty; he thought he saw her once, but it was only branches beating the windows. Davi paused by the glass. No doubt, he didn't fancy walking across campus in *that*. Lightning cracked through the black sky. For an instant, the grounds shone silver before plunging into darkness. Thunder bellowed like the final roar of a wounded beast.

Davi shuddered. At this rate, he might have to live in the library. He turned down another row, and smacked into River. "Sorry!" he gasped.

She hefted the volumes she'd been carrying. One of their sharp corners had bruised him; he forced himself not to rub his shoulder.

"Good morning, Davi. May I be of assistance?"

At least she'd said his name. "I wanted to talk to you."

"For what purpose?"

Davi ran his hands through his hair. He should've practiced. "I...wanted to talk to you about yesterday," he ventured. "You know, what happened with Volpes."

"You refer to my evaluation."

"That's right. Here, can I take those for you?" He lifted the books from her arms and almost dropped them on his foot. He managed to set them on a nearby trolley before breaking anything. Now his shoulder throbbed harder. River watched, and he could have sworn amusement sparkled in her eyes.

"They are heavier than they appear," she said.

"I'll say." He laughed, but his high spirits shrivelled quickly. "Look, River, I came to warn you. You're in danger."

Her eyes went blank. Like a soldier at attention, her voice was as rigid as her stance. "May I enquire as to how you reached that conclusion?"

"Come with me." He pulled her away from the staircase, further down the aisle. Her hand was the same temperature as the air. No blood warmed her skin, but neither was she deathly cold as most people expected. They stood in an alcove lined with shelves, somewhere in the magical communications section. That seemed safest; the com-magi were notoriously late sleepers.

"Davi," River said, "it is not standard policy to engage in private conversations during working hours."

"This is important!" Flinching, he lowered his voice. "Look, Volpes thinks you're becoming emotion-capable. They're watching you."

River's shoulders slumped. Davi could think of nothing to say. What was there to say? Her own reaction sealed her fate. The fear etched across her face made him squirm. For the first time, he hated his fellow magi. Some might call River an abomination. But now, she was just a frightened young woman.

He took a hesitant step, then abandoned caution and embraced her. "It'll be all right," he said. Even to him, the sentiment rang hollow.

She pushed him away. "May I enquire as to the basis for that assumption?"

"We'll think of something."

"I am unsure, Davi." More thunder rumbled. Davi jumped, but it didn't startle River. She continued, "The laws are very strict. Any contravention would jeopardize the Faculty of Experimental Magic, as well as the Magistatiem as a whole."

"So what? You'll give yourself up?"

"I didn't say that. I merely suggested that such infringement would be difficult at best and dangerous at worst. You yourself risk expulsion from the university, not to mention arrest and imprisonment. Do you truly wish to implicate yourself in this matter?"

"Yes. I do." They locked gazes. Davi's breath felt sharp and fast. "I won't see you destroyed."

"Did Dr. Volpes give any indication regarding the duration of his observations?"

"How long he was going to watch you? No, he didn't."

River frowned. Somehow, the sight of her furrowed brow

comforted Davi. Only yesterday, she would have hidden it from him. "Then it seems a swift course of action is advisable." She paced down the aisle. "Having considered the possibilities, it seems I have no choice. I must leave the Magistatiem."

"Leave?" Davi ran after her. "Where will you go?"

"I..." Possibly for the first time, she said, "I am uncertain."

"An inn, maybe? I have some money..."

"No." She shook her head emphatically. "I will not let you expend money on me."

Davi took her hand again. His thumb rubbed her soft skin. Exceptional.

"Davi?"

"Yes?"

"I dislike being touched without forewarning."

"Oh." He dropped it and stared down. "I didn't know."

"Do not worry. Now, it would seem passing for human is my best option. I..." River broke off, eyes wide. "Someone's coming," she hissed.

Davi heard nothing, but then, he was only human. In an attempt to appear casual, he snatched a book from the shelf at random. At the corner of his eye, he saw River shelving as though they hadn't spoken a word. He held his breath, waited for whoever it was to pass them by. Hoped they didn't need help, hoped that...

Hoped in vain. An older man approached them, panting. A dark cloak draped his shoulders; water droplets beaded the wool. While his hair had gone completely grey, he had the kind of strong jaw Davi wanted when he was in his "mature years." The man smiled at them both. "Good morning," he said. The warmth and richness of his voice disarmed Davi. Despite the interruption, he couldn't help but return the man's smile.

"Good morning. May I be of assistance?" River clasped her hands behind her back and stood at attention, all emotion wiped away.

The man bowed to her. "Thank you, my dear. Do you know where I could find a woman named River?"

Davi made frantic gestures behind the man's back, but River ignored him. "Yes, I am River," she said. "How may I help you?"

The man extended a hand. An instant's hesitation, and River shook it. The man smiled again. "A pleasure, young lady. I am sorry to trouble you so early, but I wanted to arrive before you became too busy. My name is Brother Gaelin. The woman at the front desk told me that you could help me find a particular book."

"Certainly."

River betrayed no confusion, but Davi's thoughts whirled. Brother Gaelin? The man was a monk: closer inspection revealed the tell-tale grey robes peeking from beneath his cloak. Yet he treated River like she was human. Where were the sneers? Why "young lady" instead of "MCB"? Not that Davi objected, but he certainly expected scorn from the Ecclesiat.

Gaelin glanced at the walls of books, his eyes tracing them upwards to the ceiling and the hanging chandeliers. With one finger, he stroked the velvet coverings meant to protect the rarer volumes from sunlight. "Magnificent," he said. "Simply marvellous." He moved to a shelf of exposed books. He frowned as he read their titles, but said nothing. Then he adjusted his cloak, looking up and down the rows. "Forgive me," he said, "but are there any of those artificial people about? I did hear they were used in the library."

"There are three MCBs employed as librarians and archivists," River said. "But I doubt they will trouble you on your visit here. Now, for which book are you searching?"

The monk couldn't tell. Davi wanted to laugh at this gracious, greying man. For all the Ecclesiat loathed MCBs, condemned them as atrocities against Ael, they couldn't recognize one standing right in front of them. He grinned. Perhaps River had a chance after all.

"*The Prophecies of St. Memoyah*," the monk was saying. "It's one of ours. I understand it was sent here for rebinding some thirty years ago."

"Thirty-two."

"Very well. In any case, we believe it's time it was returned to us."

"Of course. I shall show you the way." She beckoned Gaelin to follow, and then stared at Davi. "Davi, I can continue helping you with your research later. Perhaps two past noon? You mentioned Volume XVI-A of the MCB texts. They're in the vault, but one of the librarians can let you in."

"I never—"

"In the vault. I shall see you in a few hours."

"All right." The false smile hurt. "Thanks, River."

"Excellent. Now if you come this way, Brother Gaelin..."

The instant they were out of sight, Davi found a card catalogue and flipped through titles as fast as he could. The MCB texts weren't available for checkout; he'd never even read them. They were those primary sources students whispered about, but never actually dared use. Finally, he unearthed the appropriate card.

Design and Production of Magically Created Beings, Volume XVI-A: Restoration of Energy Levels in the Fully-Functioning MCB.

Davi's throat constricted. So that was her plan. Outwardly indistinguishable from humans, MCBs lacked inner organs. No digestive tract meant no food: they got their energy from a maintenance spell. If River was to survive outside the Magistatiem, she needed a copy of that spell, and a mage to cast it.

Evidently, that mage would be him.

———

In the robing room, Praeton hung his cloak and threw his surplice over his head. He yawned, wriggled his jaw, and sang a few notes. Not bad. Not great, either, but his throat always felt thick first thing in the morning. Though Brother Evander would never admit it, that was probably why they never did the

Dawn service. Everyone needed time to wake their voices up, and those who lived at home needed time to arrive.

Across the garden, a lamp burned in the dormitory windows. Praeton groaned. His warm bed called to him. Not to mention, his stomach growled on finding him awake. For a moment he considered running to the garden's fig tree. He'd climbed it only days ago, still had scrapes and everything from the bark, and the fruit had been heavy, drooping as though too tired to cling to the tree much longer. By now they were probably dripping juice: a sure sign of ripeness.

A flash of lightning gave him pause. Mud and white robes didn't mix. Either Sister Alesta or Evander would have his hide for getting his surplice dirty. And he didn't want to be halfway up the tree when thunder crashed. He wouldn't be scared or anything, but the sound might startle him enough to make him lose his grip.

A group of seminary boys trooped in, tossing wet cloaks aside and laughing. Now that they were old enough to live at the Ecclesiat, they thought they were practically full-fledged monks. Never mind Praeton, who had lived there all of his eleven years. He crept to a corner, trying to make as little noise as possible. Soon, he could wait in the cloisters without looking like a complete pet. Until then, he focused on being invisible.

"Hey, strawhead!"

He didn't look up, just read his music.

"Didn't you hear me?"

Perched on his stool, he pressed his feet into the floor to stop them trembling.

"Ah, leave him alone. He's not worth it."

"Even his own parents didn't think so!"

Praeton counted off the soprano line's intervals in his head. His cheeks burned. He was afraid to look up, in case he saw them flaming in the big mirror. A sick knot of hurt pulsed in his chest.

"Just left him here."

"Not even a week old, and they didn't want him anymore."

The hands of the clock stood at a quarter-hour to dawn. Still giving no indication that he heard them, Praeton gathered his music and headed for the door. As he passed the older boys, his shoulders hunched; he felt like a turtle retreating to its shell. They were huge, maybe sixteen or seventeen years old. One even had a beard. That boy smirked and nudged his friends.

"Look, he's not deaf. Are you, strawhead?"

He was about to say something. Really, he was. But when he opened his mouth, nothing came out. Mortified, he ran from the room, hugging his prayer book to him. Their laughter chased him from the robing room, echoing off the cloister walls.

Fortunately, they were all basses. When the call came to line up, the rest of the boys' choir, the women, and the tenors stood between them. Alesta headed the lines; Praeton couldn't see Gaelin anywhere and was too afraid to ask.

The Head Chorister, an officious fourteen-year-old named Jaon, clouted the back of Praeton's head. "Eyes in front, there."

Praeton obeyed. Jaon the Pawn got nasty if he sensed defiance. The older boy inspected the rows, yanking surplices straight and smacking those who hadn't opened their prayer books. This earned him an approving word from Alesta. Praeton seethed as a smirking Jaon settled into the middle position of the front row. It wasn't fair. His prayer book had been ready. His surplice was straight. And he'd been the first to arrive, even before any of the adults.

Mentally flicking Jaon's head as they processed into the cathedral helped some. He knew the hymn by heart, so all he had to do was look holy and angelic, and try not to step on anyone's hem. The Angel's statue loomed ahead. One by one, each row of three broke off singing and mouthed a prayer. The hairs on the back of Praeton's neck prickled as his turn came. He'd never felt comfortable around it. That vague smile. The empty eyes. Cold stone skin. It made him feel wrong, somehow, like he was singing everything a half step flat.

Seated in the choir stalls out of the statue's sight, Praeton relaxed a little. Attendance was high for a Dawn service. Normally, only monks bothered to come. Probably parents accompanying their sons. He searched his folder for the next anthem, half an ear on Alesta.

"May Ael and the Angel keep us from sin," she said.

"And redeem us when we fall," Praeton mumbled with the congregation. Definitely no Gaelin on the other side. Strange. He never missed a service.

The boy beside him nudged his ribs and slipped him a piece of paper. Eyes forward, Praeton unfolded it. He glanced down, and bit his tongue to keep from laughing. Some doubly-talented chorister had sketched the sub-prioress, with enlargements to certain parts of her body. A figure labelled "Jaon" clasped himself to her knees, little hearts floating around his head.

"You stew in pollution!"

Praeton stifled a gasp and stuffed the paper in the back of his folder. But it was only part of the sermon. Alesta paced like a caged panther before the People's Altar, gesturing to each corner of the cathedral.

"All of you who dare presume come before the Angel King are tainted, hopelessly impure!" She swung around to face the choirs. Her glare pierced Praeton, and he couldn't help a shudder. "I have had a visitation from our Angel!"

The shudder strengthened. Alesta's dreams must be worse than his.

"Last night, the Angel blessed me with a divine revelation. We have been mistaken, my people. We worship that which is unworthy of our praise, and we beg redemption of that which would gladly damn us. Ael is All. Thus, Ael is not only Angel, but Beast. For centuries, we have in fact offered devotion to our tormentor, She who corrupted mankind."

Any rustling of sheet music stopped. In the pews, people fidgeted, bit their lips. Whispers slithered across the chancel rail to Praeton's ears. Fear. Doubt. A dull pain throbbed behind his left eye. He rubbed it, but it didn't go away. A lump blossomed in his stomach. He swallowed, praying he wouldn't throw up in front of the choir.

"The Angel is our purifier. It is He who removes our flaws, and seeks to restore us to that perfect state from which we fell. Yet have you never considered that the Angel purified *Ael?* The imperfect parts of Ael became the Beast. There is only goodness in the Angel. The Angel is Ael in Ael's perfect state. Ael remains Ael in that Ael is both Angel and Beast, but Ael as Ael alone no longer exists, and has not for eons."

Gobs of spit slid down Praeton's throat. Even if he managed to hold his stomach, the next hymn would be deadly. He'd be lucky if he didn't spray all over the opposite side.

"We worship an imperfect god. We worship a dead god."

He stopped praying to keep from throwing up, and instead hoped Ael would let him die after he did. Every sound grated. Shafts of light pierced his eyeballs to the back of his skull.

"The Angel is Ael redeemed, a higher form of Ael. These final days are our final test."

The choir stalls opposite Praeton blurred. The high arches and carvings behind them darkened and spun into nothingness. Alesta's voice echoed in his head before dying away. The relief of silence didn't last long. From far off, Praeton heard screams. Men, women, and children shrieked as though their souls burned. The cries sharpened, gouged his heart and annihilated all thought. Praeton wanted to scream too, but couldn't, his jaws clamped shut as though welded together.

Ael just let me die Angelus Rex Angel King I don't know who you are but please let me die don't make me I'll be good forever I swear o Ael please please please

Flames arched across the blackness. Wherever they struck, they

illuminated horrors the likes of which Praeton had seen only in
sleep. Purpled, bloated limbs. Drool hanging like cobwebs from
slack mouths. Blood rushed from the Altar, down the aisles. An
acrid iron smell fouled the air, and Praeton gagged on it, his lungs
scorched and thickened, choking him. Like a bird hovering over
the City, he saw boiling red rivers flood the streets. Above it all,
on the Ecclesiat's bell tower, perched the Angel. Blackened blood
gummed His feathers together. His face was pointed towards the
dead and dying below, but remained as impassive as His statue.
Then He turned towards Praeton.

It sent Praeton reeling. Vomit rose in his throat, and far away
his body heaved and retched. Sweat burst out all over his body;
his skin blazed, surely he would die now, he didn't know how
he could still be alive, surely there was nothing left of him but
a pile of ash under his choir robes. A roasting wind swept over
him as the Angel unfurled His wings. He pointed to the sky.

The sun was black.

Praeton's voice bubbled up. Finally free, it erupted forth, and
he screamed and screamed. A thump to the side of his head.
Someone yelling, funny, it sounded just like him. Then cool
stone against his cheek. A bleary glimpse of shoes and the scuffs
along the bottom of the choir stalls.

Then nothing.

———

Rain woke him. For a moment, he remained still, bed sheets
cool against his skin, his limbs sinking into a soft mattress. Soft
light, like the half-light of dawn, filtered through a window
beside his head. Everything was white: the bed, the walls, the
cabinets. Everything nice and white, nothing at all like—

Praeton jerked upright. He was in the infirmary. Beloved
Angel, he hadn't fainted in the middle of service, had he? That
was a million times worse than throwing up. Dim memories
of yelling and thrashing surfaced. He groaned and pulled the
covers over his head. There, in his white cocoon, he succumbed

to tears. He'd have to run away, he would never, ever hear the end of this. And the dream itself—why couldn't it stay in the night-time where it belonged? If the Angel was angry at him, he couldn't imagine what he'd done.

"You awake under there?"

Praeton's sobs halted. It was a woman. He'd expected Brother Baeor. A sniffle escaped. None of the clergy were there for him.

"Want to come say hello?"

Not particularly. He burrowed deeper under covers, wrapped himself in coolness. A weight dropped by his legs, and a hand rested on his shoulder. "Don't be afraid. I don't bite."

Praeton emerged, wary and tense. A youngish lady rested on the end of his bed, smiling at him. Sometimes people from far-off cities found their way to the Ecclesiat, like he thought maybe his parents had, but she didn't look like any woman he'd ever seen: much taller, with deep red hair.

"Who are you?" he croaked.

The woman extended a hand. "Serafine. Your name's Praeton, right?"

"How did…"

"They told me when they brought you in. You had quite a morning." Her slender hands fluttered around the water jug on his bedside table. "Are you thirsty? I'm not really sure what I'm doing. Baeor asked me to watch you while he stayed with the Throne."

"Yes, please." The water was ice cold; funny that they'd bring up a barrel from the basement. He wiped his mouth on his sleeve. "You're not a monk."

Serafine laughed. It reminded Praeton of silvery bells. "No, I'm not. I'm just staying here for a while."

"How long?"

"I'm not sure." Serafine poured some water for herself, and sipped it slowly. "What happened to you in there?"

Praeton scowled. "Nothing."

49

"It was something."

"I don't know. I guess I dozed off or something. Had a dream. It's not worth all this fuss."

"You had a dream?" She set the cup down, gave him a look he couldn't quite read. "It must have been awful."

"I guess."

"What was it about?"

The words tumbled out before he could stop them. "Blood. Fire. The Angel."

Serafine drew back. A calculating expression flitted across her pale features, and then vanished. She started several times to say something, but broke off. Praeton stared at the rain. He shouldn't have mentioned the Angel. She'd think he was crazy, or worse.

"I'm not a monk," Serafine said. "But I've been reading the Tablet. Brother Baeor left it out; I think he was hoping I'd pick it up."

Praeton said nothing. She must be a foreigner if she'd never read the Tablet. Some places didn't have it, and that's why there were missionaries. Gaelin said he'd known one, once. In the Ecclesiat, everyone had their own Tablet, beside the bed, on top of the bookshelf. It told everything of Ael and the Angel; anyone in the Ecclesiat could recite whole passages of it.

Serafine opened a battered book. The cover dangled, but Praeton could still make out the intricate lettering on the front. "I rather liked the beginning," Serafine said. "Listen." She curled up in a chair by Praeton's bed and read aloud, "*Where there was no time, before there was any place, the first Word of Ael sounded. And all the vastness of eternity shuddered.*" Serafine glanced at him. "I've never heard the Hapax described like that."

Praeton stirred. "Hapax?"

"A Hapax is a word that appears only once, ever. That first word Ael spoke created the universe. Since there's only one universe, Ael must have spoken it just that one time. So the great Word, the…" She paged ahead. "…*sacred Word, beginner*

50

of worlds, is a Hapax. *The* Hapax."

"Oh." Praeton blinked. "I've heard of the Word."

"Same thing. *The Word was with Ael and the Word was Ael.*" Serafine closed the book. "Ever wonder what the Hapax actually was? What exactly did Ael say to create everything?"

"I don't know." His head ached, and he didn't like the way the conversation was going. "Probably you couldn't understand the Word if you weren't Ael."

She shrugged. "Maybe you're right." Pursing her lips, she added, "I didn't care for the depiction of the Flood. It just feels wrong."

"Well, it's the Beast's fault." Praeton yawned. Really, she didn't know anything. "The Angel was trying to cleanse the world, and She gave magic to a bunch of sinners so they wouldn't be drowned. She betrayed Ael."

Suddenly, the infirmary door burst open. Alesta stalked in, formal robes flapping about her legs, her mouth distorted with rage. "What were you doing?" she demanded. "We had to stop the service! If this is some sort of childish prank—"

"No, Sister Alesta, it was real!" He shoved his hands under the covers so she wouldn't see them shaking. "I didn't mean to, honest!"

"Then what happened?"

"I felt really sick." Praeton blinked away threatening tears. "Then I fainted. I never meant anything!"

"If I may speak..." With the fluid grace of a cat, Serafine slipped around Praeton's bed and laid a hand on the headboard. An ironic smile played about her mouth as she bowed to the sub-prioress. "The boy has been through a terrible ordeal. I believe his disruption of the service only upsets him further."

Alesta snorted. "A terrible ordeal? It was nothing, compared to those who have suffered for their faith."

"And he hasn't?"

"He's eleven!"

Serafine's lip curled. "Age makes no difference."

Praeton scrunched down in his bed, wishing he could fall

through and hide underneath. The two women stood above him, glaring at each other.

"I'm sorry," he said. "It won't happen again."

"See that it doesn't," Alesta snapped. "Or you may find yourself removed from the choir, if not from the Ecclesiat entirely."

He gaped at her. "But this is my home!"

"The Ecclesiat is a place of worship home to clergy and seminarians." Not a spark of warmth showed in Alesta's face. "You are neither. Believe me, it is only the self-indulgence of certain members of the Order that keeps you here. If you cannot abide by the Angel's demands for purity, you must leave."

"It was the Angel!" Praeton twisted fistfuls of sheets, the tears pricking in earnest. "I saw Him!"

Sarcasm stung him like venom. "You saw the Angel King?"

He nodded quickly.

Alesta's face tightened. "You lie."

"No!" Praeton's voice rose by octaves, ending in a squeak. "I swear it!"

Again, Serafine glided noiselessly, this time coming to stand between Praeton and Alesta. "I believe him," she said. "But even if I didn't, it would be clear that he went through something quite distressing. It would be wise to let him rest."

Redness flooded Alesta's cheeks. "You have no authority here!"

Serafine's mouth opened, but nothing came out. Whatever retort she had prepared hung forgotten for a long moment. At last, she said, "Don't I know you?"

"What? Of course not."

"No, of course not," Serafine murmured. "My mistake."

Alesta stepped away from Serafine, her lips pressed together. Pulling the blankets closer, Praeton exhaled in relief at being ignored. Maybe he could get out of this all right, and then he'd stay clear of the sub-prioress until the evening service. Maybe Gaelin would be back by then, and he could explain it to her, tell her it wasn't his fault, really.

He concentrated on lying absolutely still. Alesta broke away from Serafine's gaze, and turned her back on them. "See that it doesn't happen again," she said. The door slammed after her, and Praeton flinched.

When he was sure she wasn't coming back, he said, "Serafine?"

She stopped staring at the door, and gave him another smile. "Feeling better?"

"I think so, but..."

"Good. I guess you can run along, then. And Praeton?" She patted his shoulder. "Sleep well tonight."

IV

News that classes were cancelled spread throughout the Magistatiem before midday. Students gathered in the common rooms, giddy with the prospect of an unexpected holiday. Jokes and laughter flew through the air, as did several balled-up essays and a few textbooks. The hearth crackled, attracting a number of students who crouched before it armed with bread and pokers for making toast. Davi hunched in one of the common room's armchairs, removed from the merriment. If he had to meet River at two past, he needed her spell before then. Judging from the storm's howls, he'd be wise to leave extra time to travel across campus. So, he should leave at—

"Oy, Davi!" Tam thumped the back of his head. "You all right there?"

"I'm fine."

"You don't look it," Tam slumped on a nearby footstool. "Be happy! It's a lucky thing, this storm. A few trees go down, and we're basking in free time. Come on, let's have an early lunch!"

"You go ahead."

Tam cocked his head. "What's wrong?"

"Nothing." Davi sighed. Bad weather gave him a headache. "Is the library staying open?"

"Far as I know, it is. But you're not working!" Tam clutched his stomach. "Work's the worst thing to do on a day off—gives you cramps, it does! Then your sense of balance goes." He toppled off the stool. "And you start having fits." Davi's chair shuddered as Tam kicked its legs. "Before your tongue flops out and you die."

Davi leaned over. Tam sprawled on the floor, limbs akimbo. A few stray carpet threads clung to his shirt and pants. Just as Davi was about to poke him, he sprang up and seized Davi's arm. "Only prevention is a long meal with lots of wine."

On one level, Davi admired Tam's persistence. But he shook his friend off. "There's something I have to do."

Tam affected an expression so forlorn, puppies could have taken notes. "Will I see you later?"

An automatic "yes" leaped to Davi's mouth, but then he paused. It had suddenly hit him: these could be the last minutes he spent in the common room. His trip across the grounds could be his last. A chill swept over him, and he attempted a smile. "We'll see." On his way out, Davi stopped again. "You're a good friend, you know that?"

Now Tam looked confused, and concerned. "Well, yes, but what's the occasion?"

"No occasion." Davi saluted. "Goodbye, Tam."

He ran to the library, heart pounding. Wind tore his hat off, and tossed it somewhere in the pond. The rain fell so thick he could barely see the lights in people's windows, and the path blurred a few paces ahead. Once or twice thunder rumbled loudly enough that Davi nearly threw himself to the mud, sure a tree had been hit. They'd cancelled classes for precisely that reason: no one wanted to find a mage mangled under a downed oak or cypress.

The grounds were deserted, but a fair number of students sought refuge in the library. Caught far from their dormitories, they had decided to ride out the storm in a large, safe building. Besides, with the Magistatiem's collection, boredom wouldn't be an issue.

Keenly aware of the puddles he trailed, Davi squelched to the main desk. Keeper was on duty this time. She glanced at the line of footprints, then at Davi. "There is a mat placed by the entrance for your convenience," she said.

"I'm sorry." Remembering the way he'd crashed into her that morning, Davi strove for an extra-apologetic tone. "I didn't see it."

"Good afternoon," Keeper said. "May I be of assistance?"

"I need to get in the vault."

"Are you on the list?"

"Um." Davi considered this as a blast of thunder shook the library's hanging lamps. "Yes?"

Either he didn't convince her, or it was standard procedure to double-check. In all likelihood, it was both. Keeper consulted a ledger while Davi fidgeted, scanning the area for River.

"Here you are," Keeper said. "An entry by River of Knowledge confirms that you have permission from Dr. Volpes to enter the vault." She peered closer. "An additional notation states that you have permission to hand-copy passages from *Design and Production of Magically Created Beings, Volume XVI-A.*"

"Oh." He mentally kicked himself; he should have known River would have sorted everything in advance. Nonetheless, Volpes's name unsettled him. "Excellent."

"I will escort you now."

Contrary to the image its name conjured, the vault was not actually located in the basement. Damp and mould waged constant war on books, particularly in a building as old as the library. Instead, the Magistatiem housed its most valuable books in a secured room on the first floor.

Keeper stopped before a section of blank, grey wall. She placed her hand on a stone, apparently at random. An instant later, blue fire streamed from the wall and over her hand. Her expression never changed. Davi whistled; the security spells impressed him every time. Blue flames licked Keeper's arm. The stone shimmered and grew misty, as though turning to fog. The outline of a door materialized. When the stone had dissolved completely, Keeper selected a key from the collection she wore around her neck. The lock protested as she turned the key, but finally complied with a loud click. A hefty shove from her shoulder—a shove Davi doubted many humans could match—and they were in.

As Davi stepped inside, torches along the walls flared to life. But the blue cast to the light revealed these were no ordinary torches, which would pose an intolerable fire hazard. Another spell; some team of magi had been made rich designing and creating the vault.

Long rows of books stretched as far as Davi could see. No windows in this room, no source of natural light to bleach leather or fade print. "*Design and Production of Magically Created Beings, Volume XVI-A?*" Keeper asked.

"That's the one."

"This way, please." She led him to a collection of books with glossy red spines. Some looked too heavy to lift. Davi hoped for a small one as Keeper ran her fingers over the titles.

Luck was on his side. She handed him a slim volume, which he took to a nearby lectern. Keeper waited a respectful distance away, hands folded behind her back.

"Are you just going to stay there, Keeper?"

"It is standard policy for patrons accessing rare books to have an MCB escort for the entirety of their time in the vault."

"All right." Davi sighed. *This shouldn't take too long*, he realized once he'd located the spell. It was short, a few pages. He set to work copying it down, straining to see in the bluish light. The more he read, the more his respect for the MCB team grew. Some elegant formulae had been employed: maximum energy available for the MCB, minimal effort required by the mage. In fact, it was a solo spell. Ironic, considering the size of the group required to create an MCB in the first place. Aside from a few minor spells here and there—setting a fracture, some light repair work around the house—Davi had never cast anything significant alone. He doubted he ever would, not if he wanted a long career and a stable mind.

He had just finished when he heard footsteps. He shoved the book back in place as Volpes and Glory ambled around the corner.

"Ah, Keeper, I was wondering where you were," Volpes said. "No one's out front."

"My apologies, Dr. Volpes, I was obliged to accompany this patron."

"Davi!" The professor grinned. "Working on a free day, that's admirable. You know, a colleague passed along some fascinating articles on the nature of aither—seems it might be hiding in plain view."

Pasting a smile on, Davi crumpled the copied spell into his pocket. "Thank you, sir. I'll have to investigate that."

"Anytime. What were you reading? I didn't think there'd be much for you in this section."

"Nothing much..."

"*Design and Production of Magically Created Beings,*" Keeper piped up.

"Oh?" Volpes sauntered to the shelves, not looking at Davi. "And why would they interest you?"

"Well," Davi said, panic beating against his breastbone, "you, sir, gave me some ideas when we talked. All the differences, you know, between magi and non-magi, humans and MCBs."

"I see." The professor stroked the books' spines. "An interesting angle, one not many would consider. Out of curiosity, who signed for you?"

"A professor..." The Fox let him wait. "...in the Experimental Faculty."

Volpes smiled. It was one of the most terrifying things Davi had ever seen.

"Which professor?"

"You, Dr. Volpes," Keeper said. Davi's mouth dried. He attempted a laugh, an explanation, anything, but his jaw wasn't working.

"Did I?" Volpes shook his head. "I must have forgotten. Who marked it down?"

At that, Davi threw his remaining papers in his bag. His forced smile hurt his cheeks. "Well, Keeper, I think I've got everything. Let's go—no one's out front, you know. Can't keep people waiting!"

The MCB moved towards him, but Volpes blocked her. "Who was it, Keeper?"

"River of Knowledge."

A deadly stillness. Davi couldn't meet Volpes's face. Trembling all over, he hurried from the vault, Keeper shadowing him. Once outside, his fear solidified to anger. "What did you tell him all that for?"

"Dr. Volpes asked a question to which I knew the correct answer." Keeper touched the vault door with a fingertip, and the stone wall reappeared. "Had I not responded, he would have lacked correct information."

"That would've been fine!"

In other circumstances, he might have laughed as she tried to reconcile his statement. "That is nonsensical. What is the benefit to misinterpreting information, or possessing only that which is false?"

"Never mind. I've got to go."

A single thought pulsed in his mind. *River. Got to find River.*

His surroundings took on a dreamlike quality, dim and distant. Surely he wasn't actually doing this? A bolt of lightning shocked him back to reality. Panic would solve nothing. He leaned against a shelf and bent over. Focused on deep breaths, waited for the spots in his vision to dissipate.

"Davi?"

"River!" He grabbed her shoulders, remembering too late her aversion to touch.

"You are early."

"River, we have to go, now." The dryness of his mouth hindered his speech. He licked his lips and glanced towards the stairs. "Volpes knows you used his name."

"Pardon?"

"He saw me. Then Keeper told him."

River went quiet, the whites of her eyes stark against the brown. "Did you get the spell?"

"Yes."

"Excellent." She held out a hand. "Give it to me and I will leave immediately."

"Where will you go?"

"I have deduced that the course of action with the greatest probability of success is to leave the City entirely." Somehow, she didn't look entirely confident. "There must be magi in the other cities—and perhaps less prejudice towards MCBs."

The urge to hug her was almost overpowering, but Davi controlled himself. Still listening for Volpes, he said, "Sounds awfully dangerous, but we can discuss it later. Let's go!"

"We?"

"What, you think I'd get this far in and then duck out?" Davi shook his head. "I'm coming too. My parents live outside the City. Far outside. We can go there."

They escaped the library without attracting attention. Outside, a blast of wind walloped Davi; he nearly fell, but River hauled him up. They skirted the buildings, avoiding the path when they could. Cold mud sucked at Davi's feet; his socks were beyond ruined, his toes numb.

He trudged on, head down, following River's tracks. His satchel slapped his thigh, empty save for some pencils and assorted papers. Inwardly, Davi mourned the loss of his spellbooks, but the dormitories were in the opposite direction, too far for a detour.

At the Magistatiem's front gate, River halted. The storm played with her hair, whipping it across her face. Davi followed her gaze back to campus, but all he could make out was the Chancellor's Tower.

"What's wrong?" he shouted.

She said something, but he couldn't hear.

"What?"

"I have never been off the grounds!"

"Want me to go first?"

River nodded. They switched places, Davi leading. He felt safer once they were on the City's cobblestoned streets. Maybe he'd been reading too many adventure stories, but it seemed like they'd be harder to track without footprints. Bloated gutters necessitated leaps from curb to street. One particularly large puddle had been formed by a dead rat blocking the drain. Davi tried not to look at it as he waited for River to catch up. She gazed in all directions, her astonishment palpable.

"I cannot believe people live like this," she said. "I have read about urban life, but how do they tolerate the density of buildings? Is such overcrowding not a hazard?"

"Well, maybe. We can't all live in the halls. But don't worry, we'll be out soon enough."

They shunned the main roads. The City had an ample supply of backstreets; twisting lanes and alleys crisscrossed like cracks in dried mud. Lamps gleamed in windows, but no life stirred in the streets. People living on buildings' upper floors were probably afraid to come out, Davi reflected. Bad weather made the outdoor staircases a near-guarantee of a broken neck.

Empty squares replaced the usual bustle of markets and vendors. Davi had never realized how much the hum of hagglers and squeak of cart wheels formed a backbone to City life. The silence made him feel exposed. Only a few ragged dogs crouched in doorways, muzzles dripping. They whined as Davi and River passed, but refused to brave the deluge.

By the time they reached the edge of the City, the rain's endless hammer was maddening Davi. He rushed through the gates. Perched atop a plateau, the City resembled an island; albeit one in the centre of a valley. City-dwellers relied on wooden bridges to cross to the countryside beyond. The bridges' tendency to sway with each step made the crossing petrifying. Davi had hated them since childhood, had been glad when his family moved, and had dreaded facing them when he came to study at the Magistatiem.

But he never imagined they would be gone.

"Where are they?" he said. "Bridges don't disappear!"

River crept to the precipice and peered over. "It would seem the inclement weather has destroyed them. Remnants are visible on the valley floor."

"All right, we'll take the farmer's route." Careful of sliding stones, he edged to the end of the path. A rope ladder hung at the drop. At least, it usually did. Not even the wooden pegs anchoring it remained.

"It would appear that there are no safe methods of exiting the City," River said.

"We could just climb down."

Even as he said it he knew it was foolish. And suicidal. The rocks' wet sheen promised a fatal slip, and the wind howled as though anticipating fresh prey. Dizzy, he retreated from the edge.

"Now what?"

River looked thoughtful. "We cannot return to the Magistatiem. Agreed?"

"Agreed."

"And neither of us have money for lodgings."

Davi patted his pockets. "Not enough, no."

"Then I propose we go to the Ecclesiat."

"Are you insane?" His blood drained to his toes. "If they find out about you...River, they're worse than the Magistatiem!"

"I am aware of their views. However, one of their members has already interacted with me, and believed me to be human. Therefore, it is possible that this illusion of humanity may be maintained." With a hesitating hand, she touched her own cheek. "Perhaps not indefinitely, but long enough. Until the bridges are repaired. Assuming this condition, the Ecclesiat appears our best option."

"I don't know."

"It has sheltered the destitute and itinerant throughout its history. Indeed, part of its purpose is to provide refuge for those who need it."

Davi sighed. "Did the monk tell you that?"

"It is stated in many Aelist writings, as well as such sources as private diaries, letters, histories of the City…"

The lands across the valley called to him again. He thought of his parents' house on the coast. They lived in a small town, nothing like the City. No vengeful magi. Storms, yes, but nothing as bad as this. A haven, if only they could reach it.

"Are you sure you'll be safe?"

"No." At least she was honest. "I cannot be sure. As you noted, it is a dangerous proposition. However it is less dangerous than any option available at this time." Her gaze softened as Davi sneezed. "Furthermore, while MCBs cannot fall ill, I understand that humans are much more likely to do so after prolonged exposure to wet and cold."

Davi swiped at his nose, but his shivering persisted. "All right. We'll stay out of sight, and maybe they won't notice."

By the time they stood before the massive building, he wished he could take his words back. It overshadowed the central square like an awaiting giant, as ancient and immovable as the plateau on which the City stood. Coarse stone brooked no insult from something as insignificant as Nature. Statues bore the storm's assault with stoicism; the great bell uttered no protest as the gale screamed around the tower. Together, they stood on the front steps, River transfixed by carvings of saints and the Angel, Davi transfixed by River herself. As she muttered the names of the architectural features, he tried to imagine this slight woman triumphing over the Ecclesiat.

Tried, and failed.

———

Gaelin prided himself on punctuality. Whether for service,

prayer, or appointments, he arrived first. At the monks' assembly, however, he found the Chapter House already full. He squeezed past knees, murmuring apologies as he stepped on toes, and finally reached a free place. He frowned. This chair felt odd. His usual one, across the carpet, was near the fire: a blessing on such a dismal day.

At the front of the chamber, furthest from the doors, Alesta stood behind a polished lectern, fingers curled around the edges of the double-triangle fitted to its front. Gaelin worried for her. It could have been the greyish light spilling through the high windows, but she looked pale.

"Brothers and Sisters of the Angel!" she called. "Come to order!"

Conversation died in an instant. Chairs squeaked as monks shifted to get a better view, but not a soul spoke. Alesta smiled. "Thank you. I open this assembly by saying that Father Osvald will not be joining us."

Monks shot each other worried glances. Gaelin knew they were counting, how many weeks since he had last served, how many meetings since he had last appeared. One monk worked his jaw, raised his hand halfway.

"Please, may I ask, do you… do you know when he might join us next?"

Only the clicking of Alesta's fingernails on the wooden lectern punctuated the silence that followed. The monks beside the speaker studied their shoes as Alesta fixed the unfortunate Brother with her stare. "No. And I will thank you not to interrupt the assembly's proceedings, unless you wish to add the chamberlain's duties to your own for the next year."

Under his breath, Gaelin tutted. It had been an honest question. Surely anyone could see the concern that lay beneath. The young man went white and babbled an apology. Alesta let him go on a while before raising a hand.

"Our first order of business does concern the Throne. It is his wish that, while he is incapacitated, leadership of the Ecclesiat shall fall to me." Her smile was joyless. Satisfied, perhaps, but joyless. Waves of unease rolled over the assembly.

Alesta shrugged. "Is that not what he said, Brother Baeor?"

"Yes," Baeor admitted from his seat by the door. His face reminded Gaelin of the storm clouds outside. "I heard him."

"Excellent. Now then, before our main discussion, Brother Gaelin, may I ask where you were during the dawn service this morning?"

Heads swivelled towards him. Beneath his surprise and embarrassment, a tendril of anger took root. She had no right, neither to make an example of him, nor to stand there so serenely while she did it. Gaelin took a deep breath and folded his hands in his lap.

"I was conducting business for the Ecclesiat. I went to the Magistatiem and retrieved our copy of *The Prophecies of St. Memoyah*."

He prepared himself for the reaction. Monks shot sideways glances at him, or used their long sleeves to mask smirks. Like a cold passed from person to person, gossip dispersed through the chamber. In the centre of it all, Gaelin sat unmoving, unflinching, ignoring all but the equally unruffled Alesta.

But the jibes stung. Many of the younger monks, the ones who admired Alesta, did not bother to lower their voices.

"St. Memoyah? Well, let's just call in the Beast now, then!"

"He missed service for the magi?"

"Does setting foot on Magistatiem lands count as heresy?"

The voices whirled faster, louder, until Gaelin felt like the eye of a storm. *Go on, Alesta,* he thought, lifting his chin. *If you're our leader, stop them.*

She didn't have to speak. She simply gestured. Lightning flashed again, and the harsh light sharpened her angular features further. If before she had been Ael's standard bearer, now she was the Angel's sword.

"Brother Gaelin, you did not inform me of your intention

to visit the Magistatiem." She sounded cold and flat as the stone floor. "Considering their blasphemous work, this casts a distressing light on your actions."

Gaelin rose. "You, more so than any other, have stressed to the people that we are living in the End Days. St. Memoyah's prophecies can help us prepare for what is to come. How can you deprive your people that understanding?"

"Memoyah denied the Angel and championed the Beast."

"That is debatable."

"Her lunatic drivel cannot be shared with the people unless we are certain there is nothing heretical in its nature." She paused. "How can you poison the minds of your people against the Angel?"

The clapping began in the front. Baeor tugged his sleeve, but Gaelin brushed him off. "Very well," he said. "Perhaps, after assembly, you and I can examine her writings together, and decide what would be appropriate."

A curt nod signalled her assent. Gaelin bowed in return, and reclaimed his seat, still trembling within. Dull heat filled him from chest to forehead; he blinked away sweat. He envied Alesta's coolness; she embodied a resolution he had not seen in her before.

And she had more to say. "It is time we showed consistency in our teachings. If the end times are upon us, we must guard ourselves against the temptations of the Beast, for She already infiltrates through Ael. We must hold faith in the Angel's purification."

Gaelin ground his teeth, but didn't dare speak again. Luckily, Baeor had no such reservations. "What do you mean, *infiltrates through Ael?*"

She jabbed a long finger at him. "You did not attend to my sermon this morning. Ael is Beast and Angel. To avoid the Beast's contamination, we must worship the Angel alone, for He is the better part of Ael." When Baeor snorted, her lip curled. "Would you allow the diseased heifer to stand with the herd, Baeor? Drink the wine of the mould-ridden grape along with the healthy? This is no different."

She counted items on her fingers. "The plagues. The magi and their ungodly artificial people. The poor growing seasons. If Ael is worthy of our worship, why does Ael allow all this? This is the work of the bestial side of Ael. This is why Ael is false, if Ael even resides in our world any longer."

Another monk, Elber, raised a hand. Everyone paused to listen; he never spoke at assembly. "We have been treading down this path for years; we turn more to the Angel than to Ael. Yet Aelism as we know it would be reformed nonetheless."

A hint of insecurity revealed itself through Alesta's wringing hands. Then it vanished. She stood tall and confident as she answered, "Yes, Brother. It will be."

"Now see here," Gaelin said. "The Angel has always been an important part of our worship. But to claim He is superior to That Which is All...you have interesting points, but where is your proof?"

She leaned over the lectern, triumph brightening her features. "The Angel spoke to me."

No one seemed sure how to respond. Sister Liana, nose removed from her book for the first time all assembly, coughed. "What do you mean?"

Alesta regarded Liana as a queen might a scullery maid. "The Angel made His holy presence known to me, and told me these things. As Ael's better part, He redeems Ael. Thus, He is higher than Ael. This is the message we must shout before the Angel comes. I fear we have little time to save our people." She clasped the lectern. "Dread the passing of Ael, for Ael does not return."

To Gaelin, it was as though the skies had crashed on his head. His body felt frozen, but his mind whirred. Surely a holy vision counted as proof, and Alesta had always been spiritually gifted. Few would forget her successful anchorage. But then—

the life he had devoted himself to, the god he had loved and served—had it all been a lie?

"Come." Baeor nudged him. "They're calling for a vote."

With a queasy sensation in his gut, Gaelin forced himself to concentrate. The room felt hot and cramped. Perhaps it was humidity from the storm, but he longed to be out of the chamber, where he could tackle his confusion in peace. "What are the ayes and nays?" he asked through numb lips.

"Voting aye to preach worship of the Angel, nay to keep things they way they are."

Alesta rapped the lectern. "For the worship of Angelus Rex, the Angel King!"

A chorus of "ayes," more than half the monks. A forest of upraised arms. It took Gaelin a minute to realize his own arm was among them.

V

Directly after the assembly, Alesta steered Gaelin to her study. A bare table, a cold hearth, and two hard chairs completed the room. No personal effects distracted from the task at hand.

Gaelin's knees popped as he sat. What he wouldn't give to be in his own study. Or the padded chairs of the main reading room, as comfortable as they were popular. Then again, that popularity was probably the reason Alesta had decided against the public space.

"Well, Gaelin, let's see these prophecies."

He placed the book on the table. Dust coated his fingers as he lifted the brittle pages. "I've read a few, but doubtless you'll find others that interest you."

Alesta smirked. "Doubtless. Give it to me."

Smarting at her tone, Gaelin relinquished it. She examined the covers first. Compared to the rest of it, they were glossy and new. "I suppose the magi did an adequate job," she said. Gaelin nodded. The rebinding was exquisite—perhaps the work of a magic-made man? He shuddered at the thought, and pointed to a passage.

"There. That one could be relevant."

"*When the time of the end is at hand ye shall know it by the darkness and the barren candle.*" Alesta rolled her eyes. "Obviously, that's the point of Candlemass."

"Keep going." Gaelin sighed.

"No need for impertinence."

"I wasn't—"

"*Yea, after this shall there be Seven days before there is no more sea, nor land, nor sky, nor anything in this world, for this world shall return to void at the end of the Seventh day. And all that there is shall be naught.*"

A chill climbed Gaelin's spine. "How many days has it been?" he asked, feeling light-headed. "It wasn't yesterday; we're on the second day. Two of seven."

Alesta's forehead wrinkled. "The rest is too faded. I can't read it."

"My eyes won't be any better. Skip ahead."

She did so, and raised the lamp to the text. "Ah, here's something." Clearing her throat, she said, "*The avatars of Ael shall war amongst themselves and each shall seek the last seer among us before the dawning of the Seventh day. The last seer among us...*" A thin smile cracked her face. "That would be me. The Angel has already sought me."

Gaelin debated with himself, rereading the passage. Finally, he mustered his strength and said, "Are you certain the prophecy refers to you?" He wilted under her expression, then rallied himself. Ridiculous to cower before someone so many years his junior.

But he couldn't help a tremor of fear. The glower that belittled him was normally reserved for misbehaving boys, and he felt himself redden.

"Am I certain?" she hissed.

As he well knew, a near-whisper terrified more than any shout. He just never expected the tactic to be used on him. Affecting nonchalance, he shrugged. "It's always hard to tell with prophecies. One never quite knows how they're meant to be interpreted."

"I think it's quite clear." Her eyes narrowed. "Unless, of course, you'd like to give the people false messages. Wouldn't they feel better, safer, if the acting Throne is named in the prophecies?"

"Perhaps. But then, I thought you put little stock in St. Memoyah."

"She has a poor reputation." Alesta traced the faded letters. "But now, reading her works, I'm inclined to have a little more faith. After all…" She smiled a serpent's smile—all teeth. "You encourage open minds, do you not?"

"I do." Heat pounding his temples, he turned to open a window before remembering there wasn't one. He loosened his collar, fanned himself with the other hand. "Is there anything else?"

"Let me see." Unlike him, Alesta didn't seem bothered by the heat. Quite the contrary. "Listen to this: *That Which is All is in this world no longer. Yea, even as Ael has departed the world, so too has the Word. For as the Word was with Ael, so the Word was Ael. And the name of the Word was revealed to me, and the name of the Word is the Hapax. Yet the Hapax is not the Word, but the name of the Word. Ael alone was the Hapax and Ael is no more. As the Hapax cannot be spoken, so it must be heard. And in that place where it first resounded, it echoes still. Hearken to me, for the Hapax must be heard before the end of the Seventh day, else all shall be naught and the dwelling of the Hapax shall be naught also.*"

Her face radiated victory. "I knew it! The Angel alone resides with us. It is as I foretold. I must be the last seer."

The weight of Memoyah's revelation stunned Gaelin. Everything he had worked for—empty. Empty as the world itself. The Angel could not supplant Ael. To Gaelin's shame, he had never believed himself as welcomed by the Angel as by Ael.

"Gaelin?"

He roused himself. "Sorry, beg pardon?"

"Have you heard of the Hapax?"

"Er…" Still fighting to focus, he cast his mind back over the years. "Yes. It's a rather obscure notion. The Hapax is the Word of Ael: the Word that created the universe. Some interpret the phrase *the Word was with Ael and the Word was Ael* to mean that Ael is the Hapax itself: Ael is Ael's own creative force." He sighed. "There's logic to it. Ael is All. The Hapax created All."

There was a banging at the door. Muttering, Alesta opened

it to admit Serafine. The young woman strolled in and placed a tea tray on the table. Flipping her flaming hair, she said, "Anything to eat, sub-priors?"

Alesta scowled, but Gaelin chuckled. "Thank you."

She grinned. "Brother Baeor thought you'd need it. And it's another job for me to do. Have to earn my keep." Her gaze dropped to the book. "So, what does Memoyah say about all this?"

"That does not concern you." Alesta pointed to the door. "Dismissed."

Serafine raised her hands. "Just curious. I'll be moving on, no need to worry about me."

Gaelin glanced to Alesta. "She means no harm, I'm sure."

"This is private."

"I saw the word *Hapax,*" Serafine said.

The sub-priors stared at her. Alesta spoke first. "You can't know what the Hapax is."

"Not the actual word, no, but the concept." Her grin brightened. "A word appearing only once in a body of work. The word of creation, appearing only once in the history of the universe."

Gaelin shook his head, hiding a smile. "How do you know that?"

"I know Memoyah's work. Phrasing's a little flowery, but the ideas are interesting."

"She must have been eavesdropping." Alesta stood, and attempted to loom over her. "Out."

With a wink to Gaelin, Serafine slipped out of Alesta's reach. She paused by the door. "By the way, there's two people looking for you, Gaelin. In the narthex, a man and a woman. And," she added, "I would read a few pages on. It's most enlightening." Laughter spilled from her lips as she tore down the corridor.

Wordlessly, Alesta returned to the book. The lines in her forehead deepened. "What is it?" Gaelin asked.

"And who shall hear the Hapax? That with the ears to hear it. And when shall the Hapax be heard? When it is brought from its dwelling. And how shall it enter the world? As do all things, and

as they have done before." She slammed the book on the table. "It tells us nothing."

"Or perhaps we can't understand its message."

"I shall pray." Alesta retrieved the book, brushed some dust from its cover. "If I cleanse myself enough, the Angel may come to me again."

"Yes…" Another shiver penetrated to his bones. A peculiar feeling: sweltering in his cassock, yet icy at the core. He gulped air as the room spun. "I think I'll go to the narthex."

Out in the cloisters, a draft cooled his face and lifted some of the oppressive warmth from his limbs. The chilled, queasy sensation in the pit of his stomach had not abated, but the murmurs of monks at work reassured him. Would they still be there in a few days' time? The milky eyes of the Angel, peering at him from corners and shrines set in the walls, offered nothing. No hope, no condemnation. He was lost in the steppes with the sky lost to sight, the one star by which he had navigated for so long extinguished in darkness.

Entering the cathedral, Gaelin pushed his doubts down. People needed him. Smile in place, he drifted to the narthex. The crowds surprised him—men, women, and children surged against the stone walls. He squeezed through, offering blessings to those who swarmed to him. All the while he scanned their faces. Serafine had given no description—he waited for a hopeful nod, a spark of recognition, anything.

Then he saw them: the young couple from the Magistatiem library. Huddled against a column, they had the wary posture of hunted animals. The young man stood close to his companion, shielding her. She watched everything impassively, but he seemed to be judging every movement as one hiding a threat.

Gaelin pushed his way to them. The young woman saw him, and whispered to the man. The young man scrutinized Gaelin, and then he stepped forward, hand extended.

"Brother Gaelin?"

"Hello." He shook the man's hand. His grip was stronger than he'd expected, given the lad's lean build. The woman hung behind, clinging to the shadows. Gaelin smiled at her. "I believe the three of us met quite early this morning. Your name is River?"

"Yes." He barely heard her.

"Unusual name." Both young people tensed at that, so he hastened to add, "Very pretty, though. Is it short for something?"

"No." They spoke simultaneously, the young man's gaze flicking from Gaelin to River and back. She shook her head. "No. It's just River."

"And you? I believe I heard River call you Davi this morning?"

The lad hesitated. "That's right."

"Well then, Davi and River, how can I help you?"

They looked at each other. River's face and posture betrayed nothing, while the tip of Davi's tongue skittered about his lips. Finally, he said, "We…please, would it be possible for us to stay here for a few days? No longer, I promise, but we have nowhere else to go."

Up close, his tousled brown hair and fidgeting made him seem even younger. Really, he was just a boy. And River hardly out of girlhood, for all her solemnity. Whatever plagued them, they were too young to face it.

"Are you in trouble?"

A single nod from River. Davi scuffed his shoes on the stone floor.

"What is it?" A thought struck him. "This morning, you two were discussing something when I arrived."

More shared looks. River suddenly straightened her shoulders. "Indeed. We had come to the agreement that my departure from the Magistatiem was necessary." Her self-control amazed him. Such a poised young woman.

Gaelin took her hands in his own. "Why?"

It took her a moment to answer, her fingers twitched in his grasp. "My superior was attempting to exploit me."

"What?" He knew such things happened, even at the Ecclesiat. But the thought repulsed him. "My dear," he said. "Are you...did everything turn out...?"

"Oh yes. We left before anything of that nature occurred."

Beside her, Davi shifted from foot to foot, his eyes like saucers. "We tried to leave the City itself, but the storm's blown out the bridges."

"One thing after another, it seems." Gaelin shook his head. "Well, you two are welcome to seek sanctuary here as long as you need."

"I don't imagine we'll be staying too long," Davi cut in. "Once they repair the bridges, we'll be on our way."

Another pang of sympathy. They were so young, so alone in the world. Gaelin had long ago come to peace with the fact that he would never know fatherhood. But that knowledge did not preclude paternal instinct. These two would have made fine children.

"There are a few spare beds in our dorters. We have another guest who will show you around. Her name is Serafine; she's a red-head, you can't miss her."

They lingered in his thoughts long after Serafine collected them. Particularly River. Nothing he could put his finger on, but something about her troubled him. So reserved and distant... perhaps she had been compromised by her superior after all. The thought burned him as much as if it had been his own daughter.

Oh Ael...Angel King, let me be wrong.

⎯⎯

Once away from the narthex, Davi breathed again. Plodding up a narrow staircase behind River and the woman named Serafine, he slipped a hand in his satchel. The spell's presence reassured him. It was a link to his old life, the world he understood.

"Men sleep here," Serafine said. Her red hair and pale skin reminded him of the island-folk, but he was a little disappointed that she didn't have an accent. Twin rows of beds lined the long, low-ceilinged dorters. Davi grunted. It looked like his own dormitory. Same slanted ceiling, same starchy sheets. Even the chipped basins for washing-up were the same.

"And women here." Further along the hall, the women's dorters were smaller, but essentially the same again. Serafine wagged a finger. "There's no sneaking into the other dormitory at night. It's frowned upon." She paused. "As I discovered."

That earned a chuckle from Davi, but River asked, "Why would we wish to?"

Serafine cocked her head. "Is that a joke?"

"Yes!" Davi burst out. "Yes, it's a joke, River's very funny. Aren't you funny, River?"

Both women gave him looks suggesting they feared for his sanity. He attempted a weak laugh, which faded to silence. Serafine turned to River and continued speaking as though there'd be no interruption.

"Are you two...?"

"Are we what?"

Serafine twined a strand of hair about her finger. "What's the relationship between you?"

"Oh." River frowned. "It...I suppose it would best be termed..."

"We're friends," Davi interjected. He forced a smile over the word's thorns. "Actually, could we have a moment in private? Just to gather ourselves, you know, it's been quite a day."

"Of course." Something hid just under her smile. Before he could identify it, Serafine continued, "I'll be in the infirmary. I'll see you there."

The instant they were alone, Davi flopped onto a bed. "What have we gotten ourselves into?"

"I thought events were proceeding as planned. We are here. We have been welcomed."

"Well, yes." He propped himself up on an elbow. "Where in the worlds did you get the idea of Volpes exploiting you?"

"From a book. May I ask you something?"

"Sure."

"When you said we were friends…" She hesitated. "Did you mean it?"

"River! Of course I did!"

The ghost of a smile brushed over her lips. "I've never had a friend before."

Like so much honey left in the sun, Davi's heart felt thick and sweet. "You do now. I promise." Not trusting himself to stay on that particular topic, he said, "How are you holding up? You need that energy spell?"

She nodded. "I think that would be wise. Do you have your chalice?"

"Didn't have time to grab it. I'll just use my palm, or here, this'll work." He took a clay cup from the windowsill. It was probably someone's night-time water glass. Now it could be put to more interesting uses.

Davi held the cup in one hand and fished out the spell with the other. He reread it, lips moving soundlessly. River waited, unblinking. "Is it within your capabilities?"

"Definitely." Davi squinted at a formula. He nodded, satisfied. "It's quite elegant, when you get down to it."

"It was designed to ensure optimal MCB function even in the presence of less competent magi."

"Thanks." He rechecked one last row of figures, listened for any approaching footsteps, and grinned. "Let's do it."

The first part was easy, but he went slowly, making mental notes on his own process. There had to be some intrinsic difference between a mage and a non-mage; he was as good a subject to study as any. He closed his eyes and let his mind relax. Then he listened for the sound, a low pulse felt more than heard, like the echoes of thunder. Finding it, he locked on, concentrated all his energy upon it and—

He was in the aither. Blue flames leapt and danced about

him. A frail link to his body anchored him to reality, but it flickered. What mattered was the colour. The light. And always, the deep, deep heartbeat of the aither itself. The spell didn't call for much energy; he wanted to be in and out as quickly as possible. Like earthly fire, the aither burned.

He drew some of it into himself, siphoning it from there into the cup. With a massive effort, he cracked his eyes open. Blue fire gushed into the cup as though from a rip in space. He waited, weighing it, sensing its quantity. Noted the apparent source of the fire a finger's length or so above the clay rim. Another point for the quintessence theory: a mage was the aither's medium, not its source.

When he judged he had enough, he cut the flow. The stream petered out, and the cup throbbed with aither. Now the hard part. To keep the aither from snapping back—and burning his mind pretty badly in the process—it had to be bound. Davi's attention narrowed to the flames before him. Aither licked over the edges of the cup. For the moment, nothing else existed. In his mind, he spoke to the aither, using the written spell to solidify his thoughts, to make them concrete, better communicated.

It was like lying, convincing the aither that what it wanted to do, what it was meant to, was provide enough energy for this particular MCB to continue functioning.

It was like playing the violin, applying just enough pressure here, backing off slightly there, knowing how to stroke the right notes in the right manner.

It was like sailing, adjusting to the wind and seas minute by minute, ensuring that every rope, every sail swung to the right position.

It was magic.

A timeless period. He reached the end of the spell, gave the final instruction that sealed off the aither. Leaned back to wait. Now was the crucial moment. Would it stay bound, or ricochet through his skull to re-join the untamed aither? Lungs breathless. Exhilaration coursing through every vein, every nerve tuned to its highest pitch.

Heartbeat.

And the aither flashed, lit the room with a brilliant blue glow, and arced through the air to River. She made no sound as it struck her chest. Instead, she leaned into it, like a plant towards the sun. The aither buried itself within her. Davi watched, panting, running over the spell he'd just cast for any mistake or misdirection.

But there was nothing. The aither vanished, and River smiled. "Thank you."

"Anytime." He wiped sweat from his forehead, but found his heart and breathing already slowing to normal. River was right; the spell was within the abilities of even a marginally competent mage. "Feel better?"

"Yes." She stretched. "The spell provides sufficient energy for three to five days, depending on the level to which I exert myself."

"Good. Hopefully we'll be gone by then."

After Davi rinsed out the cup (there was no trace of aither in it, but he felt better for having done so), they left the dormitory.

And found Serafine just outside.

"I was coming to find you," she said. They mumbled apologies and followed her down the stairs. At the bottom, Serafine said, as though discussing the weather, "You know, if you're going to be doing magic, I'd keep it quiet for now. They're not too fond of it here."

River stopped dead. Davi's heart raced, faster than it had with the aither. "I wasn't using magic," he said. "Why would I? I don't need to."

Serafine laughed. "Nice try. I saw the blue under the door. As for why you're doing it..." she laughed again. "I'm sure you have good reason. You don't have to worry about me. The aither fascinates me."

"Are you a mage?" River said.

"Never formally trained, but I dabble." Serafine's smile unnerved Davi, but he found himself returning it. "What do you say we save this conversation for later?" she said. "They won't like it if the chores aren't done."

Even hours later, when he was elbow-deep in soapy linens, that smile lingered in Davi's mind, like a reminder of something he'd long since forgotten. If only he could remember what that was.

Gaelin's head felt as though a hive of wasps had attacked it. Too many things to worry about. Young River and her problems, Praeton's fit, Alesta's lectures about said fit, Father Osvald. More than anything, he yearned to return to his own room, collapse before the hearth, and inhabit the stillness of his mind. Instead, he dragged himself through the rains to the Throne's residence. The coughs rang through the garden.

Baeor bent over Osvald, wiping his forehead with a damp cloth. The Throne's torso rose off the bed each time he took a breath. Hacking bursts strangled his breathing. He was as white as his sheets, whiter than Serafine. Gaelin tapped the doorframe and Baeor spared him a glance. The healer's face was tight, his movements tense.

"Gaelin."

"I thought I should check in. How is he?"

"In all honesty…" He fell silent. A moment passed before he spoke again. "I'd begin preparing the Final Cleansing," Baeor whispered. He eyed the quaking Throne. "He'll be beyond the Veil soon."

Numbness settled on Gaelin like a dark mantle. "Are you sure?"

"Sometime tonight or tomorrow. Can't you see how hard he's working to breathe? There's something in his lungs, and it's killing him." Baeor's large hands twisted together, mixing his grief and frustration. "I can't heal him, Gaelin. Not with medicine, not with prayer. I've failed."

"You haven't." Gaelin sighed. "You've done everything possible."

"He can't die. Not when things are like this."

A kettle on the hearth shrieked, and Baeor poured three mugs of tea. One he downed, another he offered to Gaelin, and the third he held under Osvald's nose, letting him inhale the steam. The tea scalded Gaelin's tongue and palate, but he drank it anyway, if only to please Baeor. A shame the healer alone bore all the responsibility for the Throne, a shame he had only himself to count on...

"Baeor, do you believe in coincidences?"

The healer's mouth twitched, but he held the tea steady. "I believe Ael and the Angel have mastered causality. Everything happens because Ael wants it so. Why?"

"What if Ael appeared to be suggesting something heretical?"

Baeor abandoned his mug. "Like what?"

"Two young people arrived today." He straightened Osvald's blankets. "Fleeing from the Magistatiem. At least one of them must know magic. Perhaps the Angel has brought them here."

"To heal Osvald." Baeor sucked his lower lip, considering it. "Could be. He's not responding to any of my medicines. But, Gaelin, magi?"

"I know."

Neither spoke. No words came to Gaelin. The very idea made him feel unclean. And yet, and yet...he reviewed the chain of events that led to their meeting. The missing book. The youths' flight to the Ecclesiat. The Angel's hand all but smacked his face. Insane. Blasphemous. The thoughts hounded Gaelin as Father Osvald's upper body arose like an awakening corpse. Gaelin touched the double triangle hanging at his throat. The foundation that had been Ael had crumbled. Who was to say this was not a new path suggested by the Angel?

The metal dug into his fingers. "Send for them. They're in the infirmary."

"Yes, sub-prior." Baeor washed his hands and made to leave. "But Alesta better not find out."

Gaelin scarcely had time to beg the Angel for guidance before Baeor returned, dragging Davi. Soapsuds clung to the young man's hair; drops splattered his shirt. With a grunt, Baeor tossed him to Gaelin.

"Found him."

Davi blinked. "What did I do?" He caught sight of Osvald, still straining for air. "What's happening?"

"This is our Throne," Baeor said. "Now, what you can do for us, magically speaking?"

Eyes wide, Davi turned to Gaelin. "Sir?"

He prayed for calm. "Davi, Father Osvald is dying. We need you to save him." Doubt pricked his conscience. "Surely your magic will allow you to do that?"

Davi rubbed his chin. "It'll be hard by myself. And healing magic was never my specialty, I was always into meta-aithereal and theoretical…" A grunt from Baeor cut him off. "I'll do my best. But, doesn't the Ecclesiat—"

"Right," Baeor interrupted. "So you tell no one about this."

Gaelin made a soothing gesture. "The Angel's ways are mysterious, but it is better for the people if they remain unaware of this…intervention. Should they find out, there is likely to be unrest." Hating himself, but seeing no alternative, he added, "Which would necessitate the evacuation of all guests from the Ecclesiat." He mentally added an extra supplication for purity. At the rate he was going, he'd be praying until dawn.

"Do you have paper?" Davi said. Curious, Gaelin handed him a sheaf. The mage had his own pencil, and circled Osvald's bed, muttering and making notes. The two monks shot each other looks. It occurred to Gaelin that if Alesta walked in, he had no plausible excuse. A shudder rippled through him.

Baeor frowned. "You ready yet?"

"Just about."

Gaelin craned to see. Beautifully rounded handwriting filled the page. From what he read, it resembled the instructions in a prayer book, or a recipe. He clucked his tongue. "Where did you learn to write like that?"

Like twin torches, Davi's ears blazed red. "They teach us calligraphy at the Magistatiem," he said. "You don't want to burn yourself because you can't read someone's handwriting. And I used to draw, too. Do you have a cup?"

"Now's not the time for drinking!" Baeor barked.

"Brother Baeor!" Gaelin restrained him. "My apologies. These are difficult times for us all."

"That's all right." He took Gaelin's empty mug. "I can use this."

Gaelin found himself holding his breath as Davi gave his spell—how sweetly sinful the word sounded!—a final reading. Other than a few stolen afternoons in market squares, Gaelin had never seen magic performed. And that had been when he was a young boy. Part of him expected the Angel to swoop down and bear Davi to the shadows. The more rational side whispered that Alesta was more likely to do that.

For a long time Davi didn't seem to be doing anything. On the other side of the room, Baeor fidgeted and made a show of checking Osvald's pulse. The Throne's chest continued to rise and fall like bellows. Gaelin noticed with a start that Osvald's hands, resting atop his bed sheets, had taken a bluish tinge. Almost like bruising. And his breathing - he sucked rattling breaths. If it felt like it sounded…Gaelin ducked his head. How could the Angel let a good man, a warm man, suffer so?

A sudden spark drew his attention back to Davi. Gaelin cried out. Dancing blue flames filled the mug. Davi was mouthing something, his eyes half-open. The fire pulsed. Gaelin's hand flew to the double triangle hanging around his neck, and he squeezed it until it left lines in his skin. Yet he was transfixed, held prisoner by an awful yearning to see what would happen next.

The flame—no, the aither—shot from the mug to Osvald's

bed. The blue light gave the Throne an even ghostlier appearance. If not for his laboured breathing, he could have been a cadaver awaiting embalming.

Davi continued with the spell, tracing each line of his beautiful text. An unholy sense filled the room—or was that just his guilt? Gaelin shook himself and watched the aither hover over Osvald. As it sank into the Throne's chest, he imagined the flames targeting his throat and lungs, drying them out and razing the illness to ashes.

Then Davi stumbled.

Instantly, the flames snapped backwards. They passed through Davi as though he were water, and vanished in the space behind him. He tottered for a moment, ghastly pale. Gaelin caught him just before his skull cracked the floor.

Perspiration matted Davi's hair, blossomed into dark patches on his shirt. Gaelin laid a hand on the boy's forehead, and then snatched it back. Davi's skin was hot and red as if he'd had been scalded.

"Baeor! Get him some water!"

The healer already had it prepared. He wetted a rag and brushed it over Davi's face. Some droplets trickled between his lips. The boy's seared look gradually faded; he coughed and clutched his head.

"That hurt."

Gaelin held a cup to his mouth. "What happened?"

He struggled to sit up. "Aither got away from me." He touched his neck and winced. "I got burned. Sorry I couldn't do it. I think some of the spell went in before I lost control."

"You did your best," Gaelin said. "Will you be all right?"

"It takes a long time for damage to build up. I don't think my mind is completely burnt out yet." Davi staggered to his feet. "Maybe I'll go walk in the rain. That'll cool me down."

"Are you sure?"

"I'll be fine."

Baeor exhaled as the door shut. "What's the betting he'll be in my infirmary tomorrow?" He leaned over Osvald. "He's right, though. Some of this awful stuff at the back of his throat is gone."

"Good, good." Gaelin stood at the window. Across the gardens the walls of the Ecclesiat towered, simultaneously comforting and dwarfing him. *Father, I have failed you.* From a clump of cypress, Davi emerged and weaved towards the cloisters. Once the boy had made it inside, he sighed in relief. "It's getting late, Baeor. I can watch the Throne."

"No." The healer turned away. His voice sounded thick. "I want to stay with him."

The hours dragged. The rattling noise crept in bit by bit, a scout for the army of Death. Mottled purple-blue spread up Osvald's forearms. It took all Gaelin's strength to continue to hold his hands. Osvald's cold, clammy skin made him feel like he was already touching a corpse.

"Remember that Ael's Feast two or three years back?" Baeor said. "When that girl, the seminarian, scorched a hole in her glove?"

"Right before she was to make the offering to the Angel," Gaelin said. He brushed a grey curl from Osvald's face. "Father Osvald got the choirs to sing another anthem while he gave the girl his glove."

"Just like him, wasn't it?"

Conversation died. As the evening progressed, Baeor began hinting that Gaelin should find Alesta. He did so, steps heavy with the finality of what was happening.

She came bearing the sacred water. Much as Gaelin wanted to perform the Final Cleansing himself, he deferred to Alesta's seniority. The Throne's death-chamber was not the place for confrontation. And so he watched as she dipped her fingers into the water, and made the sign of the Three across Osvald's temples. The beads of water shimmered like diamonds, and then rolled down his cheeks as he endured another fit of coughing.

When the coughing eased, Gaelin knew.

Rapid breaths alternated with stretches of nothing at all. Gaelin clutched Osvald's hand, focused on sending comfort and strength through his grip. He felt a hand on his shoulder. Alesta. Dim appreciation surfaced, and then slipped away.

He thought of years past. Conversations in Osvald's study. Theological discussions, the man's alarming ability to seize upon puns. The feasts. Pink-tinged dawns of prayer. Tears snaked their way from Gaelin's eyes. Looking up, he saw their path reflected in Baeor's face. Alesta alone was dry-eyed, crouched at Osvald's other side.

All throughout that long night, the nightmare of the soul, as Gaelin thought, the space between Osvald's breaths lengthened. His heartbeat slowed.

By midnight, he was gone.

VI

No trace of morning showed above the horizon. The massive bell tolled the time: three hours past midnight. An extra bell rang, and its mournful tone penetrated to the heart of the cathedral.

In every dormitory, monks and seminarians awoke. Hundreds of knees touched cold floor in prayer. For the soul of their Throne. For the Ecclesiat. For their own future.

With an hour's sleep propping his eyelids open, Gaelin smoothed Osvald's hair one final time. The body lay on the People's Altar, beneath the sheltering wings of the Angel's statue. Dressed in robes of purest white, the Throne awaited his funeral. Countless times, Gaelin had heard of dead men looking "as though they were sleeping." He could hardly swallow the lump in his throat as he looked at Osvald. No chance of false sleep. Osvald's skin was grey, cooling with every moment he lay on the marble slab. Pooling blood left shadowy bruises on the undersides of his limbs, the back of his neck. Rigor mortis tightened his face, and Gaelin was certain the stiffness was spreading. As he folded Osvald's arms over his chest, he had to use such force that for a ludicrous instant, he feared hurting him.

Footsteps heavy with grief and fatigue, he passed by the stone calendar. The knot in his chest shifted upwards. Hand shaking, he moved the day stone forward.

"Three of seven," he whispered.

Within the hour, monks filled the Chapter House. Gaelin ignored his body's cries for rest. Adjusted his robes and clutched a copy of the Tablet. Already, he longed to read certain passages, to drink in their comfort. No one spoke much. He read quietly to a small group, his muted voice obscenely loud in the mumbling and stifled whimpers. Praeton perched on a footstool some distance away, thin arms wrapped around his knees. Tears glittered in his eyes, but he did not weep openly.

Gaelin finished the page and handed the Tablet to another monk. He knelt beside Praeton.

"How are you, Praeton?"

"He's dead, Brother."

"Yes, he is. But he has journeyed beyond the Veil, and his soul dwells with Ael."

"How do you know?" Anger rimmed the boy's voice. "What if he's just dead? Everyone dies, but no one knows what really happens. They just don't!"

Gaelin looked at him for a long time. Praeton's shoulders shook as he surrendered to his sobs, and he buried his face in his knees. "I don't know," Gaelin said. "We can't know. But I believe."

Silence.

"The faith we have in Ael and the Angel is a gift given to us. It is a different way of understanding. Different from knowing, but neither better nor worse."

"You have faith Father Osvald's all right?" Praeton whispered.

"I do."

A slamming door interrupted them. The thump shattered the gloom overhanging the Chapter House. Ceremonial white robes billowing about her, Alesta took the lectern. Gaelin regarded her in surprise—all the others wore their everyday grey robes. Her hair had been brushed until it shone like gold, and her skin glowed with a fresh scrub.

He hurried to her. "Alesta, what is this?"

"An important gathering," she said coolly. "We must choose the new Throne."

"Now?"

"Would you rather wait a few days? Perhaps when the Angel King returns?" She barked a laugh. "Of course now. We are running out of time, Gaelin."

"But—"

"I will thank you to return to your place." The smile withered. "Now."

Poisoned words flooded his mouth, but he swallowed them. Never had unvoiced speech tasted so bitter. With a curt nod, he did as she asked. It would be one of them, for the monks elected one of the sub-priors to the position. He bit his lip until he tasted blood.

"Brothers and Sisters," Alesta said. "This morning before the dawn, we mourn the passing of our beloved Throne, Father Osvald."

"When is the funeral?" Sister Liana called out.

Before Alesta could answer, Gaelin stood. "At sunset," he told her. "Today we will open the Ecclesiat to the City, so that the people may pay their final respects." He smiled at Alesta and sat.

"Thank you, Brother." Alesta's hands tightened on the lectern. "In future, I am sure you will refrain from disrupting the meeting. Our Throne is dead. It is essential we select the next one." She paused. "We shall have the vote now, and the new Throne will select a new sub-prior before noon. There are papers and writing implements throughout the chamber."

She placed a vase on the table beside the lectern. A square hole in the bottom was visible as she lifted it. In the dim light, the vase gleamed with a dull, olive sheen. The neck, wide at the base, tapered to a narrow mouth.

At the vase's appearance, the room crackled with excitement. A flush rose along the back of Gaelin's neck. Everywhere, eyes darted between him and Alesta, scrutinizing them. Probing them for strengths and weaknesses. He loosened the clasp at his neck, almost expecting to see steam rise from the gap.

The voting was quick, a haze of scratching quills and triple-folded scraps. When the last ballot had been deposited, one monk held the vase aloft, while another drew each vote through. A third sorted the ballots. Gaelin's heart pounded in his ears. He felt very far away. Almost as if he were about to pass out or wake up. As sub-prior, he could not vote himself. Praeton, who could not vote either, squeezed his hand.

"They like you," he said.

Gaelin nodded, grateful for any comfort. But deep in his soul, he knew. The results failed to surprise him. He joined in the others welcoming the new Throne. Alesta basked beneath a painting of the Angel. His blind eyes seemed to regard her alone, as though He had chosen her.

Perhaps He had.

No one was at breakfast. No one save Davi, River, and Serafine. The three of them huddled at one of the refectory's long tables, the one nearest the wall. Again, the Ecclesiat strongly reminded Davi of the Magistatiem. Remove the shrines to Ael, change the creamy stone to panelled wood, and the refectory and dining hall would look much the same.

Davi poked at a slice of coarse bread and hunted for some grapes to go with it. The Magistatiem certainly had better food. Across the table, Serafine crunched nuts, licking the salt from her fingers. She caressed a lemon, sliced it, and proceeded to suck the juice from it. Davi stared.

"Isn't that sour?"

She licked red lips. "I like it. River, aren't you having anything?"

River shook her head. She didn't even have a plate before her.

"Aren't you hungry? Here, try these biscuit things."

"No, thank you. I have eaten already."

Serafine quaffed her tea, her long neck stretching as she drank. "Suit yourself."

"Don't islanders drink tea?" Davi said.

He'd meant it as a joke, referencing their love for brews of a slightly stronger nature, but Serafine rolled her spoon around her mouth thoughtfully. "Of course they do, but I haven't had it in years." She grinned. "Time to make up for it."

Several cups later, and they were still the only ones dining. The monks kept a strict schedule; the hall should have been full. Davi eyed the doors, calculating the quickest route of escape for him and River. "Where is everyone?" he asked.

"Oh." Spooning honey into her cup, Serafine shrugged. "Probably at a meeting. Or in the cathedral. The Throne died last night, you know."

"What?" He and River spoke together.

"When?"

"How?"

"One at a time!" Serafine pointed to Davi. "When? Last night sometime. How? I don't know, this sickness he had."

Davi planted his forehead on the table. "It's my fault."

"You're a Throne-killer?" Serafine sounded impressed.

"No." He turned his head so his cheek lay against the pitted wood. "They asked me to save him. I had a spell worked out, but I ended up getting burned."

River turned to stare at him. "Really? You have recovered remarkably well. You must be quite resilient."

"Hang on." Serafine's eyes darkened. "Who's *they*?"

"Gaelin and Baeor. They told me to keep it quiet, but I figured they meant from other monks. You won't tell anyone, will you?"

Both women agreed. An awkward pause ensued. River went back to staring out the window, hands folded in her lap. "Of course," Serafine said, holding her spoon so that golden strands of honey danced in the light, "this is awful timing. Given that the world's ending and all."

Davi snorted. "Candlemass is pure superstition. Look, the world is fine."

"Apparently it's a delayed ending." She caught some honey on her finger and turned it, admiring it. "Seven days, then we finish."

"Ah! St. Memoyah!" In contrast to the heavy clouds outside, sudden energy animated River. "I read her prophecies before Gaelin retrieved them. They are fascinating."

Davi couldn't quite wrap his head around the idea of apocalypse. It was like the moment he had first fully understood that death was permanent, inevitable, and would one day happen to him. While he had accepted it, he preferred not to brood on it. But the notion of the entire world ending in the jaws of the Beast was ludicrous. He was a mage, for Ael's sake.

"You can't believe it's actually the End Days," he said.

Serafine's smile didn't reach her eyes. "It seems that way. They're all looking for the Hapax, the Word of Ael that will save them all."

"Interesting." River tapped her fingers together. "I assume this theory has been taken from the phrase *and the Word was with Ael and the Word was Ael.* As many theologians have argued, such phrasing suggests that Ael was Ael's own creative force. If the Hapax could be spoken again, presumably this creative force could be used in the formation of a new universe."

Serafine ran an idle hand through her hair. "Very good, River."

"She reads a lot." Davi sighed. "But it sounds like a sham to me. I mean, Ael doesn't actually exist. Saying some word won't make Ael exist. Anyway, things are fine. It's even stopped raining."

"You're tense this morning."

"I am not!"

Serafine giggled. "That sounds relaxed."

"I'm sorry." Every nerve felt tight. If only he could be *doing* something. "It's just—I want the bridges to be fixed. The sooner we can re-establish ourselves in a new city, the better."

"Then why don't you go see how they're coming?" Serafine stretched, catlike. "You know the way."

"It is not conducive to our safety," River said.

Serafine rolled her eyes. "All right, River, you I understand. But Davi—for Ael's sake, you're not going near the Magistatiem. Look, I'll come with you."

They let themselves out a side door. A few people meandered through the streets, shaking their heads over damaged walls and roofs. Tempers flared in the thick, humid air; more than one bellowed argument rang out from the fog. Striding along, Serafine tossed a coin to a man squatting beside a splintered wagon. Davi trotted to keep up. "You didn't need to come," he said.

"I want to."

She didn't say much else. Somewhere around the main market square she seemed to realize she didn't know the way, and let Davi lead. Backstreets appealed to him more than the main boulevards, but with the fog, he started to feel disoriented. The buildings got taller and skinnier, and packed more tightly, which suggested they were at least heading towards the outskirts. Beyond that, he couldn't pinpoint their location exactly. If Serafine noticed, she said nothing. She examined the tightly-packed stores and homes with open curiosity, lingering by the windows.

"Fascinating," she murmured.

Davi squinted through rolling fog. A fountain broke into view ahead; a young maiden placing a garland around a sea serpent. No water spurted from the creature's jaws. Of course the fountains would be down as well; it was like the City has falling apart piece by piece. Nevertheless, relief washed over Davi. They weren't lost after all.

"Come on." He banked left. "We're nearly there."

"Why didn't you say so?" Serafine broke into a run, easily outpacing him. Her clattering footsteps bounced off the cobblestones as she vanished into the mist.

"Serafine, wait!" Davi sprinted, trying to catch her. No luck. He strained his ears, listening for her voice. "You don't know where it is!"

"Found it!"

He emerged from the tangle of shops and townhouses onto the wide street that wound around the City's perimeter. Serafine waited by the wall marking the City limits. She tapped it once, and stone crumbled under her fist. "Old thing, isn't it?"

Davi approached cautiously. Serafine had already slipped through the gate, and was leaning over the precipice with a frown. Beyond the wall, the plateau's cliffs plunged to the valley floor. Vertigo twisted his stomach. Mist shrouded the valley; from here it looked practically solid. Across the abyss were more cliffs, the whole valley was like a steep bowl carved from the plains, with the City at its centre. No bridges spanned the distance.

Without any real hope that the rope ladders had been mended, Davi crawled to the edge of the cliff. Showers of dirt rained to the valley floor. He tilted over, as far as he dared, gripping an exposed root so tightly his knuckles whitened.

Nothing.

He sighed. "Well, that was a waste of time."

"Not necessarily. We know no one's been out here to fix them." Serafine flicked a stone into the valley. No echo returned. "How can we remedy that?"

"I don't know. Go to the guilds, maybe. Alert the Repair-Magi there's a job to be done." He scowled at the yawning space. "Of course, they probably already know that, which means they're too busy to take it on."

"Or maybe they don't think it's important enough. Lots of jobs out there, Davi. If they keep getting requests for one in particular, they'll probably bump it up their list of priorities."

"Fine, we'll ask the guilds. But you're doing the talking."

Wondering the whole way if he should have donned some sort of disguise, Davi led her to the guild district. Nestled far too close to the Magistatiem for his comfort, the guilds' buildings were strung with banners declaring their various specialties. An oak tree on a green background hung over Earth Magic's brightly polished windows, while across the street, the stout headquarters of the Communications Magi had been freshly painted with their shade of scarlet. Booths filled the street, each housing a lounging mage. When Davi and Serafine neared, the magi leapt up.

"Earth Magics, Earth Magics here! We'll add minerals to your farmland, we'll make sure your home's on a sturdy foundation, we'll even tackle water flow!"

"Step right in here for Life Magics, my lord and lady. Got a horse with a broken leg? Olive tree that just won't yield? Whatever the problem, if it's living, we can help!"

"Healing here, any injury or illness, from minor scrapes to life-threatening afflictions. Effective, affordable care. Why trust your health to scalpels and leeches?"

Serafine whispered in Davi's ear. "This is what they do with their gifts?"

Davi's forehead wrinkled. "Well, the guilders are a little more…commercialized. In the universities we focus on research and training. Still, it's a way to make a living." He waved the more aggressive pitchmen away and took Serafine to a three-story building that stretched most of the block. It had once been two separate stores, but the Repair-Magi had knocked down some walls, extended both buildings, and declared it the singular headquarters for their guild. More or less constant renovations provided excellent advertisement for their trade.

They walked under the Repair-Magi's flag (a blue hand on a brown field) and into the hall. Slots covered the back wall, like the mail room in the dormitories. Davi scanned the signs posted above the slots.

"I suppose putting in a request for any of the perimeter districts would work. I've never done this for a public job, though. When our chimney cracked, my father put our address on the work order, so the mage would know where to come…"

As he spoke, a man and woman entered together, the woman reading a scrap of paper. With a nod, she handed it to the man, who stuffed it through a slot. Serafine watched them intently.

"So, some mage will find that paper, and go to their home?" she asked.

"Or assign the project to another mage in the district." He stepped aside as the pair left, arm-in-arm. "It may be the higher magi who handle the bridges. Let's ask."

A horseshoe-shaped desk stood in the foyer's centre. A pale young man sat behind it, flipping through papers. Spots of ink splattered his hands and tie as his pen darted over the page. Davi cleared his throat.

"Excuse me."

The man didn't look up. "Can I help you?"

Davi frowned. Opting for Higher Studies was no reason for him to feel superior to those who'd gone straight to the guilds, but he expected a little more respect. Especially from someone his own age. "The bridges are down."

The man's pen scratched to a halt. "Again?"

"What?"

"We had a lot of complaints about them yesterday." The man pushed spectacles up his nose. "We sent out magi to fix them. Hard job it was, too. Are they really down?"

"We were just there."

The man annotated something, lips pursed. "All right, I'll pass the massage along, but they're not going to be happy. We've enough work requests as it is, seems like everyone has things falling apart. Even people who don't usually use magi are coming in."

"Good for business, I guess," Davi said, with a sinking feeling. "Thanks anyway."

When they were back outside, Serafine said, "It was worth

a try." She didn't sound as sure as before, her expression gone troubled and remote.

Davi rubbed his arms. The fog nuzzled his skin, cold and thick as ever. "I guess. Pity, though, I'd wanted to be out of the City by...Serafine, what's wrong?"

She was looking into the distance, as though straining to hear far off music. Davi listened too, but heard nothing. Something seemed off. Then he realized. The birds had fallen silent. It suddenly seemed darker, but who could tell with all the clouds?

"Davi," Serafine said. "Get down."

"What?"

"Just do it." Her teeth flashed. "Now."

He was awkwardly crouching when it started. Slowly at first. Almost imperceptibly. The ground began to shake. Serafine grabbed his hands and laced them over his head. Then she pushed him down; his knees slammed the cobblestones. Aither appeared from nowhere, encased him under a protective dome. It was almost too fast to see. He couldn't imagine how she'd done it, but waves of dizziness ended his curiosity. The earth had become a great beast, bucking beneath him, trying to throw him to the sky. A dim rumbling filled the air, deep vibrations rattling up and down his breastbone. He squeezed his eyes shut, waiting for the end.

It didn't come. A final, spasmodic shake, and the ground settled. Serafine stepped away, and Davi lifted his head. "What was that?"

"Tremor." Was that anger in her face? Or fear?

Davi wobbled to his feet as another swell of nausea crested. "We don't get earthquakes here."

"You do now. We have to get back, make sure no one's hurt."

"Was it that bad? None of those windows are even cracked."

"That's this time." She bit her lip. "There are more to come."

As she strode away, stiff-legged, Davi's question burst forth.

"Serafine, wait!" The empty look she bestowed on him deterred him only slightly. "That magic you used, what was that? I've never seen the aither handled that way."

"I know."

She said nothing more the rest of the trip back.

———

In the choir room, boys slumped over music stands, waiting for the choirmaster's arrival. A few tried to stir excitement by talking about earthquakes, but no one listened. There hadn't been any earthquakes, not here, anyway. Not one breeze came through the window left temptingly open. Praeton yawned, head heavy with humidity. He hadn't slept well the night before. First nightmares, then waking up to find the Ecclesiat in an uproar over Father Osvald's death. Jaon thumped the old piano. Notes sliced into Praeton's head. He grimaced and pressed his hand against his ear, pretending to support his head, but really blocking the noise. The progress chart on the far wall showed his blue ribbon was a few points away. That would show Jaon, with his fancy gold Head Chorister's ribbon. They'd be only a few levels apart.

A whack to the head stopped his musing. "Come on!" Jaon said in a mosquito's whine. "Master Evander expects you to be warmed up!"

The older boy was quivering, hand twitching at his side. Without saying anything, Praeton struggled to his feet. Another yawn escaped him. Jaon nodded. "Good. Get that jaw loose." Praeton rolled his eyes at the boy across from him. Some probationer, too new to know the choir's hierarchy.

Or not. The boy quickly looked down, ears red. Praeton's mouth felt dry. He swallowed, wishing it was time for a water break.

"Altos, seconds, firsts," Jaon sang, banging a chord. "On *ah…*"

The choristers were like dogs, Praeton decided as he wrenched the notes from himself. One alpha topped the hierarchy. Above the alpha was the master, whom they would follow straight to the jaws of the Beast. Not any master would do, either. It had to be *their* master, or someone just as competent. Change frightened them. Routine comforted them. They worked at the task for which they had been trained, and a scrap of the master's affection was the only reward they needed.

And so, like every other boy, Praeton exhaled in relief when they heard the *step-thump* of Evander and his cane on the stairs. Backs straightened, mouths opened further, formed better vowels. Covert horseplay ceased. Praeton concentrated on opening the back of his throat as the choirmaster lurched into the room. Jaon abandoned his place at the piano and scurried forward to take Evander's cane.

Then there was another sound on the stairs. Some notes died away. Praeton held his, singing louder to cover the section. But when Alesta followed Evander in, he too lost his pitch.

Another first, Quin, stirred beside him. "What's she doing here?" he whispered.

"Don't know."

Evander raised a finger. Silence fell in a great sheet. He looked about the room, grizzled lion's head sweeping from side to side. "Boys," he said. As always, it sounded like he was chewing his words. "As you are no doubt aware, we are to sing tonight for the funeral of Father Osvald. Our music, however, has changed."

Boys exchanged glances. Praeton fanned himself with his music folder. Suddenly, he felt wide awake. Evander fished a handkerchief from his pocket and mopped his brow. He missed the bald spot on his crown.

"At the request of our new Throne, we shall instead be singing the Angelic Chants. I also understand that the Chants will comprise the majority of our repertoire from now on."

For a moment Praeton thought he hadn't heard right. Too tired, or his brain had finally fried to a crisp, or something. The

Chants? Everyone hated them, they just droned on, and on, and on, until they were practically nodding off between notes.

Quin poked him. "We're supposed to hand in our music. What's with you?"

"Didn't sleep," Praeton mumbled. "The Throne."

"Oh…right. You'd have been up." Quin's cheeks flushed, matching the sunburn across his nose. He took Praeton's music without another word.

Praeton sighed. So what if he lived in the Ecclesiat? So what if he had no parents? Taunts from years past needled him. Difference, that was the key. Dogs always turned on the runt, or the outsider.

At the front of the room, Jaon flipped through stacks of music, passing each pile to Evander. "Choirmaster, sir," he said, sweet as overripe fruit, "I don't have Praeton's copy of *Cleanse my Heart, Angelus Rex.*"

Evander rubbed his beard. "Praeton?"

He checked his folder again, and shook out his prayer book, conscious the whole time of Alesta's foot tapping. "I…I think I forgot."

"You can give it to me at tomorrow's practice. Be organized next time. Here are the Chants, take one and—"

"Excuse me, choirmaster," Alesta said. If Praeton's neck hadn't been so damp, he was sure the hairs there would've prickled. "But it seems to me you have a chorister neglecting his duty."

"Well, he's—"

"He's been negligent. Some form of punishment is in order, to ensure it doesn't happen again." Her tone sent Praeton shrinking against the wall. He laid a hand on the cool stone, drawing strength from it. If he could just get through this without crying, please, that's all he asked.

Evander coughed. "That's a bit harsh."

"Is it? I demand the highest quality in my Ecclesiat, choirmaster. I will not have anyone, choirboys or monks, shirking their service to the Angel." She snapped her fingers. "You, boy, come here."

His feet turned heavy as lead. Sick to his stomach, he stumbled towards her. Everyone was staring. He wanted to bolt out the door, find a cool, hidden corner where he could be safe until it was all over. Instead, he crossed the room as he would a desert.

"Yes?" he whispered.

"You will pack away this music after rehearsal. You won't need these hymns and anthems anymore. My choirs will praise the Angel through Chants alone."

Evander couldn't contain himself. "There will be music other than Chants, surely!"

"No." The word flattened him. "Chants are the best form of music: pure tone and words. Anything else would be a slight to the Angel. So, Praeton, you will spend this afternoon organizing the old music so it can be packed away. You will assist one our guests; I believe her name is River. If there are further complaints about your behaviour, you will be removed from this choir and, if necessary, from the Ecclesiat. Is that clear?"

"Yes."

"Speak up."

"Yes." He studied the floor, willing it to swallow him. A quick glance showed some sympathy from the other choristers, but many more were sneering, or looking relieved it wasn't them.

Like a whipped puppy, he slunk back to his place. Quin had turned his chair away, eyes glued to the Chants. Praeton fought down a wellspring of tears and examined the new music. Oh Ael, it went on forever! And nothing fun, no high notes, no trills or swooping phrases. Just an endless line that didn't go anywhere, practically never changed notes.

Evander clapped. "If you could sight-read this."

He played the first chord. *One good thing*, Praeton thought. Sight-reading Chants was dead easy. The boys sang. They wilted fast, crushed beneath the music and the airlessness.

Normally Praeton hated the end of practice. Trooping down the stairs always seemed like marooning himself on a desert island. Sure, the choirboys teased him, but at least they were his age. In the adult world of the Ecclesiat, he was a castaway. But better a castaway than a chorister with those awful Chants. He wandered to the cloisters in hope of catching a breeze. He needed all the coolness he could get before returning to the choir room.

By the time he was due back, the sun still hadn't come out, which he supposed was a blessing. Nevertheless, he dragged himself there, muggy weight already pressing upon him. He waited outside for a few minutes. The sounds of people murmuring in the cathedral floated up the narrow staircase. When he thought he heard Alesta among them, he steeled himself and slipped inside.

The woman was already there, cross-legged on the floor with a few piles of music before her. She'd shut the windows. Blood beat a drum-beat in his temples, and he skirted the edge of the room to open one. He did his best to be quiet; he stepped over the creaky board and stayed far away from clanging music stands.

She heard him anyway.

"I closed them to prevent the papers from blowing away," she said. "But there seems to be little wind today."

Praeton nodded, and stuck his head outside. It was like leaning into a hearth. Haze settled over the City; the towers shimmered, straight edges wavering. Grit caked his tongue, and he decided to leave the window open a crack.

The woman wasn't even sweating. She smiled as he dropped beside her. "I am glad to meet you. My name is River."

"Praeton."

She was pretty, he decided. Shiny dark hair and eyes. Short for an adult. Not breath-taking like Serafine, but pretty.

"There is an inventory here. I've been collecting pieces and

placing them in boxes alphabetized by the composer's surname."
She hesitated. "That is the basis for this filing system, correct?"

"I think Evander just finds things by magic."

More hesitation. She started to frown, but then she blinked
a few times and her forehead smoothed. "I was under the
impression that the Ecclesiat prohibited the use of magic."

"I...I was kidding."

"Oh." She tied a length of cord around a completed package.
"I'm afraid I'm not very good at humour."

They worked in silence, punctuated now and then by the
request for a particular composer. Praeton toyed with the idea
of shucking his shoes and long socks, but decided against it.
River might think him rude, might tell one of the clergy.

Instead he focused on the yellowed pages before him. Each
one had a history. Through pencilled markings, he saw where
breaths could be sneaked, or where pitch was a hair higher
or lower than you thought. He saw reminders to look at the
choirmaster and wait for a cut-off. Instructions for a thousand
successful services marked those pages. And, best of all, the
doodles and notes. Stars and swords and animals, some half-
erased or scratched out. All testified to long rehearsals, boring
rehearsals, or rehearsals where another part just couldn't get it
together. He came across some of his own music and nearly
wept. Alesta wanted all this to be packed away? Never to be
pondered and sung by some future boy?

He drew a shuddering breath. River looked up.

"Is something wrong?"

"No."

Her deep brown eyes held his. There was something in them,
behind the coolness. Maybe she was nice after all.

"I'll miss this music, is all." Even to his ears he sounded like
a weakling. It didn't help that the room was suffocating him.

"So from this point forward the music used in services will consist
solely of the pieces collectively known as the Angelic Chants?"

He fought his way through her tangle of words. "Um, well, we're just singing the Chants now. Nothing else. None of these hymns or songs."

"Pity. I had looked forward to hearing them." River's voice went soft. "I never have."

Praeton picked at his shirt. Speech refused to come. River returned to sorting. In a rush, he said, "I could maybe sing something for you." She paused with a paper halfway to its destination. He gulped and continued, "If, you know, you wanted to hear something."

"I would enjoy that very much."

Praeton picked up the piece he'd been saving until last to pack. *Ael Hears All Cries*: his favourite. Summoning his courage, he dared to touch the old piano and find his starting pitch. Then, music trembling in his hands, he sang.

"Ael hears all cries, all woes and fear. My loving Ael, is ever here…"

Countless times he'd sung this to himself at night. Crouching in bed, or in the shadows of the cathedral, but always under half-voice. Now he let the notes pour from him, crest from the crown of his head. Music filled the small room. His nose and the space beneath his eyes buzzed with it. It was only as the final note died away that he realized that never again would he sing it with the choir. If it was to bounce off the cathedral's vaulted ceiling, it would be through his voice alone, and never during service.

An impossible sadness gaped in his chest. So close to the bone did it run, River's tentative applause startled him.

"Praeton," she said, eyes losing their some of flatness for the first time. "It was a privilege to hear that. Accept my congratulations."

"Thank you." A red streak outside stopped him.

River noticed him freeze. "What is it?"

"I don't know."

He hoisted himself up on the window ledge. Something had spattered on the stone directly beneath it, just beyond the reach of his questing arms. He strained to see, balancing on his elbows, the windowsill cutting under his armpits. Then there were hands on his shoulders. He twisted around and found River steadying him. The gesture impressed him. Most grown-ups would've hauled him down.

With River holding him, he stretched his arm a little further and brushed the splatter. At first it felt warm, probably from the stones. Then pain erupted through his finger. He gasped, hugged it close to him. The skin flamed red and swollen. And, coating it, ugly red-black ooze.

"What's wrong?" The urgency in River's voice surprised him. She had been so calm before.

Suddenly his head felt very light. The corners of the room rushed away, and he sank to the floor, his back against the wall. Slowly, he lifted his finger to his face. The sharp tang of iron stung his nostrils. Blood.

Darkness devoured the edges of his vision. Somewhere, far away, he heard River calling. He wanted to answer, but his tongue flopped, his jaw wouldn't unhinge. Then a deafening boom, thunder worse than all thunder combined, shattered his consciousness. Before blackness claimed him, a single word exploded in his skull: *HAPAX.*

VII

"He yelled the word Hapax?"

River nodded. "He was unresponsive when I spoke to him, and lost consciousness after his outburst. I carried him to the infirmary."

Carried Praeton? Gaelin tried to reconcile the image with the slight woman before him. "I'm impressed," he said. "You did the right thing."

"Thank you."

They lapsed into silence as Davi and Serafine returned with armfuls of books they had convinced Liana to unchain. All together, they monopolized two of the library's large tables. Liana popped around a bookshelf now and then, alternately admonishing them for noise and demanding to know if they'd made any progress.

Although it was only mid-afternoon, Gaelin squinted in the dull, grey light. The rain had stopped, but the sun refused to show itself. Appropriate, perhaps, considering the mood in the Ecclesiat. He swallowed a hard lump in his throat. The image of Father Osvald lying in state haunted him. He'd been in the cathedral all morning; only the news of Praeton's latest fit drew him from the Throne's side. And then, exhausted and spent, he had joined the outcasts in their research, desperate for a bit of peace.

That bit of peace seemed determined to elude him. He couldn't concentrate. Too many details and memories, each dragging his thoughts to a different corner. Impossible to think with a drawn-and-quartered mind. Across from him, Davi sucked his pencil, working on some magic he didn't even want to know about. Clouds rolled outside. And River—Praeton had spoken to Gaelin about her prior to his release from the infirmary.

"I like her, Brother Gaelin, I like her lots."

He selected another book at random. This was a desperate search, an exercise in futility. The Hapax could not have been written down. It was the Word of Ael, it was Ael. Ael's essence could not be bound to the confines of ink and paper.

Oh Ael, what times are these you bring upon your people?

"Gaelin, what time is this thing tonight?"

Gaelin roused himself. "I'm sorry, Serafine?"

"Osvald's funeral. When is it?"

"Dusk."

She clicked her tongue. "And I suppose Mother High-and-Mighty will be presiding?"

Mother. Alesta's new title. It caught in Gaelin's throat. Somehow, Alesta lacked an aura of maternity.

"It is a pity she has discontinued the use of hymns and anthems during service," River said. "Praeton shared some music with me, and it was quite pleasant."

Now Davi paid attention, pencil poised in hand. "You liked it?"

"Yes...I did."

For a second, Gaelin could have sworn she looked bewildered. But he must have imagined it. "Alesta's reasons for reinstating the Chants make sense," he said.

Serafine snorted. "Sure. Perfect chords, perfect beat, and perfectly lifeless. How's it going there, Davi?"

The lad rushed to cover his papers. "Fine."

"Discover the source of aither yet?"

"Only that it isn't intrinsic to the human body."

Gaelin listened with amusement. Why did magi run themselves ragged asking questions that had been answered centuries before? "Wait here," he said, and rose from the table.

He returned with a handsome copy of the Tablet, bound in supple brown leather. He placed it in Davi's hands and watched, glowing, as Davi touched its gilded edges, inspected the bookmark that protruded like a lion's laughing tongue.

"Gaelin, it's beautiful, but..."

"Read it. See where the aither comes from."

"Wait." Serafine pushed her chair back. Her pale skin, almost greyish in the flat light, contrasted with the vibrant scarlet of her hair. "I'm going to check on Praeton. Start without me."

As Serafine left, Davi set aside his notes. He sighed as he did so, but Gaelin smiled. Perhaps all they needed was education. Once Davi learned how the aither had actually come about, he'd have to look to his own heart and decide whether he could use it in good conscience. After all, despite what some in the Ecclesiat said, the magi did have consciences.

When he thought Davi had had enough time, he cleared his throat. "Well?"

Davi's brow knit. "*And so the Angel sent a great sea upon the people. And they cried: Behold! All sinners shall be cleansed from the earth, and it shall be pure as it was even in the days of the Void. And so it was, and the sinner and the impure and the flawed alike were drowned.*

"*The Beast flew over the waters, and She was red as with blood. And She clasped the sinners to Her breast until the oceans had receded back to their place. She set them on the dry land, that they might contaminate the earth once more. And She said unto them: Yea, further shall I bring into the world the aither, the purer form of fire from the...* I can't read that...I think it's *plain of the Angel. And ye shall use it that ye might taste Our power, and withstand His cleansing. And the heart of Ael shuddered with the defiance of the Beast, for Ael knew that She could not love Ael...*"

He trailed off, and stared at Gaelin as though trying to puzzle something out of him.

"Well?" Gaelin said. "What do you think?"

"I don't understand. I knew you thought the Beast brought the aither, but where did She get it from?"

Gaelin faltered. "Why...it says in the Tablet."

"But where is that plain? Is the aither there different from the aither we use? How did She bring the aither from there? Did She act as a vessel the same way magi do? Is that why we're *sinners*?" Davi offered the Tablet back to Gaelin. "You see, these are the types of questions magi ask. They're too complex to be solved by a single book."

"Elegance denotes sophistication. Perhaps your questions are complex because you're asking them the wrong way."

The mage had no answer to that; merely shrugged and resumed his note-taking. At least, Gaelin congratulated himself, he seemed to be going over them more carefully, tapping his chin and then scribbling in a burst.

Beside him, River sorted a pile of scrolls. Evidently, none satisfied, for she rejected each in turn, until she came to a slim, handsome box. "This is sealed. Can we open it?"

"Yes, Sister Liana will reseal it. Wax keeps the dust out, or so I'm told. Here's my pen-knife, do you mind slitting it? You're younger, your hands are steadier."

"Certainly." She slid the knife into the wax. "A pity you object to the use of magic, it offers much better protection. I find—" A gasp strangled the rest of her sentence. The knife clattered to the floor.

Davi was at her side so quickly, Gaelin didn't see him move. "River! Are you all right?"

"No, I—"

Some horrible, pragmatic instinct rose in Gaelin, and he moved the box aside, safe from any spilt blood. Then, ashamed, he touched River's shoulder. "Are you bleeding? Let me see."

"No!" River pressed her injured hand against her stomach,

curling her body around it. "It is nothing. Davi can take me to the infirmary and bandage it."

"Don't be silly, let me see it."

He tried to ease her hand up, but she clenched it tighter. Remembering her past, he backed away. Did he remind her of the man she'd fled? He didn't want to dredge up bad memories, but her wound worried him.

Then he saw it. Something blue shone on her skin like a tiny tropical sea. Cold, metallic fear dried his mouth. As if in a dream, his hand wrapped around her wrist and wrested it towards him. She cried out. Davi pulled her arm back, but his angle was wrong. Time slowed to a crawl. With a thud, Gaelin forced River's hand to the table.

She had cut herself. Two flaps of skin, thin and translucent, guarded the gash. But no blood. There it was, as he had glimpsed it. Under her skin. It was almost like jelly. Pulsing, shining, but never spilling beyond its confines. Blue that meant only one thing.

Aither.

"You're one of them," he whispered.

"Brother Gaelin, I..."

"Get back!" His gaze darted about the room, searching for protection. He grabbed the nearest chair and tried to lift it. A spasm of pain shot through his back and he dropped it with a low moan. All the while, River advanced, hand outstretched. He stumbled backwards, kept a table as a barrier between them.

Davi approached, palms pressed together. As if he wouldn't use magic. "Brother Gaelin, please."

"Stay away from me." His voice shook. "What are you doing here? Magistatiem spies? Agents of the Beast, sent to wreak destruction in the last days? Tell me!"

"We no longer have any association with the Magistatiem," River said.

"No longer?"

"Davi was a student. I was…created and employed there. But we have left the Magistatiem. Permanently."

"We can't go back," Davi said quietly. "They'll kill her."

The boy glanced at River, and then away, sighing. His hair fell into his eyes, hiding his expression, but his jaw tightened. Gaelin's fingers unclenched. Tiny indents marked his palms.

"You lied to me. She's one of those…things, and you said nothing."

River looked at him with disdain. "With all due respect, sir, I am a Magically Created Being, an MCB, and I will thank you to refer to me as such."

"An MCB then. Nevertheless, you lied to me. You abused the Ecclesiat's hospitality and goodwill."

"Would you have let us stay if you knew?" Arms folded across his chest, feet planted, Davi challenged Gaelin.

"Of course not. Beings created not by the divine, but by man, are an affront to Ael and the Angel King."

"But she's still a person."

"Actually, Davi, I'm an MCB."

The young mage faced her. "The terms aren't mutually exclusive. You're a person, River. A wonderful, living person." A note of pleading entered his voice. "A few days, that's all we need. Just until they repair the bridges—we were just there, checking, and they're out again. Give the guilds some time. Then we'll leave, and no one will be the wiser. Please, Gaelin."

An MCB in the Ecclesiat. Her false feet treading the stones of the sanctuary. Soulless life untouched by Ael. She had manipulated him, allowed him to worry over her, to feel outrage at the circumstances driving her flight. All lies. She presented an impeccable replica of a human woman, with none of a real woman's heart or morals. Perfect mimicry. Perfect mockery.

He shook his head. "I'm afraid that will not be possible."

Davi cursed. "I didn't want to do this."

At that, Gaelin retreated further. Would he end up a toad?

Could magi even do that? He braced for the blue fire that would obliterate him, but Davi continued to speak. "You asked me for a spell, Gaelin. To heal Father Osvald. I'm pretty sure that's also forbidden in the Ecclesiat."

"I acted in the Ecclesiat's best interests!"

"I know. But I'm betting you wouldn't like Alesta to know about it."

No one spoke. The three of them—mage, monk, MCB—stood locked in a triangle. Gaelin and Davi panted, River was rigid and untouchable. At last, Gaelin broke the silence.

"Blackmail. Not very honourable."

"No. Pretty effective, though."

"How do I know you're not working for the Beast?"

Davi laughed, low and bitter. "I don't believe in the Beast, the Angel, or Ael. How about you, River?"

"The divine by its very nature can neither be proved nor disproved. However, I assure you, Brother Gaelin, that if the Beast does exist, I am not in Her service."

His head throbbed. Such a sweet young woman, yet such an abomination. How was it possible? He ached with the weight of the years, of the pressure of keeping the Angel's sanctity. He collapsed into a chair, stiff and chilled with the fight fled from him.

"Three days," he said. "You have three days. I will not have you here past then."

River nodded. "Understood."

Ael must have been merciful for the creature to agree so readily. Davi, on the other hand, sneered. "Don't want us here on the day the world ends?"

"I do not."

He pulled himself up and lurched away. Then a thought struck the breath from his lungs. He whirled around, to where River was organizing the now-abandoned books.

"Davi!"

The mage's scowl intensified. "Yes?"

"That spell—you wrote it down. What did you do with it afterwards?"

Lines of confusion etched themselves into Davi's forehead. "I don't know. I was pretty burned, remember? If you or Baeor didn't take it, it's probably still in Osvald's room." He paused. "Why?"

Gaelin had a hard time swallowing. He licked dry lips. The room swam before him. "Because that room belongs to Alesta now."

He couldn't get to the Throne's lodgings fast enough. His senses felt hyper-aware. He smelled the spiced smoke of candles lit for Father Osvald. He heard boys' shoes slapping the cloister floors. He saw the leaves of the fig tree shudder in the breeze. All everyday things, so ordinary he never really paid attention to them until the moment he needed to focus most.

The Throne's door was unlocked. He let himself in, his fingers trembling on the latch. Surely Alesta would still be in the cathedral. All he had to do was get to Osvald's room, find the paper, and get out unnoticed. He'd destroy the spell later. His breath wheezed as he mounted the stairs—

And met Alesta on the landing.

"Brother Gaelin." Emotionless. "What are you doing here?"

"I'm, er, looking for you."

Her eyebrows lifted. "A coincidence indeed. I wanted to find you."

He prickled all over. Tasted the sour tang of his lunch rise in his throat. "Ah. Then we are both in luck."

"Come with me, Gaelin."

She led him downstairs, and along a corridor to a small room in the centre of the house. Gaelin knew it well: windowless, completely sealed within the interior. Dust-filmed lanterns cast muted, sinister light. Three chairs occupied the room:

two beside each other, the third a distance away, facing them. Nothing on the walls, nor the floor.

When he'd presided over trials here, there had been four chairs.

Brother Elber was already there. He smiled weakly at Gaelin, but at a glance from Alesta, the monk became engrossed in his fingernails.

She directed Gaelin to the lone chair, and then seated herself beside Elber. "Gaelin, I have selected Brother Elber as my successor to the sub-priory."

"I see. Congratulations."

"If I were you, I would not be so light-hearted," Alesta said. She drew a slip of paper from her robes and pressed it on him. "Do you recognize this?"

"What is it?"

She leaned forward. Her fingers curled around the arms of her chair like claws. "It looks very much like a spell. But that is impossible."

He said nothing. Elber coughed and flicked his eyes to the door. Wait it out, just wait it out. Gaelin almost laughed. In all likelihood, they were both thinking the same thing.

"Answer me, Gaelin."

"Very well." He felt like a bridge collapsing under too much weight. Thorns were everywhere on his path; why travel carefully when he'd be wounded no matter where he stepped? "It is a spell. I asked a mage to heal Father Osvald."

Elber reeled and made strangled sounds. By contrast, the admission passed over Alesta with the insubstantiality of smoke. She blinked once, then spoke. "I hope you are aware how grave this is. Magic, Gaelin? Have you lost your mind?" New emotion crept in, salting the gashes she'd opened.

Not anger. Something worse.

Sorrow.

"I acted in good heart." Inside, Gaelin cursed himself. Fool. Just an old fool, ready for pasture.

"According to Divine Law, you should be stripped of authority, if not banished from the Ecclesiat. By all rights, Elber and I should be holding your trial right now." And here Gaelin sensed sheer *calculation*, rolling off her in palpable waves. "However, these are unusual circumstances. If you were attempting to save the old Throne..." She let the sentence hang. "The Ecclesiat must survive the End Days any way the Angel commands. Even if those orders feel uncomfortable. You comfort the people, Gaelin. They respect you."

Unbelievable. More blackmail. "I'll be pardoned if I endorse you?"

"No, no. That would be immoral." Alesta smiled. "You're too valuable to lose right now. Of course, if you were to cease being valuable, I would have to reconsider your motives in engaging with a mage. If you were seen defying the Ecclesiat, well, perhaps you truly are a heretic. Perhaps you even orchestrated Father Osvald's death."

"I never!"

"I'm not saying you did." Her face looked different. More angular. Predatory. "But it might seem that way to others. To ensure stability, I might have no choice but to remove you."

Gaelin slumped.

"So?" she hissed. "Do I have your support?"

His throat closed. No help from Elber, who was pressing himself into his chair like he wanted to sink through the floor.

"I will strive to carry out the wishes of Ael and the Angel, as my soul can best interpret," he said.

She considered that. A panther, faced with unknown meat. As she tilted her head from side to side, Gaelin noticed her double triangle was gone. So was Elber's. Gold medallions, no bigger than a thumbnail, rested at the hollow of their throats. Gaelin had seen them before, but infrequently. He knew the image upon it, etched in impossibly fine lines. Angelus Rex, the Angel King.

"Good," Alesta said. "I do, however, think that some form of penance is in order."

Something in her tone alarmed him. Hunger. He kept his voice mild. "Penance?"

"Oh, yes." From within the folds of her robes, she drew a silver knife, the length of his finger. Pearls studded its handle like dozens of blind eyes. She handed it to him. "Your palm," she whispered. "Purify yourself."

Gaelin gripped the knife in one hand, stared at his palm. Had the Angel planned this? A cut on the palm. One on the back of River's hand. Mirror images. Was he truly the reflection of such an abomination? Or would his own blood wash him?

The blade was cool. Clean. The knife quivered in the air, threw the lamplight back on the walls.

"Go on." Alesta's lips pulled back from her teeth. "Do it!"

The blade sliced through his flesh. He gasped, pain radiating from the thin red line, crackling up his forearm to explode in his shoulder. Blood dripped to the floor. The knife landed next to a perfectly round splatter. Under Alesta's triumphant grin, Gaelin clutched his hand, all too aware of how closely he resembled River. Elber began tearing a strip from his robe, but Alesta threw out her arm and caught him in the stomach.

"Let his sin be carried away with the blood."

And so Gaelin pressed his thumb to the cut. Gradually, the bleeding slowed. He unstuck his thumb from the congealed blood and lifted his gaze to Alesta.

"Am I cleansed, Throne?"

"For now." She plucked the knife from the floor. Ran her finger over it. "So much pollution in our world. So little time to cleanse it."

His hand throbbed. Perhaps he would be fortunate, and avoid scarring. "Mother Alesta?"

She started. "What? Oh. Dismissed. I expect you in the cathedral at one before dusk."

As he trudged to the infirmary in search of soap and bandages, Gaelin wondered whether River's cut had hurt as badly.

VIII

Hand securely bound, Gaelin stood in the cloisters outside the cathedral at the appointed time, marshalling monks and choirs. How many days had it been since he'd last done this? Two? Exhaustion blunted the pain, but didn't erase it. A day ago, Father Osvald had been alive. Grief surfaced through his churning emotions. He hadn't even said a proper goodbye to his friend and mentor. Too many others needed a repository for their sadness.

Deciding the choirs could fend for themselves for the time being, he slipped into the dim cathedral. The massive space enfolded him, the emptiness a balm after the chaos outside. He acknowledged the Angel, and then proceeded to Osvald's side.

The paleness of death had claimed him completely. The embalmers had ministered to him earlier in the day. Now their fluid stiffened his limbs, the rigor mortis worn off. Gaelin laid his uninjured hand on Osvald's shoulder. Cool, but not the frigidity he expected. Then again, with the summer heat...

He cried, then. Quietly and steadily. It had been years since he had cried for himself. He'd shed tears for others, on behalf of others. But now, he wept only in part for Osvald.

"I need you now, Father. We all do. These times, these events... how are we to endure them without your guidance? How can I show our people the way, when my compass has been taken from me?"

No answer. Merely a tepid, hardened body. From nowhere, fear choked Gaelin. The terror of the grave. Osvald had been perhaps fifteen or twenty years his senior. His own mortality loomed large, an icy touch on his lungs.

A candle flickered, tossing the Angel's shadow over Osvald's face. He must be beyond the Veil, with Ael and the Angelus Rex, sheltered from the suffering of mortal life. He must be. He had to be.

"Forgive me, Osvald." His voice broke. So did something in his chest. Hollow inside, he made perfunctory motions to ready the chancel. Checked the choir stalls for debris. Squared the corners of the altar linen. Secured the door to the inner sanctum, which had been left ajar.

The funeral began at dusk. Attendance exceeded even that of Candlemass. Trudging up the aisle with Alesta and Elber, Gaelin glimpsed Davi, River and Serafine in a pew. Dull anger surged, only to dissipate. Anger had no place here. This was a time of mourning.

His arms felt too light without the double-triangle standard. "In your name," he whispered to the Angel. The notice had gone around earlier—the second part, "and the name of Ael," had been excised. He longed to trail his fingers over the slab bearing Osvald's body, but protocol bound him. Head bowed, he staggered to his seat.

So far, the boys across the chancel were behaving. No poking or chatting. Their little faces were serious, focused on Evander. Strange music, though. He was no expert, but the high treble of a young boy didn't seem suited for the Angelic Chants. Praeton must be suffering, with his light voice.

Gaelin frowned, and squinted. Cleaned his spectacles and looked at the opposite stalls again. Praeton wasn't there. Normally his blond hair made him easy to spot, but no, even after Gaelin had counted every boy, he was nowhere to be found.

Not this, too. Not now. Another fit? If he had fainted in some out-of-the-way corner, he wouldn't be found for hours. The entire body of the Ecclesiat packed the cathedral.

There was nothing he could do. The thought clanged in Gaelin's head like the Ecclesiat's bell. He couldn't leave. Of its own accord, his thumb stroked the gash on his palm. Fool. The vastness of the Ecclesiat, so awe-inspiring before, now served only to mock him. The great statue of the Angel reproached him. He had welcomed a mage and a monster to His home. And for what? He hadn't even saved Osvald. All his efforts had produced was a pitiful body so stiff the finger joints wouldn't even bend.

Old fool.

Alesta assumed her usual position, a ways down from Father Osvald. She moved slowly, like a queen, robes trailing behind her. Her sleeves brushed the floor. No wonder she wasn't gesturing as much.

"The Throne has died." Instead of making the sign of the Three, she acknowledged the Angel again.

"Angelus Rex made Father Osvald Vilenard the seat of His power in our world. As the Angelus Rex is King, so was Father Osvald His Throne."

"Light be upon the soul of the Throne."

"And the Angel King, He of perfect being, called His Throne back to Him, that he might serve beyond the Veil."

"May the soul of the Throne pass through the Veil."

Incense bearers materialized from the edges of the chancel. They processed towards each other, meeting before Osvald's body. After bowing to the Angel, they swung incense over the altar. Smoke wreathed Osvald; an ephemeral effect, as though his soul clung to the home it once knew.

The prayers continued. Gaelin had to admit that Alesta spoke with skill and precision. And her memory—she showed no hesitation at all. Her clear voice offered a fine contrast to the choirs. The Chants droned endlessly. Evander kept time with a flick of his wrist. Gaelin was sure the misery on the choirmaster's face wasn't entirely due to Osvald's passing.

Then another procession. Every monk in the Ecclesiat filed past the body. The public's chance had been earlier. With Alesta and Elber, Gaelin guarded the altar. Faces passed him. Tearstained and shocked, marble-pale and blotchy red. But all grieving. Their heavy hearts touched his own, until he thought he would collapse with the weight.

And always at the back of his mind, prodding him: where was Praeton?

Towards the funeral's close, he and Elber readied the symbols to officially transition Alesta to the position of Throne. She knelt before the Angel's statue, head bowed. As the more senior of the two sub-priors, Gaelin laid his hand on her neck. The delicate veins there throbbed.

"Do you accept the call of your Brothers and Sisters to serve as vessel and vassal of Angelus Rex, the Angel King?" he said.

"I do."

"Do you swear to guard the most sacred and holy Ecclesiat of That Which is All, to protect the beliefs and worship of Ael..." He stopped himself. "...of the Angel King?"

"I do."

"Do you swear to strive for complete, total, and perfect purity, in accordance with the divine will of the Angel King?"

"I do."

There Gaelin paused. Several more questions were supposed to follow, but even in the days of Osvald there had been talk of removing them. Some theologians argued they implicitly bound the Throne to the Beast as well as Ael. Alesta had simply ordered them cut.

"Do you swear to uphold these oaths past the moment of your death?"

"I do. And should I break them, I commend my soul to full annihilation in the darkness of the Beast."

Elber retrieved a bowl of sacred water and a ladle, both crafted of gem-studded gold. After checking his gloves for holes through which his bare skin could contaminate the holy instruments, Gaelin ladled some of the water. He had imagined this moment before, had always envisioned feelings of solemn joy, a deep spiritual connection with all surrounding him.

Tonight, he just felt empty. He poured the ladle over Alesta's neck. The sight of the droplets running down her skin failed to stir anything. Something had died within him. The thought unsettled him, and to conceal it, he plunged the ladle in again. This time, Alesta held her hands cupped before her, and he dribbled water into them. She wrung her hands, coating them with the water. Cleansed without tainting the source.

For the third ladling, he poured more water into her hands. This water, she drank. Beside him, Elber watched with open awe. Only the Throne could taste the sacred water and be purified from within to serve the Angel. Once, Gaelin had spent long hours contemplating how the water would taste, how he'd *feel* after it was inside him, touching his soul.

Nothing.

Alesta looked up, blonde hair falling away from her face.

She licked her lips.

She returned to the chancel rail. Surveyed the people, her people.

"I have taken the oaths," she said. "I will serve the Angel King as His Throne, as I have served Him all my life and shall continue to serve Him after my death. Osvald served Him well, yet he served in different times. These times are the last the Angel's people shall ever see.

"We must grow to survive, purify ourselves to win eternal life. This purification may disconcert the faithless among us..." He swore she glared at Baeor. "But does the gold that was once iron regret the refining fire? We must become fire by fire. I shall lead you to the Angel, my children. For He is with me—behold!"

She thrust her arm up, pointed to the Ecclesiat's dome, so high and dark that the walls disappeared into shadows. Gaelin heard his own heartbeat.

An almighty roar. Fire leaped into being at the top of the dome, and streaked to earth in a flaming column. Gaelin stared, frozen. His mind worked desperately to comprehend, and failed. Screams erupted, the congregation roiled with people seeking escape. A rush of heat and crackle of flame knocked Gaelin to his feet. From the floor, he saw the fire strike the crossing, between the chancel and the aisle.

The instant it touched the marble, the flame disappeared, vanishing into the floor. The shouts died away. A scar, as long as the altar, blackened the stones.

Slowly, everyone in the cathedral turned to Alesta. Her face flushed, her arm lowered to her side. Triumph and awe mingled in her expression, and her chest rose and fell in rapid bursts. She bowed to the Angel, and then stretched her arms to the cathedral.

"Are there any among who doubt your senses?"

No one answered. The black mark confronted them all.

"I am His Throne, He is King above all, and the pure of us shall be His own."

After that demonstration, anything to do with Osvald smacked of anticlimax. Several monks bundled his body into a wooden casket; he would spend another night in the cathedral, and then be laid in the crypts at dawn. Gaelin suspected the closing of the casket lid went unnoticed. Certainly the weeping had subsided. As the choir and monks processed back out of the cathedral, people strained to see Alesta, reaching over each other to touch her robes. A small smile twisted her otherwise perfect mask of solemnity.

He restrained himself until the door between cathedral and cloisters closed. Then he pounced. "What—how? Are—"

She silenced him with a wave. "The Angel."

"But—it's a miracle."

"Naturally. Do you have faith in your gods, but not their works?"

"It's not that." Gaelin struggled to phrase his thoughts.

"It's—I never thought I would see one myself. Did you know it would happen?"

"No. I believed it would happen." She glowed. "The Angel has revealed much to me. We haven't much time."

"Day four tomorrow."

Evander interrupted their conversation, thumping towards them. Gaelin wasn't sure which was more frightening: his glare, or the way his cane swung as though he'd dearly like to take someone's head with it.

"I'm missing a chorister."

"Praeton," Gaelin said. "I noticed that."

Alesta sneered. "That boy is more trouble than he's worth."

"Fine treble, though." Evander shrugged. "Train that breathiness out, and he'll be even finer."

"The problems he's caused..."

"He hasn't been sleeping well," Gaelin said. "Nightmares." A thought struck him. "Perhaps the Angel has visited him, too. He mentioned the Hapax in the last one."

Alesta's face darkened. The storm outside, just picking up again, mirrored her change in mood. "His *bad dreams* cannot be compared to my *visions*. The Angel King has *not* come to him; he is nothing but an ill-behaved, attention-seeking child."

"Mother Alesta?" The young monk waited a respectful distance away. She bowed, hair swinging forward to brush the stone floor. "Please, Mother Throne, they're asking for you in the cathedral."

"Oh? And who are they?"

The monk's chin quivered. Gaelin prepared to catch her if she fainted. "Please, it's...it's your people."

Alesta smiled. "Do you hear that, brothers? My people are waiting. Mine." She sailed off after the monk. Evander scratched the head of his cane, muttering.

"I've got to rehearse the boys—middle section was atrocious—and I'm still missing a treble!"

"I'll look for him," Gaelin said. "I trust that Alesta can handle the cathedral for now."

"Much obliged. Anyway, he likes you. If he's hiding, he might come out."

Such optimism soon proved misplaced. Gaelin checked Praeton's usual haunts, but found nothing. Not in the bell tower, nor the space under the stairs to the choir room. With the rain starting, he doubted he'd be hiding in the reeds by the pond—and he was right. The dorters and refectory were empty, and all he got from the kitchens was the unsettling news that some loaves and cheese had gone missing.

The problem was that Praeton had had eleven years to acquaint himself with the Ecclesiat. And unlike the monks who had been there longer, he hadn't been interrupted by constant prayer and study. Even the Ecclesiat's school was connected to the main building. As boys will, he had explored every nook and cranny. The Ecclesiat was his home, his playground, his princedom. If he wanted to remain lost, then lost he would remain.

Gaelin returned to the cathedral. The black scar on the crossing drew large crowds. Some were kneeling to kiss it; others made the sign of the Three while touching the charred stone. He dodged the line that trailed from the Angel's statue all the way to the stone calendar. Scraps of prayers and speculation buzzed. Excitement hummed in the air, but so did something else.

Fear.

While monks and public alike swarmed Alesta with questions about her "miracle" and requests to see it again, a few huddled in shadowy corners, casting nervous glances at the dome. The line to see Osvald's casket inched forward, slowed by sobbing cries that he had left when his Ecclesiat needed him most. Mothers thrust their children on monks carrying sacred water, demanding blessings and purification for their offspring. More than once, Gaelin was approached with variations on the same questions.

What had happened? What was coming? When would it arrive? To all of which, he had but one response.

"I don't know."

He knew their frustration. He felt it each time he asked whether a young, blond boy had been spotted. Again, there was but one answer.

"No."

A new idea whispered to him, chilling his veins. What if Praeton had left the Ecclesiat? In all his life, he had ventured outside its walls only a handful of times. If he was alone in the City...Gaelin didn't want to think about it. His eyes itched again, tired from searching, tired from holding back tears. Each step on the hard marble jarred his shins and knees. Maybe he should get a cane like Evander's.

Exiting the public chapel after another fruitless hunch, he glimpsed Serafine's fiery hair in the narthex. River and Davi were with her. He pressed himself against the wall, hoping to escape to the cathedral unseen.

Naturally, Serafine called out, "Brother Gaelin!"

Tense, ready to flee, he approached. River gave him a tentative smile. He ignored her. Either way, as mere mimic of humanity or artificial human, her audacity appalled him.

"Can I help you, Serafine?"

"Just wanted to know what you thought of Alesta's show."

"Miraculous."

"I see." She sounded disappointed. "Do you believe it was the Angel?"

"What else could it be?"

"You're right, of course." A pause. "But what did He want to accomplish?"

Time gnawed at him. So many places left unsearched, and he wanted a proper discussion with Alesta. Best to leave, but not without information. "Have you seen Praeton?"

Three negative murmurs. River glanced to Davi, then spoke.

"Is he missing?"

"Yes, he is."

If he didn't know better, he'd testify before the Angel that the creature was worried. "May I offer my assistance in finding him?"

He had to laugh. "Why would you want to help?"

"So that he may be found faster, which would be to his benefit."

"He's a sweet child," Serafine added. "I like him."

Gaelin found himself looking at Davi. The mage studiously avoided his gaze. When the silence reached a breaking point, he mumbled, "I'll help too."

"I know the Ecclesiat far better than you, and I've had no success."

"Think he went outside?" Serafine asked.

He couldn't answer.

"Is there anywhere in the Ecclesiat you have not searched?" River said.

Oh, those magi. She sounded so genuine, he was almost comforted. "The Throne's lodgings. The inner sanctum and crypts."

"Considering the Throne's antagonistic nature towards him, it is highly unlikely he is in her home. I therefore propose we search there last. Thus, our next step is to investigate the inner sanctum and crypts."

Cold logic. Cold, but correct. "I'll do that. You aren't allowed in there."

He left them, pushed his way to the back of the chancel. It wasn't until he was halfway down the corridor to the inner sanctum that he remembered: the door had been open before the funeral. He had closed it himself. *Oh, Praeton...* He hobbled as fast as his sore legs would allow, lamplight casting monstrous shapes on the walls. Even this deep in the Ecclesiat, fresh bursts of thunder interrupted his thoughts. And was it his imagination, or did the walls themselves shudder? There'd been rumours of earthquakes. But here?

At the sight of the inner sanctum, his breath caught in his chest. The High Altar was undisturbed, wood still piled upon it. But the trapdoor was open, the lid flipped up like a laughing mouth. Yawning darkness swallowed his lamplight; the steps faded to obscurity.

Lifting the hem of his robes with one hand and holding the lantern high with the other, Gaelin descended. It had been some time since his last visit. As always, there was the sensation of holiness lurking just beyond his grasp. He paused on the stairs. His senses deceived him. Was that breathing he heard, or his own blood rushing in his ears?

"Praeton?"

No answer.

He continued on, imagined the fear a small boy must feel down here. Alone, in the dark, on the edge of the Angel's sacred presence. At the bottom, he stopped again and lifted his lantern to each of the three passages. The two outside ones went off to the catacombs. Reason told him to search them first. After all, Praeton wouldn't dare enter the Angel's Sepulchre.

Something stronger than Reason argued differently. Gaelin wasn't sure whether to call it intuition or revelation, but he started down the centre passage. Its narrowing reminded him of a dragon's gullet. Though it was summer, the air sparked gooseflesh. He held the lantern close to him, for warmth as much as light. The passage felt endless—the lamp was an oasis of light in the void. The life and movement in the cathedral above grew incomprehensible. And at the end, drawing him onwards, the spirit of the Angel, waiting. Dreaming without sleep.

A small shape sprawled before the ebony door. Gaelin hurried, his lamplight skittering over the boy. He almost wished he hadn't found Praeton. Not here, where he was guilty of sacrilege. He knelt at the boy's side. No visible injuries. His breaths were shallow, but regular.

"Praeton."

The boy didn't stir.

He shook him gently. "Praeton, wake up."

Nothing.

The darkness deepened. He nearly burst into the sepulchre to beg the Angel for help, but stopped himself. No. Not now. To enter the holiest of holy spaces in such a state of mind would taint it beyond repair. That was not an option. Not when he had seen His power that very night.

"Come, Praeton."

He needed a miracle.

"Gaelin?"

He almost smashed the lantern against the wall in his rush to turn. "Serafine?"

She emerged from the blackness, clutching a lamp of her own. Alone.

The gooseflesh on Gaelin's arms rippled. "What are you doing here?" He pointed to the ebony door. "This is desecration!"

"Don't worry."

"Don't worry? Do you have any idea what place this is?"

She winced. Taking deep breaths, as though dredging each one from the bottom of her lungs, she forced speech out. "All too well. You hold my light, I'll take Praeton." Bewildered, Gaelin found himself with hands full as Serafine stroked Praeton's hair. "Praeton," she said. "It's time to get up."

And he rose.

"Serafine? Brother—I'm sorry! I know it was wrong. I...I wanted His help. Just to make the dreams stop."

"Shh…" She laid a long, pale finger on his lips. "We'll take you out. Gaelin, if you'll lead?"

Swallowing his anger, Gaelin guided them back to the world of light. Relief and reprimands battled for supremacy. The catacombs were supposed to be the purest part of the Ecclesiat.

The fact that they had been twice defiled sickened him. True, Praeton was only a boy, but he should know better. And Serafine—Ael only knew what myths she'd learned on whatever storm-tossed rock she called home.

The cathedral still hummed when they emerged. Serafine touched Gaelin's arm. Her hand was ice cold. "River and Davi are in one of the anchorage cells," she said.

"What? Why?"

"I asked them to wait there."

He hooked the lanterns back in their sconces. "I ask again. Why?"

"Just come, Gaelin. You too, Praeton."

Somehow, she knew the way. Beside the stairs to the choir room, another staircase wound beneath the Ecclesiat. The anchorage cells lined the space under the nave. Doors peppered the narrow halls; years of delivering bread and water to the anchors had grooved the floor. Gaelin sighed. He considered himself a man devoted to Ael, yet the anchors' piety astounded him. To remain in such a small space for a year with no human contact, save the monk who brought food, required true commitment to Ael. Few elder monks attempted anchorages. Fewer still lasted the year.

Small wonder the Angel deemed Alesta worthy.

At last, Serafine ushered them into a cell. Davi and River crouched in the far corner, examining the stone. Phrases from the Tablet covered the cell's walls.

"Look," Davi was saying. "It's that bit about the flood, only here the aither comes from the *plane* of the Angel. Not *plain* like a field, *plane* like a state of being."

"What is all this?" Gaelin rounded on Serafine. "I have been patient with you. I have welcomed you, allowed you to seek sanctuary within our walls. My patience is now nearing its end. I have people to serve, matters to attend to."

Praeton, avoiding Gaelin, paced from one end of the cell to the other. "It's small."

Serafine laughed. "It certainly is."

"How did you rouse Praeton when I could not? Where did you come from?"

"Are we questioning Serafine?" Davi left his place at the carvings. "I'd like to know exactly how you use the aither. It's got pretty important implications for my research."

Serafine's blue eyes danced. "I've told you again and again."

"It doesn't help. You're not a mage. Serafine—what are you?"

"What am I?"

Her hair blazed crimson, as though made of flames. A reddish glow replaced her paleness. Gaelin backed against the wall. The urge to flee thrummed in every nerve, but he was paralyzed. Bizarre shadows on the wall behind her added to his fear. Something was happening to her back.

Whispers filled the cell. A pair of wings, scarlet as her hair, arched over her shoulders. The wingtips, sharp as daggers, crossed over her breastbone, while softer feathers curtained her face. As Gaelin watched, another pair emerged. These wings wrapped around her thighs, and cascaded over her feet. Where was Praeton? Safe, and gazing open-mouthed as a third pair of wings unfurled. This central pair dwarfed the others, and Gaelin knew that they were the wings that lifted her into the air.

"What am I?" she asked again, and it was her voice, but richer, and deeper, and higher, and filled with such powerful, awful beauty that Gaelin wept to hear it. A shining smile lit Praeton's face. At the edge of his vision, Gaelin saw Davi with a protective arm around River. The mage was ashen; River simply stared.

"I am the shadow of the turning," the thing that was once Serafine said, "the darkness of the dawn. I am the ending that begins, and the hope of the grave. I am the destroyer who creates.

"I am the Seraph."

"The—the Beast!" Gaelin choked out.

Her gaze washed over him, bluer and brighter than a thousand summer skies. "I am called the Beast. I *am* the Seraph."

Praeton stretched a hand to touch Her feathers. Acting on instinct, Gaelin yanked him back, and sheltered him in his arms. He turned his back to the Beast in an effort to shield the boy.

"Gaelin!" Praeton whined, voice muffled by Gaelin's robes.

They were going to die. The thought overwhelmed everything else. Deep in the bowels of the Ecclesiat, buried beneath a manmade mountain, the Beast was going to kill them and gorge Herself upon their souls. Gaelin gulped lungful after lungful of dust-filled air. No matter how musty and dry they were, they were precious.

"Angelus Rex," he prayed. He squeezed Praeton closer. "Hear your servants at their deaths. Angel King, I commend to you my soul. At the ending of my life, I call upon the mercy which is yours to give as you see fit."

"Oh, be quiet, Gaelin." With a sigh, Serafine beat Her wings. The shock wave nearly knocked them all to the ground. She hovered close to the floor, wingtips making a soft *shh shh* on the stone walls. "I'm not here to harm you."

"Then why are you here?"

River? Gaelin chanced a look. The young woman had her arms crossed and an exasperated expression on her face. Mentally, Gaelin gave himself a good slap. She was *not* a young woman, and she could *not* be showing an expression of any sort. Deceit, false facial movements, that's all it was.

He didn't quite believe himself.

"The same reason as last time."

Now Davi crept beside River. Unlike her, he kept his face pointed towards Serafine's feet. When he spoke, Gaelin had to strain to hear. "Didn't you bring about the contamination of humanity last time?"

Brave words for a terrified lad. Praeton had stopped struggling, now listened just as carefully. "Pray to the Angel,"

Gaelin whispered to him. "He'll protect us."

"I'm not scared."

"It wasn't contamination," Serafine said. She fluttered to the ground. Every inch of Her shimmered. "None of you would have survived without me."

Gaelin lifted his head. "That's a lie. The Angel wished to exterminate the sinners, nothing more."

Her silvery laugh hadn't changed. "And how many do you think lived up to His standard?" When She didn't receive an answer, She continued, "The flood was meant to destroy the world. Every man, woman, and child. What does the Angel love, and strive for, above all else?"

The word forced itself past Gaelin's lips. "Perfection."

"Precisely. What's more perfect than nothingness? It's even in your Tablet. *It shall be pure as it was even in the days of the Void.*" One of Her bottom wings extended towards Praeton. His hand darted forth and seized it. Serafine smiled. "I don't like the Void. It's staid, boring."

"But you defied Ael," Gaelin said.

The colour faded from Her feathers. "I did," She whispered. "But *He* forced my hand."

Davi snorted. "Ael couldn't control Ael's own creations? Some god."

"No, no." Serafine held up three fingers. "Ael is Ael, and Ael is the Angel, and Ael is me."

The mage's mouth moved as he worked it out. "You're Ael?"

"In a sense."

"I thought you were the Seraph."

"I am."

"Then..."

River reached for Davi's shoulder, then pulled away. The mage didn't notice, but Gaelin suppressed a snort of his own. Who the MCB thought she was fooling was beyond him.

"Davi," she said. "I believe this is a manifestation of the

'mystery of Ael.' Ael becomes the Angel and the Beast, who are then by definition Ael. Yet Ael also remains Ael."

Serafine clapped. "Ever consider becoming a theologian, River? Just one thing: I'm the Seraph. They only called me *the Beast* after I brought the aither."

To Gaelin's discomfort, Praeton was still stroking the wings curled about Her shins. At this remark, however, he dropped them. "Why did you bring aither?" he asked.

She knelt beside him. "Because without it, you wouldn't have stood a chance against the Angel. Once He saw what I was doing, He gave up cleansing the entire world, and settled for what had already been destroyed. But He made sure He got power other ways." Her smile turned hard and sour. "That was about the time of Ael's passing."

"What?" Gaelin gaped at her.

"Ael is That Which is All: Ael can't turn against Ael's own self. When Ael saw the fighting between the Angel and me, Ael left. I'm not sure where."

The double triangle at his neck suddenly felt ridiculous. A golden lie had been nestling next to his skin for all these years. "Then the Angel King is more powerful."

"I don't know about that." Serafine shrugged. The movement bent Her wings against the ceiling.

"Wait!" Davi burst out. He quivered with unconcealed excitement. "This means, it's all real. That story, how the aither came. The first magi. You're real, you really did it."

"And you're just now realizing it?"

With a wave, Davi dismissed Her. "Do you have any idea what you could do for my research? How did you do it? Where did you get the aither?"

Serafine gestured vaguely. "The aither's everywhere. I just helped people see it. Then some of their children could see it, and so on..."

"So it is passable traits! But, what do you mean, it's everywhere?"

"It is. Their eyes were opened to it when I moved it through my soul, but it's always been everywhere."

Davi frowned. Taking advantage of the pocket of silence, Gaelin jumped in. "This is all fascinating, but you never told us the reason for your return."

"Oh. Right. Sorry about that." Serafine smiled. "The world is ending, so I thought I'd save you."

"With more aither?" Praeton asked.

"No. We need a new world; this one's run its course." She bit Her lip. "The only problem is, only Ael can create a new world."

"And Ael is either unwilling or unable to do so," River said.

"Ael is. But if I found the Hapax..."

All the air whooshed from Gaelin's lungs. "The Word was with Ael, and the Word *was* Ael!"

"Exactly. Tomorrow's day four of seven? The Angel made His position very clear to me tonight. He wants His Void again. And the way things are going, He is very likely to get it." One by one, Her wings retracted. The brilliant glow left Her body. Her voice thinned, became human again. "Shall we?"

They followed her from the cell. Gaelin could barely place one foot before the other. The Beast was walking just ahead of him. Suspicion coiled about him like a serpent. How much truth had she told them? The writings all concurred—she was cunning. Dangerous.

Behind him, he heard Davi mutter to River, "It doesn't make sense. The aither *isn't* everywhere!"

IX

⁓

The blood started in earnest the next morning. Thick red streaks dripped down the windows, congealed in the crevices of walls. No birds braved the bruised sky. None that Davi could see, anyway. The air burned his nose every time he breathed. He swiped the sweat beading his forehead. Sticky. Everything too cramped, too dense... The open plains past the horizon had never seemed so seductive. Or so unreachable.

Thunder. Clouds clenched like fists, threatening. He imagined the first raindrop as a pin pricking an unbearably stretched tension. And waited for it, peering past the scarlet smears. The thunder growled again, yet the rains abstained.

The world was holding its breath.

Even in the dorters, the mumblings of those at prayer reached him. So did shrieks and screams - the lifelong pious confronting the realization of their worst fears, and the unbelievers grappling with mental vertigo as the foundation of their world shuddered. He sympathized. Ael was real. Or had been. The Angel, the Seraph, the Beast. So much for the world following nice, clear-cut rules. Just when he thought he understood, his feet had been yanked from under him. Vertigo indeed.

Four of seven.

A low groan escaped him. She had said the aither was everywhere, but it wasn't, it simply wasn't. And she was a goddess, or as good as. The gods were supposed to be something you believed in, they weren't supposed to sit beside you and brightly explain how they planned to save or destroy the world. And the terrible heat crushing his head, the damp sheets under his legs—he couldn't even crawl back in bed. The very thought of cocooning himself in sweltering blankets suffocated him.

A knock at the door. "Yes?" Davi said. Probably the monk who slept a few beds over and was always forgetting some essential part of his attire.

He glanced up, and his breath caught.

River peered in. Her lovely dark eyes blinked. The tips of her hair swung forward past her chin. In that moment, his apprehension ebbed, and a thrill of delight took its place.

She wavered on the threshold. "May I come in?" she said. A simple sentence, but obviously one that taxed her. Davi nodded, and she entered. Paused again a few steps from him. He patted the bed, and she lowered herself next to him, back rigid and hands clasped in her lap. If she'd had blood, Davi mused, her knuckles would've whitened.

"What is it?" he asked.

"Nothing. I did not wish to be alone. Irrational, perhaps, but nevertheless…"

He squeezed her hand. River's body tensed, but the hand went limp. He dropped it, and forced a smile. "Not irrational. Not now."

"I suppose there is little that is rational about blood pouring from the sky."

"River…" His hand inched towards hers again. "Was that a joke?"

"An observation." This time, she let him hold it.

He had no answer to that. Blood dripped, tainted their view of the outside world. But something in Davi sang through the disgust. He had her hand. In his. Wonderfully soft, warm from the heat of the day, and dry as bone. His heart swelled and thumped. Surely she heard it. But if she did, she gave no indication.

Just when he was about to cough, or move, or do anything to break the silence, she spoke. "I have not seen Serafine today."

He swallowed his wooziness. They had to get a pitcher of water up here. He didn't know how the monks could stand it. "Really? I thought she'd want to see us."

"Perhaps. However, it seems futile to predict her actions. Presuming she has correlations with human behaviour is a flawed assumption at best."

"Right." His thoughts kept drifting. With a pang, he let go of her and rubbed his temples. A wash, breakfast, and fresh air, preferably in that order, and he'd be fine.

He could tell himself that.

"Listen," he said. She trained those eyes on him, and he choked on his sentence. The dry heave of his throat ached. Three words. Three impossible words. Cursing his cowardice, he changed tack. "What she said about the aither. Does that make sense to you?"

"No, but our understanding of the aither is incomplete."

The academic side of him rebelled. Though he tried not to show it, her remark stung. "I know. We're working on it. But it's not everywhere."

"How do you know?"

"Well…" He gestured around the room, at the rows of beds. "Is there any here?"

Dutifully, she surveyed their surroundings, gaze travelling from the rafters, to the crisp white coverlets, to the floorboards. At last, she shrugged. "I don't see any, but that should not surprise you."

"Yes, yes, MCBs don't have magic." He sucked air through his teeth. Once his mind had a problem, it worried it like a hound with its game. "What do we know?" he said. Rhetorical question; he didn't wait for an answer. He paced, not seeing much of anything. "Before the flood, no one had magic. Then Serafine *gave* it to people. How?"

"She said she moved it through her soul."

"*Through* her soul. Which implies it's not everywhere, it came from somewhere."

"Or that it wasn't everywhere then, but has since spread."

His head hurt. "If it's everywhere, why can't I see it? I'm a mage."

River looked thoughtful. "You can use aither anywhere, yes? Have you ever considered from where you actually draw it?"

"From…inside."

"Inside what?"

"I'm not sure. We just…reach inside." He grimaced. "Hence the old arguments whether or not aither is a physical part of us. Do we have a second stomach filled with aither? Is it something our brains produce?"

"I wonder if it would be possible to draw aither from something else."

The thunderclap outside was nothing to the one that resounded in Davi's skull. Possibilities kindled, thousands of bright flashes blinded him. "Maybe," he said. He cast about, settled on a stubby candle. Cupping his left hand, he gripped the candle in his right and concentrated on it. Narrowed his attention to such a degree that he could almost ignore River leaning towards him.

Almost.

He loosened his shoulders, breathed, and tightened his grasp until wax softened against his palm. The temptation to close his eyes was tremendous, but he forced them to stay open. The low beat of the aither boomed in his ears—but that was the old way, it was coming from inside of him. He had to fight, had to ignore the guiding signal calling from within his own being. Lock onto the candle. But the damned thing wouldn't sing to him.

With a cry, he pitched the candle across the room. "Useless."

River retrieved the pieces. "It appears your experiment was unsuccessful."

He laughed hollowly and collected some of the wax fragments. "That's one way to say it. And I broke their candle. Naturally. Now I'll have to fix it." The pulse came to him right away, but then he paused. "River, have you ever tried magic?"

She stepped away from him. "Of course not."

"Could you?"

"Any attempt on my part to access or manipulate the aither directly contravenes the policies for MCB function."

"Whereas escaping the Magistatiem and hiding in the Ecclesiat because you're starting to have emotions is perfectly acceptable."

To his astonishment—and delight—she smiled. "Well argued. How do I begin?"

Davi fought to find his tongue. "Um. Listen, I guess. It's like a heartbeat. Sometimes novices actually hear their own heartbeat and think they're getting close, but you shouldn't have any trouble with that, because—" The realization of where this path headed made his lips clamp tight.

River went still. "Because I lack a heart."

He nodded. His cheeks burned. River's eyelids fluttered, and she seemed to draw everything inside of her further inwards, leaving her outsides blank and empty. Before Davi could apologize, she motioned for him to be quiet. Minutes passed.

And then: "Nothing. I'm sorry."

"Nothing to be sorry about," he said. Lightning clashed, painting the room silver. The eerie light lit River's disappointment in crystal-sharp detail. More readable emotion. He tucked that away in a corner of his mind. "It just proves my point. Aither's not everywhere. Yes, it's the fifth element, but it looks like it's found in magi. Not as part of our bodies, but maybe it's attracted to us? Like how lightning's attracted to metal. You don't even find air throughout the whole world— not underground, not underwater."

"She wouldn't lie, though." River turned away. "It is an

139

irrational conviction, and should not influence your theory. Yet, I know she wouldn't lie." She turned back to him, and she looked too young, far too scared. "Davi," she whispered. "What is this?"

Fearful thrill and thrilling fear fused in his veins. "I'd say intuition."

"No. MCBs don't have intuition."

The urge to hold her returned. His hands clenched and unclenched by his sides. "Most don't. But in case you haven't noticed, you're unique."

Tremors rattled her body. "This must be fear. It's—how do you do this?" Her voice broke. "Every minute, every day, from every side. No wonder the early MCBs lost their minds! Davi, what if it happens to me, too? What if I'm another Emerald?"

Not quite certain of his actions, Davi took her by the shoulders and drew her near, into his arms. For a moment he thought she would break away, or break him, but then she slumped against him.

"You're not another Emerald," he said. "You're stronger. Look, it's not that you can't handle emotion. It's that you've never had to. Things will get better, you'll see."

"But it was so much simpler before!"

She buried her face in his chest; he leaned down so that his forehead brushed her hair. Hair utterly devoid of the perfumes and feminine scents he'd known in the Magistatiem common rooms, but glossy and silky and—

That was it. Thought ceased. Emotion reigned.

Forget the aither. Forget Serafine. Alesta, Gaelin, and the Ecclesiat, they were nothing to him. Even the raging storm and raining blood, even the end of the world itself, he didn't care. All there was in that moment *was* that moment.

"Things were simpler before," he whispered. "But were they better?"

No response beyond increased quivering. He fumbled for

some way to comfort her. "Don't worry," he said, stroking her hair. "Once the bridges are fixed, we'll get away, as far as we can. We'll make a new life."

She disentangled herself for an instant. "Without the others? We seem to have become enmeshed with them. Would you leave them here?"

Thunder. Senses and arms still filled with her, Davi forced himself to think. The roaring at the end of the world rang in his ears. Leaving the City had been his only goal since their flight from the Magistatiem. It was the closest thing they had to a plan. But then he imagined a void where Serafine had been. Praeton, struck dumb by apocalypse. And Gaelin, who was such a threat, but tried so hard...

He made a decision.

"No. I guess I wouldn't."

She nodded, and seemed about to say something more, when the floor pitched and threw them from their feet. The floorboards struck Davi's palms and kneecaps. He winced and fumbled for something to shelter them both. A desk or table. Nothing. He scrabbled at the ground, clung to the legs of the nearest bed so tightly that splinters pierced his fingers. Vague memories of advice and folklore surfaced—he had to protect his head. That's what Serafine had tried to do the last time. Shoving his upper body under the bed, he waited to die.

He didn't. The quaking ceased as suddenly as it had started. He crawled from under the bed, dust coating his shirt and hair. River had crouched on the floor, head tucked under. She uncurled cautiously. "Another earthquake," she said. "And stronger this time, suggesting an increase in seismic activity. Are you injured?"

Davi shook his head. "We'd better go downstairs. See that no one else is."

And, he added to himself, to find Serafine.

Wails from the cathedral reached them before they had left the cloisters. As they slipped through the connecting door, Davi scanned the crowds for Serafine's fiery head. No luck. It was possible he missed her in the crowds—they were big enough—but not likely.

People clung to monks like drowning men to flotsam. Moans and tears reverberated off the dome. Sickness twisted in Davi's stomach as he spied bloody footprints leading from the narthex. The stain on the pale stone glinted, fresh. He stopped a nearby woman.

"Excuse me, what's happening out there?"

The whites of her eyes showed stark and wide. "The Angel is come upon us with His rightful anger. We have not been pure enough, we have failed."

He bit back frustration. "Please, miss."

"The earth quakes, the clouds bleed, all is darkness and death..."

Outside the Ecclesiat doors, hail struck the square. Chips of pink-tinted ice bounced off the cobblestones. Waiting horses stamped and whinnied, and the wealthier Ecclesiat-goers covered their heads as they scurried to their carriages. Davi redoubled his efforts to find Serafine, frowning. If she really was the Seraph, why wasn't she stopping this? The Angel could make Alesta control bolts of fire; where was Her power?

He retreated to the narthex. And had an idea.

"Praeton." He hadn't realized he'd spoken aloud until River frowned. "It's worth trying," he said. "He's had all these dreams about the Hapax. As far as I know, he's never been tested for magic. Maybe he can clear this up."

She considered him as though he'd joined the shrieking, desperate masses. "Am I to understand that you intend to conduct an investigation based on a child's dreams?"

"Well—" He wandered into the public chapel. More noise there, less chance of being overheard. Pretending to admire an ossuary, he continued, "It's not like we have anything better to go on."

"While I admire your zeal for your area of study, may I suggest that there are greater priorities at the moment?"

He leaned his head against the cool stone. Then he realized how little distance separated his face from a casket of bones, and drew back. "It's all connected, somehow. Serafine. Her aither that's supposed to be everywhere, but isn't. The Hapax." He felt old. Probably had a few worry-lines by now. Grey hairs, too. "Look, Serafine changes everything. If she's real, maybe Praeton's dreams are, too."

River stepped closer to him, and his breath caught. But she had just been avoiding a matriarch trailing her children and grandchildren. "A tenuous assumption, if you'll forgive my saying so."

"An irrational conviction, right?" He grinned. "Call it intuition."

For the second time that morning, River smiled. "Very well. Let us find him."

It soon occurred to them that they had no idea where Praeton might be. The mourners and monks gathered by the chancel railing served as a reminder that Osvald had been interred mere hours earlier. So Gaelin was probably occupied. But had the choirs been involved in the ceremony? Were they rehearsing? Davi didn't know. He'd never had much of a spiritual upbringing. His parents had ensured the majority of his time was spent with his hands full of aither, not being washed before the Angel.

His parents. Semni, their town, was a few days' journey at least. The earthquakes couldn't have affected the coast. Right?

Begin at the start, he told himself. Take the information at hand. Praeton was a boy. What's more, he was a boy who knew the Ecclesiat far better than they did. So, if he were Praeton, where would he be? Not, as Davi discovered, in the public chapel. Nor lurking about the chancel. In the aisle, River halted him and pointed. There, in the shadows between the columns and the wall, lounged a group of boys. Davi squinted in the dimness. They looked about Praeton's age.

Their high-pitched voices subsided as Davi and River approached, and they flattened themselves against the wall. One of them, a curly-haired boy who seemed to be the leader, stuck out his jaw.

Davi held up his hands. "We just wanted to ask you something."

"It wasn't us!"

How often he'd uttered that defence, and really, not that long ago. With a jolt, he realized these boys saw him as an adult on the same order as Alesta or Gaelin.

River cleared her throat. "Do any of you know Praeton?"

The boys cast side-long glances at each other. The curly-haired boy shrugged. "Sure. He's a first soprano."

"Do you know where he might be?"

Pure bewilderment this time. "Why'd we know that?"

"Don't you play with him?" Davi said.

Sniggers broke out as the leader smirked. "No. He doesn't play with anyone. He's weird."

Davi's brain churned helplessly. A twelve-year-old had just rendered him mute. He tried to come up with a rebuttal, but River got there first. "Praeton is a fine example of an Ecclesiat chorister. Now, can you tell us where he is habitually found?"

The boy looked at Davi. "Where is he normally?" Davi translated.

More laughter. The boy pointed. "Right there."

Davi turned and saw Praeton wandering up the opposite aisle. A begrudging thanks to the boys, and he charged after him, River in his wake. They dodged crowds, their footsteps stark and swift on the stone. Praeton heard them long before they reached him. He waited, brow furrowed far too seriously for one so young.

"Davi? River?"

"Praeton!" Davi skidded to a halt beside him. "What's going on, are you needed right now?"

"No." The boy checked the altar behind him. Davi followed suit. No one there he recognized, but Praeton shuddered.

"Can you help me with something?" Davi said.

Praeton blinked. "What?"

Just as Davi opened his mouth, River touched his arm. He gulped as she leaned towards Praeton and lowered her voice. "This is perhaps best discussed in private."

Now they had Praeton's attention. The boy practically squirmed. "No one's in the refectory!"

The refectory was a little more open than Davi would've liked, but the three of them could sit there without arousing suspicion. If a hungry monk wandered in, they could pretend to be eating. His stomach rumbled. Perhaps they could actually eat.

They took the long way through the cloisters, rather than cutting across the gardens. By unspoken agreement, it seemed better to stay indoors. The great cloister windows facing onto the gardens were so smeared with blood, dirt, and rain, Davi could hardly see out of them.

True to Praeton's word, the refectory's long tables stood empty. No smells wafted from the kitchens below, though a forlorn loaf and basket of fruit lay on the sideboard. Praeton grabbed the heel of the bread and headed for the room's far corner. He swung his feet up on the bench, leaned against the wall, and began disassembling his bread, eyes on Davi.

Somehow, Davi couldn't shake his nerves. He reassured himself that the refectory was empty save for them. Not even the mice poked from their hiding spots. Across the table, River nodded at him. He forced a smile, and faced Praeton.

"Praeton, have you ever been tested for magic?"

Crumbs flecked the boy's grey shirt. He stuffed the bread in his mouth and shook his head emphatically. Davi sighed.

"Want to do a little experiment, then?"

Praeton swallowed. "Something to do with magic?"

"Yes. Have you had any more of your...dreams?"

Praeton went quiet. His eyes flicked to River, as though seeking comfort or confirmation. Receiving a "go on" motion from her, he took a breath. "Maybe."

Davi willed himself to be patient. "A little more detail, please."

Praeton wiped his mouth and curled himself about his skinny knees. "I had the one in the choir room. And then...I don't know. Maybe another? It didn't make sense, though." He glared at them. "Don't think I'm stupid."

"We won't," River assured him.

Mollified, Praeton picked at the table-top. "Streams of light, all wrapped around each other. White light, but there wasn't anything outside of it."

"Then how could you tell they were streams?" Davi said.

"I don't know!" His voice rose. "I just could."

"It's all right, just asking."

"Davi, isn't magic bad?" There was that far-too-serious look again. "Only, if it is, how are you good? And how is Serafine?"

"And me," River said quietly.

In retrospect, Davi supposed he shouldn't have been surprised. The boy had been indoctrinated in Ecclesiat beliefs since infancy. That didn't take the sting from his question. Davi cast about for the best way to explain. Again, some theological experience might have helped.

"Serafine brought the aither, right? And people thought that she disobeyed Ael by doing that. And she did. But that might not have been a bad thing."

"Really?"

He bit back a sigh. "Well, she's why we're all here."

"Oh. How am I supposed to help you with magic?"

As nice as theological knowledge might have been, experience with children was what he needed now. He kept his voice light.

"First let's see if you can use the aither. Don't worry if you can't, it's pretty rare."

"How?" Praeton wriggled on the bench. "I know it looks like blue fire, but—"

"That's great—close your eyes and listen. Try to hear something like a drumbeat, but not." Sure. That would help him. "Like a low throbbing noise, repeated over and over," he corrected himself. "Like the lowest note on a fiddle or violin, a sort of thrumming."

He held his breath as Praeton concentrated. The boy's hands clenched on his knees. His jaw locked. Once, Davi had done the same. Only he'd been in an office at the Magistatiem, with his parents and a tutor watching. That first time he'd followed the pulse to the gulf of sapphire flame - he'd never forget it. Summoning up the memory, he offered Praeton all his hope and goodwill, and then something he'd never offered before.

A prayer.

"Do you have it?" he said.

All he got was a dismissal like someone shooing a gnat. He waited. Often focus ran so deep, it completely cut the mage off from their surroundings.

So he was startled when Praeton muttered, "I hear it, but I can't find it."

River moved closer to him. "Could you elaborate?"

It sounded like Praeton was speaking from a long way off. "It's here. The thrumming. Like a chord, like when you have a soprano split, and then the altos underneath." Eyes still shut, he shook his head. "Only I don't know where it's coming from. Can't follow it."

A few more minutes of breathless silence from Davi and River, and Praeton jerked upright. Dampness darkened his hair, glistened at his temples. His lower lip trembled. "I couldn't do it. I'm sorry."

"It's all right," Davi said. "You did a lot better than most people." Not only was Praeton's lip quivering, so was his whole body. Davi nudged him towards the sideboard. "You'd better get something to eat."

As Praeton weaved through the tables, Davi dug out a small notebook and pencil from his pocket. He licked the pencil's tip. "Thoughts, River?"

She watched Praeton root through the fruit bowl. "It seems he is sensitive enough to hear the aither, if not to use it. I did, however, note something of interest."

"What?"

"He described the source of the sound as being impossible to localize. Therefore, the aither was similarly impossible to pinpoint." She stopped, apparently for Davi to fill in the blank. An idea struggled to dawn on him, but he squashed it. They'd been over this—it wasn't possible, nor was it helpful. When he refused to answer, River continued, "While it is possible he simply couldn't locate it, from his perspective, the aither was, indeed, everywhere."

X

He endured as long as he could. But eventually, Gaelin needed to leave the cathedral. After Osvald's interment in the crypts, he couldn't focus. Couldn't bring himself to care. Twice he didn't hear a junior monk ask a question, and the answers he gave were nonsensical. The massive Ecclesiat felt too small. Somewhere, he knew, the Beast was lurking. He didn't know which would be worse: if this was another one of Her plots, or if She was telling the truth.

So when Alesta instructed teams of monks to trawl the City, to spread the teachings of the Angel and direct refugees to the Ecclesiat, Gaelin jumped to volunteer. A pang of uncertainty shot through him as he strode into the square. The light outside had a yellowish tint, as though the air were jaundiced. This despite the twisted knot of clouds. Heat stuck Gaelin's tongue to the roof of his mouth. Yet he shivered as blood splattered beside him. Sticky warmth soaked his toes.

Drawing his hood over his head, Gaelin plunged into the City. Since entering the seminary as a young man, he had ventured beyond the Ecclesiat's walls only to fulfil its work. The house of Ael was practically a city unto itself—few felt the need to explore the godless one surrounding it. Turning constantly to keep the bell tower in view, Gaelin followed half-forgotten alleys and laneways. Solemn-eyed children and wary mothers watched him from glassless windows, faces half-hidden by tattered curtains. The fathers lounged on corners before their homes, daring him to stop.

He did. Block by block, home by home, family by family, he explained the holy danger that was to come, and urged them to seek safety in the sheltering arms of the Ecclesiat. Some listened. They were the ones who had seen the blood drench their children, stiffening their hair to foul spikes. They were the ones whose houses had succumbed to the shaking of the earth. At one dwelling, Gaelin helped pull a little girl from the rubble of a collapsed staircase. Her family lived on the second floor of the house; she had been trying to enter their apartment when the quake struck.

As he clasped the girl to him, brushing dust from her tearstained face, Gaelin had one question. *Why?* Passing the girl to her mother, another question formed. *Who?*

Angel or Beast? King or Temptress? The Purifier or the Polluter?

Around mid-morning, as he shared some cold ham with a group of young carpenters, he noticed the silence. No birds. No buzzing insects. Uneasy, he tried to remember if any stray cats or dogs had crossed his path since leaving the Ecclesiat. None came to mind.

"Quiet today," he said.

One carpenter laughed. The rest hid pitying smiles in their skins of wine. A few streets over, Gaelin saw why. Blood clogged the gutters, but it hadn't all fallen from above. Now that he looked, he saw where the animals of the City had gone.

Lost to the flood.

Stray dogs curled by buildings, fur matted into sticky red clumps. Atop ledges and under stairways, cats stretched out cold and stiff. He stepped off the street and into a garden to inspect one, the hot, wet earth sucking his feet. Its glassy gaze reminded him far too much of Osvald. The scarlet rains half-drowned its tabby stripes, but there was no obvious reason for death. It was as though it had simply slipped into a deeper sleep. The stench of rot and congealing blood forced Gaelin back a step. Not even the vermin had escaped. Mice floated in the fountains. In drains, he glimpsed sodden, unmoving lumps of fur.

Eventually he reached a clearing in the City streets. A stone wall challenged the troubled sky. The Magistatiem. His lip curled at the sight of it. Such ostentation. They had no need to enclose their entire organization. If the Ecclesiat was a city unto itself, the magi were trying to make their Magistatiem its own kingdom. Stained flags fluttered from the top of the wall: the once blue Magistatiem falcon now a tired red, the sandy background the brown of old wounds. Trust them to have their own coat of arms. Imitators, that's all they were, despite their protests to the contrary.

But there were more neighbourhoods between the Magistatiem and the City's outer walls. Sighing, Gaelin plodded along the Magistatiem's border. Magi dashing to and fro like mad ants went out of their way to avoid him. Speckled with blood, all of them. Some pointed at his robes from a safe distance. Gaelin squared his shoulders to it. He did wish he could reach out to the ones that visibly paled as he neared, but he had his instructions. Besides, he realized with a twinge, this was the place from which Davi and River had come. He had pitied them, admired them even. For their resourcefulness in escaping, for Davi's adoration, obvious to all but the Object herself. But their actions...mocking Ael by making life. Lying to him. Abusing his trust.

He wondered why a part of him still liked them.

A pattern appeared in the throng of magi. They fanned into the streets strategically. Handheld bells clanged, voices boomed through amplifying horns. Through the din, Gaelin caught a few words:

"All available magi to the Magistatiem! Spellers to Orsus Hall! Casters standing by!"

None of it meant anything to him. All he had to do was keep walking, maybe cut down a side street to avoid the place altogether.

Instead, he stopped a man about his own age. He seemed respectable enough. Much taller than Gaelin, with a thin face. He looked down on Gaelin.

"Yes...*Brother*? Are you lost?"

He understood the coldness. The same frost threatened to colour his own speech. "Excuse me. I know a mage. Is he supposed to be here?"

He registered some surprise at that. "You know a mage?" Chilly grey eyes evaluated him. "How old?"

"Twenty?"

A nod. "A young one. Good. Send him along."

"What shall I tell him?"

"That he's needed, as long as he can reach the aither or write a formula."

He waited, but no further information seemed forthcoming. He cleared his throat and sidestepped a swelling puddle of blood. "What is the Magistatiem doing?"

The man grinned. "We're trying to save the City. Our teams think more earthquakes are coming. Tell your mage—never thought I'd say that—tell him to get here as fast as he can. He'll get more information then."

Four of seven. The thought appeared from nowhere. A threatening growl came from the ground. Gaelin quickened his step, hip protesting from the morning spent walking on hard paving stones and climbing stairs. Five days ago, he would never have imagined acting as a messenger from the Magistatiem.

He didn't want to imagine seven of seven.

"What?" The monk was insane. He had to be. "Return to the Magistatiem?"

"That's right."

Davi shook his head. He had sought refuge in the library. The lectern before him, chains snaking down to books stored on shelves below, created an impenetrable shield. Or so he thought. River, at the lectern beside him, also raised an eyebrow at Gaelin.

Too many possible traps occurred to Davi all at once. "They know River's here."

"He mentioned nothing about your...associate. And indeed, there were many magi. I believe they are genuinely planning something." He shrugged. "It might buy us time to find the Hapax."

"Too dangerous. I'm not going."

"Excuse me," River said.

Gaelin didn't look at her. "Yes?"

"With all due respect, I would ask that you not refer to me as Davi's associate. I have a name, as you well know. Moreover, until recently, you were quite comfortable using it."

The monk's mouth flapped like a landed fish, which made Davi suppress a laugh. Every so often, River surprised him. It was happening more and more lately.

"I apologize." A blush tinted his cheeks. Better yet, it sounded as if he meant it. "I didn't think it would bother you...River."

"I accept your apology. Thank you."

Instead of leaving, as Davi expected, Gaelin continued to stand before them. Rolling his eyes, Davi returned to his work. The Ecclesiat had a handful of books concerning aither. All of them dealt with the subject from the angle that it was temptation offered by the Beast, but another angle was always helpful, even just as contrast. Besides, with his own books stuck at the Magistatiem, he was desperate for reading material. He was halfway down the next page when Gaelin cleared his throat.

"If I may ask, what are you doing?"

"Working," Davi said.

River frowned at him. "We are investigating Davi's theory that the aither is somehow linked to the Hapax."

"It's not just my theory. You think there's something there as well!"

"Please." Gaelin's face hardened. "The Hapax and the aither? The Word of Ael and what was brought by the Beast?"

"I only brought what Ael had made." Serafine stepped from behind a shelf. Her blue eyes locked onto Gaelin's. "The aither is Ael's creation as much as earth, air, fire, and water."

Five elements. Four visible in the world around them, and one allegedly everywhere, but really inside something, somewhere. Davi's thoughts wandered. He wondered what Tam was doing, if there was any way to contact him. He would know what the Magistatiem was planning.

"Serafine," River was saying. "The writings of St. Memoyah say the Hapax echoes *in that place where it first resounded.* Where was that?"

She shifted. "I don't know."

"Don't know?" Davi slammed back to reality. "How can you not know?"

"I wasn't there when Ael spoke the Hapax."

"You are Ael!"

"No, I'm the Seraph, which is what Ael became. And neither the Seraph nor the Angel was there at the beginning of creation." Serafine shook her head. "We don't know the Hapax any more than you do."

"And what about the aither? It's not everywhere!"

"Yes, it is. I don't know how to make that clearer. You might as well ask me where up is."

A rustling startled them all. Praeton peered around the same shelf that had hid Serafine. He coughed and picked at his shirt. "Are you fighting?"

Serafine smiled at him. "More like talking."

"Oh." He went straight to Davi. "I wanted to help more. Can I?"

Much as he liked the boy, Davi wished he hadn't appeared. Now Gaelin was polishing his spectacles, his face stern and severe. He guessed what he was in for. Regret for his endangered soul, astonishment that he was corrupting a child of the Ecclesiat, and worst of all: bitter disappointment.

He was right.

"You've been involving Praeton in your magic?"

The words were supposed to induce shame. And, truth be told, a smidgen of discomfort niggled at his conscience. But then he swung around, jaw set. The monk had no business making him feel ashamed of his magic. Magic had created jobs for countless people. It had improved healing, communications, buildings. It had made River. And, if Serafine was right, it had saved them all from extinction.

So Davi's answer rang out firm and clear. "Yes. I have."

The response was simple, but no less authoritative. "Why?"

"Because we're running out of time!" He didn't care that Gaelin had stepped away, shock and hurt written all over him. "Everything affects everything else. He's been having these dreams, and I thought, well, who knows? Maybe he would have magic and an answer that would save us. You know, something a little better than 'the aither is everywhere!'"

"Listen here young man, I—"

"Stop!"

The high-pitched shout shattered Davi's thoughts. Praeton had his fists balled up. The boy wavered, clearly unsure whether to run away, or keep shouting. Sister Liana marched over, disapproving comment all ready, but when she saw the five of them, she fled. When she had gone, Praeton flushed. He looked feverish.

"Stop fighting! It's all my fault. I'm sorry I have dreams. I'm sorry I let Davi test me for magic. I'm sorry I don't have any." Far from halting at the collective murmurs to the contrary, he launched off again. "I'm sorry the Ecclesiat has to take care of me. I never asked for this. I—I should run away!"

A stunned silence followed this finish. Davi groped for something to say, and failed. He never was good with children.

Gaelin, who should've had more experience, offered Praeton a chair, but the boy pushed it away. Then, River rose and went over to him.

"Praeton, you know those statements are nonsensical."

He turned his back to her, too.

"Listen to me. Dreams are uncontrollable. Therefore, you cannot take either responsibility or blame for having them. Merely testing for magic is not prohibited under Aelist teachings. Not having it is no shame; the ability is rare. As for the circumstances under which you find yourself in the Ecclesiat's care..." Here, Praeton whimpered. Undaunted, River continued, "My understanding is that you remain in that care because the Ecclesiat willingly provides it."

Slowly, Praeton's fists unclenched. He looked at River as though he'd never seen her before. "Really?"

"Really."

"Come on." One of Serafine's slender hands nudged the small of Praeton's back. "Let's go for a walk in the cloisters. Cool off."

With a dazed expression, Praeton allowed himself to be led away. Both Davi and Gaelin had forgotten their argument. Instead, they focused their attention on River, who had gone back to her books. Keen awareness of the changes occurring in her gripped Davi. This wasn't just emotional capability. At least, he suspected it wasn't. True, MCB logic coloured her statements, but he swore there was something else. Something very much like empathy.

Gaelin said nothing. Just frowned, and followed Praeton and Serafine. Davi doubted River even noticed him go. He breathed deeply, reined in his thoughts. Back to work. Work always soothed him. No matter how complex the question, the answers were simple: right or wrong. Black or white, with none of this moral ambiguity.

But soon he found himself distracted again. His line of thinking, once interrupted, refused to materialize again. Instead, he doodled in the margins of his paper. He'd been a pretty decent sketcher once, and now he jotted a portrait of River. With considerably more passion than he felt for the aither at the moment, his pencil flew over her fine features, shaded in the darkness of her eyes and hair. The lips received special care. Full and sweet, for all her mouth was small.

Of course, he'd have to tear the page out and hide it somewhere. That was all right. It was worth it. Satisfied with his rendering, he moved on to stupid, pointless drawings. A map of the Magistatiem. An ornate spell-casting chalice. A wild boar. A hunter confronting the animal, bow raised. Not bad, not bad at all, though they were awfully flat. Creating forms with his pencil made him feel vaguely godlike, and he played with the idea of living as one of those drawings. Living on a piece of paper.

For starters, he thought, adding a house for the hunter, it'd be hard to move. You'd be stuck to the page, unable to raise your head or your hand. You couldn't jump. Then again, that probably wouldn't be so bad. After all, you'd have no concept of the third dimension, wouldn't realize it existed. If you'd never seen it, you'd never miss its absence.

You might as well ask me where up is...

A thunderbolt rooted him to the floor. Suddenly, he couldn't breathe. If drawings lived, they'd only see two dimensions; they simply wouldn't be able to conceive of any others. But what if there were some drawings—a very few—who could lift their heads up, even for a brief moment? They would see the third dimension. And it would be everywhere. It had to be, for it always existed, even if they couldn't see it normally.

Davi tore out his drawings and wrote so hard and fast he scored lines in the lectern What if the aither existed in a dimension that humans couldn't see until Serafine's intervention? They'd never realize it was there, any more than his drawings could conceive of the notion of "up." And even now, magi were unaware of it in their day-to-day lives; they only noticed it when they "stuck their heads up," so to speak.

"River!"

She leaned over. Half a dozen open books were fanned precariously on the lectern. She'd probably been reading them all simultaneously. "What is it?"

"I think I found it—I know where the aither is!"

Breathless, he explained, showed her the allegories with sketched people. A light gleamed in her eyes, and she studied his papers as though they contained the Hapax itself.

Maybe they did.

At last, she nodded. "This is quite elegant, and justifies the aither's nature as understood by both the Magistatiem and the Ecclesiat. My only question is this: where is this dimension?"

He hadn't thought of that.

"I mean," River said, "your allegories suggest a world surrounded by other dimensions. The missing third dimension is greater than the experience of the two-dimension people."

"Right. So maybe it's the same thing again?"

"Perhaps."

She did not twitch, or breathe, or shift in her seat. Far away, leagues away from him and this dusty library corner, her mind was whipping through possibilities at a rate his could never hope to match. She gazed past him, into space, off through the narrow stacks.

"It's like time," she murmured.

Davi frowned, awaiting more explanation. "What do you mean?"

"We live in time. It is everywhere, an integral part of everything, yet as with aither, we cannot see it." Her mouth fell slack, her eyes bright with wonder. "But they can. Ael and the Angel and Serafine, they are within and of the aither, experiencing it as we experience the regular four dimensions. Hence her insistence that aither is everywhere. She didn't bring the aither, Davi; she brought the ability to reach the dimension in which it is found."

What he did next was something he'd never planned to do. Dreamed about, sure. Seriously contemplating it made him want to laugh and cry at once. But now, with the sheer joy of discovery flooding his veins to the bursting point, he did it without thinking.

He kissed her.

Tingling spread through his body. Her lips were soft against his, not as soft or warm as other women he'd kissed, but that didn't matter. They were her lips. Unspeakable love for her flowed through him. *Oh,* he pleaded, before his swollen heart trampled rational thought, *let her feel some of this. Just a little bit.* With a trembling hand, he touched her hair. It smelled of nothing. That didn't matter either. He inhaled the scentless air around her like ambrosia.

Until she shoved him. Hard. He slammed against the bookshelf. Chains jangled and a sharp corner somewhere jabbed his back as joy curdled to mortification. His skin felt clammy, too tight.

River blinked rapidly. She stepped forward, then away. "I apologize." She sounded more than distant. She was glacial. "I was unprepared."

"No, I'm sorry. I should have warned you." He picked at a fingernail. "But now that you know…"

"With all due respect, may I suggest that it is in our collective best interests to continue the investigation into this new discovery?" She gathered her books. "I will be working in the women's dormitory."

The words cracked over Davi's skull with the weight of a falling tree. The women's dormitories, forbidden to men.

Then, just before she ducked out of sight, she held his gaze and whispered, "I'm sorry."

⁓

The prospect of an extra service did nothing to cheer Praeton up. The walk through the cloisters with Serafine had been nice. He'd

159

hoped she would show off her wings, but she made no mention of them, and he was too shy to ask. Now, he stood at attention in a service that had been announced about an hour in advance. With such short notice, only a few trebles dotted the choir stalls. Probably most of them were at home. Praeton couldn't imagine many parents had let their sons go to school today.

More chants. At least singing them, if you could call it singing, allowed his mind time to wander. The sheet music in his hands drifted lower and lower. After the service, he wanted to find somewhere and have a good think. Somewhere safe. Possibilities teased him. The bell tower, or maybe the basement near the anchors' cells. He'd been drawn to the cells lately. There was something about them, he wasn't sure what.

A happy thought occurred to him. If Serafine really was the Seraph, maybe she could help him. She had to know a lot. They said Ael and the Angel knew just about everything. Maybe she knew who his parents were, and why they'd abandoned him to the Ecclesiat. Maybe she knew how to stop his nightmares.

Two C sharps hurtled towards him out of nowhere. Praeton barely made it, sliding his voice up a half step. Normally sharps made things interesting—they always sounded mysterious and creepy to him. He loved creating that effect. But in the Chants, everyone got a new note. The chord remained exactly in tune. Just like it had been for pages. Just like it would be for pages more.

He stifled a yawn, and Evander shot him a warning glare. Praeton flinched reflexively. The choirmaster was handing out reprimands left and right. Even Jaon had got one, until Alesta ordered it removed from his record.

It wasn't fair, though. This service was only for monks. Only a few pews in the front were filled, it wasn't like they had a huge audience to inspire. Half the monks didn't even look like they wanted music. They were all sour and pinched and hunched. Praeton worried one or two might even throw up. The new, strengthened incense certainly made him fear for himself.

A chill hung in the air. The tips of Praeton's fingers tingled; turning pages became tricky. He wished the candles were closer to the stalls, rather than down by the altar. Actually, the altar was different. A new cloth covered it: white like the old one, but much shorter. Instead of draping the altar's sides, it barely covered its top.

The Chant ended and Praeton sank back. The other trebles promptly went glassy-eyed with daydreams, or began poking wars with each other. Not him. Something was wrong. A few of the prayers were ones he'd never heard before, and he thought he knew them all. You didn't live in the Ecclesiat your whole life and fail to learn how things worked.

He studied the clergy. Alesta wore her second-fanciest stole: the thinner blue and gold one, with embroidery that gleamed in the candlelight. Gaelin and Elber had their usual white robes and gloves. Odd, though, that no one else was at the altar. Where were the monks that helped with the sacred water? He twisted around to view the back of the chancel. The double-triangle standard wasn't in its usual place. The choir had entered far later in the service than they normally did. Hadn't a sub-prior, or the Throne, or someone brought it in?

At the rear of the nave, the narthex doors opened and a sheet of light spilled into the Ecclesiat. A single column of monks entered. Now other boys roused themselves to stare at the procession. A single question passed from chorister to chorister through nudges, shrugs, and pinches. They did everything in threes at the Ecclesiat, so why one column?

As the processing monks neared, Praeton picked out a strange sound. A clip-clopping on the stones. Having spent hardly any time in the City, he couldn't place it. Not until the monks swarmed into the chancel, and he saw it.

A white goat tripped up the chancel steps. A number of boys whispered and giggled as it tossed its head, tiny horns glinting in the light. As the goat passed Gaelin, its nose brushed his knee. It had to be a baby goat. Praeton grinned as the monks led it to the altar, but his smile faded when he saw Gaelin. The monk's mouth was thin, his lips so whitened Praeton barely made them out. Gaelin's eyes narrowed, his face dark and tense as dammed rapids. Any second, Praeton sensed, the floodgates would break.

But Gaelin merely turned away as Alesta lifted the goat to the altar and bound its legs with golden rope. She moved aside to let the Angel's sightless eyes fall upon it. A heady animal smell floated above the incense. Alesta placed her hands on the goat's back. Praeton envied her; that fur looked soft.

"Angelus Rex, the Angel King," Alesta said. "Our transgressions are greater than we can atone for in all eternity. Therefore, let us place our sins onto this creature in Your sight. In our stead shall it be punished. The innocent blood of this creature, spilt for us, shall go some way towards cleansing us, for the pure blood of this creature is more precious than the soiled blood of your flawed servants."

The word *blood* set Praeton's heart pounding. Surely she wasn't talking about literal spilt blood. Monks loved symbols and metaphor. That had to be it.

The anger in Gaelin's hunched shoulders and stiff movements told him otherwise.

He gasped when Alesta drew a silver knife from her robes. Evander glared at him again, but Praeton wasn't the only one. No one daydreamed or studied their music now. Frozen, he watched as Elber sprinkled the altar with salt. Alesta ladled sacred water onto the blade. It curved wickedly—more an undersized cutlass than a knife. The goat paid no attention, merely stretched its neck towards the praying monks in the pews.

Gaelin stood off to the side. Saying nothing. Pale with rage.

A quiet prayer on his lips, Elber seized the goat's hind legs. Another monk pulled its leash forward. Caught between leaning forward and shrinking back, Praeton found he had to watch.

His eyes wouldn't leave the goat, so small and white. Its dark eyes with their lovely long eyelashes met his, and the animal bleated. Not worrying whether he looked stupid, Praeton gave it the tiniest wave.

Alesta slashed the knife down.

The goat collapsed like a puppet with cut strings. Its knobby legs buckled and splayed to the sides. The head didn't simply fall, as Praeton expected. It bounced. Out and down, off the altar. For a second, there was no blood. Just two white blobs where a moment ago, there had been one. Then a scarlet stream sprayed from the stump. Blood drenched the altar covering, spurted onto the robes of everyone nearby, and splattered the floor all the way to the edge of the chancel. Redness spotted even the statue of the Angel. The sharp, iron tang made Praeton's stomach revolt. Goosebumps erupted across his arms and legs, and dimly, he heard his teeth chattering.

"Gross!" Quin whispered from beside him, breathless and horrified. "Look what it's doing!"

Praeton did. And sorely regretted it. The goat's legs jerked and kicked, as though it were running on its side. The hind legs pushed; the front stretched out, as though imploring, reaching for the choir stalls in a dance of death. The fur around the oozing hole was almost black now. He didn't want to stroke it anymore.

Somehow, he made it through the rest of the service without fainting. There wasn't much after that, anyway. The goat's beheading seemed to be the climax. Instead of going down the centre aisle as they always did, Evander had the choir process out the side. Better for avoiding the pitiful body on the altar. As he replaced his music and surplice in the robing room, Praeton revisited the image of the bouncing head over and over. It burned in his mind's eye as clearly as if it had been branded there. And the blood on the Angel…Praeton shivered. Maybe Brother Baeor had some tea to give him, something to calm his stomach.

He slipped into the cloisters, and came across Gaelin and Alesta. He knew he shouldn't eavesdrop. But despite his horror at the service, part of him was dying to hear what Gaelin would say about it. At least, what he'd say about it when children weren't around. He ducked into an alcove and pressed himself to the stones. Outside, a mix of rain, hail, and blood continued to tear chunks from the garden lawns.

"Sister, what were you thinking?" Gaelin hissed. "A sacrifice?"

"Mother." Her voice was cold and sharp as the sacrificial blade. "May I remind you, *sub-prior*, I am the Throne."

"My apologies. But nevertheless - there has not been an animal sacrifice in decades! Certainly not in my lifetime."

"Our practice is not founded entirely on precedent." In his hiding place, Praeton gulped. That tone meant someone was in for it. "I need hardly remind you that these are unusual times. Unusual measures are needed."

"Indeed. And beheading a goat will help? I cannot believe the Angel would approve of such wanton cruelty towards an innocent being."

"It was not wanton, nor was the thing innocent. That was the point, Gaelin. When we sin, we must punish ourselves to atone for it and cleanse the stain from our souls. Clearly, our souls have reached such a state of pollution that the Angel has seen it fit to bring the End of Days upon us. That goat carried our sins for us— had you listened to my sermon instead of sulking in the corner, you would have heard me say that it was being punished in our stead."

"But there were children there…"

She laughed, hard and brittle. "Worried for your little orphan? It's a small price for him to pay considering the time and money we've spent on his care. Frankly, I cannot imagine why Father Osvald thought it fit to keep him here, instead of finding a family to adopt him."

A lump squeezed Praeton's throat. He wiped his eyes. This was what he'd tried to tell them in the library. River had been really nice about it, but hearing Alesta brought all his old doubts back.

"Father Osvald must have had his reasons, and I believe Brother Ioren was particularly sympathetic, having been the one to find him. In any case, you cannot discuss it with either."

She was quiet so long Praeton almost peeked out. "Better the choirs see a dead goat than their own souls annihilated," she said at last.

"Then why didn't you perform the sacrifice in front of the general public? Why a private service?"

"I realize it is a...controversial ritual. Now that it is completed, we shall see if it appeases the Angel King. If it does, all well and good. If not..." Her twisted smile shone through her voice. "Next time won't be private."

XI

All she could ever give, and still it was never good enough. Horrible irony struck Alesta as she ladled sacred water onto the necks and hands of the penitent. Such presumption in her attempts to cleanse others, when she herself was as tainted as the lowest among them. The water fell like diamonds into a young woman's cupped hands.

The Throne closed her eyes and suppressed a shudder. What should have been her time of glory—stained, forever corrupted in the mind of the Angel. His presence burned a hole between her shoulder blades. The thought of turning and facing Him filled her with cold dread. Being so unworthy, she could not dare to stand before Him. And leading His people through the End Days—the idea was laughable.

The black stain at the crossing continued to captivate onlookers. Instead of the pride she expected to enjoy, Alesta cringed. They would see through her soon. Not a holy seat for the Angel King, but as besmirched as any. Atonement was needed. Nothing else conquered the estrangement induced by sin. Only when the self-induced suffering equalled the anger of Angelus Rex could the sinner be reconciled to Him. Her sin was great. Her penance must be greater.

At her feet, the young woman paused in washing her hands and sniffed. The scent of the sacrifice hung about the altar. The woman looked questioningly at her. Outwardly Alesta betrayed no emotion, merely motioned for the woman to vacate her place so that another might be cleansed. Inside, stirrings of panic wrapped icy fingers about her. After talking to Gaelin, she had the impression of a thousand carefully spun threads, all unravelling and disintegrating before her eyes. But no, that time had passed. She must be pure. She was pure. Her clean state was bought and paid for by daily purification by pain, hourly recriminations, and constant atonement to the Angelus Rex.

So strange, that something so small cast so large a shadow. Her hand tightened on the ladle, as though once again holding the sacrificial blade. That shadow would not darken her soul in this critical time. If that which cast it must be destroyed, then so be it.

A sharp poke to the ribcage woke Davi. He bolted upright. The poker had a cold finger—a chill was already spreading through his abdomen. His bleary eyes focused on Serafine. Normally, Davi supposed, one could say something like, "She was silhouetted against the rising sun." But it wasn't the case that morning. The sky had blackened further overnight, more than he'd believed possible.

Then his slowly-awakening mind clunked forward another cog, and he gathered his blankets around him, blushing. He glanced left and right. The monks slept, their peace undisturbed aside from a few mumblings and snores.

"Serafine!" he hissed. "What are you doing?"

"Waking you up."

It took all his restraint to keep from snapping at her. Reminding himself that she probably had more power in her baby toe than he did in his entire being, he positioned the blankets more securely. "What time is it?"

"Two before dawn."

Early. So early, there'd been times when he'd still been awake at this hour, having just transitioned from staying up "late." He rubbed the stubble invading his chin. "Want to tell me why you're here?"

He didn't like the way she avoided his eyes. "The Magistatiem is burning."

"What?"

In his haste, the blankets fell away. Cursing, he fought to rearrange them as the monk in the next bed rolled over and muttered something. Serafine pressed a frigid fingertip to his lips. Without looking down, she tossed a blanket over his lap and motioned for him to join her outside. He waited until she had gone, then struggled to slip on some pants and a shirt as noiselessly as possible. By the time he made it out, stumbling but clothed, she was pacing and wringing her hands.

"What happened?" he said.

Her red hair hung in dulled sheets, the vibrancy leached away. Uneasily, Davi wondered how much staying in their world strained her. Spending too long in the aither caused burnout. Could something similar happen to her?

She started down the stairs. "Fire strike. They'd been trying all day to calm the earthquakes and stop the blood. Thought it was something to do with underground fault lines—nothing supernatural of course—and got several teams working at it."

Davi slowed. "That's what Gaelin was talking about."

"Right. They wanted every mage in the City."

"I thought it was a trap."

"It wasn't." She steered him through the cloisters. Wind wailed against the ancient walls. "Not on the Magistatiem's part, anyway. But then…my best guess is that He noticed what they were doing. I was out, I saw it. A bolt of fire from the sky. Not unlike the one we saw for our dear friend Alesta."

With a tremor, Davi noticed a lamp burning in the Throne's window, but Serafine pushed him past it, towards the side door leading out to the City.

"It hit the library."

No. The information refused to sink into Davi's brain. It was impossible. He lost his voice, settled for shaking his head.

Serafine gave him a quick hug. Her skin felt nice in the heavy air.

"Sorry, Davi," she said. "They're trying to put it out."

He whirled on her. "Why can't you?"

"Because I vowed to play by the rules this time."

"And the Angel didn't?"

"Apparently my usual ways aren't so unappealing after all." She smiled crookedly. "But more importantly…It's a big job. Holy fire and all that. I can't risk losing this body to save some old books."

"Old books? They're the most important collection of magical knowledge we have! They're…"

"I know." She opened the door. Hot, muggy air plugged Davi's throat. He coughed, and she pounded his back, seemingly without much thought. "That doesn't change the fact that I need to prioritize. And so…" She pointed to the pre-dawn darkness. "Get over there, young mage."

The streets felt alien: dark and twisted. At least the blood had stopped. Davi's feet slid on wet cobblestones—he nearly slipped several times. The tiredness had left him now; everything seemed hyper-real, sight and sound and scent too vivid for the waking world.

He smelled the fire before he saw it. Thick smoke poisoned the air. Then came the cries. Shouts splintered the early morning. The gates were wide open, and he charged through them with scarcely a moment's hesitation. He didn't know how he'd be received. It didn't matter. His home was dying.

Once past the gates, he saw the red glow. Flames crackled against the dark sky, bisected by the silhouette of the Chancellor's Tower. Ash wafted on the winds, and he coughed. Magi fled in all directions. He recognized some guild members by their uniforms: the white vests of the Healers' Guild, the short sleeves and caps of the Repair-Magi.

Circles of spell-casters sprang to life on the lawns. In some, magi bound the aither informally, desperately, without the help of written spells. Other magi darted from group to group, thrusting sheaves of papers at them. Blue flames met red as the bound aither snapped towards its targets. Where aither met fire, the flames died away, hissing and sizzling. It wasn't enough.

Smoke and soot seared Davi's lungs; he could picture them blackening in his chest. He loped towards the library, and the wall of heat that rolled from it struck him like a slap across the face. He'd never seen uncontrolled fires, had never imagined how intense they were, how *hot*. Flames licked the library's widows like dragons' tongues.

A mage grabbed him. A Healer: Davi vaguely recognized him from some lower-year lectures. Always a well-dressed young man, but grime now streaked his face and hair. His customary jacket was gone completely.

"Davi?" he said. "It's me, Artur. Aren't you—I heard you were expelled."

"Not the time. How can I help?"

Artur pushed his hair back. Ash smudged where his hand had passed. "Um, um, we've got spell-casters on the fire. Pick a group, I guess. And there's a bucket line, for water. In case you're burnt out."

Davi nodded. A quick check for Volpes revealed nothing. He eased his way into a group full of people he didn't know. They were about his own age; no point in joining the older magi, where he'd stand out like a dog in a wolf-pack. He bet these young magi had completed their four years and gone directly to the guilds, already earning a living with their magic.

Copies of a hastily-written spell circulated. Davi traced the rows of figures and description. The spell proposed constructing a barrier between the flames and the surrounding air. Cut off, the fire would die out.

"Can you handle the third part?" a girl asked him.

"Yes." Davi frowned. "But it's not going to help. This'll only dampen the flames already outside the building. It's not going to do anything for the inside, and that's where all the damage is happening."

The guilders edged tighter together, away from Davi. The girl sniffed. "Look, maybe we didn't opt for higher studies, but we know what we're doing. We're professionals."

Screams shrilled against Davi's patience. In the hellish light of the fire, he made out the hands of the clock tower. One to dawn. Shouldn't the sun be rising now? He shook himself.

"It's not a matter of being professionals. This spell won't work."

The mage next to Davi grabbed his copy of the spell at that. Totally ignoring him now, the guilders banded into a circle, their backs to him. He caught mutterings from their midst. Soon enough, ropes of aither stretched over the library. Any flames that hit the barrier sputtered, but Davi's eyes locked onto the lower levels. Deep within the core of the library, the fire was alive and well, merrily destroying everything within. The building itself was stone; it probably wouldn't fall, but he hated to imagine how many books had already perished.

Teams inched nearer to the library. The closer they could get, the less energy they'd squander setting parameters for distance. A plume of flame swept out of a window, scattering magi across the lawns. A few reunited, scuttled over the spiky grass, and poured aither on the fire. The plume quailed and retreated back within the building, but not enough. They needed to be there, to see with their own eyes where the fire was strongest, to divert as much power as possible to fighting it. Otherwise, they were wasting their strength on blind guesses.

They had to get inside.

Heat crackled over his cheeks. His heart pounded. Penetrate the heart of that inferno? It was suicide, idiotic.

Necessary.

Gritting his teeth, Davi trawled the magi for anyone as insane as he was. A few here, a few there. Some promised to write the spell, if he rounded up more helpers to actually go inside.

"This is our legacy we're talking about!" he yelled at one point. "We can't let it die!"

"I should say not!" came a familiar voice.

He spun around. "Tam?"

"At your service." His friend winked. "Could've asked for better circumstances, but then, I never thought I'd see you again!"

The pair of them managed to find a handful of magi willing to brave the flames. They assembled on grass that crunched beneath their feet, bone-dry. A sick odour stung their nostrils: burning blood. Davi shuddered. Had the flames claimed anyone yet? Anyone burned to death, either by earthly flames, or the divine fire of the aither? He pushed the thought away. If he dwelled on it, he'd never act.

"Here are the spell-parts," he said. "It's pretty similar to one some guilders were using, see, we're cutting off the air. But…"

"We'll be in the thick of it," Tam told the other magi.

Artur folded his copy inside his breast pocket. "Cutting off the air while we're inside will be dangerous. Huge risk of suffocation. Tamus, you're a Healer too. You know what that smoke will do to us, even if we're not siphoning out whatever pure air is left in there."

Tam nodded. "I've been working on it. Anyone in the proximity's at risk, so I made a nice little spell to keep us breathing easy. And that group there…" He pointed. "Is right now working on some flame-resistant magic. Probably won't last long, but it'll give us a chance."

A chance. They all seized on the word. That was all they had. Not a guarantee. Not even a very good probability. A chance.

"Well." Davi clutched his part. "Let's go."

He had thought the fire was hot before. Now it wasn't just a physical feeling—it was like a demon had possessed the building. The harsh smell of his own singed hair made him gag, but he was breathing all right. For now. Smoke attacked his eyes, and tears blurred his vision so much he could hardly read his spell. The magi clustered inside the main foyer. At the end of the hall, flames and smoke billowed towards them. Davi took a step forward, but the heat pushed him back. The crackling and roaring which had been mere background noise now overpowered any attempt at speaking. Heat rattled the building like an ogre punching the foundations.

"We'll have to do it from here!" he shouted.

Scared nods. But nods nonetheless. Artur distributed a few chalices he'd brought, while Davi cupped his palm and listened for the aither. The full impact of his earlier discovery struck him suddenly, weakened his knees. He was reaching to another dimension, forcing matter to stay and do his bidding in a plane of existence entirely alien to it. Ridiculous to think of such a thing when he needed to focus on his job. He siphoned the aither into his hand. The blue flames disoriented him. A fifth dimension. This had to be why magi burnt out; the sheer magnitude of what they did was unimaginable. It was insane. So far beyond insanity, Davi's stomach dropped out and his mind seized.

"Come on, Davi!" Tam shouted.

Right. He read, pressing and prodding the aither with his mind. The silent symphony rose and fell around him. He sensed the other magi exerting their own influence. Once they had the aither before them, they persuaded it to assume a new shape, a new function. They suggested new ways for it to behave. They bound it into their world, their four dimensions.

Azure barriers erupted in the air. Another thrust from the magi, and the magic lengthened and stretched. The barriers shot down the corridor to the library proper. Flames hissed into nothingness on contact with the spell. The magi advanced, casting as they went. *Break its back*, Davi thought in fragments. *Break the fire's spine, and we'll get out. We'll be fine. Break the spine, we'll be fine.*

173

His eyes streamed. He was surprised he had any liquid left in his body—surely it had all been scorched away. Shock choked him at the sight of the library's main hall. Heaped piles of ash looked ready to blow away any second. They sickened him, for not long ago, the black dust had been books. So much research and work, so many hopes and dreams, lost forever.

One of the beams over the doorway cracked and narrowly missed them. The front desk and work tables blazed; he hoped they'd all been empty when the fire struck. Then his eyes widened.

"Tam!" he said. "Where are Glory and Keeper?"

Layers of dirt and soot split around Tam's mouth as he spoke. "Don't know. Haven't seen them."

Beside him, Artur closed his eyes. The barrier shifted upwards to defuse the flames licking the second floor. "Forget them, Davi. We can make more."

He wanted to listen. To shrug his shoulders as Tam was doing and save what little of the library's collection remained. The knowledge was important. Everything else paled in comparison.

Even as he made these arguments to himself, he knew otherwise. His own evidence overpowered any wish to do the easy thing. Odd as it seemed, Glory and Keeper were the closest thing River had to relatives. They might not have had her emotions, or her spirit, but they were important to her. And now, they were important to Davi as well. Not as tools, not "just" as MCBs. As people.

"I'm going to find them."

"Have you burnt out already?" someone yelled. In the smoke and confusion, it was impossible to tell who.

"I'm coming with you." Tam jostled him in his eagerness. "Look, I don't know what kind of thing you have for MCBs. First River, now those two? But I'm not letting you go alone."

A shelf collapsed in a shower of sparks and flame. "Fine." Davi ran before his courage could desert him. "Come on!"

Row by row, they searched and called for the MCBs. Each charred book sent a twinge through Davi. In the main reading room, Tam halted before the tapestry that had been a Magistatiem treasure. It had adorned the wall since before their grandfathers' time. Only the brass rail from which it had hung remained. A few scraps littered the floor beneath. Tam pocketed one.

"Did you ever think?" he said. "I thought it'd be here forever..."

There was nothing he could say.

They renewed their search, but hope slipped away. Flaming wreckage barricaded the staircase, and the heat crushed them between inexorable palms. Just as Davi was about to succumb, he caught sight of something in the Weather Magics section. Two somethings.

"There they are!"

He jogged down the row. Abruptly, the air turned thicker, more pungent. He gasped and wheezed; scrambled to think of a way to keep Tam's spell from disintegrating further. Already, it felt like a tangle of smoke had settled in his chest. Like an octopus, it writhed and squeezed him from within.

A hand on his back. Tam crouched, other palm cupped and already full of aither. "I've got you covered," he said, eyes fixed on the MCBs. "Go!"

Sweet, pure air rolled through Davi's lungs. Springtime bloomed in his chest. He didn't know what spell Tam was casting, but he knew from his friend's pinched expression that it was costing him. He sprinted forward. Bolts of heat shot through his feet every time his shoes touched the floor. No surprise—the soles had mostly been burned away.

Glory lay face down. Her dark hair flowed over her shoulders like a funeral shroud. Next to her, Keeper was motionless, face vacant and empty, even by MCB standards. "Come on." Davi shook them. "Wake up."

Keeper's lips moved. Davi patted her cheeks. "Let's go, Keeper. On your feet."

"Function...impaired."

"No, you'll be fine, you just need a few spells."

"Spell-structures damaged." Her voice faded in and out. "Total failure imminent."

"Don't say that. Look at Glory, she's..." He rolled the other MCB over and gasped. A scorched hole gaped at him where her face used to be. All her features dissolved into a bluish-grey soup of burned aither. A scream froze itself in Davi's mouth.

"Keeper, let's go, now!"

Like a ghoulish puppet, Keeper's upper body juddered upright. She blinked at Davi. His breath was getting short again—Tam's strength must be waning, the smoke was winning. He got as low to the floor as possible, and repeated, "Now, Keeper!"

A spark wafted and settled on her shoulder. There, it burst to life. She regarded it as though a fly had landed on her. No evidence of comprehension. The flames feasted on her, her skin blistered and peeled away to reveal jelly-like aither that shone brilliant sapphire before shrivelling. Suddenly, she looked far too much like River, and Davi backed away, strangling a sob.

"Total failure..."

She never finished the phrase.

Half-blind and fighting for air, Davi ran. He leaped over broken shelves and burning books. Suddenly, his dwindling pocket of clean air vanished completely. Smoke assaulted his eyes and nose like a living thing. Sputtering, he crawled the rest of the way. Tam sprawled on the floor. "Thank the Angel," he muttered as Davi neared. "I lost it."

Davi felt his friend's forehead; Tam leaned into his touch. Hot, red skin, like a fever. Impossible to tell whether it was from the fire, or the aither. Tam closed his eyes and shuddered. "It hurts."

"What hurts?"

"My brain." He laughed weakly. It lifted the hairs on Davi's neck. "All those little connections, Davi, all fried. All burned up."

And he fell back. His skin blistered now, angry and red under the grime. Hot, far too hot—how much magic had Tam done? Davi tried to remember, to think clearly with panic knocking at the door. Definitely some spells outside. Maybe more before he'd arrived. The main one inside the library, and this last one. Davi groaned. Normally, magi burned out over the course of years; they might get acute burns from individual spells along the way, but complete erosion of the brain's ability to handle aither took time. Damage needed to accumulate. But none of the acute cases Davi had seen involved such aggressive searing.

He didn't dare use more magic himself. Cowardly thought, but dominating. He grabbed Tam's collar and pulled. Step by agonizing step, he dragged his friend through the dying library. Burning wood and parchment fell all around them; Davi cried out as smouldering debris bore holes through his clothes. He kept an ear cocked for mumblings from Tam; he had to wake up soon.

He didn't.

Shapes emerged through the haze. Davi squinted, tried to focus. His eyeballs felt frail in their sockets, as though they might drop from his skull at any time.

"Davi?" a voice called. A minute passed before Davi recognized it. Artur.

"Here," he said. Too soft. He mustered his strength and pushed the word out again. "Here!"

The shapes resolved into magi, begrimed and exhausted, but stronger than him. They took Tam from him, an act for which Davi might have wept with gratitude, had there been a spare drop of water in his body. All higher thought gone, he followed them, placing his feet wherever their footprints disturbed the ash. He didn't trust them; trust required more mental capacity than he had at the moment. He simply reacted.

He didn't know how he made it through the long hall, or the

foyer. Somehow, he found himself outside. Too many people, all shouting and running. The glow of aither hurt his head, he just wanted there to be darkness.

His stomach heaved, and suddenly, there was.

———

A slap to the face. A shock of silver hair wavered in his vision. Dry grass itched the undersides of his arms. Another slap. Davi winced. "Stop," he mumbled. "I'm awake."

"Good. Get up."

That voice. Davi struggled to his feet. Too quickly—his legs wobbled and he toppled over. With smoke and clouds painting a grim scene behind him, Volpes glowered, his arms crossed.

"So. You came back."

"Yes, sir." Davi vowed not to look away. "When I heard about the fire. It was my duty to help."

The Fox's lip curled. Davi met his sneer steadily and braced himself for the next onslaught.

It wasn't long in coming. "How very good of you. Clearly your presence has been most beneficial to us."

He gestured behind him to the library's smoking shell. Glass littered the ground; none remained in the windows. Even from a distance, the building radiated emptiness. Traces of ash drifted on the smothering wind.

"Utter destruction," Volpes continued. Pain etched lines in his forehead, turned him from fox to wolf. "The entire collection, gone."

"I'm sorry."

"Are you?" He turned from Davi, watched the magi sifting through wreckage. "You aided the flight of a renegade MCB. Frankly, you should be clapped in irons right now. You would be, if not for this disaster." Volpes paused. "How fortunate for you."

It took Davi's aither-fogged mind a moment to process the implication. "Wait, are you saying I started it?"

"Without a library and archives, we have no practical use for the MCBs. Even if we were to reclaim River of Knowledge, she would have no purpose here."

"I didn't! It was the Angel."

"How burned did he get?" Volpes asked a nearby mage. The woman shrugged and felt Davi's forehead.

"Not as bad as the other one. He shouldn't be delusional."

"Other one?" His heart thudded. "Tam. How's Tam?"

"Still unconscious. Unlikely to use aither for a while." The woman shook her head. "And neither should you. The Angel, indeed."

"A few days ago, I wouldn't have believed it," Davi said. Neither Volpes nor the woman interrupted him, but neither seemed inclined to continue the conversation. Fighting the raggedness creeping into his voice, he continued, "The blood, the earthquakes, that stupid candle ceremony. Don't you see? It's the End Days."

The woman glanced to Volpes. "We did have that monk in looking for the *Prophecies of St. Memoyah*."

"Nonsense." Volpes brushed her aside. "Now, Sanders, you're coming with me. I want—"

But Davi never found out what he wanted. From the sky erupted another flood of flame. Without thinking, Davi dragged Volpes down. The air withered with the rush of heat. Magi screamed as flames fell on them; their cloaks and gowns carried parasitic fire as they ran for cover. Where moments before the grounds had been shrouded in grey dawn light, they now blazed with a sickly glow.

"Fire at the Life Magics buildings!" The cry hurt Davi's ears.

"Get someone to Physical Magics, now!"

Then, a screech that pierced him to the core: "The Regis Building's aflame! Aither Studies is being destroyed!"

Chaos descended on the Magistatiem. Volpes seized the scruff of Davi's neck and hissed, "If you still have aither, you get out there!" He pushed Davi towards the inferno.

"Where are the injured?" Davi shouted. "Where's Tam?"

The woman lifted her skirts and barrelled down the path. "The dormitories. Oh, please don't let them be hit..."

Davi followed her, muscles already protesting. Then something, some awful premonition, compelled him to stop. He felt like he'd seen this all before. The racing magi, now organizing into teams; the burning buildings on every side; none of it seemed real. He looked up.

Directly overhead, the clouds had parted. A black rift tore the sky. In that rift, the moon shone red as blood. Thought would not come. He simply stared as the rift filled in again, hiding the moon from view. Another blast of flame spewed from the clouds' underbelly.

As precisely as if it had been aimed, it shot towards the Chancellor's Tower. Struck it dead centre, about halfway up. With a horrible creaking noise like that of something dying, the Tower fractured.

"No!"

Like a collapsing behemoth, the fire-struck Tower crumbled. It hit the ground with a thud that shook the Magistatiem's foundations. The great clock lay smashed, hands frozen at the moment of its demise. Heedless of the glass and flames, Davi charged towards it. Already he could see people crushed under the fallen Tower, blood and bone and burning assaulted him on all sides. Bricks scraped his hands as he dug through the ruins.

Exhaustion beat at him, its wings enfolding him, tempting him. So tired. How easy it would be to move back, find a clear space on the lawns, and escape into sleep. Just for a minute. No more noise or confusion, just the healing shadows.

Weak scratching below him jolted him awake. He tossed bricks like a madman, fingers red and raw. People were trapped inside; the Tower now their tomb.

The clouds parted again and the moon gazed on the crippled Magistatiem.

It was still red.

XII

News of the fire reached the Ecclesiat as it became apparent that dawn wasn't coming. Another deluge of people poured into the cathedral. Some had lost their homes in similar fires; others sought counsel, a sympathetic ear, anything.

Gaelin did his best to provide.

A queer feeling had settled upon him. Something like suffocating, though he was breathing fine. Lungs a little cramped perhaps, but nothing he didn't expect at his age. He had just finished blessing an older couple when he glimpsed her lurking behind a column.

River.

The familiar bramble of emotions prickled him. At times like this, he wished he had someone to whom he could whisper his doubts. Too many questions surrounded the young woman, if she could even be called a woman. Which would be worse: if she was soulless, or if she had an artificial soul? Did it even matter anymore? Serafine had shaken his understanding of the world; his trust in his own teachings had been compromised.

It scared him.

He didn't let the fear show. Instead, he plastered on a smile as River approached. Offered a hand to her when she stumbled. "Hello, River."

"Hello." She shifted from foot to foot. "Are you counselling at the moment?"

"Not this moment."

"Could you...Would it be possible for you to offer guidance to me?"

At first he wasn't sure he'd heard her right. But he glimpsed hope in her dark eyes; tentative hope, but hope nonetheless. His tongue felt awkward, unsure how to respond. She didn't rush him, just waited silently until he nodded.

"But not here," he said. "Come. We'll go to my study."

This was better, he decided, closing the study door. He was rather proud of the space: a cosy little room where they would not be seen or overheard. River was treating the room to her quick, dark gaze. She drank in the volumes displayed on his bookcase, and eyed the figurines of saints parading across his desk.

"Sit," Gaelin said, indicating a chair by the fire. He had two: simple, yet handsomely padded. A pity the comfort would be lost on an MCB. "How can I help you?"

She started and stopped herself several times. "Doubtless you have heard the news regarding the Magistatiem."

"The fire, yes. I am sorry."

"It was my home. Davi's as well." She shook her head. "I never intended to return, but I assumed it would always be there. Now it is damaged, perhaps irreversibly, and I feel..." A sharp laugh broke through. It was short, but the first Gaelin had heard from her. It seemed to surprise her as much as it did him.

"I feel," she continued. "That would seem to be the crux of my problems, would you not agree?"

"You're the first of your...kind to feel, aren't you?"

"The first to survive feeling, at any rate. Yet, it seems a curse. Such inner turmoil; how do you bear the constant noise from within? How do you find a pocket of peace?"

"Well," Gaelin said, after a pause, "some of us turn to Ael."

Her mouth twitched. "I doubt Ael would be an appropriate recourse for me."

"Perhaps not." He hated saying it, hated the flicker of disappointment that ruffled her face. But it was true. "Perhaps, with time, you will become accustomed to your emotions."

"I believe the other MCBs are dead. For all I know, Davi is as well."

She blurted it out. Gaelin tented his fingers, digesting that. On the one hand, if the MCBs had been destroyed, there were two fewer affronts to Ael. On the other...he sighed. "Were you close to them?"

"MCBs don't have families. Until recently, they didn't have friends. Glory and Keeper were my colleagues. If they have indeed perished, I am the only MCB in the City." She rubbed her eyes. "At times such as these, I regret my inability to cry."

His heart went out to her. Abominable creation or not, she suffered. As a monk, and as a human being, he had vowed to end suffering where he could. He patted her knee. "The fact that you mourn them attests to their importance to you."

"What do you think occurs after death?" With gentle, but firm fingers, she removed his hand and edged her chair back. "I am aware of the physiological changes, and of Aelist teachings. However, I am curious as to your personal beliefs regarding the fate of the soul or consciousness."

"I am a monk of Ael, River. I believe that after death, the worthy soul passes through the Veil and returns to Ael. As Ael is All, the soul then dwells with and in Ael. It could be described as a paradise. The unworthy are cleansed by the Angel, and then they too join their fellow deceased with Ael."

Her expression didn't change, but he knew she'd absorbed every word. "What if you didn't have a soul?"

"I wouldn't know, but I would assume that the being would simply cease to exist." Maybe not the most comforting answer, but an honest one.

"Then Glory and Keeper were in all likelihood obliterated." She rose and walked to the door on stiff legs. "I believe I shall continue my research. St. Memoyah's writings have offered some interesting possibilities."

"I am sorry, River." The words popped out unplanned, but no less genuine. "Please remember, my door is always open."

Too late. She was gone.

———

She hadn't asked him the question that had truly been haunting her. Did she have a soul? She almost preferred not to know. The idea that Glory and Keeper no longer existed in any form disturbed her concentration. Foolish, really. They, like her, were tools. Did magi grieve when one of their chalices broke? Did the farmer mourn a broken plough? Of course not.

Work wasn't as absorbing as it should have been, but it was better than waiting by the gate for Davi's return. If only those thoughts would go away. The sense of wrongness, that this was some fruit forbidden to her, marred the happiness he brought. That, and the ever-present fear that she would lose herself to emotions as her predecessors had. She understood, now, what might drive an MCB like Emerald to seek solutions in a plunging dagger. Rejected the notion, feared it, but understood it nonetheless.

MCBs, history showed, could not be trusted with feelings.

In any case, no satisfactory answer existed. She would outlive Davi, she could not bear his children, and she'd already made herself look like an utter fool by panicking at his kiss.

The shame of that memory was potent as ever. She buried herself in books to escape it. Searching for the Hapax was logically futile, but it gave her a distraction. By definition, the Word had only occurred once in creation. If it was gone, it could therefore never come back. And it was certainly gone: if it was not, it would not need to be found.

She turned another page. Having exhausted the Ecclesiat's collection of aither-related texts, she'd moved on to other topics. Chronicles of the Ecclesiat seemed as good a place to start as any. Whatever the Ecclesiat's attitude towards MCBs, she had to admire their record-keeping. Weekly entries by a chronicler detailed events and life within the Ecclesiat's walls; each record was numbered, dated, and catalogued within their system. An MCB would be hard-pressed to do better.

Though the shelves held chronicles dating back centuries, the volume she was examining was just over a decade old. She'd faltered before choosing it, for relevant references to the Hapax were not likely to have occurred so recently. But then— perhaps there would be something about Praeton. Something about Alesta and Gaelin. Some clue that would help her to understand them better. She didn't have that option with Davi, useful as she'd find it. It certainly didn't exist with Serafine.

Therefore: she read.

The text wobbled in her vision. She blinked, and paused a moment to steady her hands. The sun still hadn't risen, but the great bell tolled five past dawn. She hoped Davi would return soon, both out of irrationally overstated concern for his safety, and also real, logical concern for her own. Ignoring the trembling deep in her core, she focused on her work.

Alesta had spent one year alone in the anchorage cells. Most humans River had met expressed amazement at this feat, including the chronicler. Personally, River envied Alesta. An entire year to read in the comfort of solitude sounded like the paradise of which Gaelin had spoken. Insulated from the stress of others, she could forget the interference of grief and fear, know a measure of peace for once.

What about love?

What about it? River told herself. *It is irrelevant.*

Then why do you think about it so much?

I will decline to participate in further conversation with myself, thank you. She flipped ahead so violently the page nearly ripped. Little to see, at any rate. Alesta had stayed in her cell. The raising of tithes had allowed a section of crumbling wall to be rebuilt. Father Osvald had given a St. Bailero's Day feast with the most succulent veal ever tasted. A baby had been found on the Ecclesiat steps.

Interesting as Praeton's history may have been, it was not particularly useful. Alesta posed a greater threat; she needed information about her. She searched for the chronicles from a few months prior. Yes, there were a few references to Alesta's anchorage: primarily anecdotes from a Brother Ioren, the monk who supplied her with food. Any information recorded by the chronicler, River realized, would therefore have been filtered through this intermediary. None of the information regarding Alesta was first-hand. Opportunities for bias grew exponentially, and she didn't have enough information to compensate for it.

River closed her eyes. Her head didn't hurt, she never felt pain, but her thoughts were becoming disconnected. Harder and harder to string words together in her mind, or follow them on a page. She managed to find some scrap about Alesta suffering from illness, and then the letters wriggled too much for her to decipher them.

She abandoned the chronicles and staggered down the hallway. Her feet refused to go where she directed them. Fear stabbed her abdomen. No matter how much she went through, she never accustomed herself to the feeling. She never truly accustomed herself to any feeling, come to think of it.

Increasing incoherence. Naturally.

At the end of the hall, Alesta had Praeton cornered. The boy shrank back, eyes bright with nerves. The Throne's lips moved, but the sounds coming from them were a tumble of consonants and vowels. No sense whatsoever. River tried to hurry, but her body felt too heavy. Her stride slowed to a crawl, perhaps better to keep pace with her thoughts.

Davi. The concept shimmered in the mental fog, and she clung to it as though to a lifeline. She needed to find Davi. Impossible to count days, had it been four? Five? Surely it was too early for another energy spell. She'd exerted herself more than usual, but she should have had at least another day. Useless to fool herself; the signs were unmistakable. Intuition again: if that didn't scare her so that she thought she'd collapse, she might have laughed.

The two humans turned as she neared. Praeton's face shifted; concern and fear creased his forehead.

Alesta's eyes narrowed. "Move along."

"Please," River whispered. Her lips tingled. It felt like far too much air filled her head, leaving her consciousness in the grip of vertigo. "Please, where is Davi?"

"I'm sure I don't know." Alesta sniffed. "Perhaps you'll see him later...as you do your chores."

Show nothing. No fear for herself, no pain. No worry for Davi, fighting an unnatural fire. A section of her mind flickered to dim life. He could be dead. If so, she'd share his fate soon enough.

False assumptions. Poor reasoning. She nodded, as much to clear her head as out of politeness, and tried to walk. Hardly two steps later, her feet tangled. She fell. The *whump* as she hit the floor reached her ears, but she felt nothing of the impact in her arms or knees, which meant the spell's functions were shutting down. A vision of her body's future flashed before her: an empty shell, inanimate as a puppet. Without aither, she was a husk, her mind asleep without dreaming.

Praeton ran to her. She wasn't sure if the warmth flooding her body was gratitude or aither-deprivation. The boy stooped, and his breath brushed her cheek. "River? Are you all right?"

She tried to answer, and failed. Her mouth opened a crack, but nothing came forth. Haze descended like someone had drawn a veil over her. Even a blink proved beyond her means.

Alesta floated into her line of sight. The Throne appeared as an oval framed by golden hair; River couldn't see her expression, but she made a calculated guess.

"She must go to the infirmary, of course," she said.

The infirmary, full of healers all too eager to examine her. River's shout of *No!* echoed only in her head. Praeton touched her shoulder. "Maybe she should just go to bed?"

"You dare question me? Double chores and half-dinner. Get to work!" The last vestiges of hope left River as Praeton scurried away. The greyness leaped and devoured her final traces of sight. Blind and immobile, she could only listen as Alesta called for monks to bear her away.

Davi had not come. A fresh gouge where her heart should have been, and she threw herself into the darkness. And welcomed it.

<hr />

"What is it, Serafine?" Gaelin sighed. Since his talk with River, he had not moved from his chair. His conscience nagged him on two fronts. The look in River's eyes, while artificial, had unsettled him. Moreover, he should be in the cathedral with the other monks. But the comfort of his study called louder. Sleep had not been his friend of late; all he wanted was a few moments alone.

Evidently, that wasn't going to happen. Serafine prowled his study. A statuette of the Angel attracted her attention. She fingered it and pursed her lips.

"Serafine."

"You know He'll be after the Ecclesiat, right?"

Behind Serafine's back, Gaelin checked the clock. Not even noon. He massaged his temples. What he wouldn't give for some of the vigour of the old days. "I'm afraid I'll need more explanation."

"He's gone after the Magistatiem. The Ecclesiat will be next."

"If you're referring to the Angel, I'll have to disagree. Why would He attack His own order?"

Her face hardened. "It's not an order in His eyes. It's chaos."

A weight settled in his chest. The world was a narrowing

tunnel; all options dwindled to a single, inexorable path. For all his prayer and hope, he was as lost as any in this frightening new world.

Maybe that was why his temper frayed. "Serafine, there are people out there who need my help. I cannot give it to them unless I renew myself. Unless you have something important to tell me, I will ask you leave me in peace."

"Davi's not back, is he?" She tossed the statuette from hand to hand. "I'm getting worried."

Gaelin shifted his chair so he stared at the hearth. "Then go look for him."

"I want to stay here, I..." She stopped. "Listen."

Footsteps clicked in the hall. He barely had time to rise when Alesta wrenched the door open. She panted, face flushed and eyes blazing.

"With me. Now."

"Mother, I—"

"*Now!*" She seized his shoulder. Her fingernails dug through his robes and into his flesh—the ball of his shoulder throbbed in her grasp. Shocked, Gaelin cried out. With more force than he thought possible in a woman, she wrested him to his feet.

Serafine was between them in an instant. "Stop that. You're hurting him."

"Silence," Alesta hissed. She shoved Gaelin forward. "To the cathedral."

No further information came. Any questions or comments broke against a grunt and a face of stone. Gaelin racked his mind for explanations, but found nothing. He twisted around, searching for Serafine. She wasn't there.

The cathedral's dome amplified a torrent of agitated voices. Hardly anyone lingered by the public chapel or rested in the pews. Even the throng around the infamous black mark had thinned. Whispers stung Gaelin like the drone of mosquitoes. He squinted. Although the crowds circled the altar, no one ventured too close to it. They hung back, as though frightened.

When the masses parted, Gaelin's heart sank.

She lay on the altar, dark hair fanned behind her. Her eyes were closed. The sight of her motionless chest panicked Gaelin for a moment, until he remembered: she had never drawn breath.

"Look at her arm," Alesta snapped.

"But..."

"Look at it!"

With trembling hands, Gaelin tugged at River's sleeve. The skin underneath was tepid; it was like touching a mannequin. On her upper arm the Magistatiem falcon unfolded. Its wingtips encircled her arm; its stylized beak opened wide. Quietly, Gaelin replaced her sleeve.

"Well?"

Calmness had come into him. He straightened River's tunic, as though it would make her more comfortable. Then he raised his eyebrows at Alesta.

"Why is she here?" he said. "Should she not be in the infirmary, or even her own bed?"

The crowd surged forward, eager to hear the Throne's response. Alesta batted them back, indiscriminate in whom she struck. "Why ask questions to which you know the answer? Tell me what she is, Gaelin. Tell the people what abomination our Ecclesiat has harboured."

"I don't know what you're talking about."

"No? Then watch." With a movement so deft it could hide in a blink, Alesta had her sacrificial blade in hand. Silence fell, total and paralyzing. Gaelin wanted to leap up, to knock the knife to the ground, but his body refused. He could only watch as Alesta pricked River's palm. The crowd gasped. Several shielded themselves. Others craned forward, a thirst for blood shining in their eyes.

But of course, not a drop spilled. Blueness throbbed inside

the cut. That was all. And it was everything, for Alesta looked at Gaelin with a face of marble.

"She is aither."

The words unleashed a frenzy. Half the people trampled their neighbours in their rush to escape the presence of the MCB, while others swarmed the altar, eager to shred River with their bare hands. Gaelin threw himself on top of her. Alesta had foreseen this. Fear bred loyalty; a sick, poor form of it, but loyalty nonetheless. An MCB on the altar mixed the sacred and profane—small wonder the people responded so violently. He bent his head over River's. She had become Alesta's prop.

"Wake up. In Ael's mercy, please wake up, River."

A sharp clap cut the air. The crowd retreated, all dragging heels and curled lips. Alesta waited until they had moved behind the chancel railing before speaking.

"This creature is a testament to man's arrogance. What are the magi to think they may create life in the fashion of the Angel King? She is not of His. She was not created of Him. And so, she must die."

Tentative applause goaded Gaelin to action. He ceased his attempts to revive River—clearly magic was not as infallible as the magi would have them believe—and drew himself up. "She is not a creature of the Angel," he said, "but we are not His arbiters. The Angel judges for Himself. Send her from the Ecclesiat; let the Angel do what He will."

"The Angel judges for Himself, but I judge for the people!" The tendons in Alesta's neck stretched to breaking point. And then, abruptly, she relaxed. She smiled at Gaelin, smoothed River's hair. "Now we know the source of our pollution. As she befouled us, so she will cleanse us."

Gaelin hovered by the altar. He didn't understand. Or maybe he didn't want to.

The blade glittered. "She will be sacrificed."

The walls of the Ecclesiat seemed to gasp. Amongst the storm of faces and whispers, horror and exhilaration, Gaelin caught sight of Praeton, squeezed against the edge of the chancel rail. The boy was staring at River with eyes bleak as the streets outside. Gaelin cleared his throat.

"The goat was one thing," he said. "But a human sacrifice is unacceptable."

"First, she...*it* is not human. Second, you do not tell me what to do." Orange shimmered along the blade's length as Alesta turned it in the candlelight. "The sacrifice of the goat failed. After all, the End Days draw on. If a manmade being shelters within our gates, we have failed to a greater degree than a mere animal sacrifice can remedy."

Failed. She waited, allowing the word to sink in before continuing. "Today is five of seven? It will be destroyed on the dawning of the seventh." She snapped her fingers and Brother Elber bobbed at her elbow. "Take it to my lodgings. Ensure it is bound, in case it awakens."

Elber bowed. He was approaching the altar when Alesta halted him. "But first," she said. "Fetch my lash."

Coldness swept through Gaelin's bones. He stood rooted to the spot, one hand half-snaked towards River, as Elber disappeared into the choir stalls. Elber emerged a moment later clutching a braided black whip, which he held out to Alesta. She grabbed it and offered Elber a perfunctory blessing. While her mouth formed the appropriate prayer, her eyes did not leave the whip, and her fingers did not cease rubbing its plaited leather.

She spoke to him almost casually, as though discussing theological semantics over tea. "Well, Brother Gaelin, do you deny your prior knowledge of this creature's true nature?"

A way out. He scarcely believed her discretion. Yet something within him rebelled at taking it. To do so placed him even more under her thumb. And by Ael, after all he had lost and seen in the past days, he would not lose his integrity at this critical moment.

"I deny nothing."

The whip's end trailed along the floor. "Then you allowed it to remain here, even knowing what it was?"

"When she first came, I believed her human." Seeing her now, he almost believed it still. "I learned only later that she was not."

He expected the reaction of the congregated people. The looks of dismay and betrayal from many he had counselled. He read their feelings as clearly as the prayers in his service book. Some of the people clustered on the black mark had received his blessing as infants. The older amongst them had sought him for advice on their love, their work, their faith. Together, monk and people, they had laid a foundation of trust. A foundation generations in the making was shattered in an instant. He did not bow his head. He owed them his strength.

"Why did you not bring this attention to the Throne?"

"I considered it." His gaze dropped to River's palm; the mark of her previous injury was nowhere to be seen. "In recognition of her essential goodness, I gave her three days to leave the Ecclesiat."

"Essential goodness?" Alesta smirked. "She is empty, Gaelin, she has no *essential goodness*. You bargained with the children of the Beast. You committed a fault. And so..." The whip cracked. "You must redeem yourself."

The sound echoed like a thunderclap in the suddenly silent Ecclesiat. At that moment, another earthquake would not have surprised Gaelin, so unsteady did he feel. "I beg your pardon?"

"Your punishment. You must be brought into atonement with the Angel. Remove your robe and shirt, Gaelin."

Fighting to keep his face impassive, Gaelin peeled off his robes. The air was like water against his skin. How else could his chest and neck be so slick with sweat; how else could he move so slowly? His shirt stuck to his chest. He had to wriggle out of it; he stumbled as he did so. A few snickers drifted from the nave. Gaelin swallowed, throat tight. Dignity. He must keep his dignity.

So, he folded his shirt and robes neatly and placed them on the floor. A few wispy hairs glinted silver on his chest. Glancing down, he winced. Softness replaced much of the muscle of his younger days. He looked old. Vulnerable.

"Against that pillar," Alesta ordered.

Silently, Gaelin obeyed. He braced his elbows on the cool stone, touched his forehead to it. Gazes and judgements pierced his back like daggers. His breath sounded fast and shallow in his ears; he forced himself to breathe normally. Anything to deprive Alesta of the satisfaction.

Her footsteps struck the marble like a knell. Gaelin closed his eyes, sought refuge in the blackness behind his lids. A trickle of sweat stung his upper lip with salt. A sliver of doubt needled him. Maybe he was deserving of this punishment. He had violated the law; he must accept the pain, both to show his remorse and self-loathing for having committed such a sin, and to cleanse and redeem himself.

No! He told himself, clenching his fists on the pillar. *I have done nothing wrong in Ael's sight. Perhaps in the Angel's, but not in Ael's.*

He clung to the thought, wrapped it around his mind as a balm to the horror. Behind him, he heard Alesta measuring paces. Total silence fell. They waited, all of them.

"May my act cleanse your unworthy soul, Gaelin. May you accept it with the knowledge of your flaws, and the determination to purify yourself of them."

He tensed.

The lash tore the air. This was no sibilant hiss. It was hard and harsh as lightning. Gaelin heard it strike his flesh before he felt it. For an instant, there was nothing but shock. The shock of his mind that she'd actually done it. The shock of his body as it scrambled to register what had happened. Then a line of fire erupted across his back.

He bit his lip to keep from crying out and shut his eyes tighter. He was deaf to all but the slash of the whip. For it snaked back across the floor, back to Alesta. Another pocket of silence, and she struck again.

This time, something wet trickled down his back, and cooled in the air. He knew what it was without touching it. Blood. The whip changed from fire-bringer to ravenous mouth, ripping strips of flesh from his back. Again and again the waves of pain submerged him. Each blow threw him forward. His wrists ached from supporting his body; the beginnings of a bruise throbbed on his forehead. And through it all, the terrible muting of every voice.

No one spoke. Not to cheer Alesta, nor to comfort him. Alesta herself had gone voiceless as the grave after her last pronouncement, while Gaelin strove to dampen his urge to scream.

And then the lash failed to strike. He waited, blood and sweat merging into poison on his raw back. A single word battered him, over and over: *excruciating*. It blotted everything else out, all rational thought, all resistance. He awaited his fate.

But then Alesta finally broke the silence. "Put on your clothing and return to your duties." He reached to feel the shreds of his back, but she interrupted. "Leave your wounds be. They will serve as a reminder against sinning again. Go."

Now he noticed the reactions. They spanned the gamut from horror to glee. He collected his clothing. Pain shot through the tears in his skin, pulsing with every heartbeat. He struggled to get into his shirt and robes. The combination of agony and humiliation thickened his fingers, made him almost too dizzy to see.

River was gone. Elber, too. He supposed the monk had removed her during the flogging. The word curdled in his stomach. *Flogging.* Punishment of criminals and the basest base of archaic times. Apparently, he now counted among them.

Finally clothed, Gaelin strode towards the cloisters. He kept his pace fast, better to hide how every footstep jarred his back. At the door, he risked a glance back.

Alesta had her face craned towards the Angel's. Even from this distance, Gaelin could see: they shared the same smile.

XIII

Once the lash appeared, Praeton bolted. Squeezing between pews and dodging people, he ran down the aisle. He wasn't sure where he was running. He didn't care. All he wanted was to escape Alesta. Waiting tears burned his eyes. In the moment Gaelin removed his robes and shirt, Praeton's perception of him changed. Suddenly, Gaelin wasn't the all-powerful, all-knowing sub-prior. He was human. Just a man, and an older one at that, riddled with flaws and weaknesses. It was as though someone had come along and scooped the catacombs from under the Ecclesiat. With its heart and foundation gone, there would be nothing to stop it tumbling into the void.

People turned to stare at him. He ignored them, focused on his pumping arms and legs. The doors to the narthex gaped like a mouth, and he whipped through. A short dash past some monks receiving refugees, and he was out the main doors.

There he stopped. Clouds were barely visible in the darkness of the sky. Only a few swirls of deep grey against the black shattered the illusion of a starless night sky. The clouds coiled like snakes dancing on the rim of a vortex. The rains had stopped; dried blood coated the City like rust-coloured dust. It plumed around the feet of people running across the square, clung to their clothes. They wiped smears of brownish-red from their noses and mouths, occasionally frowning at the place the sun should have been. Praeton guessed by his rumbling stomach it was around noon, maybe a little later. His eyes' insistence that it was closer to midnight unsettled him.

It felt like the entire City streamed past him. Old people all by themselves, pairs of men and women, whole families. All had the same desperate look. All ignored him. Their cries sliced through the distant thunder.

"Mamma, I want to go home!"

"Came right from the sky, it did, set everything on fire."

"My father! Where is my father?"

"The Angel has him, Carra. Hurry, bring the children..."

"Oh Ael, let it end, let it end..."

Praeton hugged his knees. Plumes of smoke scraped the clouds' bellies. Not the gentle columns of chimney smoke, though. This smoke was thicker, oily. Just the sight of it made him want to cough. He sucked in some rancid air. It smelled the way Father Osvald had at the end.

Then, on the lowest step, he spotted a familiar flash of red hair. He bumped himself down until he was next to her. Serafine didn't look up, just kept gazing across the square. Blue veins traced spider webs under her skin. Her resemblance to a glass sculpture was so strong, Praeton was afraid to tap her. He coughed a little instead.

"Uh... Serafine?"

She still didn't speak, but fixed him in her sapphire stare. Praeton wilted under its force, and felt his own speech shrivel in his chest. "What are you doing out here?" he said.

"I had to get out." The flatness of her voice scared him. "Couldn't watch."

"Me neither."

"But you're a child, I..." she sighed. "I should have been there. I'm a coward, I admit it. Nothing's turning out, Praeton. He got to the Magistatiem, and I couldn't protect it. Then River, I couldn't get to her in time either. And Gaelin...I don't even know what's going on with your dreams." A little of the life drained from her. "Maybe I was wrong. Maybe Ael *wants* Him to win."

"No!" In his rush, he forgot his earlier fears and clung to her arm. "Serafine, no. Please don't say that."

"It was my fault. I thought sending Davi off would save the Magistatiem. But it didn't, and River paid for it. Gaelin, too. All my fault." Her voice shook. "I'm no saviour."

Praeton shifted to let a lady with a cane by. His fingers curled around the lip of the stone step. "Look at me, I'm nothing. No one even wanted me. And I'm such a runt—everyone has bad dreams."

"Not like yours. And people do want you."

"Well, maybe *you* can save someone." He thought. Anything to stay outside longer—he wasn't returning to the nave until he had to. He couldn't face the thought of River on the altar.

"Wait!" he said. "River."

Serafine raised an arched eyebrow. "What about her?"

"She's being kept in the Throne's house. Alesta even said so. We'll save her!" He deflated a bit. "Only...will she be all right? River, I mean. She wasn't waking up."

A spark glowed in Serafine's eyes. "She'll be fine, she just needs aither. I didn't think she'd run out so quickly. Come, let's see if they've taken her."

Traversing the aisles of the nave was like slogging through water. So many people, eddying and flowing in and around the pews. It felt like they were using too much air. Praeton clung tight to Serafine's hand and fought the urge to hold his breath. He couldn't see the altar, but Serafine nudged him and said, "She's gone. So is Gaelin."

Praeton squirmed. "Where's Alesta?"

"Up at the front. Being pandered to, it looks like." She clucked her tongue and pulled Praeton towards the cloister doors. Scraps of conversation floated past.

"Never thought he'd betray the Ecclesiat," one man was saying to another. "But to let something so unholy within our walls...can you imagine consorting with something that doesn't have a soul?"

The other man shook his head. "Just serves to show how these end times have corrupted even our most trusted. Did you see his back, though? He's been aptly punished for that little transgression."

Serafine squeezed Praeton's hand as the first man laughed. "Well, he'll be back to the fold with a reminder against straying again. Good for the Throne, she's the kind of spiritual leader we need now. When the Angel comes, and mark my words, it'll be any day now, He'll lay His hand on the Throne first. The Throne and all who stand by her."

"Agreed. Osvald was too soft with them..."

Praeton's free hand clenched to a fist. Cowards. The way they talked, Gaelin sounded like a real heretic. And all he'd done was open the doors to someone who needed help. True, she was a little different, but he didn't believe all this nonsense about River being an abomination. The word curdled in his stomach. Ael had to like River; she was *nice*.

No sign of Gaelin in the cloisters. A few seminary boys lounged by the windows, staring at the sky with expressions of dismay. However, embers of derision flickered as their focus shifted to Praeton and Serafine. Serafine ignored them, lifting her chin and tossing her flaming hair like a queen. Praeton wished he could be so brave. He tried: setting his jaw in what he hoped was a manly fashion and lengthening his stride. It didn't work. Their sneers stung as much as always.

"It's not fair!" he hissed as he followed Serafine into the garden. "I've never done anything to them."

"Of course you haven't. They don't like difference, that's all. Not many here do." She sidestepped a huge bush. Dried blood crusted its leaves. "Anything that deviates from the norm is flawed. Anything flawed is imperfect and must be purified. He..." Praeton knew she meant the Angel. "He hates the imperfect, so they do too."

"What about you?"

"I love it."

She pulled Praeton into some shrubbery across from the Throne's lodgings. The small house nestled into a corner of the gardens; the Ecclesiat's walls seemed to have sheltered it from some of the raining blood. Suddenly, the quality of light changed, grew misty red. Praeton glanced up. The clouds had parted. Like a heart veiled by smoky gauze, the moon glowed red.

Wrong colour. Wrong time of day. Praeton shivered in the blazing heat.

Serafine's eyes narrowed to blue slits. "Elber's still in there, I think. Someone else, too."

"River?"

"No, another man. What's-his-name...the healer."

"Baeor?"

"That's the one." Catlike, she crouched beside him. "Wait, there goes Elber. Get down!"

Praeton ducked. His heart hammered. With a sneer wrapped about his lips, Elber walked so close to their hiding place that Praeton could've spat on his shoes. They waited until the sound of the sub-prior's robes swishing the gravel had subsided. Then Serafine crept forward.

"Wait out here," she whispered.

He frowned. "I want to come."

"Too risky."

"It's just Baeor in there."

Serafine froze, apparently listening for something. She spoke from between clenched teeth. "I've got to move fast. I won't hurt him, but I may need to...slow him down."

"Fine." Praeton crossed his arms and sat in a huff. He stabbed at the ground with a stick as Serafine darted across the path and into the house. It wasn't fair. Finally, a chance to prove he wasn't a baby, and he was stuck outside. He could be making himself useful, not grinding a twig into the dirt.

Why didn't he make himself useful, then? He stood and brushed the dirt from his pants. Checked the path. No sign of anyone coming. Figuring he'd lose his nerve if he thought about it too much, Praeton dashed through the door. He paused just inside, panting. He'd spent some time in here with Father Osvald, listening to stories, occasionally getting invited to have some milk while Osvald sipped wine. It'd been a while ago, but he called up his memories of the place.

There was a chamber in the middle, he remembered, with no windows. Serious, secret things took place there. He'd bet his highest note that's where she was keeping River.

Floorboards creaked beneath his feet. The halls were narrower than he remembered: more like a maze. Baeor slumped by the chamber door, his back against the wall, and head lolling to the side. No cuts or bruises anywhere. Praeton put his ear by the healer's mouth. He was breathing. Probably Serafine had done something to him, but Praeton didn't want to risk awakening him. Just in case.

A sudden, delicious thrill of fear shot through him. He was in *Alesta's house*. And she didn't even know. He had an unconscious monk at his feet, and the Beast and an MCB in the next room.

Hardly aware of himself, drunk with excitement, he eased the door open. It took him a moment to adjust to the shadows; no candles or lamps burned within. Only aither dancing on Serafine's fingertips gleamed off the polished wooden walls. River sagged on a chair—Praeton had heard many tales of people awaiting punishment on those chairs. Just the sight of it made his bottom ache. Cords lashed her wrists and ankles to it; he worried about the rope cutting into her skin. He knew she didn't have blood or anything, but couldn't she feel pain?

Serafine hunched over her. Aither glowed not just on her fingertips, but all over her body, like an aura. She fought the ropes, the sound of her nails digging into the tough cord carried in the silence. Praeton considered walking over, announcing his presence in some way, but he held back. She'd tell him to leave. Instead, he peeked around the doorframe, ready to run at an instant's notice.

Cords slithered to the ground like dead snakes. River didn't move. Honestly, Praeton didn't see how she was still alive. She didn't look dead, exactly, she looked...unreachable. Like everything that made her *River* was frozen in ice, and no matter how big a fire they had, they'd never thaw it. A lump formed in his throat. He'd liked her.

Now Serafine was kicking the ropes' remains to a corner of the room. She extended an elegant finger and touched River's forehead. Serafine glimmered bluish-white in the light of the aither; it contrasted even more with River's coppery skin. Praeton strained forward. Was it time for the magic? Serafine's back was to him, but he saw a spark of aither. It hung in the air like a blue pearl, and then melted into River.

Their fire was big enough after all. The MCB began twitching and muttering. She reminded Praeton of a sleepwalker he used to know. That monk had had terrible dreams, almost as bad as Praeton's. Did MCBs dream? He slammed his fist into his palm. There was so much he didn't know. So many times he felt useless.

Serafine hushed River, laid a hand on her arm. The MCB stopped moving, and Praeton just caught what Serafine was saying. "It's all right," she whispered. "You're safe. I'm here."

"Serafine? Where are we?"

"The Throne's house."

"This is not safe." A shade of emotion there. Fear. "We must leave. Does she know that I..."

"That you're an MCB? Yes, she's realized that. Come on, I know a place we can hide." She turned then, and her brilliant eyes captured Praeton's. "I thought I told you to wait outside."

"I..."

"Never mind. You come, too. We're leaving."

"Wait." He looked from Serafine to River. "Leaving this house, or leaving the Ecclesiat?"

Serafine's voice was tight and clipped. "The Ecclesiat."

He withdrew until his back hit the wall. "No. No, I live here."

"Praeton...five of seven."

"Then the Ecclesiat's probably the best place to be!" Wild panic beat his ribs. He shook his head vigorously. "I'm not going."

River was clenching and unclenching her hands, and taking some tentative steps around the room. Apparently satisfied, she said, "If the Angel is indeed the harbinger of ultimate destruction, it appears that the location most conducive to survival would be that which Serafine occupies."

"To summarize, stay with me. I'll protect you." Serafine beckoned to River and seized Praeton's hand. "Look, we need you. I need you."

"Why? My dreams? I didn't ask for them, I don't want them."

"And yet, you have them. Off we go."

When they reached the gardens, he wrenched his hand from her grasp. "You don't care about me. Not really. All you care about are my stupid dreams! If you really liked me, you wouldn't make me leave. This is my home!"

Serafine sighed. "I do care for you. But between the Angel and His handmaiden, your home resembles a snake pit more than a sanctuary. Besides, we—" Gravel crunched on the path. "Quiet."

Grey flashed at the edge of Praeton's vision—and there was Elber. His mouth fell open when he saw them; he didn't seem to notice his robes trailing in a blood puddle. Then his face hardened and he bellowed, "The fiend is escaping!"

"Time we left," Serafine muttered. Aither flew, seemingly from nowhere, and struck Elber's chest. He dropped like wet robes: a sodden thump to the ground. Serafine pushed River ahead and ran after her. She extended a white hand to Praeton. He snatched it, and did his best to keep up.

River ran far faster than any human woman he'd ever seen, and Serafine swifter still. His feet barely touched the ground; he was flying, bound to Serafine only by their interlocked fingers. Bushes, trees, walls rushed past in a blur. They were nearing the side gate, they were nearing the outside.

Monks streamed from the cloisters and threw themselves before them. Aither flashed like lightning. They fell. Serafine smiled grimly. The thud as the monks hit the ground unnerved Praeton; he recognized every face there. He almost slowed, but Serafine pulled him on. Ahead, River was already scrabbling with the gate. She managed to unlock it, and darted through. Serafine's steps ate the distance between them and freedom in giant bites.

Then Praeton slipped.

A stupid, stupid piece of ill luck. He was wearing his short pants and socks: no robes to trip on. His shoes actually fit for once. Yet with his eyes on the beckoning gate and his attention on the monks, he lost his balance on a patch of mud and blood-slicked grass. He went down hard. Pain erupted in his knee, and his hand tore from Serafine's.

She didn't notice at first. Just kept running. He scrambled in the dirt, fingernails digging for traction. Small stones slid under his feet; he slipped again, and cool mud caked his cheek. A strong hand clenched his shoulder. Someone hissed in his ear, "Stop, or they will die."

Alesta.

Her breath on his skin petrified him. He went limp. Now Serafine was turning, now she was growing paler, if that were possible. River was also losing speed. Both were outside the gate; Praeton could practically put out a hand and touch the wall. At least, he could've if he'd dared move. He prayed Serafine understood the message he was thinking with every fibre of being.

Go away! He cried silently. *Get out of here, she'll kill you!*

River's brow creased. She ran towards him, but Serafine's arm shot out and caught her in the chest. The two women stared at him, one showing mere traces of concern, the other white with wrath. The scarlet of Serafine's hair seemed to intensify, ignite against her deathly face. Praeton's eyes remained dry, but he drew breath in shuddering gasps.

Go away!

Serafine lowered her head. When she lifted it, only her eyes were alive in what could have been carved marble. Twin pools of pain, regret, rage...then she signalled to River. They sprinted into the haze and darkness.

"So," Alesta said, "it seems that *thing* was an instrument of the Beast."

"No, please, she..."

"Quiet." She threw Praeton to the ground. A stick stabbed his bruised knee. Ignoring his whimper, Alesta summoned a monk and wiped her hand on a white cloth he offered her. She stood over him, as immense and impassive as the Angel's statue.

"You were helping them." Not a question, not exactly an accusation, but a statement weighted with certainty. "Nor is this the first time you have sought to undermine the Ecclesiat."

One of the monks felled by Serafine struggled upright. She bowed. "With all due respect, Mother Throne, he is only a boy."

Alesta snapped her fingers. The monk cowered. The snap resounded again. Desperate glances to her fellow monks got the young sister nothing. She stumbled towards Alesta.

Crack! The smack rang in Praeton's mind long after its echoes rebounded off the garden walls. The monk scurried back to her place, Alesta's handprint burning on her cheek. Praeton cringed on the ground, half-thinking of raising his arms to shield himself. Something told him that if he attempted such defiance, he'd pay double for it.

Alesta delivered a short, sharp kick to his ribs. "Disrupting the service the day that red-haired demon arrived, fainting and shrieking at every turn, failing to repay the generosity of those monks who insisted you remain here..." Another kick. "Damn that Ioren! Foundling, how are we to know you aren't possessed? How are we to know you are even of the Angel?"

Praeton groaned. Hot, splintery pain ran along his ribcage. He'd give anything to be safe in his own bed, or letting his voice free in the choir room...anywhere but here. Where was Gaelin? He needed him. With Serafine and River gone, with even Davi gone, he needed him.

"Damnable wretch," Alesta muttered. She motioned to Brother Elber, whose feet had crossed the edge of Praeton's sight. "Take him away. Keep him where the creature was being held."

"For how long, Mother Throne?"

"Until the sacrifice."

———

The base of Davi's skull pounded. Hopefully it wasn't burnout; he'd stopped using aither hours ago. A precaution, really, but he felt safer saving his magic. Instead, he'd carried buckets and lifted rubble until every muscle throbbed. The fire still burned. Even now, collapsed a short distance from the ruined library, he could see flares erupt from buildings across the pond. An empty bucket rolled beside him. He should take it over, fill it, and find some flame to douse. After all, he had his pick of them.

Wordless columns of magi passed him. He strained to rise. No time for lying around, even if he might keel over at any moment. Smoke rose from the library's shell. The reminder of failure cut Davi. No matter how many buckets they carried or spells they cast, the truth was inescapable. The Magistatiem was dead.

A group was assembling by the pond. Davi shook his head. Such a short time ago, students relaxed here. The charred stump of his favourite tree listed to one side, nothing more than a relic from a place that would never be again. Just as the Hapax would never be again.

He smiled bitterly. They had all placed their hopes in the Hapax. And it had come to nothing. Sure, he had a new theory on the nature of aither, but that was useless here. Explain the fifth dimension to the rows of fallen magi. Sketch the analogies to the kin who would bury them.

Artur stood by the water's edge, staring at the campus opposite. Reflections of flames danced across the mirrored surface. "This isn't right," he said, without looking at Davi. "Where is the sun? What caused the fire?" A note of trepidation sounded. "Do you think...could it be something, er, supernatural?"

"Yes." The glow surrounding the Regis Building subsided momentarily, then reignited. Davi winced. "It's the End Days, Artur."

"Some people were saying that." Artur's face tightened. "But I didn't believe them. We're scholars of science and magic, not... fanatics mooning over Angels and Beasts. How is this possible?"

"I don't know."

"So many deaths, Davi..." A moment of silence lapsed between them. "There's already talk of turning the back field into a cemetery. And who knows what's happening in the rest of the City? I'm pretty sure I saw other fire strikes." He sighed. "I never thought the world would end while I was still in it."

"We all think we're immortal...until we die."

Artur grimaced. "I guess nothing's immortal. Not even MCBs. You did something with River, didn't you?"

Davi's jaw clenched. He shrugged and strode away. On the bank, people were talking about new strategies for battling the flames, or caring for the injured. He didn't join them. Tam was unconscious, but safe. As safe as he could be, anyway. Unease over River was starting to creep in, to replace the adrenaline and desperation of the past few hours. How long had he even been gone? Without the sun or the Chancellor's Tower, time slipped from him like a ship missing its anchor. It had probably been too long.

No one was paying attention to him. Dirty as he was, and tired as they were, he doubted more than a handful recognized him. He slipped past the ruins, occasionally crouching behind tumbled stone as yet another recovery team marched by. He expected to leave the destruction behind on exiting campus. Artur must have exaggerated, or been hallucinating from exhaustion and burnout.

The neighbourhoods surrounding the Magistatiem's wall were gone.

Not gone, precisely, but certainly no longer standing. Shapes of houses were no longer discernible; it looked as though a giant foot had simply kicked a collection of blocks into a heap.

That probably wasn't far from the truth.

Although he tried not to look, the devastation captivated him. Flashes of colour poked out from the rubble. Scraps of cloth, bits of furniture...and what might have been flesh. Torn between conscience and horror, he called out, "Is anyone in there?"

Only the wailing wind answered him.

He closed his eyes for a moment, to order his thoughts, when something freezing touched him. A cry escaped him, and he spun around to find Serafine and River.

"Don't *do* that!" He glared at Serafine. "What are you doing here?"

"We're no longer welcome at the Ecclesiat," Serafine said. "We were discovered."

"What? How?"

"It was my fault," River said quietly. "My energy levels dropped too low and I ceased functioning in Alesta's presence. She was thus able to determine that I am not human."

Davi felt like he'd been punched in the gut. "River...River, I'm sorry. That's not your fault, it's mine." He kicked a section of wall. "I should've been there. I shouldn't have left you."

"You did what you thought best," Serafine cut in. "Both of you. Now, we have more pressing matters. We'll need to save Praeton."

"Praeton too?" Davi struggled to keep afloat. "What happened to him?"

"He was caught when he and Serafine attempted to rescue me."

"He's in danger." Serafine gave him a sidelong glance. "She was going to sacrifice River."

"*What?*" Fury like he'd never known coursed through Davi's veins. River was looking down, avoiding his eye. He stretched a hand towards her, brushed her hair from her face. For an instant, she stiffened, but then she relaxed. A little. Davi took that as a sign of acceptance and gave her a brief, light hug. She didn't pull away.

"How could she?" he whispered.

"Because I'm not human, I'm something unnatural." River's voice cracked. "Moreover, my actions have cost us our sanctuary."

"We'd have been forced out sooner or later." Serafine tapped her foot. "I have a place, and now we've got you, Davi. Let's go."

"To save Praeton?"

She snorted. "Yes, with you dead on your feet and River running on aither I threw at her. No, you need to eat and rest, and River needs her levels checked by someone who actually knows what he's doing." At their protests, she gave them a withering look. "You won't do Praeton any good if you collapse right into Alesta's arms."

"A logical argument," River muttered. "Infuriating, but logical."

"Glad you think so. Now, follow me."

XIV

No one came to him. Gaelin stood in the public chapel, waiting to help. Many refused eye contact with him, though a few glanced at him nervously. Children occasionally approached him, only to be yanked away by their parents. Gaelin sighed. His back throbbed, pain clawing through him with every movement.

And everywhere, the Angel's milky eyes.

He hadn't been outside, but judging by the haggard looks of those entering the Ecclesiat, things were deteriorating. More injured to send to the infirmary, more traumatized victims to listen to. At least, there would be if they didn't shun him like a carrier of plague.

A sudden commotion disrupted his thoughts. The chapel and nave were emptying. People rushed from the Ecclesiat, shouting and clutching icons of the Angel. Alesta followed in their wake, regal in freshly-washed robes. Gaelin's were bloodstained and filthy.

He stumbled after them. So many people packed the front steps that there was hardly a place to stand. Noise roared in his ears, impossible to distinguish individual voices or words. Muggy air clung to him. Outside the sheltering stones of the Ecclesiat, his head spun from the heat. Odd that it could be so warm, yet so dark. He spied Baeor in the crush and sidled next to him.

"What is it?" he asked.

Baeor pointed upwards. "A miracle."

Light pierced the black vortex of clouds. Like lines of fire in the sky, an outline formed itself. A head, torso, two wings. Its hand was raised to condemn and restore. Pure contour, no detail, yet the form was unmistakeable. The Angel blazed above the Ecclesiat.

The form hovered in the void, unmoving. If it heard their clamours, it gave no sign. Nor did it react to Alesta falling to her knees, praying feverishly. The people around her followed suit, dropping in waves like ripples across a pond. Gaelin tore his eyes from the Angel and saw that he was the only one still standing. Yet he could not offer obeisance to this thing. Instead, he found himself groping for his double-triangle—the double-triangle he had long since removed—and praying for protection from Ael.

Fragments of phrases he had never heard spooled themselves from the inner cave of his mind. Not the Angel's words; he sensed that much. Someone else's small, powerful voice spoke amid the tumult.

And so the candle burns, yet behold, at the very centre of it is blackness. Yet there is also the light unending, that light which defines and challenges the shadow. For as the shadow is in the light, so too is there light in the darkness. Both are in us, and both are in all…for between the potential and the actual is the choosing. Your *choosing.*

Blessed coolness spread over him, as though he'd plunged into a pool of fresh water. Above, the form of the Angel wavered, and shrivelled to nothingness. For an instant, only the wind and thunder spoke. Yet even they died away as Alesta rose.

"A sign from Angelus Rex, the Angel King," she said.

"He redeems us!"

"Mother Throne, has He found us worthy? Are our sins forgiven?"

"What of the dead? Have they joined Him?"

She raised her fist. When she had recaptured their attention, she cleared her throat. "It is a sign He approves the new sacrifice. Not the polluted artificial creature; it was not fit for Him."

"Must be why it escaped," Baeor whispered to Gaelin. "The Angel wanted it out of His home."

Gaelin hushed him. Dread knotted in his stomach. No news of a "new sacrifice" had reached him. While River's escape relieved him, he wasn't sure he liked where Alesta was going.

"What sacrifice?" he called out.

A woman standing beside him edged away, closer to Alesta. Some seminarians stared at him, goggle-eyed. For her part, Alesta ignored him, answering as though someone else had asked. "Eleven years ago, the Ecclesiat took in an orphan. Since then, he has dwelled within our walls, eaten at our table, and walked amongst the Angel's glories while offering nothing in return."

Gaelin hardly believed what he was hearing. The coolness turned to ice. "He's offered nothing?" He elbowed closer. "What of his voice? What of his kindness?"

"The boy then betrayed the trust we placed in him by aiding the abomination. Because of him, it stalks free in the City of the Angel King."

Shocked, Gaelin looked to Baeor. The healer bit his lip. Nodded. A wave of despair rolled over Gaelin. But Alesta wasn't finished.

"Therefore, tomorrow, he shall be sacrificed to Angelus Rex, the Angel King."

Discomfort rippled through the crowd. Several looked again to the sky, as though seeking reassurance from the Angel's apparition. They found none, for it had not returned. Others then glanced to Gaelin. He felt their eyes upon his back, registered fresh doubt and sympathy in their faces. He wished he could give them something, anything. But he could scarcely breathe.

Alesta seemed to sense her people's uncertainty. She smiled. It had the same forced quality of a festival mask. "I know he is a child. It is for that reason that he is a fitting sacrifice. By willingly depriving ourselves of that which we value most, we show the Angel the true depth of our devotion to Him. Further, the child himself has sinned. Offering his life to the Angel will restore his soul to purity. We would wish him cleansed enough to join Ael, no? And he shall save us all."

At her words, sympathies shifted from Gaelin back to her. A few still looked unsure, but many, many more were smiling and nodding. Gaelin felt ill.

"She can't do this!" he muttered.

Baeor shrugged. "She can do anything she likes. And perhaps she has a point."

"You can't mean that. He's a boy!"

"He was with the abomination. And that woman who, if she isn't the Beast Herself, is surely Her tool. Besides, Gaelin do you really think you...never mind."

Anger pulsed in his chest. "Go on."

"Well, it's just..." The corners of Baeor's mouth twitched. "I don't mean to offend you, but you can't be objective about this. You were closer to Praeton. And..." His gaze drifted over Gaelin's shoulder.

"And I have already been punished for helping the same creature myself. That changes nothing. Human sacrifice cannot be part of the worship of Ael."

"I wasn't discussing Ael." Alesta hissed directly in his ear. "Remember St. Memoyah? Ael is no more. There is only the Angel."

"No." Energy he had not felt for years returned to him. His hands shook, but his voice remained steady. "There is more than Him. I worship That Which is All."

"Ael is imperfect. Ael includes the Beast."

"So be it."

Baeor had disappeared into the crowd, which now circled the pair of them like spectators at a dog fight. Danger glittered in Alesta's eyes. "Our Ecclesiat," she said, "does not tolerate the impure."

"Then this is not the same Ecclesiat to which I gave myself." Alesta was tall for a woman, but Gaelin did not let himself be cowed. "Let Praeton go."

"I am the Throne. I am the seat of the Angel in this world. I choose."

Between the potential and the actual...

"You choose against Ael."

"There is no Ael."

The tension between them was almost a tangible thing, a barricade. No one moved; the square was a yard of statues. Perhaps they were stunned into immobility. Pinched by fury's grasp, everything about Alesta had narrowed - her eyes, nostrils, lips.

"Let Praeton go." Sureness graced his mind for the first time in days. "End this now."

"You defy me?" He expected to see her flush, but she calmed herself. "Very well," she said. "If you claim to serve Ael, then you are no servant of the Angel. Therefore, there is no reason for your presence amongst us here. Brother Gaelin, you are banished."

Banished. The blood drained from Gaelin's face. Self-assurance followed. No monk had been banished in living memory. It was the worst punishment the Throne could bestow: something that might happen to those who broke their vows of celibacy, or attacked or violated another. Never in his life had Gaelin imagined he might receive it.

There was no reply possible. He did not bow his head. He did not plead for mercy or forgiveness. He simply turned and walked down the steps. The crowd parted before him as though afraid of touching him. One old woman pressed a book in his hand: a copy of the Tablet. Gaelin smiled at her and made the sign of the Three. He would never again handle his own Tablet; he was no longer allowed into his dorter or study. Tucking the book under his arm, he crossed the square. On the other side, he allowed himself to say farewell to the Ecclesiat. Not the one that was now. He said farewell to the Ecclesiat that had been. The tears he shed, the grief that he felt, were for *his* Ecclesiat.

Once he entered the labyrinth of streets that comprised the City, he realized he had no idea what to do next. He had no family outside his Brothers and Sisters. The few friends he had amongst the laity would doubtless shrink from helping him; they would want to avoid Alesta's wrath, particularly in times such as these.

Times such as these indeed, Gaelin mused. The gutters ran thick with congealed blood. The stench of rot polluted the air of the City, seeped into its foundations. *These are strange times, End Times.*

Ash encrusted him. It was inescapable. Every time a building collapsed or caught fire, more plumed into the air. He approached a fountain hopefully. A nest of beetles writhed in the bone-dry basin, metallic wings gleaming. They almost covered a small bloody mass—maybe a weasel, possibly an undersized kitten. Their grasping mandibles clicked as they devoured it; they were as efficient as soldiers. Gaelin shuddered and stepped down from the fountain.

On the other side, he found the dead man.

The corpse sagged against the fountain, empty bucket by its feet. Empty sockets housed buzzing flies. Thin, purple lips split in a travesty of a grin. Then again, it might have been a scream.

He had to do something. Close the man's eyes? Impossible with nothing left in the sockets. Bury him? Breaking the plaza's cobblestones wasn't an option, nor was he strong enough to drag the man to a cemetery. Bless him? Gaelin was already forming the motion when he stopped. Everything to which he had pledged himself was gone. His nice, firm ground of faith had been shaken more than the City. With a heavy heart, he lowered his hand.

Ael was gone. If the Angel demanded innocent blood, Gaelin could not bring himself to serve Him either. As for Serafine, his years in the Ecclesiat had left a deep mark upon him. She was the Beast. Perhaps her intentions were better than he'd believed, but that changed little.

He moved into the tangle of alleys beyond the fountain. Here, the houses leaned into one another, practically meeting overhead.

One could almost step from one balcony to another, going from apartment to apartment without ever touching the street. They reminded him of walking in the nave, under the vaulted roof. Eventually he would find his way to the edge of the City. Past the valley surrounding it lay other lands. He could become a missionary, like Ioren, spreading Aelism throughout the world.

If there even remained a world through which to spread it.

"Gaelin!"

He saw nothing. No one in the windows, or in the shadows below staircases. In this part of the city, where he could stand in the centre of the street and touch the houses on either side, there were few places to hide. He mustered his courage and called, "Who's there?"

She jumped from a balcony, red hair streaming like wings. Gaelin sighed. Somehow, he'd expected her.

"What now?"

"Where's Praeton?"

"In the Ecclesiat, as far as I know." The implication struck him fully for the first time, and he wilted. Serafine bore his bulk without protest. "I was banished," he said. "I can't save him. He will die."

"Not if I can help it." She patted his cheek. "Glad I found you, actually. I was just heading to the Ecclesiat to see if you'd come."

"Come where?"

"My new safe house. Davi and River are already there."

She led him through twisting side streets and lanes. The streets narrowed until they had to walk single file. Even then, it was a tight fit. Gaelin's gaze flicked over familiar scarred doors and windows covered by tattered cloth. In his years serving Ael, he'd spent long hours here, listening to families with sick children, sitting with those who had one foot already beyond the Veil. The reek intensified: illness and death had their stronghold here.

It's the end, he thought, as Serafine leaped over an unmoving bundle. *We...the Ecclesiat should be here, reaching to those who can-*

not reach us. And instead? Alesta wishes to add to the toll...

Serafine skipped up a staircase that led to a second-floor apartment. It had no door, merely a blanket hanging limp in the still air. She ducked under the ratty fabric and called, "Found him!"

It took Gaelin a moment to adjust to the gloom. No candles here; he couldn't even imagine having them in such a cramped, hot space. Debris from broken furniture and torn clothes littered the floor. As far as Gaelin saw, there wasn't an intact object in the room. After the majesty of the Ecclesiat, the space seemed even smaller.

River sat in a corner, cross-legged. Davi lay by her feet, either asleep or unconscious. Dirt lent his dark hair an oily sheen. The MCB shifted her feet, inching them closer to the mage.

"Gaelin, you joined us," she said.

"Apparently it is what Ael wishes. I have no other options."

Serafine straightened the hanging blanket. "None of us do. What's happened to Praeton?"

Saying it aloud made it real. His tongue was wooden. "Alesta intends to sacrifice him."

River jerked her head up, away from Davi's still form. "I thought human sacrifices were not condoned under Aelism."

"Not condoned, but not condemned either." Gaelin shuddered. "It stuns me, how something as beautiful and meaningful as the worship of That Which is All can be perverted into something so barbaric. So terrible."

"It shouldn't." Serafine wiped her hands on her skirts and joined them. "You're too idealistic, Gaelin, that's your problem. When is it?"

"Dawn of the seventh day."

"Nice timing. Well, we'll rescue him, don't worry." A thought seemed to strike her. "How did the people react?"

"Variously. Some seemed eager, others...less so."

Serafine's red lips compressed. "Maybe we can get a few on our side, then. What?" she added, reading Gaelin's noncommittal shrug. "You think the four of us can take on Alesta and the Angel? Besides which, I'd like to save more than three humans and an MCB."

Davi stirred. After extending and retracting her hand several times, River stroked his back. He smiled faintly and went quiet. Gaelin shot her a look, which she avoided. "He spent the day spell-casting at the Magistatiem," she said. "And then restored my energy levels. His risk of burnout is heightened; he needs rest."

Serafine nodded. "We were going to leave him another hour. That gives you a respite, too."

The urge to do something, anything, as long as it was *now* thrummed in his blood. He paced the room, irked by every sound, every non-productive movement from the other three. Finally he could bear it no longer and cleared space in the corner opposite River. He eased himself down on a pile of filthy rags and opened the copy of the Tablet he'd been given.

The texts still ignited the sense of awe and the holy within him. Even if Ael as Ael's self was no longer in this world, at this moment, reading the words inspired by Ael gave Gaelin some peace. At least Ael had once been. Flitting from section to section, he concluded that was better than nothing.

When Davi began moving in earnest, Serafine slipped away. She returned a short time later with a small sack, and dumped its contents on the floor. A few bruised apples, some premature grapes. A loaf of bread that had been dry for what looked like years. Gaelin picked at the fruit, keeping his nose firmly in his book. Grumbling, Davi sat up and reached for the loaf. He banged it against the wall. The mortar flaked, but the bread was unharmed.

"What are you reading?" River asked Gaelin suddenly.

He nearly winced. Such a painful attempt at conversation. But then he sighed, and showed her the cover. "The First Tablet. I thought that if our world is to die, I would remind myself of its birth."

"*Where there was no time, before there was any place, the first Word of Ael sounded,*" River quoted. She waited, as though for approval.

Davi looked up from the loaf, which he was wrapping in scraps of cloth. Clearly, it served better purpose as furniture than as food. "The Hapax," he said.

Serafine scowled. "What did St. Memoyah say? *And in that place where it first resounded, it echoes still.*"

"So the Hapax is where there isn't any time," Davi said. He slouched so that his head rested against the wrapped loaf. "Unfortunately, that's not going to be anywhere nearby. We've had time since, well, the beginning of time. It's one of our four...five dimensions, for Ael's sake." He paused. "Gaelin, what's the order Ael created things in?"

"You don't know?" Gaelin nearly dropped the Tablet. "That's fundamental knowledge!"

"For an Aelist perhaps. I've never been very religious."

Gaelin shook his head. What kind of education had Davi's parents given him? "First there was nothingness. Then Ael separated the aither from the Void."

"Then us!" Serafine interjected. "I mean..." She flushed. "Ael then became the Angel and I."

"And remained Ael." Gaelin stroked the Tablet's threadbare spine. "Then, Ael parted the four lesser elements from the aither. Ael gathered them up into their places, and then Ael created life upon and within the four elements."

"Then the first thing Ael made was the aither," Davi said. "Is an echo of the Hapax somehow still there?" Suddenly, he bolted upright, mouth falling open. "Is that what makes the aither magical in the first place? Some influence of Ael's own self?"

"A divine influence," Serafine mused. "Interesting."

"Then, wouldn't it be possible to hear the Hapax within the aither?" Davi was pacing now, his gesturing hands in danger of smacking Serafine and River. "And if we had enough magi, maybe we could do it ourselves. Create another world, I mean."

220

"What about Praeton?" Gaelin intercepted Davi. "Wherever the Hapax may be, he is in danger."

"Look, no Hapax, no new world when this one ends."

"So, you too would sacrifice him."

"No, I'm just saying..."

"Enough!" Serafine separated them. "I refuse to let anything happen to Praeton. But he's a prisoner of the Angel, against whom the Hapax is the strongest weapon we have."

The room's shadows shrouded Serafine, hid her expression. Gaelin twisted the hem of his sleeve, frowning. "While the Angel is not the deity I devoted myself to, must we attack Him? He is still an aspect of Ael."

"The Angel demands what is not possible for this world; His desires preclude life itself." Serafine leaned against the wall. Showers of dust rained on her, streaking her hair with grey. "The Hapax is in and with Ael. Its return is Ael's return."

"Then what of Praeton?"

Dust motes danced in the air. Serafine watched them as though hypnotized. When she spoke, her voice seemed to come from far away. "He has until tomorrow. Perhaps an assembly of magi may disquiet the Angel, make Him hesitate." She smiled faintly. "He fears that which He has not seen."

Davi gathered the remains of the food and started for the door. "There are still magi at the Magistatiem. We can talk to them, see if we can get a spell going. But..." An internal tussle played itself across his face. "They'll want proof. They'll want you, Gaelin, and Serafine as well. Especially Serafine. It'll take a miracle for them to trust us."

"Then a miracle," Serafine said, "is what they'll get."

Rope sliced into Praeton's ankles and wrists. Fear filled him from the soles of his feet to the crown of his head. A particularly thick lump of it lodged in his chest, constricted his heart. He had sung at first. Out of instinct maybe. For comfort. For defiance. But his mouth and throat were too dry; his tongue felt like the shrivelled worms you found on the garden path after rain.

Rain. He'd love some now. Any water, really. The musty airlessness of the Throne's inner chamber had him on the verge of screaming. He imagined himself out in the gardens, in the sunshine. Or, for the first time, entirely beyond the Ecclesiat's sheltering arms, in the valleys that surrounded the City, or the plains that stretched past the horizon.

Praeton squirmed. The waiting was the worst part. Not knowing what Alesta would do next. And the darkness. He kept thinking he heard someone in the hall. Given that this was the Throne's house, he tensed up every time, sure that Alesta's cold eyes were seconds away from meeting his. Maybe it was ghosts. After all, Father Osvald had died in this very house.

He'd be a good ghost, though, he told himself. *He'd haunt Alesta, not me.*

The argument didn't convince him.

Salty tracks itched his cheeks, just out of reach. He fought the cords binding him, failed to move his wrists more than a hand's breadth. No more tears, he promised himself. In some ways, it'd almost be worse if he had parents. Parents would worry about him; their heartache would make him feel even sicker. At least this way, he was the only one to suffer.

When he was little, he'd pretend his parents were the King and Queen of a far-off land, who'd been forced to abandon him for his own safety. To protect him from some usurping relative, or a military coup, something interesting like that. Or maybe they were powerful magi, and they'd made enemies in the guilds or universities. The Ecclesiat would be the one place magical adversaries would never think to look. No matter the scenario, his daydreaming always concluded with a joyful reunion, when his parents emerged from danger to collect him from the Ecclesiat.

Then he got older. Learned more about the world. A few run-ins with older boys had cemented his suspicions. He was nobody special. There weren't any monarchs watching political currents, waiting for the right moment to reclaim their son. No magi were arranging safe-conduct to another city, ready to snatch him as they fled. Probably it had been some street walker and a merchant who weren't going to get married and didn't want a child out of wedlock.

No one really cared about him.

The corners of his eyes tingled. He snuffled and blinked, tried again to move his limbs. Light shone under the door. That didn't mean much; without the sun he had no way of guessing the time.

Maybe a few people cared. Gaelin, for one. He thought Baeor had too, but the healer hadn't even looked at him when he came to talk to Alesta. Even when he'd called his name. But then, there was Serafine. River too, and maybe even Davi.

It hurt to think about them, but he couldn't stop. For having known them only a few days, they'd made their way surprisingly far into his heart. A smile crossed his face as he recalled the morning he'd spent with Davi and River, when Davi had tested him for magic. Even if he'd failed, he'd enjoyed the time with them. Enjoyed feeling like he belonged for once.

He sighed, tapping his toes on the floor. Maybe the mix of terror and boredom was another of Alesta's tricks. He closed his eyes. If he had magic, he'd be out of here faster than a star fell. The idea tugged on him. He slumped, thinking. He'd been nervous that morning. And sometimes while singing, it took a few tries to know your range.

A final tense minute watching the strip of light under the door, waiting for the dark blobs of approaching feet. Nothing. He made himself as comfortable as possible, leaning back to relieve some of the pressure on his wrists. Squeezed his eyes shut. Davi made it seem so simple. Just listen. If he was good at anything, it was listening.

At first the whisper of his own breathing dominated the soundscape. He ignored that, plunged himself deeper *inside*. Inside what, exactly, he didn't know. But it felt right. Wood creaked overhead. Trees brushed the sides of the house. The wind howled, commiserating with him. And at the centre of it all, his heartbeat. A constant pulse, slowing as he relaxed. And then—

The humming.

Not just one note. He'd already told Davi, it was like a chord. Multiple notes, all in glorious harmony with each other. It was familiar. Sort of like the vibrations from a plucked string. It felt eternal, like it'd been playing in the background all his life. Ael knew, it probably had been. This was where he got frustrated. Magi said to follow the humming to the blue fire. But Praeton couldn't sense a trail. It had no origin, no destination. The sound simply *was,* everywhere and in everything. No magical blue fire revealed its source to him.

He quit, letting his head fall forward. The humming died away. Once more, his breath covered all other sounds. The room wavered; shadows pulsed with each heartbeat. A heartbeat that rapidly increased, moved into his throat.

A black hole in the centre of his vision spread, consumed the wooden walls and floors. The last thing to go was the sullen candle placed in a corner wall bracket. Then he floated.

The streams of light again, three twisted about each other. The purest, most beautiful white he had ever seen. And the humming again, louder and truer than before. It didn't make any sense, though. Aither was blue, not white. He hovered outside the lights. Where he was, there was nothing. No light, not even darkness. He was in Void.

Yet something was in there with him. He strained, casting his senses in a widening net. The Void was empty save him. Yet there was something in all the nothingness. Or rather, the echo of something that once had been.

The humming grew louder, roared in his ears and soul.

Overwhelming, intoxicating, obliterating all thought and feeling. The braided rope of light twisted and revolved. Somehow he drifted closer to them. One took a bluish tinge. Another shimmered, became clear. It was like gazing into a column of glassy water. Praeton's attention fastened itself to that one. People moved inside. Coming and going, in what he recognized as the Ecclesiat's halls. He reached for it and suddenly, he was inside.

The crystalline pictures vanished. All he had now were smears of colour, flashes of shape. And silence. He tried to blink away the blurriness, but couldn't move his eyes. Where was he? Somewhere in the maze under the Ecclesiat. Rows of doors, it had to be the anchors' cells.

A man with curly brown hair went by. He carried a tray with a bowl, a heel of bread, and a cup of water. At one cell, he knocked, waited a few moments while mouthing a prayer, and entered. Before the door shut behind him, Praeton saw her.

She was younger, but it was unmistakeably Alesta. Same sharp features, same golden hair spilling down her back. This had to be her anchorage, which meant that the man had to be Ioren.

The image buckled and paled. The colours and lines leached away, and Praeton floated in the abyss once more.

When he awoke, his hands and feet were numb. And he was still alone. *Where are you all?* He raged silently. *Gaelin, Serafine…* *Ioren.*

Anybody?

XV

"Are you certain about this?"

Davi smiled, faking a confidence he did not feel. "Of course. Trust me, they've got bigger things to worry about than you."

Tilting her head from side to side, River observed the shattered remains of the Magistatiem's walls. "It's been destroyed," she said softly. "Not just destroyed...*annihilated.*"

Semantic quibble or no, Davi concurred. Soot and ash blackened the stones. They looked like fungus, or ulcers poisoning the Magistatiem's outer layer. The gates lay in shambles. A briar patch of splinters poked up, wickedly sharp. Through it all, people moaned and wept. Serafine's jaw set as they neared; he saw her eyes flash over a small band of children slumped against the walls. Their clothes were torn, their faces so dirty and ragged he couldn't guess at ages or genders.

"Refugees, this way; families keep together," someone called. A man leaped from rock to rock, skipping over the damage and jollying bewildered people past the gates' remnants. "Injuries report to the white tent by the pond. Fighting will result in your expulsion from the camp. Be sure to give your names to anyone wearing the Magistatiem falcon."

"I don't believe it," Serafine whispered. Her hard edges vanished in a cloud of joy. "They've organized an encampment. Shelter, medical attention, ten times more than the Ecclesiat's doing!" Her sigh rippled with contentment. "I knew I brought aither for a reason."

Gaelin frowned. "The Ecclesiat is also offering itself as a place of refuge."

"But the Magistatiem's far more efficient," Davi said. "That's how we operate." He nudged River. "Isn't that right?"

She didn't answer. She had frozen in place at the mage's appearance, fingers curled by her sides. "I cannot go in there."

"What?" Davi offered his hand. After a moment, she took it, but remained tense. "Why not?" he asked, wishing he could pass reassurance skin-to-skin. "They're not likely to notice you, and if they do, they're too busy to care."

She squeezed his hand tight enough to make him gasp. His stricken expression didn't seem to register with her. "The risk is too high. I have crossed all points of no return with the Magistatiem. I am afraid, Davi." To his amazement, she edged closer to him. "Despite the imminent threat of total destruction, I have…enjoyed the last few days. I do not wish my existence to cease."

Neither do I. He held her. His own emotions twisted too much to sort through, a maelstrom of desire and dread and love. At Gaelin's exasperated sigh, he broke contact.

"So, what you do you propose?" he asked.

"I don't know."

"I think you're forgetting something." Serafine shrugged elegant shoulders. "Me. I'm not going to let them hurt you."

Davi wished he could say the same. Breath held, he watched River deliberate. Finally, she nodded. "Very well. I shall trust in you."

If only she'd said it to him.

Gaelin's mouth tightened as they joined the clumps of refugees. Everything, from the walkway leading to the stump of the Chancellor's Tower, to the tatters of Magistatiem flags, seemed to spark his distaste. He shied away from the magi, stealing glances when he thought they weren't looking.

Davi fell into step next to him. "Well? What do you think?"

Gaelin started, nearly tripped over a pile of bricks. "It is larger than I expected. More structured." He pointed to the shattered clock. Fragments sparkled like tears on the dead grass. "What was that?"

"Clock from the Chancellor's Tower." Seeing Gaelin's quizzical expression, he added, "Mostly used for administration, but it was a key part of campus. One of our landmarks, physically and emotionally."

"It must have been hard."

Davi snorted. "You don't know the half of it." Speeding ahead, he slipped behind River. "How are you?" he said quietly.

She kept walking, betrayed no tremble or quiver. "The Library is gone. As are many other essential buildings." A flicker so fast he almost missed it. "Perhaps I should not feel such attachment to buildings. They are inanimate objects: stone, wood, brick... nothing that warrants this reaction."

"I had an attachment to those buildings.'

"Yes, but you're supposed to."

"You can, too. You spent your whole life here."

"Three years. Insignificant on the grand scale. Undergraduate degrees are four." She covered her face as they passed another mage. "You've been here six."

Down by the pond, white tents had sprung up. Several of these bore the chalice-and-heart of the healers' guild. Boxes and crates spilled from others. Lines snaked slowly through these tents as magi distributed rations. There wasn't much. No meat that Davi could see, a bit of cheese, lots of the rounded white loaves so common in the dining halls. Most people huddled on the lawns. They clustered in families, blood-related or otherwise. All had lost, frightened looks, as though all the world outside this oasis of grass and rubble had fallen away.

Magi patrolled the lawn, breaking up fights and singling people out for healers' attention. Despite their reassurances, a tense atmosphere had settled over the Magistatiem. Everywhere

Davi looked, he saw faces at the breaking point, heard words sharp as arrows and as carefully aimed.

He hoped Serafine knew what she was doing.

She smiled at the hive of activity. The contrast between her serenity and Davi's anxiety rankled him. She beckoned. "Davi, find out who's in charge, will you?"

His forehead wrinkled. "Of the whole Magistatiem? That's Chancellor Pare. Why?"

"You'll need to tell him why we're here."

"Me?"

Silver laughter burbled forth. "Of course. You know him better. You'll need to make the introductions."

The thought of introducing the Magistatiem's Chancellor to the Beast left Davi unsure whether to giggle or cry. Part of him wondered whether the Final Day had passed without his realizing, and left him to bumble through some limbo of absurdity.

He questioned the touring magi. Most seemed reluctant to reveal the Chancellor's whereabouts. At least, they were reluctant until Serafine sauntered forth. An air of enchanting sensuousness and gentle authority clung to her like perfume. When she asked, the magi were more than happy to point her in Pare's direction.

Serafine dragged Davi to a tent set apart from the others. Bricks from the Tower studded the lawn; it was like walking through a quarry, or the badlands beyond the City. The scarlet moon struggled from behind roiling clouds. Reddened moonbeams washed the Magistatiem in an eerie, pale light.

The Chancellor hunched over a table with several Heads of Faculty. Volpes was not among them, to Davi's relief. The Heads—all grey, craggy men—were so deep in conversation they failed to notice Serafine and Davi standing by the tent flaps. Then Pare fell silent. The discussion tapered as one by one, the magi fixed them with questioning stares.

Davi rocked on his heels. If another chunk wanted to

plummet from the Tower and crush his skull, that'd be fine with him.

A red trickle oozed from a gash on Pare's forehead. The other Heads showed no sign of injury, though Davi noticed many torn academic gowns and hoods. Pare cleared his throat. He was a tall man, but lean, and the richness of his voice surprised Davi.

"Yes?"

Serafine nudged Davi, her hand like ice in the small of his back. Words garbled and stuck between his teeth. She touched him again, and some of the embarrassment ebbed away.

"Chancellor Pare, sir. My name is Davi Sanders..."

"He's the one!" the Head of Weather Magics exploded. "The one Volpes was talking about. Ran off with a renegade MCB!"

A polite cough was sufficient to quiet the man. "You have been brought to our attention," Pare said. "Why are you here?"

Davi gulped. "Sir, the End Days are here, but we think we have a way to stop them. Or at least avert the crisis."

That was as far as he got before guffaws drowned him out. The Head of Weather Magics slapped the table; Life Magics' Head rocked back so much he was in danger of tearing through the tent's sides.

"End Days, help us all, we've a theologian among us!"

The Head of Earth Magics leered. "Must be why he took the MCB—she was an affront to Ael."

The howls that followed that remark would not be silenced by a subtle gesture from Pare. He waited patiently, but Davi saw his jaw clenching. When the laughter did not subside, he stood. The full effect of his height served to reduce the gales to a smattering of hiccups. He gave the men a warning look, and then turned to Davi.

"Do you have proof?"

"Um." Davi felt like he'd missed a step going down stairs. His mind raced for an answer. All he'd seen—how could he prove any of it?

"He doesn't." Serafine's voice matched Pare's for calm and command. "But I do."

"A foreigner?" someone at the back muttered. Davi suppressed a groan and hoped Serafine hadn't heard.

She had. And she smiled. "Not quite."

Remembering her revelation in the anchors' cells, Davi scrambled aside to avoid unfurling wings. But she didn't release them this time. Instead, an orb of light shimmered in the air. Faint shapes flowed within. Pare raised an eyebrow.

"Impressive magic, but hardly proof."

Serafine laughed. "Oh, I'm just getting started." A marble chamber appeared within the orb. An altar stood at its centre. "Five days ago, the ceremony of Candlemass was performed at the Ecclesiat. For the first time, the new fire failed to light."

"We know that," the Weather Head grumbled. "But the world didn't end. It's superstition."

"Following that," Serafine continued, "this world saw unseasonal weather, a few *miracles*, and the destruction of your institution."

"Fine. I'll give you that."

"We know all this," Pare interrupted. "Where is your proof?"

"Getting to it. My goodness, you magi are impatient." She stroked the orb as one would a cat. Then she pulled it and stretched it. It turned clear as glass. Davi saw through it and to the table beneath as clearly as through a window. "Watch," Serafine said.

The section of the table top visible through the orb seemed to magnify. Tiny details enlarged, as though they were pressing their faces to the grain of the wood. Soon the image changed. No longer was it crystal-clear, but oddly muddled. Something wiggled, as though tiny vibrating strings had been dropped in front of the wood.

No, Davi realized. *It's as though tiny, vibrating strings are the wood.*

A familiar humming filled the air. Every pair of ears in the room pricked. The magi swung towards Serafine, confused. It was the sound of aither.

Serafine smiled.

Now the strings were growing, filling the space within the orb. As they got closer, Davi saw they weren't colourless, as he'd initially thought, but definitely tinted. There was a jump, and he gasped. They were blue.

One string in particular dominated the field of vision. As though they were running towards it, it appeared to get closer and closer, until it seemed a collision was imminent. Several magi drew back with small cries.

Then they were inside it. And now, the only thing Davi saw through the orb was aither. Blue flames leaped and danced; the sight was so similar to casting a spell that he blinked a few times to ensure he hadn't fallen into a trance of some sort.

The humming of the strings—of the aither—never stopped.

But the demonstration did. Serafine nodded, and the orb fizzled to nothingness, taking the image of aither with it. Several magi prodded the table, their noses pressed against it in close inspection. They cast spells of their own, examining the area Serafine had showed them. Others, Pare included, just stared at her.

Smirking, she rubbed her neck. "Told you it was everywhere. Your mage here figured it out on his own. Davi, why don't you tell them?"

"Um...all right. Sure." Quickly, Davi outlined his theory of the fifth dimension. *Extra-Dimensional Aither Theory*, he heard himself call it. Under normal circumstances, he would've been elated at the prospect of sharing ground-breaking research with the Heads. Not to mention the Chancellor himself. That elation was hard to find now. All he wanted was to make them see it, as fast and clearly as possible, so that they would help him. The nods and racing pencils encouraged him. Even the Weather Head grunted approvingly. A miniscule portion of Davi's ego swelled at that. No matter what, they were all academics at core.

His mouth felt dry from talking so much, and the beginnings of a headache throbbed in his temples. Still, he continued, relating what had been happening at the Ecclesiat. When he came to Serafine's part in the events, he tripped over his words.

Pare motioned for him to go on. "What is it?" he said. "What was in the cells?"

"Me," Serafine answered. "I'm the Seraph."

Fully expecting more guffaws, Davi cringed. But all she got were quizzical looks. Maybe a little condescension thrown in.

"My dear," Pare said. "The Seraph does not exist."

All right. A lot of condescension.

"Oh, really?"

The six great wings bloomed into being. Crimson feathers strained against the fabric walls; the tent actually lifted off the ground slightly. Davi couldn't help a laugh as the magi shrank back with round, frightened eyes. And yet, it lacked the theatricality of her first revelation. Perhaps she too was feeling the weight of time. Or perhaps she was growing tired.

"Davi," she said in that unearthly voice, "tell them about the Hapax now."

And he launched into explanation and examples afresh. Here he was on shakier ground. Lacking River's memory and Gaelin's training, he had to rely on Serafine for some of the Aelist specifics. It was almost better that way. She had not withdrawn her wings. They fluttered, occasionally brushing Davi with heartbreakingly soft feathers. Hearing her recite passages from the Tablets, with the light of divinity so bright about her, nearly had him considering conversion.

"Then, this Hapax is absolutely essential for the creation of another world?" Pare asked when they finished.

"Yes."

"And you believe that it is linked to the aither."

"It must be," Davi said. "The aither is the first thing Ael made. The echo of the first word has to be there."

"Very well," Pare said. He laid several sheets of paper on the table and distributed pencils to the magi. Pride trilled through Davi when the Chancellor rolled one to him, too. "To work, then."

Grinning, Davi seized his pencil and jostled for a space at the table. He hardly noticed Serafine shake her wings and perch on the rubble outside. He certainly didn't notice the time creep past midnight.

———

Bits of paper littered the ground. So did shards from everyday life: a smashed mirror, scraps of cloth, someone's trampled textbook. River sighed inwardly. She had never seen the grounds this messy. She had to fight an upwelling urge to pass the matter along to one of the groundskeepers. As much as she wanted to, drawing the Magistatiem's attention was suicidal. The restoration of her ordered home had to wait.

She'd found a sizeable piece of black fabric; most likely ripped off someone's cloak. Now, it covered her hair and part of her face as a makeshift shawl. Nevertheless, she kept her eyes down, towards the debris. If her presence here was obligatory, she would take as few risks as possible.

Gaelin yawned and fastened his cloak. They were among the refugees, just two specks in an endless sea of them. "What time is it?" he asked.

"I am unsure. However, I would estimate half past dawn."

"Day six, then."

"Yes."

"Where's Davi? And Serafine?"

The same question burned her. "I don't know."

With a low grumbling that River suspected had more to do with age than exasperation, Gaelin hoisted himself to his feet. "I will offer some praise for you magi," he said, watching a pair come around with a basket of buns. "You are exceptionally well-organized."

"Thank you," River said absently. She wasn't a mage herself, which rendered Gaelin's comment technically incorrect, but she let it slide. Something was bothering her, though she couldn't identify the source of her unease. Naturally, there were many possibilities: Davi's absence, the ever-looming threat of discovery, the world's imminent destruction, the scheduled sacrifice...to name but a few. Yet there was something else. She had the unnerving feeling that she was forgetting something, that there was an important fact she'd overlooked.

I am an MCB. I neither forget, nor overlook.

Then what is it?

"Excuse me." Gaelin was holding a bun he'd received. "May I offer you some?"

"No, thank you."

"Oh, yes... Of course." He bit into it, and winced. "Perhaps it's just as well. These could take the teeth from a bear."

She didn't laugh.

Having eaten as best he could, Gaelin brushed the dust from his robes. Together, they searched the campus for Davi and Serafine, attempting to give the impression they were stretching their legs after a long, cramped night. Maybe Gaelin really was; River supposed she wouldn't know. Her own limbs were functioning well since the last energy spell. So much so, she continually slowed her pace to accommodate the monk.

"Thank you," he wheezed. "Most considerate."

But was she truly considerate, or just well-designed? Humans agonized over the possibility of free will in a universe that contained That Which Was All. Yet their gods' designs might well be nuanced enough to allow their creations freedom of choice. She, conversely, was the product of mortals, not gods. Humans had designed her for a set of specific functions, using strict formulae to bind the aither. Her memory, penchant for organization, politeness, and deference were all means to an end, rather than components of her individuality.

The more emotion assaulted River, the more she wondered:

at what point did the spells stop and the "I" begin?

They rounded the pond and returned to their starting point. The library's shell trailed wisps of smoke that melded with the blackened sky. A stiff wind threatened to snatch the shawl from River's head. It was all so *different,* seeing it this way. A fugitive in her own home, an exile. Abruptly, she realized Gaelin likely had similar thoughts.

"Is it hard?" she asked, staring at the ruined library, "to know you will never return to a once-cherished place?"

He pulled his robes tighter about him, shivering. "Are you speaking of my banishment?"

"I was drawing parallels between our situations." Some of the confidence left her. Discussion of emotions was best left to humans. But, conversation begun, she couldn't abandon it. "I was obliged to leave my home and now court danger by returning. You were forced from yours. I am unfamiliar with protocol regarding banished monks, but I assume your return would not be met happily."

"You're quite right. Like you, it seems I must find a new home, a new family." He joined her vigil. "Apparently, similarities exist between us that one...that I...wouldn't imagine." Waving a hand towards the lawn full of refugees, he continued, "Neither I nor the Ecclesiat would expect such empathy, either from the Magistatiem, or from you yourself."

Empathy. I am capable of empathy.

River had barely digested this notion when shouting broke out on the lawns. The ordered rows of seated people dissolved into a pushing, scrambling mass. Magi ran through their midst, shooting blue sparks in the air and yelling for order, but the refugees ignored them. Several even knocked the smaller magi down.

River and Gaelin glanced to each other.

"Davi and Serafine?" he said.

"There is a distinct possibility."

They hurried across the lawns. Dry grass pricked River's ankles.

She lengthened her stride, then worried about leaving Gaelin behind. The monk wheezed, face red and shiny. The crowds parted, and she glimpsed Davi. That was enough; Gaelin would find her. She shifted into a sprint. Here, her facility with patterns and spatial relationships shone. People generally moved in subtle patterns; she dodged through the gaps that appeared between them.

She slowed just as she neared Davi. In truth, she wanted to fling herself at him, have him hold her. She restrained herself. Those arms held comfort and safety, but they burned.

Then she saw the true cause of the disturbance. Following behind Davi and a group of the Magistatiem's principal magi was Serafine. She ambled along, picking her way carefully over dropped travelling cases and food. Her wings rose like sails, feathers and hair melding into a blaze of scarlet.

"The Beast!" The scream wrenched itself from uncounted throats.

A selection of rough-looking men pushed the women and children to one side, and advanced on Serafine, fists raised. A few magi joined them, aither already glowing in their palms. In the leaping magic-light, Serafine looked wilder, more dangerous. Davi swung his arms in a circle, calling, "Get back! It's all right, don't hurt her!" River wanted to help, but fear rooted her to the spot. Any one of the Heads would recognize her in an instant.

She secured the cloth about her head and slunk towards the other women. The sense of unease, of missing something, nagged at her. She pushed it aside; rationally, she was forgetting nothing. There was no reason to feel this way.

Feeling again.

Are these emotions even worth their price?

Gaelin forced his way through to Davi. The two called something to each other, but River couldn't hear over the shouting. Terror gripped the carefully-balanced structure of the Magistatiem and squeezed until it burst.

The Chancellor himself mounted a small knoll. The bump

was an aberration, an unsightly bulge in the otherwise smooth lawns. Yet it served its purpose admirably.

Pare did not waste words. "Your attention...*please!*"

A tenuous silence fell. River edged back. The Chancellor had always intimidated her, towering over her while she worked, auditing evaluations, folded in the corner like a waiting spider. If there were papers for the creation or destruction of an MCB, his hand signed them.

"Thank you. Now, we are all aware of the unusual events of the past days..."

"The Beast!"

"No." He glared at the speaker like a professor with an unruly student. "It seems there is an element of truth to the Ecclesiat's superstitions."

"Kind of an understatement, don't you think, Chancellor?" Serafine's central pair of wings beat the air. Wind from their flapping forced River's head down. When she raised it, Serafine hovered over the lawns. The lowest pair of wings covered her feet, the uppermost veiled her face. And the third, largest pair maintained a steady rhythm, each flap like a heartbeat. Dust flew from the ground; people shielded their eyes. River imitated them; she felt the grit, if not the sting.

"Don't kill us!" A mother shrieked, throwing herself between her ragged girls and Serafine. Her voice trembled. "Take me, spare the children!"

The wings covered Serafine's mouth, but River imagined her grin. "I'm here to save you, not hurt you."

"Where have we heard that before?" a man snarled.

"Good question." Serafine gestured to the whole campus. "As I recall, it was during the Angel's flood. And if I remember correctly, it resulted in all of this."

People looked at the Magistatiem as though seeing it for the first time. The magi especially looked as though they'd all been burnt out simultaneously. A young mage next to River cupped some aither in her palm, and stared from it, to Serafine, and back.

"Now then. We haven't much time. All of you, listen to me." Her voice carried throughout the grounds, rose to the wall of clouds overhead. "This world is ending, and in that end, none of us shall be saved. Unless," she continued, surmounting the chorus of dismay, "we can make another world. A new one. To that end, we need magi. We have a spell, and we shall cast it together."

Pare showed no consternation at a divine being speaking from above him. "Each Head of Faculty has a section of the spell," he said. "Find your Head and receive your copy. We shall meet on the North Lawn in two hours' time."

Amidst the controlled chaos that followed, River heard one of the ragged little girls ask their mother, "How did they make copies so fast? Where are they?"

Before she could stop herself, River answered, "Each Head has only a single copy, but will duplicate it as needed by means of a simple replication spell. It is standard practice."

The girls and their mother regarded her with open, stunned faces. "Are you a mage?" the girl asked.

She should have remained inconspicuous. That was what the situation demanded. But no, she had to volunteer the information. Just as her spells directed. "No. I am simply knowledgeable about the aither."

"Hello, there!" Davi jogged over, and after raising his hands to show his intentions, took River by the arm. Pure emotion sparked wherever his fingers touched her skin. "May I borrow her? Thanks." He led her away to a relatively empty patch of lawn. He seemed incapable of standing still, compulsively shifted from foot to foot and rubbed his hands.

"I think we have it," he said. His joy was so obvious, she almost felt it. "The spells make sense, and I—I was writing a spell with Pare himself! Can you believe it? I was one of them, and they said my Aither Theory was *very well-reasoned,* and I could be in academic journals for this, and..." He deflated. "My future just got so much brighter, but if we can't do this, it's only going to last two more days. Tops."

Impulse battled caution and lost. Instead of hugging him, River clasped her hands behind her back. "If the spell works, you can always pursue your research in a new world. Consider the opportunities."

"That's true. If it works." He bit his lip. "We'll know soon enough."

XVI

This was her day. Alesta sipped a cup of water, alone in her dining room. The massive oak table comfortably seated a dozen or so, but she never had guests. Never would, in all likelihood. While in her younger days she had enjoyed Osvald's dinners as a chance to make connections with higher-placed monks, she saw little use for them now that she herself had attained her pinnacle.

Frivolous distraction. Fostering the flesh's drive to dominate the spirit's desires. An opportunity to lose the control she prized so highly.

No more.

An oil painting of the Angel occupied nearly a whole wall; the heavy frame, carved into art in its own right, stood in stark contrast to the lighter walls. Captured in rich swaths of colour, He seemed almost alive, a prisoner of the canvas. His golden hair, so like Alesta's own, tumbled down his white neck, reflecting the light of a promised paradise. Alesta carried the message in His stern gaze wherever she went.

Few may enter here.

Alesta shook her head, as though it would dislodge the breathless anxiety within. The apprehension was like a rat, monitoring her with red, pinprick eyes, snapping at her soul whenever the faintest thought of sin brushed by her.

"I am good," she said aloud. Too late, she considered that the boy might hear her. But no, he had gone quiet during the night. Hopefully not dead. Not yet.

A wave of anger and shame flowed over her, thick and hot as lava. All around, her grip was slipping. The monks, the choirs, the people, everything. And at this critical time, too. Obviously, she was unfit to serve the Angel. She had failed to carry out His most basic commands. She was a fraud, a nothing.

Worthless.

A cry broke in her chest, and she wept. Wept for her human flaws, for her sheer incompetence. But she would be sanctified. Fittingly, perhaps, her blood would redeem her.

Those few who cleaved to His standards enjoyed His rewards.

Davi couldn't believe his eyes. Magi converged on the North Lawn, so many he couldn't begin to count them all. At least one representative from every faculty and guild crammed onto the stretch of grass between the pond's northern edge and the academic and residential buildings. On the south side, from the pond to the Chancellor's Tower, the refugees and non-magical waited. The hopeful looks and words they gave the magi simultaneously flattered and worried him.

The spell was complex, but rough. Serafine was the key to it all. She was, in St. Memoyah's words, *that with the ears to hear.* He studied his part of the spell. Consensus was, if they could mimic the world's initial conditions closely enough, with the aither, any echo of the Hapax should come to the fore.

Which meant stopping time and space. The dimensions were linked: no time, no space, no aither. Whatever would be left to the fill the Void had to be the Hapax, which Serafine could then pick out.

Or so they hoped, anyway.

Madness.

He took his place. All the faculties grouped together. Tam saluted as he left his friends in Life Magics. Blistered skin peeled on his nose and forehead; he was still too burnt-out to cast anything. "Good luck!" he called.

Davi gave a small wave. Time to focus. He scanned the lines of text and formulae again. Everything added up. Pare himself had done the final check-through, after declaring Davi "a sound and ready mind." Just remembering the praise made him beam. They'd survive this, and when they did, Davi had a feeling he'd made a powerful new ally.

The ally in question was clearing a space in the centre of the lawn. Pare raised a single red flag. Silence. Davi was acutely aware of his own breath. A checked blue-and-red flag. Davi readied his chalice. His own lay somewhere in the rubble of the dormitories. If there was time later, he'd go look for it. In the meantime, he had Tam's.

Hundreds of magi gripped their chalices, rims open to the moaning sky. Every calibre from rough-hewn wood to bejewelled silver, every size from a child's drinking cup to basins on sticks. Those without chalices used their own palms. Davi gripped Tam's chalice. His friend's was made of oak; the stem felt warm and smooth. Comforting.

Blue flag.

Davi's gaze dropped to his spell. He listened, caught the sound of humming aither. Smiled as he remembered the tiny strings. Who'd have thought something so small could hold such power? But no time for that now, that was for the articles he'd write after the fact. The humming grew in Davi's ears, more forceful, more insistent.

Then he had it. He could have wept. This was what he was meant to do. The aither's song was as well-known to him as his mother's lullabies. He measured out as much as he could, and plunged back to his reality.

The aither followed him, burbling from a slit in space into his chalice. He spared a glance at the other magi. So many streams of aither poured into the sea of magi, the air looked like a dripping sponge. Eerie blue light lit the campus; the aither leaped in chalices like flames burning on torches.

Now the real challenge began. Persuading the aither to assume the form it'd had at the beginning of creation was difficult enough. Keeping it stable enough for Serafine and safe enough for the magi was another challenge altogether. He prodded the aither, stretched it, reminded it how it felt at the beginning, when those vibrating little strings were still, and it was the only thing in creation.

He was entrenched in that section of the spell when the trouble started.

It was nothing major at first. Simply a matter of taking a firmer hand with the aither, upping his force a bit. Or maybe it was someone else, another mage out there who wasn't as convincing as his colleagues. Davi kept going, confident the problem would disappear.

It didn't. The aither grew unsteady in his chalice. No longer waiting for instructions, it looked almost as though it were boiling. Deep in his mind, Davi felt the spell structure shattering.

"Come on," he spat through clenched teeth. "Like at the very beginning..."

The aither bucked. Whole spell casting webs unravelled, and around him, Davi sensed magi losing control. Aither snapped back to its own dimension. Right in front of him was a young man, had to be a first year. He went down hard. Tell-tale burns were already spreading over his neck and arms. More magi collapsed, the effect rippling from a few key points.

They were reaching the critical juncture. Davi was struggling to keep everything together, throwing together new instructions to compensate for the burnt-out magi. No use. He may as well have been keeping floodwaters back with a bucket.

"Davi!" Serafine's voice. "Get clear!"

"We can do this, we—"

"Now!"

Shocked into action, he severed the connection with the aither. Not clean or fast enough: it cracked to its own dimension like a lightning bolt. It caught Davi, and his head exploded with fire and flashing lights. He had just enough time to mourn losing control of the aither in front of Pare, and then thought was impossible. The pain seemed to melt his brain; his skull was an oven. Heat scorched him within and without. A final, cataclysmic burst of white. Then he sank to the ground, wrapped in darkness.

———

He was still on the ground when he awoke, lying spread-eagled with a rock digging into his back. An attempt to sit up brought waves of nausea and worsened his headache. The campus swam in and out of focus.

Sitting was too much effort. He collapsed again. A layer of heat prickled, trapped between his guts and skin that felt two sizes too small. Vomit surged over his tongue. He turned his head, got most of it on the grass.

"Davi?"

River crouched beside him. She'd lost the shawl she'd been wearing, but he couldn't form the sentences to ask where it'd gone. He reached for her face. Shyly, she guided his hand to her hair.

"River...what happened?"

"The spell failed."

He didn't think he could get more out, so he tossed his hand. Apparently, she understood, for she continued, "There was a massive breakdown in the spell's structure. I'm surprised you're awake, most are still unconscious. How do you feel?"

"Not great." Twin fists of pain slammed into his temples, and he groaned. "Pretty bad headache."

"You're talking, though. That's good. Can you walk?"

"If you help me."

She offered her shoulder. Gasping, he pulled himself upright. Her strength caught most people off guard; River was a small woman, but she supported him without a hint of strain.

Cautiously, Davi lifted his head. A stab through the eyes and forehead, but he managed to stay standing.

River fumbled in a small satchel with her free hand and withdrew a flask. She snapped the top with her thumb, and then pressed it on Davi. He lifted it to dry lips and drank. Water. Cool, pure water. As it rushed down his throat, he felt life return. The headache didn't abate much, and his feet were unsteady, but he felt less like a lurching corpse.

With a sigh, he wiped his mouth. "Where are the Heads?"

"Most are in the Healers' tents. Pare is organizing non-magi to attend to the burned."

"So he's all right?"

"He abandoned the spell and braced himself when it first disintegrated. He was unconscious for perhaps four hours."

"Four... River, what time is it now?"

Those lovely dark eyes had never frightened him more. "Five past noon." The unspoken question hung between them. Perhaps knowing he wouldn't ask it, she said, "According to Gaelin, the sacrifice will occur at dawn."

He let loose a long string of curses. Ignoring them, River led him to a Healers' tent on the other side of the pond. Cots spilled from the tent onto the grass. Red-faced, blistered magi moaned and feebly grasped for water.

Serafine and Gaelin drifted through the rows, offering drinks and cool cloths. More non-magi had formed a bucket chain from pond to tent. Pare emerged from the tent. Before Davi could hide his face, or River's, the Chancellor spotted them. He strode towards them with the patience of a panther on its prey.

"This Hapax was not in the aither."

Davi tried to turn River around, to think of some way to distract Pare, but the Chancellor gave a humourless laugh. "I know about River, Sanders. The Seraph there told me exactly what to expect if we attempted to dismantle her...as we should have done, by law, days ago."

Something unreadable passed over River, but she said nothing.

Pare was waiting for an answer. Davi worked his jaw and ignored the hammer pounding his brain. "I'm sorry, sir. It doesn't make sense, it should be there. St. Memoyah says...um, River?"

All expression was drained from her voice. "...*in that place where it first resounded, it echoes there still.*"

Gaelin and Serafine had joined them. A good thing, for Davi was beginning to feel slightly hysterical. "So the Hapax has to be part of the aither. It's what Ael made first. Right, Gaelin?"

With his hands tucked inside his long robes, his silvery hair and beard dishevelled, Gaelin looked like the archetypal man of wisdom. He pushed his now-filthy spectacles up his nose. "The Tablets state that, yes. After *the first Word of Ael sounded,* we are told, *Ael separated aither from Void, and lo, the universe was aither.*" Gaelin regarded Pare calmly. "So you see, it seems Davi has reasoned this quite well. A fine scholar."

Gaelin defending him? Well, with the Last Day approaching, he should expect the impossible.

River frowned. Pare caught her expression and glared. His fingers started to cup, and then he glanced to Serafine. He clenched his fist instead. "Well then, if the aither was the first thing Ael made..."

"It wasn't."

At River's words, Pare made a sound as though choking. He wasn't the only one surprised; Davi saw his own shock reflected in Gaelin's open mouth. River fidgeted, awkward at finding herself the centre of everyone's focus.

"It wasn't the first thing Ael made," she repeated. "That's why the spell failed. That's the reason for my irrational disquiet."

"Intuition?" Pare snapped.

"Her intuition may save your life," Davi shot back. Then the blood drained to his toes. The aither must have burned him worse than he thought—such insolence with the Chancellor? Yet his doubts melted under River's smile.

"Well then," Gaelin said, in a patronizing tone, "if the aither wasn't Ael's first creation, what was?"

"Ael's own self." River sounded more confident now; she was on ground supported by text. Davi hoped she knew where she was going with it. "Recall the first sentence of the Tablet: *Where there was no time, before there was any place, the first Word of Ael sounded.* Aelism also informs us that *the Word was with Ael and the Word was Ael.* Therefore, it is the Word, and thus Ael, that makes the first appearance in the universe. Not the aither."

"Fine," Gaelin said, "but then the Hapax echoes within Ael's self. If Ael is the Hapax, then both are lost. And if the Hapax echoes in Ael, both are lost forever."

River shook her head. "Not necessarily. Consider where the Word sounded: the Void. It is this Void that lacks time and place, it is this Void from which Ael separated both Ael's self and the aither, and it is therefore this Void in which the Hapax echoes."

More than anything, he wanted to sweep her from her feet, but even in the depths of burnout, he sensed that wasn't a good idea. Instead, he forced whatever remained of his intellectualism to the fore.

"So far, I agree with you," he said. "Wholeheartedly. But then, where is this Void?"

River was silent a moment, and then her eyes widened. "Ael separated the aither from the Void, and then the other four elements from the aither. Am I correct, Gaelin?"

"Yes..."

"The aither supersedes our own dimensions. Would it not then be possible for the aither itself to be within another dimension? The Void?"

"Yes!" Serafine exclaimed. "That's why the Angel and I can't hear it—it's the same reason you're mostly unaware of the aither."

"Or my sketch people and the third dimension," Davi said.

Pare did not join the excitement, although a begrudging tone of admiration sounded as he said, "Assume your *nesting doll* theory of dimensions is correct. The problem remains: how do we get the Hapax to our dimension?"

"St. Memoyah answers that," Davi said. He thought a moment, and then ceded to River with a small bow.

She looked alive. Even inches from the Chancellor, emotion was getting the better of her. "*And how shall it enter the world? As do all things, and as they have done before.*"

"Helpful," Davi muttered.

"It is, actually," Gaelin said. "I don't know much about dimensions, or aither, but I know of one time when someone eradicated certain boundaries..." He smiled at Serafine.

She blew a lock of red hair from her face. "True."

"Could you do it again?"

"No."

Pare folded his arms and gave her the same look Davi had seen him give to underachieving students. "Why not?"

"Because I was already in the aither's dimension. I've never been in the Void." She shrugged. "If it overarches the aither, you'd need to pass it through aither." A blue spark danced across her fingertips.

"Serafine..." Davi said slowly, "how exactly did you get the aither through?"

"Through love. A love strong enough to breach the boundaries between dimensions." The spark erupted into a brilliant blue sphere. "The aither is between the Hapax and us, just like I was between you and the aither. So if it's your medium, you need aither capable of loving. You need aither with a soul."

Pare sighed. "Then we're at the beginning again. It's hopeless."

Agreement danced on the tip of Davi's tongue, and then died. A chill swept through him, expelled his burned-out fog as effectively as a plunge in the ocean. He didn't want to say it. He wouldn't.

But, naturally, River had seen the solution even faster. And, naturally, she would not keep quiet. "I am aither," she said. "I am aither made flesh: a Magically Created Being. If I loved, I could act as a conduit for the Hapax."

He didn't know what to do. The campus, even the City itself, shrank in significance. Instinctively, Davi checked Serafine. She was impassive, in stark contrast to Pare's open disgust. The Chancellor snorted. "Of course. The last time an MCB loved, innocent people were killed. And I'm to believe another MCB will save us?"

River's face became stone. Any light the thrill of discovery had sparked in her withered and died. Davi fumed, ready to take Pare to task, but Serafine shook her head behind Pare's back. Biting his words back, Davi gripped River's hand.

Gaelin coughed. "River, I may be wrong but do you not already have certain...feelings for Davi?"

Serafine stepped in, ready to rescue. "Not enough," she said. "Take it from someone who knows. The kind of love we're talking is a full, pure love. None of this tentative affection you've been feeling, River. You have to open yourself up to it. Embrace it fully. And that's something you haven't done yet."

"And what if she did?" Davi said, more urgently. "What would happen?"

A grim, distant look settled over Serafine. "The Void, carrying all things, including the Hapax, would pass through her soul. That's the point, you see. Anything that can love has a soul, love supersedes dimensional boundaries...and so the need for a soul."

"And then?"

"Then, since it's the Word, and the Word is with Ael and is Ael..." The pause that followed stretched too long. "It would be a very powerful force."

"Would she survive?"

Serafine did not address him, turned instead to River. "If that Word were to pass through your soul, it would overcome you. And you, as we know you now, would cease to exist."

250

River froze.

"She'd be annihilated?" Davi said.

"Let's think of it as apotheosis."

A cold lump slid from his throat to his stomach. "Then we need to think of something else."

Gaelin stirred, regretful wisdom pasted all over him. "Davi."

"No!"

How dare the monk look so smug and sure of himself? Didn't he realize? Didn't he care? The headache returned full force, and Davi's knees wobbled.

"It's the only way," Gaelin said.

"It can't be. We'll find another. Right, River?"

She had retreated into herself. "I observe that I have yet to be consulted for my opinion on this matter."

Pare shrugged. "What opinion? You'll do as you're told."

Before Davi could protest, Serafine's stance went tense and dangerous. "I like you, Pare, but let's get something straight. River isn't your ordinary MCB. You'd better remember that. Now, River, what do you think?"

"I cannot easily reach a solution. If I fully accept my developing emotions, I will be destroyed. If I do not, the world will be destroyed."

The intensity of Serafine's stare rattled Davi, even though it wasn't directed at him. Serafine lowered her voice. "You can't force it, you know. If it's there, you can suppress it, but you can't make something from nothing."

"Well, if the fate of our world rests with Emerald's successor, I'm off to tend to the survivors." Pare wiped his hands on his pants, his nose wrinkling. "Not that there's much point. Good evening."

When the Chancellor left, Davi was ready to begin a thousand-item list of reasons why River should save herself, when he stopped. If loving was going to let the Hapax through, that meant she could never love...*him*. Not the way he loved her.

Her choice. It had to be her choice, or he was as bad as Pare.

But that didn't mean he wanted her to destroy herself.

"River," he said.

She ignored him. "We should discuss Praeton. Our plan to confront the Ecclesiat with magi is no longer feasible."

Serafine nodded. "Too many burned. All right then, we'll use trickery. Let's see now, Gaelin can't go; he'd be recognized and ousted. I can't go, same problem. That leaves you two."

"Wait a second," Davi said, "can't you just disguise yourself?"

Raging winds tore at Serafine's hair. Her brilliant blue eyes dulled, and she rubbed her arms. "I'm very tired, Davi. I need to keep something for tomorrow."

Seven of seven. Unreal to think of it. "Then how do we save him? I'm too burned for magic right now, and I doubt Alesta will hand him over if we ask nicely."

Gaelin coughed. "I have an idea. It's sacrilege, and breaks countless rules, but...it's better than the alternative." He knelt in the dust and traced an outline of the Ecclesiat. "Enter the main doors, like everyone else. Then go to the catacombs, they're open to the public. The entrance is...*here*." He stabbed the dust. "Will you remember all this?"

"I will," River said.

"Good. Now, there are a series of tunnels..." Lines swirled in the dust, snakelike. Gaelin frowned, paused with his finger in mid-air. "You'll need to bypass those on watch duty. The network runs under the nave, and merges with the crypts."

"And the Angel's Sepulchre," Serafine said.

"Yes, but you needn't go in there. Follow the stairs into the inner sanctum. From the sanctum, exit at the back of the chancel." He added in more details. Davi squinted, envisioning the Ecclesiat, imagining himself there.

"We'd be behind Alesta," he said.

"Yes, the element of surprise. In the confusion, you can remove Praeton." The monk pointed to a spot on his diagram. "Up to the choir room, and along the corridor. There's a staircase that leads to the bell-tower. Follow it down, there's a door to the narthex."

"Why can't we get in that way?"

"Because that door is locked on the narthex side. We don't want the laity getting into the tower." He patted Davi's arm, a paternal gesture that was somehow irksome and encouraging at the same time. "Any other questions?"

None. Between the four of them, they figured they had enough time for a scanty meal—even the white rolls were running low, now—and a quick nap for Davi and Gaelin. Davi protested this, but secretly he was grateful. His body craved sleep. Needed it to heal from the trauma it'd borne. He reclined on the scratchy, dry grass. The hulking carcasses of Magistatiem buildings reared to the dark sky.

Something moved in the gloom, high overhead. Many somethings, tiny and glittering. One touched Davi's cheek: a cold pinprick that vanished in an instant.

It was snowing.

XVII

The snows fell steadily through the night. Sleep was out of the question, but Davi found himself fighting to stay awake. Closing his eyes for ten minutes seemed like an excellent idea. Let the snow blanket him. He curled under an overhanging section of wall and alternated a trancelike half-sleep with fits of wakefulness. Every time he woke, River was next to him, regarding him as seriously as a guard dog.

He wasn't sure what she was thinking. He wasn't sure he wanted to know.

Partially-glimpsed forms haunted the border between nightmare and reality. Tongues of fire lashed the sky, blasting the snow to steam. The ground rumbled as though the soil itself was groaning in pain. A family huddled not far from Davi. With each jolt to the waking world, he saw the snow cover them a little more. He almost got up to help them, or mentioned something to River, but he was too tired to think, let alone move. And so he fell into slumber, not convinced it wasn't all a dream.

By the time River murmured, "Time to go," they were completely buried.

Davi winced. Snow continued to drift through the predawn night. Now that he was awake, he heard more than the earth's moans. All the world wailed through screeching wind and the scream of splitting rock. Rifts ruptured the ground, devouring buildings that tumbled down in cascades of stone, along with unwary men and women who fell with truncated sobs. He shivered again, the cold and the sound as keen as a knife's edge in his ribs.

Stumbling over, Gaelin skirted one of the chasms. The tip of his nose looked wrong: waxy and white. The lines in the monk's face were etched deeper, and his entire body shook.

"Are you leaving now?"

Davi forced a reply through chattering teeth. "Yes."

"Serafine and I will come. We'll wait across the square."

Brushing snow from her shoulder, River said, "We're losing time."

If anyone noticed the four of them go, they did nothing. Unseasonal winter strangled the City in a freezing embrace. The Magistatiem's walls offered some protection from the wind, but outside, snow throttled the streets. In some places the drifts were as high as Davi's waist. They fought their way through the streets, moving so slowly that Davi despaired of reaching the Ecclesiat in time.

Everything felt too heavy. The snow that grabbed at his feet and blocked his way. The enormity of the task ahead. His own limbs. And most of all, the sentence that endlessly chased itself through his thoughts.

Seven of seven.

He fell to his knees. "I can't do it."

Serafine prodded his back. She blended with the City so well, only her flaming hair distinguished her from the snow and shadowed, broken buildings. "Yes, you can."

"No."

"Praeton's waiting for you. Up." Hooking her hands under his arms, she hauled him to his feet. "Not so bad, is it?" she said, patting him on the back.

Warmth spread through his thin shirt, through his chest and along his limbs. The pinched, tingling sensation in his fingers and toes dissipated, replaced by gentle heat. Davi flexed his fingers, bewildered. Serafine patted him again, and the feeling intensified.

"You're welcome."

They met few people between the Magistatiem and Ecclesiat. Few living people. They avoided human-sized lumps, bowed their heads as they walked by arms and legs that poked from the snow like monstrous blackened flowers.

Gaelin made the sign of the Three. "None were prepared for this. It's summer, who would fear the cold? And this far south?"

No answer was necessary. It wasn't just that there was a blizzard in the summer. It wasn't just that the snowfall was greater than the scanty film the City normally received. An eerie tension hung in the air. The gentle snow was made even more twisted by its play at innocence.

Serafine halted at the edge of the square, in front of a store. The front window was smashed and the sign torched, but Davi remembered it had been a cobbler's. Nothing remained of the neat rows of shoes. The shelves lay in splinters, even the meanest bits of leather long stolen. Serafine guided Gaelin inside. Broken glass framed her; Davi saw she'd have a good view of the Ecclesiat.

"We'll wait here," she said. "When you find Praeton, get here as fast as you can."

"And then?"

She rubbed her shoulders, where her wings would be. "We hope for the best."

"Thanks for the encouragement."

Other footprints crossed the square. Small ones that stopped halfway. Larger ones in pairs. They were in various stages of being filled in. Cobblestones poked through some; Davi guessed those were the most recent. They clambered through the Ecclesiat's doors. No hesitating on the threshold this time; the Ecclesiat's warmth sucked them in.

Even now she was prepared for opposition. Threats of flogging, forced fasts, banishment—she carried a full arsenal to the Chapter House. Sometimes it took several examples to get a message through. No need this time. Her hand-picked monks mutely accepted her instructions. Strap the boy to the altar. Knock him unconscious if need be. And then—

The blade.

———

The narthex was so crowded that it had been easier to move through the snowdrifts. River strove to hide her face, but Davi suspected she needn't have bothered. Frozen skin, exhaustion, and missing family members demanded people's attention far more than one more couple trudging into the cathedral.

Candles glowed in the aisles, but they did little to illuminate the Ecclesiat's darkest corners. If anything, they accentuated the shadows, allowed things to hide in the contrast they created. The statues of saints and paintings of the Beast and Angel had a sinister cast to their features that Davi hadn't noticed before.

He glanced up the aisle. Monks busied themselves around the altar, positioning candles and urns of sacred water. No sign of Praeton or Alesta. River squeezed one of his fingers.

"An hour to dawn," she whispered.

The stairs to the catacombs were along the northern wall. They battled the flow of people going eastwards towards the altar, and cut across the cathedral. Too many people. The smell of their closeness permeated the air, its cloyingness both agitating and sedating. Sweat and other bodily smells mixed with incense to set Davi's head throbbing again.

There was some relief as they descended to the catacombs. A few monks stood watch, stepping forward whenever someone drew too near to the coffins. Coarse-bricked walls muted the noise from above. It was like stepping into a pocket world; connected to, yet separate from, the Ecclesiat above. Recesses punctuated the walls. Stone coffins lay within them, covered in angular carvings that boxed the name of the deceased.

"Relatively important monks are interred here," River said,

"those who held middling positions." She jerked her head towards a smaller, winding corridor. "The higher one's position, the closer one is interred to the inner sanctum."

Davi pretended to inspect the coffin before him. *Sister Ema.* Feeling the attention of a monk upon him, he moved his lips as though in prayer. River copied him. The monk wandered off, but Davi knew better than to relax.

"He said there'd be monks watching. How do we get past them?"

"Like this." River strode away from him, down a broader tunnel. Davi stared at the ceiling, trying to realign his inner compass. She was moving away from the inner sanctum.

He chased her. "What are you doing?"

Around the corner, she paused in front of another coffin, one set at about chest height. *Brother Honrael, Chronicler.* With a murmur that Davi couldn't make out, she pushed at the coffin lid.

———

The boy slumped in his chair. Faint purple mottled his fingers; perhaps she'd tied the ropes too tight. No matter. The extra pain just eradicated more sin.

His head lolled, and his hair stuck up in sweaty spikes. Alesta's lip curled at the sight of him. Thank the Angel his eyes were closed and not beseeching her, meek and brown as a fawn's.

A cuff to the side of his head woke him. He recoiled as far from her as his bonds allowed. The action stirred no sympathy in Alesta. Only disgust. As disappointing as the abomination's escape had been, she had to admit the boy made an excellent sacrifice. Young and fragile, yet also soaked in sin requiring extermination.

No. Not an excellent sacrifice.

A perfect one.

———

Aghast, Davi whispered, "You can't do that!"

"I am sure, considering the circumstances, Brother Honrael would overlook this disrespect." The lid shifted slightly to reveal a sliver of blackness.

Gooseflesh prickled on Davi's neck and arms. He felt ghoulish, like a grave robber. Utterly calm, River dusted her hands and strode back the way they'd come. She marched to a monk and, with assertion Davi had never heard before, gave him what could only be described as a talking-to.

"I must say, I am appalled at this treatment of the Order's deceased."

The monk looked as shocked as Davi felt. "Excuse me?"

She pointed down the hall. "I went to pray at the tomb of Brother Honrael, and saw that someone has prised his coffin lid off. Vandals, no doubt. Most likely after some relic to protect them in these End Days." She rose on tiptoe, battling for every inch of height. "I find it blasphemous that such disrespect is allowed to flourish beneath the Angel Himself."

The monk cowered, flustered. "Of course, miss. I agree, miss. Let me see to it." He shuffled down the hall and out of sight.

A huge grin eased some of Davi's discomfort. "River, that was incredible! *I* was scared of you."

She offered a slow, shy smile in return. "I'm glad I was convincing. But come, while he's gone."

The ceiling sloped downwards; Davi's hair soon brushed the top of the tunnel. The corridor also narrowed, giving him the uncomfortable feeling of walking into a coffin himself. Eventually they reached a point where the wall sconces stopped. Davi unhooked the last lantern and carried it with them.

Lamplight played across the rock, the flame sputtering as the wick burned lower. Though he longed to hold the warm glass close to him, Davi lifted the lamp high, spreading light as far as he could. From the corner of his eye, natural irregularities rearranged themselves to look like grimacing faces, or writhing demons. No sound penetrated here. Aside from their footsteps and Davi's rapid breathing, the silence was absolute.

"Look," River said. "The tombs are more elaborate."

The coffin-filled recesses had given way to proper chambers and shrines housing effigies of the dead. Iron gates set into the rock sealed them off from the corridor. Jewel-encrusted reliquaries bore whatever sacred scraps the deceased had left behind, and rubies and sapphires winked through the gloom. The number of open tombs decreased the further in they went. Imposing seals replaced them, heavy doors of wood and stone bearing names, epitaphs, and the double triangle. The markings were shallowly-cut, obscured by the dust of years long since passed. The hand of the ages pressed on them both, and their attempts at conversation faltered and died.

Something was watching them.

Davi initially dismissed it as paranoia. Understandable, given how little sleep he'd had, not to mention the after-effects of burnout. Some magi who'd had severe, repetitive burns simply ended their careers by going mad. It was no surprise he was jittery.

But the sense of something lurking just out of sight refused to leave him. They'd taken so many twists and turns, he doubted he could find the path back. Not by himself. He walked so close to River that he stepped on her heels.

She sighed. "There's nothing to fear. The deceased are incapable of causing harm."

"I'm not worried about them."

He thought he heard rustling. Like wings.

———

Alesta slashed the cords and growled, "Move."

The boy climbed to his feet, cringing. He stepped forward and nearly fell. Trailing a hand on the wall, he hobbled from the room. Alesta kept the knife close to his throat.

"Elber!" she called. "Get over here."

The sub-prior hastened from the second floor. He flicked beads of sweat from his brow. "How may I serve you, Mother Throne?"

She thrust the boy at him. For the first time, Praeton cried out. No tears, but a whimper. Alesta's eyes narrowed. "There is a pail and robes in the front room. Prepare him. And then bring him to the cloisters."

Praeton would weep yet.

———

"Davi, the Angel has not manifested Himself in a physical form. He cannot be here."

"Just tell me where His sepulchre is, all right?"

As soon as he'd spoken, he regretted the tone. But he didn't apologize. Too nervous to stand still, he paced in circles. The massive weight of the cathedral crushed him. How could it all remain standing? Surely there was less air than before. The Ecclesiat must be sinking, the stones overhead rushing to flatten him against the core of the earth.

River caught hold of his arm. "The Angel's Sepulchre isn't far. By Gaelin's map, one simply has to follow that corridor." Ahead, three passages split in separate directions. The centre one, Davi knew in his bones, led to Him.

He started for it.

"Davi, what are you doing?"

"I want to see it." His heart thumped against his ribs like a frantic, caged bird. "I need to see it!"

"There is no reason to."

"I just...just need to make sure He's still there. That He's not stalking the darkness." And, unable to contain himself any longer, he broke into a run.

———

Seven of seven. The phrase pounded a triumphant tattoo, matching Alesta's heartbeat. They had nearly made it. She had led the Ecclesiat through the End Days. Soon enough, the Angel King would rise, and her sins would be obliterated for eternity.

No choirs today. No music of any sort for this service. Just a few loyal monks to tend to the candles and mop up the blood. They were already forming their lines in the cloisters. Alesta polished her new Throne's standard, a small smile her only outward sign of the rapture within.

I have not failed You. She kissed the figure of the Angel adorning the staff. With careful, loving movements, she wiped a particle of dust from between His wings. *I have not failed.*

They were early, but the lines were ready. Standard in hand, Alesta inspected them one by one. The Angel seemed to observe as well, from His perch on her staff. At last, she nodded her approval.

"We are ready. All we lack is the sacrifice."

―――

He couldn't see where he was going. The lamp bounced as he ran, swinging too much to be of any use. The air chilled, and the passage constricted further. His elbows scraped the sides of the tunnel, and he felt the cool wetness of blood pool on his skin. He ignored it, just as he ignored River's shouts behind him.

At last, the passage ended against a black mass. A few moments passed before he realized it wasn't the end, but rather, a door. Under the lamplight, the wood gleamed, dark and beautiful.

"Davi!"

He paid no attention, threw his shoulder into the door. A dull ache reverberated in the ball of his shoulder. He paid no attention to that, either. The presence engulfed him. The Angel was so close, he sensed Him, removed from him by nothing but wood. He had to see Him. Need raged through his veins, seeped out through his steaming skin. There was supposed to be a statue. What if He was there, but His statue was not? Another shove, and he was in.

―――

Alesta was on the verge of sending a messenger to fetch Elber when the sub-prior arrived. He carried a thick cord that wound about Praeton's neck. A precaution, as Alesta had ordered, though it didn't look like the boy was interested in escaping. Circles like bruises ringed his eyes, an irksome contrast to his pink, scrubbed face. He stood quietly, listlessly, while Alesta issued final directions. She slapped the flat of the blade against her palm as she spoke, but the boy gave no reaction.

"On this final day of the world, we perform this duty for Angelus Rex, the Angel King."

"Ruler of us all," the monks answered.

Praeton's lip quivered. Alesta smiled.

They entered the cathedral.

———

Davi panted, his chest heaving. His eyes and brain were talking in different languages. He knew he was seeing something, but he couldn't understand what. Gold dazzled him, everywhere gold, on the ceiling, the walls, the floor. Gradually, a shadow overtook him. He followed it towards the back of the room, until his eyes came to rest on an enormous statue.

It loomed larger than Davi; its wings touched the ceiling. The entire statue was cut from white stone he could not identify. The suggestion of movement haunted the Angel's stone robes, His curling hair. The statue almost breathed.

It was here. Not roaming the catacombs, but locked within His sepulchre. Davi shuddered. The thought had occurred to him: perhaps the Angel's statue was kept here not for His protection, but for the Ecclesiat's.

A tap on his elbow made him jump. River had entered the room unheard. Her mouth opened as though to speak, but then, catching sight of the Angel, she closed it with a snap. Blinking furiously, she turned her back to both Davi and the statue.

"Are you satisfied?" she said. "The statue is here. As I told you it would be."

Her dark head, seen from behind, seemed as impenetrable as the Angel Himself. Davi approached her. The way she stiffened sent a pang through him, but like sunlight piercing mist, it diffused some of the panic. He began to wonder if he'd been acting the fool.

"I'm sorry," he said. The fog in his brain retreated, hovering at the edges. He shook his head. "Must have been the air down here. Kind of thick, don't you think?"

"I wouldn't know."

An air of brittleness pervaded her every word, every movement. Davi wanted to go over and touch her, but he was afraid she might break in his arms. Instead, he awkwardly followed her from the sepulchre. She shut the door with a deliberate *thud*.

"I... I guess we should get to the inner sanctum," he said. "What time is it?"

She was already striding away. "Nearly dawn."

In all her years, she had never seen the Ecclesiat so full. The pews groaned and creaked under the burden of far too many people. Those who hadn't arrived early enough jammed the centre aisle, or clung to the bases of columns. Hands emerged to grab her robes as she led the procession, fingers tearing at her like thorns. She swallowed her irritation, offered her blessing as she went.

Coughing, sobs, and whispers eroded the usual solemn silence of procession. The ordinary sounds, amplified by acoustics and sheer numbers, buzzed in Alesta's ears like a horde of locusts. She gritted her teeth. They were approaching the altar now. Nearly there, then she could speak, and this racket would fall away.

The hem of her robes slithered over the chancel steps. She hitched them up, praying no one saw the undignified gesture. These robes were the most formal of the Throne's vestments. Heavy, bejewelled fabric dragged her arms down, slowed her walk. The stole hurt her shoulders, but she never once longed to remove it. She bore it for the Angel.

As she made the acknowledgement to Him, thunder rattled the Ecclesiat. A monk behind her risked burns as he jumped too near a candle. This was no thunder like she'd heard before, not even in the nightmares of childhood. This was thunder like

264

an almighty beast shaking the cathedral in its jaws.

The sacrifice had to be done now.

Elber dragged the boy forward. He was rough; the boy tripped on the steps and went sprawling in front of the altar. Ear cocked, Alesta stood ready to pounce on any sympathetic murmurings. There were none.

Praeton had always been a weakling, small for his age, but next to the Angel he looked frail, as though the darkness and promise of what was to come had aged him to a weedy old man. Perhaps this lulled Elber into false security, for he loosened his hold on the rope.

Alesta's reaction was slowed. Praeton's was not. He wrenched himself free of Elber and hurdled over the chancel rail. Monks were still processing up the side aisle closest to the cloisters; he sprinted for the side nearest the catacombs, the rope trailing behind him.

A cathedral full of people, and all they did was sit mute and useless as rocks. The ceremonial robes hindered Alesta; walking was a trial, let alone running. Rage simmered. To come this close and lose it to a fool and a child...she would not let it happen. The awful, unearthly thunder rumbled again, closer this time, and her cheeks flushed.

In a voice that matched the storm, she bellowed, "In the name of the Angel King, stop him!"

Finally, the congregation was goaded to action. A burly young man half-fell from his pew as Praeton ran by, but the boy weaselled from his grasp. More people were on their feet now, beginning to give chase. Praeton cast a pale, terrified glance over his shoulder, and dashed straight into a clump of men.

He veered away from them, but they had blocked his path. The crowds forced the boy against the north wall. He backed into the stone, as though hoping there was a secret door. A thin smile settled on Alesta's lips. He was a fawn indeed—a fawn finally cornered by her hounds.

And, just like hounds, they sniffed at her feet for approval as they dragged him forward. He wasn't listless now, kicking and punching like the demon-child he was. It took half a dozen men to strap him to the altar. Even then, he refused to lie quiet, gnashing his teeth and shouting a name, over and over. Alesta couldn't quite recognize it. Something like Serafeem.

Another check to his bonds satisfied her. Let him writhe and struggle all he liked; the ropes would hold. Thus appeased, she launched into her sermon. She was rather proud of this one. She should be, for it was one of the last she would give in this world.

Anticipation cloaked the Ecclesiat. She sensed that few were actually listening to her. They were waiting for the main event, the act that would save them.

Well. Why make them wait any longer?

She withdrew the blade.

———

The steps leading to the surface seemed endless. Rough stone threatened to trip him, send him stumbling back to the labyrinthine darkness below. He concentrated on following River. Wherever she placed her foot, he placed his. So much of his attention was devoted to this task that when she pushed open a trapdoor, it took him a moment to notice the faint stream of light.

Another chamber. Like in the Angel's Sepulchre, a single colour ruled here. However, the inner sanctum was lined not with gold, but with white marble. A ghostly altar dominated the chamber. A few sticks from the Candlemass wood pile spilled from the altar to the floor.

They hadn't agreed to silence, but neither spoke. The domed ceiling caught every sound they made and threw it back ten-fold. The chamber's atmosphere set Davi's teeth on edge. No matter what they might find in the cathedral, he wanted out.

The passage was too narrow to walk side by side. Davi went first. If they met any danger, he stood a poorer chance of protecting River than she did him, yet he felt better for being her defence. Romantic nonsense it might be, but if this was the Final Day, he planned to indulge in it.

At the end of the corridor, he whispered, "Ready?"

She nodded.

"River..." He held her hand. Her arm hung limply, but she didn't pull away.

They shared a silent moment, there in the dark. Together, and yet alone. On the other side of the door, Davi heard the drone of Alesta speaking, monks moving through the chancel. Sounds that, right now, had little bearing on reality. For reality was the absolutely noiseless, absolutely motionless woman standing in front of him. The woman whose love would destroy her. The immensity of it all broke over Davi like the Angel's flood.

The end was now. Their ending would not, could not, be joyful.

He dropped her hand.

"Let's go," he said, and eased the door open.

<hr>

Alesta stroked the blade as she would a lover. On the altar, Praeton squirmed, shaking his head from side to side.

"As payment for all our imperfections, Angelus Rex, we give to You the life of this boy. We are not worthy to be saved. By rights, we do not deserve to live. However, on this Final Day of creation we offer this sacrifice in vain hope of Your mercy."

She raised the knife high.

<hr>

After the dim light of the catacombs, a blaze of colour assaulted Davi. Candles burned like stars in the void of the Ecclesiat. The Angel's statue blocked Alesta from view, as though it were sheltering her. Terror and anger and sheer energy blended to flood Davi's veins with a potent mixture.

He sprinted from shadow to light. The chancel gaped around him, the walls so far apart it was like being outside, between two separate buildings. A dim roar reached him. The congregation had seen him. No time to worry about that now.

Rounding the Angel, he saw an evil-looking blade flash. With a cry like that of an animal, he lunged forward and slammed into Alesta. Her arm jerked. The blade sliced through the air, uncontrolled. It missed Praeton's neck, but nicked his side. Blood seeped through the boy's white clothes.

But he was alive, grinning hugely. Davi forced Alesta to the ground, a dim part of him horrified that he was wrestling a woman, and the Throne at that. Monks advanced on him, but there was River between them.

"He's tied," Davi gasped. He stomped on Alesta's hand. The crunch of her fingers beneath his heel sickened him, but she let go of the knife. He kicked it towards River. "Your hands are steadier."

In one fluid turn, she scooped it from the ground and neatly severed Praeton's bonds. The boy was babbling something, but Davi's ears didn't seem to be working properly. The sneer on Alesta's face was so wolfish, there had to be an accompanying snarl, but all he heard was a faint humming.

River had Praeton off the altar, and they were running towards the north wall. Davi fought the instinct to freeze and raced after them. The aither tempted him. It would be so easy to summon some, quickly instruct it to hold these people off. But when he tried listening for its song, a warning ache pulsed in his skull. Not yet, then.

Somehow, the stairs to the choir room were much easier to climb than those to the inner sanctum. Davi wasn't sure if his feet touched the ground. He was flying on exhilaration, and he feared that if he stopped an instant to think, he'd plummet to earth like a stone.

"Turn left!" River shouted. Praeton was lagging, clutching his side. Without breaking stride, she turned and picked him up. His legs dangled; suddenly, he looked like a much younger child.

Davi didn't ask how far they had to run. It didn't matter. He could have run to the moon and back.

At the corridor's end now. Stairs spiralled upwards to the bell tower and down to freedom. The steps twisted treacherously, stealing speed. Davi's momentum, now held at bay by the risk of a broken neck, rebelled within him. He was alive, every sense heightened, mind comprehending everything and nothing around him. And then River was fumbling with the latch on the door. They were fighting their way across the narthex, dodging latecomers who hadn't fit within the main cathedral.

They covered the square as though they had wings strapped to their feet. Snow invaded Davi's shoes, resumed its attack on skin that had just begun to thaw. The air was frigid enough to freeze his lungs.

Light spilled onto the snow. A mob streamed from the Ecclesiat, many brandishing weapons. Some, probably farmers and hunters, wielded knives, but many more clutched brass candlesticks, portable statues, even hefty prayer books.

Davi locked his gaze across the square.

Now, Serafine!

XVIII

Outside the cobbler's shop, the thunder continued. Gaelin shivered, leaned against an empty shelf and tugged his robes tighter. He counted the seconds between thunderclaps while blowing on his peeling fingertips. The storm was on top of them, its teeth inches from their collective throats.

Serafine let out a dramatic sigh. She kicked over a crate and flopped on it, head in her hands. "Are you all right?" Gaelin asked.

"I hate the waiting," she said. Her feet drummed the floor, sending up clouds of dust. "I didn't think it would take this long."

"I understand. I never imagined these circumstances myself." Refusing to abandon the hope of warmth, he tramped up and down the room. Anything to get the blood flowing.

Serafine eyed him. "How so?"

"Well, I never thought Alesta could commit such acts. She was a promising young monk, you know. I suppose you've heard about her anchorage."

"Youngest anchor ever. Yes, yes." Serafine yawned.

Memories slowed Gaelin's legs. Moments of years past overwhelmed him; for an instant, he was there again. Back in a time when this present was inconceivable.

"Maybe she was too young for an anchorage," he said slowly. "She seemed to change afterwards."

Now he had Serafine's attention. "Oh?"

"Yes. She became…more rigid. More demanding. Not just of herself, others too." He shook his head. "Before her anchorage, she was friends with another monk, Ioren."

"Her link to the outside."

"Precisely. They grew apart, after. She criticized him to no end." The old regret resurfaced. "Between you and me, that's probably why Ioren became a missionary. The bitterest enemy is he who was a friend." Gaelin shrugged. "I always thought it a pity. They were quite close. I don't think she's had many friends since."

They didn't speak much after that. Serafine guarded the window, staring across the square. Gaelin found some empty sacks and laid them across his lap. The warmth they offered was negligible, but better than nothing.

He thought. He revisited the choices he'd made, and people he'd known. Osvald and Alesta, Praeton and Ioren. Baeor. So many moments to compose a life, and in a few short hours, they would be wiped away like marks upon the sand.

It was too bad about Alesta and Ioren. He held them in mind as his eyelids drooped. Particularly Ioren: he had been so dedicated during her anchorage, so hurt when she emerged. Gaelin hoped he was safe, wherever he was. And happy.

The world wasn't fair. A lifetime erased in an instant, under the gaze of an absent god.

Serafine cried out, interrupting Gaelin's thoughts. "They're coming!"

He struggled to her side, arms and legs numb. "Is Praeton with them?"

"River's got him." A sharp intake of breath. "They've got a mob after them! How many people did she cram into that place? It looks like the whole City!"

She vaulted through the glassless window. Snow sprayed in a shimmering cloud as she sprinted across the square. After his shock faded, he struggled after her. Now he could make out the desperate trio fleeing the Ecclesiat. River was in front, carrying Praeton. Gaelin exhaled in relief. The boy was pale and scared, but alive. Davi battled to keep up with them, falling further and further behind.

Serafine stopped in the centre of the square. Her red hair whipped behind her, a flood of flame in the wind. She stood tall, defiant. Their shield.

Gaelin took Praeton from River and enveloped him. The boy trembled in his arms, and he hugged him tighter, trying to squeeze the fear from him. "My boy, my boy..."

"I dreamed again, Gaelin, the lights again, and Alesta, and..."

The chatter slid over Gaelin's ears. He was much more interested in the events occurring over Praeton's shoulder. Serafine glowed like a beacon in the night. He wondered if the wings were coming, and then they burst forth. All six of them unfolded in the crisp air. The oncoming mob halted. Those in front stopped so suddenly they slid on the ice and tumbled. The mob fractured, thrown into chaos by people trying to flee.

Alesta shoved her way to the front and faced Serafine across the snowfield. Although she headed the largest congregation Gaelin had ever seen, she seemed oddly small. Pinched and wizened, as though she'd given all of herself.

Her lip curled. "I was right. You do work for the Beast."

"I'm not the Beast, Alesta." Serafine's voice was pure honey. "I'm the Seraph. Completely different thing. There's still time. Let me help you."

"We don't need your help!" Her shrillness shattered the frozen air. "We have the Angel. Return the boy."

"No." Serafine's wings sliced trails through the snow as she stepped towards Alesta. "That gets you nothing. Trust me."

Alesta's eyes burned. "I don't trust."

In Gaelin's arms, Praeton shivered. The thin robes he wore offered no protection from the wind. Gaelin held him closer, and rested his chin on Praeton's head. The boy's hair carried the scent of incense. He prayed Alesta would stop her fight. She had fallen so far, she who had once been the Ecclesiat's golden star.

272

Suspicion uncoiled in the depths of Gaelin's mind. Dark and slick as oil, it spoke to him with utter confidence. Bits and pieces, whispers and glimpses; they fitted together in new ways, took on new meanings. It couldn't be. He had seen many impossible things in the past week, but this, this he would not believe.

No matter. Belief was irrelevant. He *knew*.

He spoke before he realized what he was doing.

"He's your son."

The fact, once voiced, was irretrievable. It echoed in the square. He sensed countless eyes upon him. Nudging Praeton back to River, he went to Alesta. Met her face to face.

"Praeton is your son."

Alesta's features—features that Gaelin saw mirrored Praeton's—dissolved into a mask of fury. Unrest rippled through the crowd; they balanced on tiptoe to see her better, or deserted her on the spot. The mood shifted, the entire square now rang with the anxious, unthinkable question.

Alesta turned to placate them. Then she addressed Gaelin. "You lie."

Certainty thrummed through Gaelin's bones. "It was during your anchorage, wasn't it?" He was surprised at the way he sounded, so old and resigned. "Ioren fathered him. He was the sole person to see you. In your twelve-month anchorage, it was possible to hide a nine-month pregnancy."

"You lie!"

More pieces fit, the pattern surfaced. "After you bore him, Ioren took him. Pretended to find him, abandoned on our doorstep. Convinced Osvald to keep him here…Osvald knew, didn't he, Alesta?"

"No!"

"Is that why you were so cruel to Ioren? Because he reminded you of your actions? The shame of breaking your vows of celibacy? By all rights, Alesta, you both should have left the Ecclesiat eleven years ago."

273

Spasms distorted Alesta's face. "I didn't...I am pure, I..."

Serafine lifted off the ground and landed softly beside the Throne. "Listen, the Angel might care, but I don't. It's not too late."

"I will never crawl to you!"

The crowd surrounded them now, like wolves. Gaelin recognized the looks of dismay and betrayal far too well; but now, they were not directed at him. Suddenly, the mounting tension was broken by a shriek.

Praeton, from within River's arms, had gone white. The Angel's apparition blazed in the sky. But unlike last time, it was no mere silhouette. Details materialized: His feathers, His curling hair, His unseeing eyes. A deathly hush descended. Gaelin reached for Praeton. The boy was staring not at the Angel, but at Alesta. Lips trembling, Praeton touched the cut on his side.

The Angel spread His wings, and He was no longer a shape in the clouds, but a form as solid as Serafine. He drifted as gently as the falling snowflakes, until he hovered over the crowd.

Alesta's mouth went slack, her eyes shone with frenzied ecstasy. "Angelus Rex!" she sobbed. "My Angel King, I have sinned, yes I have sinned, but I..."

The Angel turned His eyes upon her.

She crumpled. Gaelin rushed to her side, scrambled to feel her neck. No pulse. No heartbeat. No expression of peace, but only that final mask of horror.

The Angel soared over the commotion. Poised in midair, He threw His wings wide and pointed to the Ecclesiat. The bell tower buckled and fell backwards, onto the roof of the nave. The great bell gave a final death knell that vibrated into a ghastly parody of its former glory. The cathedral cracked with a sound like a breaking spine, and the Ecclesiat disintegrated in a tumble of falling stones.

Praeton screamed.

After the crash of stone, there was a terrible silence.

No breath of wind disturbed the air.

Not a soul moved.

The Angel alighted on a spire of stone poking from the rubble that was once the Ecclesiat. There He crouched, utterly immobile. His milky eyes swept over the City. Davi felt sure that any moment, he was going to either awaken or faint. There was no way this could be real. And if it was, there was no way his mind could cope with it.

Praeton's whimpering broke the spell. Automatically, Davi ruffled his hair, hair that had undoubtedly come from Alesta. He shuddered. That idea was something he wasn't ready to contemplate yet.

"Davi?" the boy whispered.

"Yes?"

"If she was my mother, why did she hate me so much?"

Davi had never truly understood the meaning of the word *helpless* until that moment. In the most literal sense, he had nothing to offer Praeton: no help, no solace. Tears trickled down the boy's cheeks.

The people in the square seemed lost. Some were already scaling the ruined Ecclesiat in an effort to reach the Angel. Others edged towards Serafine. Snow howled over the square. Hardly anyone seemed to notice the cold anymore. Many simply sat where they were, smothered by snow, empty in mind and appearance. Understanding dawned on Davi.

This was what lay past despair.

River clutched his arm, her fingers like shards of ice. "It is past dawn. We need the Hapax."

"No. Not yet."

He took her face in his hands, touched his forehead to hers. Lacking blood, her skin had assumed the temperature of the air. The coldness penetrated him to the core. It didn't matter. Emotion seized his heart, seized it, and crushed it between

275

jagged teeth. Tentatively, River entwined her fingers in his hair. He closed his eyes, lost in the moment.

And then he remembered.

The lump in his throat was so great that he struggled to breathe. As he recoiled, he hated himself, hated Ael's very self. "We'll figure something out," he muttered. "Anything."

The Angel had not moved.

An hour or so later, a long, low moan rattled the foundations of the earth. A trumpet blast like none heard by mortal ears reverberated over the globe. The vibrations knocked Gaelin flying. The Tablet he'd been holding slipped from his grasp and sank in the snow. The small group listening to his attempts at comfort cowered like dogs anticipating a kick.

Atop His perch, the Angel unfurled His wings. The black sky burned with scarlet streaks. They hurtled to earth, sparking explosions that threw off clouds of dust and chaos.

"What are they?" Gaelin shouted to Serafine.

She looked grim. "Pieces of sky."

A molten rock smashed into a row of buildings not far from Gaelin. It ploughed straight through its upper floors. Bricks melted on contact, liquefied glass dripped to freeze on the snow below. Thick, ugly smoke poured from the ragged wound in the building's side.

More meteors pummelled the buildings lining the square. The stupefied mood of moments before was gone. Now all was turmoil as people fled in every direction, covering their heads and screaming pleas to the silent Angel.

Sulphur stung Gaelin's nostrils. He fought his way through smoke, and snow, and panicking hordes, back to the spot he'd left Praeton. Serafine sheltered the boy beneath Her wings. He'd expected Her to seem harried, as petrified as he felt. Instead, Her radiant face showed only the trace of a frown.

Davi, palm out and eyes closed, looked on the verge of

collapse. Blue sparks quivered in his hand, but refused to coalesce into more substantial aither.

The chorus of screams intensified. The plummeting meteors now seemed to be targeting individuals. As Gaelin watched, a ball of fire flattened three men dashing for the shattered cathedral. Hot blood scalded the snow, rendering it a sticky red mass that stretched as far as Gaelin could see.

The world had degenerated to burning, blood, and dying. Cries, ranging from highest treble to lowest bass, gouged Gaelin's soul. He wasn't aware of his tears until they froze on his cheeks.

"Stop this!" He tugged Serafine's wing. "Won't you stop this?"

She gently prised him off. "I can't. I can do nothing without the Hapax."

And so the maelstrom raged unabated. Severed limbs leaked torrents of blood onto the snow, the stones, and anyone brave or foolish enough to aid the wounded. Purplish-red innards steamed, their vapours rising to the wall of smoke that hid the sky from view.

Gaelin shielded Praeton as best he could. But there was no escape from the smell, or the sounds. The deadly mixture of abyssal cold and hellish heat consumed them. Hissing erupted as the rains of fire seared the snow. Praeton wept, and clung to Gaelin as though the Angel Himself could not break his grip.

In their corner of the City's main square, in the shadow of the dead Ecclesiat, Gaelin commended his soul to Ael. He offered his thanks to the god that had been, but was not, and seemed unlikely to ever be again. One by one, he thought of those he had known, and gave gratitude for the time he'd had.

Innumerable moments to compose a life, and each one was a gift. He prayed to Ael that these final moments not be filled with too much suffering. Arms securely around Praeton, Gaelin waited for the world to end.

More than ever, River wished for tears. How humans took them for granted: a way to unleash the torment within, to let agony wash away instead of festering and rotting the mind itself. She held Davi's free hand. Privately, she doubted that he would even be able to access the aither. Not now, not when he was stressed beyond belief, exhausted beyond human limits, and burned on top of it all.

The devastation in the square shocked her. She could hardly conceive of the end arriving throughout the City. Throughout the world. Across the land, seas leaped free of their bonds to devour coastal towns. Mountains crumbled to dust, and flames consumed the rest.

And they would all die.

She had been all but assured of immortality, once. The spells that had transformed aither to flesh prevented her aging. She had no organs that would weaken and cease functioning. There was nothing within her for parasite or plague to exploit. So long as she revealed no emotion, she could, in theory, live forever.

Live to watch institutions and empires blow away like sand. Live to stand on the grave of everyone she'd ever cared about. Live to feel lost love gnaw at her sanity until she succumbed to the haven of madness.

An endless life was no life at all.

And they would be safe. Revelling in the preciousness of existence as she could not. River stroked Davi's face. Eyes closed, deep in concentration, he smiled.

It would be enough.

She slipped away from them. She did not look back. There was no need; her memory was perfect. The cold did not bother her, nor could she smell whatever was making the humans blanch white as the snows. At the base of the Ecclesiat, she paused to gather herself.

And so, at the end, I choose.

She climbed.

The aither taunted Davi, eluded him by inches. The humming was there. Flashes of aither mocked him, but he could not reach it. He lacked the necessary focus; it was impossible to zero in on that hidden dimension. A far-too familiar throbbing in his temples and at the base of his skull warned him against trying further.

He opened his eyes. Gaelin and Praeton huddled under Serafine's wings. The monk and child were either asleep or unconscious. A few snowflakes filtered through Serafine's feathers and salted their hair and clothing. Praeton's lips were turning blue.

Davi swore under his breath and turned to ask River her opinion on returning to the Magistatiem. There might be standing buildings to hide in, maybe even some magi who'd recovered from their earlier burnout.

She wasn't there.

A set of tracks led towards the Ecclesiat. Unease settled over Davi like a shroud. He yanked Serafine's lowest pair of wings. They flexed irritably, and She flinched away from him.

"Why does everyone do that?"

"Serafine—where's River?"

Her silence told him everything. "No," he said, feeling his chest constrict. "No, she wouldn't. She didn't. Not yet."

Through the haze and smoke, the crumpled remains of the Ecclesiat were barely visible, but straining to the utmost, Davi just glimpsed a figure scrambling up the pile of stone and wood. His body seized. Then the full impact struck him, and he was running, snow spraying under his heels, lips splitting in the wind.

"River!"

The earth bucked beneath his feet, flinging him forward. Snow drove into his nose, his mouth. The hard cobbles underneath scraped his elbows; bruises were already forming around his kneecaps.

He didn't feel any of it. He was up before he realized he'd gone down, and re-engaged in the battle against the elements and his own screaming muscles.

A fireball struck the ground so close to him that he heard its whistle, felt its heat and steam as it burrowed into a drift. He dodged more streaks of fire that scarred the earth on every side. Despite the cold, sweat streamed down his face and neck, where it promptly froze. He wouldn't have been surprised to find himself ice through and through.

The Ecclesiat loomed in the darkness, like a ship appearing over the rise of a storm-ridden sea. River was nearing the Angel, her ascent strong and sure. The Angel swivelled towards her.

"No!" Davi shouted.

But He simply alighted from His spire. His wing beats forced Davi to a stooping shuffle. Light bathed Davi as Serafine hovered across from the Angel. The two divine beings faced each other over the charred fire-pit that had been the City.

The light and the dark. The cold rigidity of the Angel King, and the Seraph's warm livelihood. Terrible perfection and glorious flaw.

An unbalanced symmetry.

Skin tore on Davi's hands and arms as he attacked the Ecclesiat. He hauled himself over vestiges of columns, sliced his knee on the edge of a painting's broken frame.

"River!"

Balanced on a narrow outcrop, she glanced down at him. There was no blankness in her face now. It was alive, suffused with emotion. Pain. Sorrow. Fear. Pride. So many experiences, so many sensations she had not allowed herself to feel until that moment. At last, she was *River*, not the renegade *River of Knowledge*.

And it was too late.

The wind screamed around Davi's head. He hung from the rock like an insect, tears blurring his vision. He was so tired. So sore.

"River!" The cry was ripped from his throat. The wind stole it, echoed it back at him. He prayed she heard.

Her dark eyes found his. Amidst the shrieking, amidst the horror of a world about to fall, they were together. It was an eternal moment that ended when she looked away from him, to where Serafine and the Angel swooped in the tormented sky.

"Please," he whispered. "Please, River. Don't."

He couldn't hear her over the gale. But he saw her lips form the words, "I love you."

And then she exploded in a searing blaze of light.

XIX

"No!" Someone was screaming as though their soul was on fire. The most inhuman screeches Davi had ever heard, without any sign of ceasing.

"No, oh please, no!"

It was not until he drew a gasping, shuddering breath that he realized the voice was his own.

He clambered over the rocks as though they were pebbles. Lead weighted his limbs; his skull was on the verge of bursting. Surely no one could see what he had seen and keep their sanity. Half-blind, he collapsed on all fours on the spot where River had been.

Nothing.

No charred markings. No scratches. Not even a coating of ash.

Was there to be no sign of her existence? Was she simply wiped from the earth? He beat his fists against the stone, until the knuckles were red and raw and blood trickled down his forearms. He bellowed his anguish to the heavens.

"Serafine! You let her—you made her—you..."

Serafine wasn't listening. Not to him. Her head was cocked. She seemed to stare through the fabric of the world, to whatever lay behind. For there was something there. A new note entered the groaning of the earth and the howling of the sky. Out of reflex, Davi grappled for the aither.

It was different. The same as he'd always known it, but *more*.

The Hapax was in the world.

Serafine threw back Her head, triumph written in the

spread of Her wings, the azure glow to Her eyes. Shades of consternation crossed the Angel; He rubbed at His ears as though clearing water from them. Then He snarled.

Angry light broke over the City, etched shadows sharp as knives. The blast sent Davi soaring backwards, smashing into one of the Ecclesiat's ribs. A sphere of fire, mammoth compared to its predecessors, shrieked through the air. Bits of it broke away to form fiery trails of their own. It was as though the Angel had thrown the sun itself at the City. Walls of heat flattened Davi to the rock. He welcomed them. Wherever River had gone, he would surely follow.

Gravel skittered beside him. Serafine delicately picked Her way to the top of the Ecclesiat, where the spire had once been. She smiled at Davi, Her six wings flared wide. She was no longer bathed in light, She seemed to have become light itself.

And She spoke the Word.

It filled the universe: the Word that had been; and always was, in silence; and now had come again. The Word no longer a Hapax, as Serafine reintroduced and reaffirmed it to all the dimensions. It was a Word of light and life, of creation from destruction.

Davi's ears could not hear it; his mind could not comprehend it. It was vaster than human understanding. He was aware of it, aware of a force that suffused everything, of That Which Was All returned, but the Word itself eluded him, deafened him by its power as the daytime sun blights out the stars.

Serafine sang on, but She was no longer just the Seraph. The Word was with Ael, and the Word was Ael. As Davi watched, She became more, as the aither was more. Her wordless song of the Word deepened and strengthened, and in it was the creation of a new world.

Blackness appeared before Her: an abyss in the air. As it had done before, as it always did, the purest light sprang from the darkness. For it was only through each other that each existed at all. The shimmering, new-born world expanded. Aither pulsed within. Still, the song went on, and the aither twisted into tiny, vibrating strings. Around them grew a whirl of the elements; the fire, water, earth, and air that formed the bones of the new world.

Davi grew conscious of the square below. Farmers and merchants, councilmen and aristocrats, monks and magi, all peered upwards. He picked Praeton from the crowd. The boy ran from Gaelin's side and began climbing the Ecclesiat's ruins.

He expected Serafine to send Praeton back, but She extended Her arms to him, still singing. Davi caught glimpses of the new world now: a soft, dawn-lit forest barely visible through the shimmering portal. Light spilled from its edges, illuminating Praeton's grin. Serafine swivelled the boy around to face the portal.

Without a backwards glance, he jumped through.

Praeton's departure to the next world unleashed a floodgate. Lit by the deathly comet still hurtling towards them, the people of the City began their ascent. One by one, they passed Serafine and entered Her world. Davi hung back, still sheltered by the stone rib.

All of them were afraid. That much he gleaned from their expressions, their restrained movements. For some it was the death promised them by the Angel's final weapon. For others, it was Serafine; or the next world itself. Yet as each person stood on the threshold of the worlds, their fear melted, and was replaced by something else.

Hope.

Serafine's words of a few days and eons ago haunted Davi. *I am the ending that begins, and the hope of the grave.*

I am the destroyer who creates.

Golden light erupted from the portal and arched across the earth in shining rivers. Wherever they touched ground, new portals formed. From his perch, Davi saw the souls of the City abandon their world for the next. Some hesitated a distance away. Others leaped through as Praeton had done. Impossibly, he watched those at the Magistatiem enter, Tam and the Heads, and all the magi and refugees who had sheltered there.

He saw his parents, walking over the sea into the new world. And in the valleys, those who had fled the City found passage.

And in every other town and city,

And by the sea,

And in the mountains,

And in the shrouded northern forests,

And the blistered southern deserts,

And in the lands beyond the ocean, which had no name,

An instant and eternities later, the exodus was complete.

A sickly glow heralded the comet's collision. The reek of decay overran the City. At last, Death had claimed this world for His own. Davi shivered in his pocket of stone. The last man in the world.

The portal glimmered, an oasis in the forsaken desert this world had become. It held no temptation for him. All he had cherished was gone. He wept, his sobs the sole living sounds on the earth. Salt stung his lips, seeped into the cuts along his arms. An icy fist squeezed his heart.

There was nothing left for him.

"Davi..."

He did not answer.

"Davi."

If Death would take him now...

"Davi!"

Serafine pulled him into the open. Warmth from Her hands and body roused his blood, but his mind clamped down, and he pushed Her away. There was no room for warmth anymore.

"Are you coming?"

He turned to the wasteland. His kingdom. "No."

Serafine was changing again. Becoming something he couldn't begin to imagine, let alone see. "It is her gift to you." With that, She entered the portal. The beams of light that connected it to its brethren winked into darkness. Only the one, original portal remained.

She had left the door open.

Davi wavered before it. Could he even trust Her, She who had allowed River to rush headlong to her doom? The Beast?

On the precipice, his heart lurched. He looked again to the oncoming comet, now so close it blotted out most of the sky. Hell over earth. Here, there was nothing but death. There, nothing but potential.

Nothing was as terrifying as what *might* be.

And yet, River had accepted it. So had untold millions. Already his skin was blistering, peeling away. Another few moments and he would be dead.

Time had run out.

He stepped through the portal.

Behind him, the world died.

———

It had taken no more than an instant. Truthfully, Gaelin had barely noticed what lay beneath his feet as he entered Serafine's gateway. One moment, the world was an angry red, boiling over with death and flames. The next, cool, blue light embraced him.

Slender trees beckoned him from veils of mist. He moved towards them, as though in a dream, and laid a hand on their smooth bark. As he did so, he noticed his robes were free of rips and dirt. His skin was unblemished. Even the aches in his limbs had subsided.

A smile tugging at his lips, Gaelin drifted through the glade. Soft grass left dew-drop kisses on his ankles. Laughter floated through the trees. He emerged into a clearing. Pinkness warmed the sky over the treetops, fading into a pearly periwinkle. A few low notes of birdsong sounded.

Further on in the endless forest, he saw others. Even at this distance, their joy was palpable. He glimpsed Praeton running through the trees, alive and free, and singing as loud as he could. The world seemed whole again: the morning after the nightmare of the soul.

"Thank you," he whispered.

A breeze caressed his cheek. He breathed the dawn's scent,

filled his lungs with it. The sunrise spread, merged with the light of the morning star. With the idea of finding those in need, he looked about for a path.

There was none. Instead, at the foot of a towering tree, a book rested on the grass. Not the Tablet, nor the prophecies of St. Memoyah, but a book of poetry. A book for pleasure.

Gaelin whispered his thanks again, and finally took his peace.

———

Davi awoke on a golden beach. Thick, coarse grains of sand brushed his legs. A sun like a polished shield rose over the ocean, turning it to a mirror of amber.

In the tranquil glades behind, Gaelin was reading, pausing every now and then to dispense a kind word. Faint strains of Praeton's singing floated over the meadows. Throughout the lands, life began anew.

Yet Davi felt soulless.

He traced patterns in the sand. Watched the dawn of time. And fervently wished it would end all over again.

"You are unhappy."

His shoulders hunched. "I don't want to talk to you, Serafine."

"Oh?"

He turned... and stared.

It was Serafine, and it was not Serafine. He gaped, and asked stupidly, "Who are you?"

The being laughed. "That Which is All."

"Ael?" He was too stunned to move.

"I am the Seraph." The voice was Serafine's, yet it was more than hers. It was the voice of the Word. "I am Ael. I am the Angel."

Davi backed away. "The Angel?"

"The Angel is part of all things. Without Him, I am not."

"What happened to Serafine?"

"I spoke the Word, and the Word was with me, and the Word *was* me. And as the Word is Ael, I am become Ael also. For I have always been Ael."

"And yet you were the Seraph." Davi sighed. "I know, I know."

"Tell me why you grieve."

"You know why!" Davi's voice rose. "This new world is great, but without River, it's empty. Sure, she sacrificed herself, and I love her for it. But I can't be happy about it."

The being he had once called Serafine smiled.

"What?" Davi demanded.

"I am all things that were, are, and shall be. And, as I am *all* things, so too am I those things which are not."

Davi frowned, trying to make sense of it.

Then he heard a voice. "Davi?"

Hardly daring to hope, he turned. There she was: a little further up the beach.

"River!"

His legs could not carry him fast enough. She was there, kicking the ground uncertainly, rubbing her arms as she craned to better view the endless ocean. It was though she had never left. At the last moment, he skidded to a halt, sending the sand flying. The liquid darkness of her eyes was more beautiful than any of the marvels around them. Tentatively, far too aware of his heartbeat, he held his hand out.

She batted it aside, and embraced him fully. The breath rushed from his lungs. They held each other, talked over each other. Davi didn't think he was making real speech, but he didn't care.

He took River in his arms, and she pressed into him, warm from the rising sun. On that golden beach, on the first day of the new world, Davi knew happiness.

Suddenly, River broke away from him, touching her eyes. A sudden remoteness settled between them. The fire in his chest dimmed, and a shadow of fear stole over him. "What's wrong?"

"Look." She showed him her fingertips. Drops of water glistened like pearls on her skin. He looked into her face. Now they shone in her eyes, coursed down her cheeks.

Tears.

Made in the USA
Lexington, KY
08 March 2013